THE
TYPEWRITERISTS

David N. Martin

Forged Truth Publishing

Follow us at www.forgedtruth.co.uk, or scan
below:

To Kathy, Jonny and Rebecca —
my family who are everything.

Chapter One — Cambrai, December 1917

After the retreat, he was hailed a hero and billeted in a makeshift bedroom that had once been a pigsty in the outbuildings of a grand château. The animal afterscents lingered under those of bleach and carboxylic scrub, but any room with stone walls was better than a tent and any tent better than the insides of a tank along the road to Cambrai. To Eustace Havershall, the lottery of survival felt absurd, but the absurdist thing of all was the typewriter on the three-legged table, its corner propped up by a hay bale.

"What's that for?" he asked.

"Oh, that," said the batman assigned to show him the room. "We found it in the wreckage of the main house, Sir. Frog contraption. The Major's not so taken with 'newfangled mechanical writing' — that's what he calls it — but he says it'll look more official. On letters to families, you know. I understand there's a letter to write for one of yours."

Eustace surveyed the man — the uniform unfeasibly neat, the bowling-ball face well shaved, the cap just so. *Out of place. So out of place.* Everywhere the world lay in pieces.

"I wouldn't know how to use it."

"Orders," the batman said.

"Damn it! Fancy writing won't make my gunner less dead."

"No, Sir. I'd say not. But I wouldn't be caught saying no when the Major wants it his way. That thing's been passing from room to room. Some days it moves quick. Everyone hates doing them, see. Everyone hates the letters."

Eustace perched himself on the edge of the narrow bed, testing the springs with his weight, assessing his new quarters, cold as hell, but this was as much as he could hope for — an oil lamp and a chair, a cracked shaving mirror and a bowl to wash in. His hands looked ugly and scarred against the creamy mattress.

"Who had this room before?"

"A Captain, Sir. Captain Evans. Missing in Action, which means—"

"It means he bought it in the advance, most probably."

"Yes, Sir. We wouldn't normally, not with you being a lieutenant, only we heard you was in line for a medal, see. Military Cross, isn't it?"

"I wouldn't know."

"The Quartermaster, he says, 'Best look after him', so here we are. We was told you're the youngest lieutenant the Tank Corps has ever had, the only one who earned it on his own bootstraps?"

"The Tank Corps is four months' old. There's not so much history to get past."

"Yes, Sir."

Eustace blinked his eyes shut, and when he opened them again, he said, "Have you seen action… ever?"

"Always a Base Rat, Sir. Unfit for Active Duty."

"Well, let me tell you. I stick my head up through a turret. I shout, 'Fire'. And then I shout, 'Fire,' again. Care to try it? If you can shout loud enough, you could be a lieutenant."

The batman stared at him in confusion and Eustace felt ashamed of his own anger. He had never considered himself cruel. A killer, yes, by necessity. But not cruel.

"The thing is, a Kraut officer like me is probably writing that letter right now. Same letter. Different uniform. Different boy."

"Yes, Sir."

"You have nothing better to say?"

The batman said nothing at all.

Eustace felt his eyes begin to leak. Numb and unexpected, wasn't that the way of it? He felt nothing, even though beating the odds was everything. There was no grace to it, other than the grace of better luck.

Several minutes passed him by. The batman was nowhere to be seen, but in that time, Eustace Havershall had hardened the armour needed for living. He would be alright.

That morning, twenty-five Mark IV tanks had limped back here to safety, his own among them. More than four hundred had started the advance. He had seen most of them broken or burned out between here and Cambrai. Now the chill of evening was biting hard and there wasn't even the roughest alcohol to be had.

He lit the oil lamp and sat at the table with a bartered cigarette on his lip. Its smoke danced above the lamp shade as he tried to fathom how paper was supposed to roll around the typewriter's platen. Mechanical writing or not, the letter had to be written.

The label on the machine said 1895, the year of Eustace's birth. It looked and felt solid — a polished wooden casing, a galvanised steel chassis, ivory keys on metal levers, their associated typebars resting in a semi-circular cut-out above the keyboard. He had to press a key down almost two inches to swing a typeface up to hit the page. Key strokes came with a mechanical thwack.

'dear mrsmast…'

Dammit! Scrap that sheet. Try again.

'dear mrs masterson,we regr et …'

Three attempts failed before he realised he had to hold down a special key to make capital letters. Typing 'Your son did his duty' revealed a problem with the 'H' and 'Y' keys. The typefaces stuck against the platen and refused to return until Eustace poked them with his finger. His hands were shaking against the cold. The truth was a larger problem. Mechanical words could not capture the shape of loss.

He was staring at another hopeless attempt when the Sergeant coughed to announce his arrival. There was no door to mark the entrance, only a tattered curtain that hung lopsidedly.

"Permission to disturb you?"

Sergeant Joseph Woodmansey was a northern lad, runtishly slight, acne from cheek to cheek, lost half a big toe a month previous. But a whiz with machinery, always talking about cars and motor cycles, smelt of pickles even when pickles had not been in the ration for weeks. Out in the field, he was the saviour of their tank.

"The men sent me to ask. We've all got passes out tonight and—"

"And what, Woody? You can talk freely here."

"I know it 'ent regular, but none of it's regular."

"You're off to the village? Well deserved."

"Madame Franny's. We thought you might like to… to remember Masterson, you know? It 'ent regular, officers and other ranks together, but the thing is, you 'ent a toff like the others."

Eustace smiled. "I think of myself as a temporary gentleman. I don't presume to have the breeding to make it stick."

"Well, Sir, we know what you done. We'd all have done it. In your place, that is, and it's just between us, that's what we decided. This place in the village, the *maison tolérée*, it's a bloomin' good one, I'm told. They have musicians and we want to give him a send off. A wake, you know? Him being Irish."

Eustace gestured to the page on which he'd got as far as 'Dear Mrs Masterson…' before the 'Y' of 'Your' had stuck again.

"Know anything about these things, Woody? You're the engineer. I'm told it's use is a Brass Hat order." He released the 'Y' and then pressed its key — same thwack, same jammed result. "It seems you can fix anything."

"Not really. I had a piece of good fortune fixing the tank, that's all."

"Nonsense. We were stranded otherwise. If you stop, you're dead, isn't that what they say?" He waited a while, then added, "It seems the Brass is putting me up for a medal, maybe a promotion. Captain Havershall, how would that sound?"

It sounded to Eustace like dead man's shoes. He laughed to drown the thoughts that came echoing in its wake.

Woody shook his head, expressing no opinion. He lent over the typewriter's mechanism. "I reckon Heath Robinson would be proud. Happen I know about things that move and shoot. War things. If it doesn't blow up or kill you, it's useless out here. Same goes for the soldiers."

Useful things you win medals for...

Ten days earlier, within the ungodly confines of a Mark IV tank, Eustace had led seven crew across the soft-walled ditches on the way to Cambrai. Fascines of brushwood gathered for the purpose bore them across trenches and ditches. On the flat, they swept aside the barbed fences. Advancing miles over the line in a morning, the supporting foot soldiers and cavalry slipped back out of sight. The army command had not planned for such success — one bold tank that made it further than the rest.

Eustace stood up through the hatch in the front turret, tin-hatted in the gunpowdered air, metal mesh above his head to deflect grenades. He gulped for oxygen. Briefly free. He surveyed the mud fields of smoke. Below, men awaited his command. Blenkinsop, Jones, Masterson, Mulgrove, Priestley, McAllister and Woodmansey — all his responsibility.

Without warning, their tank was hit low on the starboard side near the sponson. His head jerked sideways. Vision blurred. It felt like falling. He couldn't breathe for the sudden showers of dirt. His ears were ringing.

It took seconds to realise the tank had tipped up on one side then crashed back to the ground. The mechanical rumble supporting him clanked itself into silence.

"Fuck. Fuck. Oh, God, fuck," he heard from below. Someone screamed.

Stay calm. Maintain command. An officer had tricks to avoid the experience of fear. Two flies landed on the exposed back of the turret lid. Eustace watched the gently flexing wings and rubbing legs, took another few seconds to refind rhythm in his breathing.

"Is there a problem, Lads?" Quite matter-of-fact as he ducked into the tank's innards. The confinement down there terrified him. He always had to hide it.

Masterson, the gunner, had slumped from his position in the starboard sponson. He'd fallen back into the narrow gap between his big six-pounder and the tank's engine bay. Everyone had rushed to get a look. He was twitching when they got a torch on him.

Eustace saw it all — the flesh torn off the cheek, smashed bone visible, caught by the shell splatter, oozing blood. Moments before Herbert Masterson looked young and perfect, as the world had done before the war.

More failures with the letter brought Eustace to a frustrated intermission. He stopped and looked at himself in the mirror. Like all the men — officer or not — he had descended to hair lice and grubby fingernails. His fingers held tracks like black veins, filled with trench dirt and powder burns that couldn't be scrubbed out by the mobile bath units that occasionally rolled in on the back of lorries. The best moments of his days were the first brief seconds of the morning before he remembered his sins.

Eustace's forefathers were devoutly religious lace makers, the factory masters of Victorian Nottinghamshire. Although profits in the cloth trade declined with the new century, the Havershall boys — a trio of brothers — were sent to third-tier public schools, raised on sermons from the pulpit, the restless cane of gin-soaked headmasters and the rationed attention of parents.

As middle son, Eustace always knew he was the least favoured, neither heir to his father's remaining fortune nor his mother's darling. He tried to fit in. When the stiffened resolve of recruiting officers helped school friends sign up, he bit on the lie — the Church first, King and Country close after. He signed for the short campaign they were promised. He thought his father would approve, might perhaps be proud, even if his mother worried. The stoic Christian faith of the family remained.

Belatedly, examining the man he had become in that mirror, he decided he would take Woody's invitation. He reached in his pack for a cleaner shirt, pulled on his boots and set off into the evening with his men, his letter unwritten on the typewriter's platen.

* * *

So the survivors of Cambrai introduced themselves to the whores of Madame Franny's. As a group, his tank crew sat and talked, drinking in the salon. Eustace listened, learning their truths as he hid his own.

They seemed to get louder and his thoughts grew more troubling. Soldiers still, they might never reach home, because there was another war tomorrow. Every day, another and another, and the only ones who escaped were dead, or shipped away in pieces or both.

A sweet copper-haired girl — she smelt of rosewater and called herself Maisie — slipped her hand inside his. He sat sipping vinegary red wine from a grubby glass. A one-eyed pianist played popular English tunes on a nearby upright while the singer took a break. Maisie's soft fingers worked their promises against Eustace's palm.

"When I'm free of this..." Woody piped up. He was sandwiched between two working girls on a stained velvet sofa. Small he might be, but the lad consumed vast quantities of alcohol without apparent effect.

"If you are, if we're ever bloody free," said Priestley, their port side gunner.

Mulgrove, the tank's driver, the most obviously drunk, said, "We're none of us free. We're not fighting for ourselves. We're fighting for *them.*"

'*Them*' was not defined. '*Them*' was an assumed and hated '*them*', a privileged '*them*'. Eustace's companions shook their heads in dull agreement.

After a while, Mulgrove ran out of words and began to paw at one of the girls, pulling aside her shapeless blouse. She smiled professionally.

Woody said, "I've been wondering about your machine, Lieutenant. Not the tank, the writing machine."

"I thought you'd condemned it useless."

"Aye, it is, out here, Sir. But afterwards, when we get home... if we get home."

"If..." Priestley repeated. "*If...*"

Priestley was older than the rest, mid-thirties. He had fought the Boers in South Africa. His uncertainty sent them all into silence.

Eustace could see now. He had been but half-weaned into the world when war plucked him from his parents' house, and in France, he had become that half-and-half creature that belonged no where. Not Mulgrove's 'them', but certainly not 'us' either.

He remembered the leather-bound library his grandfather had assembled and abandoned in that Nottinghamshire house, folios of Shakespeare and Milton that no one but Eustace attempted to read. And, oh yes, the tired soap-box seditions of his mother's drawing room where rich folk played the bleeding heart. Lunch with the vicar; tea with the revolutionaries. The family talked and talked, paying liberal service to women's rights and Irish home rule, pretending to demand progress. The change his parents craved was a little advancement, a recovery of due privilege, maybe a royal honour for his worthy father, while all the time, the industry that had supported his ancestors edged into decline.

On Eustace's first trip to London, his father had argued with policemen about the inconvenience of a suffragette rally crossing their path. The parlour talk, it seemed, did not extend beyond the family's front door. Certainly not as far as Piccadilly Circus. Or to women chained to railings.

That was 1913. He was seventeen. He had already begun to hate his father.

A society girl in summer dress and yellow bonnet was distributing 'Votes for Women' leaflets. She dropped her pile.

His father tapped him on the shoulder, pointed her out, laughed at her dilemma. Eustace rushed forward to help her. She smiled at him as he picked up the leaflets, her painted eyebrows arching into brackets. He wanted to introduce himself, shake her hand perhaps, but a girl like that would think it forward. She never offered.

His father told him, "You're knocking on the wrong door, Son. Don't you always?"

Here's the truth his father would deny: the girl was old money and of a class Havershalls would never reach. Lace mills and Christian industry had failed to make gentry of the manufacturing classes in Victorian England. Havershall money had looked too new while they had it, and now it was dwindling away before it had a chance to be old.

Eustace carried away the idea of her — her wealth, her poise — and he liked the way she annoyed his father. She was the real 'them', a toff his father would have said, seductive and wrong and out of reach. Eustace had wanted that, if only for a moment, or maybe several moments, or maybe he still did. Did it matter out here in this hell? Here, they were all dying one at a time. Here only tomorrow mattered. The men had invited him to this wake. He belonged with them. Almost. But not quite.

* * *

When Eustace snapped out of his daydream, it was still Maisie with her fingers against the scars in his palm. He noticed now how young she looked. Too young for this, but then everyone is too young for war.

It wasn't that he hadn't 'indulged' before. As a new recruit, it had been a rite of passage, thirty feral seconds to plant a flag. It might be all you got. He had racked up a minute and a half in three years. Stealing more time seemed wrong now. After Cambrai.

Maisie's copper hair brushed Eustace's cheek. She started to whisper in his ear.

"Tu es troublé? You wish to forget?"

She promised a menu of delights in the upstairs rooms, things that might remove his troubles. A stirring of desire, yes, but his troubles and desires were tangled up in yellow bonnets and money, and all the things that might set himself apart from his father and everything else.

In the background, Mulgrove was shouting, "D'you think she's been handed to you for your pleasure? No, boys. Who gets your daily sixpence, while you're busy getting *syph* spots on your knob? These places are run by the Frog government. *They* give. And take back. And we fight for *them*. We die for *them*."

There were moments inside the stricken tank that Eustace constantly relived — the smell of fear and lost dignities and hot greasy metal reshaping everything; the air thickening. Would the Germans get to them before the British advance caught them up? Masterson moaned, dying slowly.

Priestley and Blenkinsop were kneeling over the boy, trying to raise his head. Priestley grasped him by the hand. Masterson mumbled, "Please, please…"

"Help the poor bugger, Lieutenant… someone… for God's sake, help him."

"Please, please…"

All eyes fell on Eustace. He had no answer. Woody leaned in at his ear.

"It wasn't the blast, Sir. It was when we tipped. It must have knocked something loose. In the gubbins underneath, I reckon."

Masterson had taken Eustace's attention. He'd forgotten for a moment that the engine had stopped. Masterson was lost, but all eight of them were doomed.

Woody said, "I can fix it, Sir, maybe... if I go outside... crawl underneath, like."

"You can't go outside, Woody. I wouldn't send–"

"No, not an order, Sir. I'm a volunteer. If we do nothing... well, we're all like Masterson."

Seconds passed. Outside, the guns boomed. Eustace had never sent anyone to die, not even a volunteer.

"Alright," he said. "You go. I'll deal with this."

He looked down at Masterson and then at his own hands. His beaded sweat seemed to want no part of the pitted skin, no part of what must be done. He unfurled fingers one at a time, rubbed together the slickness between their tips, then unclipped his Webley revolver from its holster.

And the rest? What happened afterwards?

Well, he remembered Woody's return, that moment when Sergeant Woodmansey ducked back inside through the manhole in the middle turret.

"Try it now," he said with surprising confidence.

And the engine started. On the third turn of the starting handle.

Ecstasy came out of despair. Unexpected and undeserved. The survivors whooped for joy like Lazarus. The roar and rattle remade everything.

Nearly everything. Everything but Masterson.

The British support never arrived. The tank trundled into retreat — men, like Lazarus reborn, their steel walls suddenly a comforting shield. By now, Eustace had seen too many cycles of war. The gain of territory always reversed; human loss was permanent.

In seventeen days, the Germans would take back the land they initially conceded at Cambrai. The cost: one hundred and twenty-five thousand casualties. Tanks were supposed to change the equation, so said Winston Churchill. But everyone in the Tank Corps knew Churchill had pushed these new machines on the army too soon, and the army adopted them because Churchill was doing the pushing. The Mark IV pretended advances in engineering, but the three 'marks' that went before were all terrible machines, each new one a few months after the last, and each adopting a fraction of the improvement learnt from failures. The Mark IV was still the Mark III which was Mark II in disguise, a slightly refined Mark I.

The wags among the ranks pointed out Churchill was running the navy at the time. Ships only had to float, not cross ditches, flatten wire or cope with boarders willing to drop a grenade down the spout. The wags were wags because what else did you have out here but humour?

The men stayed on at Madame Franny's while Eustace trudged back to camp with French money unspent in his pockets. He didn't suppose restraint made much of a difference, yet it mattered to him.

He sat up past midnight typing his letter. Straight backed. No more cigarettes. A dozen attempts approaching success. He had mastered the mechanism, but could not quite master the words.

This is why your son died…
Thou shalt not kill…
…for King and Country…
…for God…

He jerked forward, trying to sweep the typewriter from the table. Fifty pounds was too much to move. The table slid an inch on the stone floor, that's all. He laughed suddenly. How could anyone believe this stubborn machine could make butchery look official? Or be a better means for recording it?

He was lost in thought when Woody's flushed-red face appeared again in the doorway, peeping around the curtain. He must have barely made the curfew.

"I came to report, formal-like. We're all back now, Sir. Safe and sound. Six of us. Well, seven counting you."

Eustace said, "Thank you, Sergeant."

"Sir? If you don't mind… Are you alright?"

"There'll always be one missing, Woody, won't there?" he said.

"Yes, Sir. Always one missing," Woody agreed. "But seven of us made it."

Chapter Two

Eustace's elder brother, John, named after their father, had received a swift discharge for medical reasons no one ever explained. His younger brother William joined up when he came of age in 1918, with just enough time to die before the war ended.

The news arrived in Nottingham on the day after Armistice. A shaky handwritten letter from Eustace's mother took another two weeks to return to France, though he was by then no more than twenty miles from the *Sambre–Oise* canal where William had drowned in phosgene gas.

Eustace returned home a captain, cast among the courageous, awarded the Military Cross with three bars. A handful of men received the honour with multiple commendations, each repeating, "For conspicuous gallantry and devotion to duty…"

A cartoon of a dashing Captain Havershall spread in propaganda, his name becoming an advert for the Allied victory. Passing posters of himself in the street, he enjoyed only the ones people had defaced — glasses and beards and devil horns. His first commendation was for the single-handed advance at Cambrai, his last was for driving his tank between straggling British soldiers pinned down in bomb holes and thirty Austro-Hungarians who were closing in. The stragglers were led by Major Peregrine Squires, nephew of a Government minister back home. Tank fire scattered the attackers. Arms and legs and whole bodies were left behind. A week earlier, Eustace had made a daring manoeuvre to relieve fifty trench diggers of the British West Indies Regiment, outnumbered three to one by advancing Germans. Saving common men, especially black men, got no mention in despatches. Saving a favoured nephew won medals. He would always remember the lesson.

The lice washed out of his hair and the black scars on his hands began fading. Eustace swore he would never return to the family business. He wasn't wanted there and he was no longer sufficiently delicate for lace. With his medals, he had more than a few job offers and he needed to make a living of his own.

He moved to London and joined Weatherstone & Hoare's bank as a junior executive, knowing nothing about banking. He was good for the bank's business — their man, the war hero — providing the illusion of a changed world, while invoking the national pride of the old. He shared an office with Archie Hoare, the son of the managing partner, a tall young man of his own age who sat at his desk chair like a stick insect rearranging its limbs. Archie knew the bright young things of London, had been to school with half of them, the other half being sisters and cousins of those who had shared his education or sat in the same ministry jobs while the fighting was in France.

From the off, Eustace showed a natural understanding of money. Battlefields and lonely billets had nurtured a talent for stillness. He had learned to listen and wait, and to seize the moment when the moment was ripe. He proved himself the perfect dealmaker.

By the time the Social Season renewed its usual splendour in 1920, Eustace was climbing the lists of eligible upstarts invited to débutante balls, even to the special enclosures at sporting events, his red industrial blood mixing with the blue. Weatherstone & Hoare's encouraged him to accept the more prestigious invitations.

He grew a moustache in the style of Douglas Fairbanks. Young women above his station were introduced. He danced with them, or spoke politely, but he found himself looking for that girl in the yellow bonnet. How well did he remember her? Her face had faded. The idea of her remained. Meeting her again, it seemed, might prove something about the 'them' and 'us' of the new order. He wasn't sure what, or indeed, if the new order differed from the old.

Interminable dinner parties with knights of the realm, two shooting weekends, the Grand National, then Ascot — Eustace Havershall did them all. Henley came next.

The Henley Regatta was another toffs' event. The toffest of toffs' events, that's what his father, John Senior, had called it when Eustace mentioned his invitation. All about money and power, not sportsmanship.

"*Esprit de cours* has boundaries, you'll see," his father said.

He was right. The rules ensured that those of raw talent, without money or privilege, would never be allowed on its eccentric one-mile-550-yards of water. Working class boys who may have supplemented their athletic endeavours with coaching or teaching were declared 'professional'. Those working around boats for money, even in the boating lake hire business, were forbidden. Muscled young gutter snipes who had been 'by trade or employment for wages a mechanic, artisan or labourer' were banned by the amateur code of

1879. Physical work for one's own financial subsistence amounted to cheating.

In the regatta of 1920, the talk among the crowds was of American Olympic champion John B. Kelly, excluded because he had once apprenticed as a bricklayer. He was, by the rules, a professional.

Eustace was invited to the Stewards' Enclosure. *You're knocking on the wrong door, Son. Don't you always?* He accepted anyway.

He arrived at the regatta with Archie Hoare, both guests of Sir John Bowles. After lunch, he slipped away to the riverside to watch the spectator boats casting off as the Eights were due to race. It felt cooler by the water. His lounge suit, dictated by the dress code, was thick and itchy. He had been unable to afford another in lighter cloth, having purchased four outfits for the season already. He was sure he must be the sweatiest man in Henley.

A launch of a dozen people was leaving a pontoon. He gazed after it.

And there she was.

He felt impossibly certain, even at this distance, and even though the yellow bonnet had gone. Yes, it was her, today wearing a blue straw boater, blue dress, a clutch of men surrounding her among the other gaily dressed ladies. He rushed forward along the pontoon, almost failing to stop at the edge.

"I say. I'm sorry, but that young lady, I'm sure I know her."

The launch had puttered away out of reach. Another young woman remained ashore, seemingly left behind.

"Now, would that be the skinny girl in the green hat, or the fat one with the pink head band? Some men prefer that kind," she said.

"The blue. The blue, of course."

"Oh, my dear Sir, we do tilt at windmills."

"Windmills?" he repeated.

"That would be Caroline Buckley, Lord Montague Buckley's daughter. Viscount Fairchild's fiancée."

"She's engaged?"

"That's usually part of the arrangement, so I understand. It isn't different in England, is it?"

"You're American?" he said, belatedly catching her mid-Atlantic accent.

"Not really."

"Not really?"

She allowed him a sardonic smile. She appeared awfully young, he thought, to be unescorted. The rules of youth and protection were so different here, of course. This was *Society*. She was undeniably pretty, though — violet eyes shaped like almonds, bobbed dark hair peeping from beneath a linen cloche hat. She wore an ivory drop-waist dress in the season's style, just long enough to meet the code.

"I think my father liked the idea of cowboys. Took us West before the war." Shaping her fingers, she fired an imaginary gun. "Never got further than New York."

"So you *are* English?"

"Disgraced English."

His confusion made her smile.

"I've been sent to the old country to improve myself. Tell me, is it usual here for a gentleman without a formal introduction to accost ladies with questions about their cousins?"

His gaze strayed to the back of the straw boater and blue dress of the soon-to-be Viscountess Fairchild, holding until she was nothing but a coloured hat in that highest clique he could not access.

"I was sure it was her," he said. He had begun to have doubts.

"Perhaps, Sir, you could dive in gallantly and maintain the pursuit," his companion suggested. "It happens in all the best tales of unrequited love. Did you never read that novel? What's it called? It's by Beerbohm?"

A first edition of 'Zuleika Dobson' — the novel in question, a scandalous satire on the love lives of Oxford undergraduates — had been added to the Havershall family library before the war. Its publicity underlined everything his father believed: *'Breeding failed to produce thoroughbreds.'* Only Eustace had read it.

"The men in that book come to a deliciously sticky end," she continued. "Mostly they drown. Such is the course of true love, I suppose."

A moment later, she was off, marching up the grassy bank towards the Steward's Enclosure.

"Cousins?" he repeated to himself, as the relationship registered. "Cousins!"

He hadn't got her name, too slow to spot the old world leaving and the new arriving.

He compared blue dress to yellow bonnet, but came to no conclusion other than that Viscount Fairchild's fiancée was gone. Beyond him, clearly. Perhaps she had never been anything other than an idea. He was a fool. Not so far from the young men in Beerbohm's novel, only poorer and considerably more scarred.

He spotted the girl in the cloche hat again a half-hour later. Since racing had started, the enclosures were almost deserted. She was standing outside a drinks' marquee, hand resting on a stand-up table, smoking a cigarette and clutching what he took to be Pimms. There was fruit decorating her glass. He grappled with his courage.

"May I begin again?"

She gave him a puzzled look.

"A gentleman without formal introduction…" he explained.

She granted permission with a nod.

"Eustace Havershall at your service."

"Oh, I know who you are," she said.

"You do?"

"Golly, I should think most of Henley has pointed you out, Captain Havershall. England is so proud of her heroes. You're quite the bee's knees, I've been told."

"So you didn't need the formal introduction after all?"

"What one does or does not need is hardly the issue. It's a question of entitlement."

"And you are… entitled?"

After holding his gaze a moment, she burst into laughter. "Oh, it's all balderdash, stuff and nonsense from the stuffier classes!"

She looked around as if expecting someone to arrive and, finding no one, extended her hand. "Virginia Buckley. Ginny. You may kiss it or shake it, as long as you don't make it too beastly."

Thrown for a moment, he took the hand and kissed the back of it.

"Most chivalrous," she remarked, seeming very pleased with herself.

"Do not tempt me, Miss Buckley. I cannot swim," he said.

"What?"

"Earlier, you quoted that Beerbohm novel. Everyone drowns. For love, or for romantic foolishness. It does not seem *delicious*."

"You are mocking me."

"A little. Dying is a serious business for a soldier. I hated the novel. It reminded me of the idiots in charge of the war. We jumped in and they insisted on holding our head under."

"Oh, dear, you are far too—" She stopped herself. He was still clutching her hand. He let it loose. An uncertain smile lingered on her face. "I know I am forced to spend far too much time with English aristocracy and its stupidity, Captain. Perhaps you are the smarter man? If you'll excuse me, I should drink this before I am recaptured and returned to the mill. I went to all this trouble to lose my chaperone."

"You lost your chaperone?"

"Yes. You do seem to have the habit of repeating parts of my every sentence. Is that also terribly English?" She thought for a moment, then said, "If you wish to become my best friend, you could be a brick and buy me another Pimms while I finish this one. I'm afraid the barman in there thinks I am under age."

"Are you?"

"No," she said. And then, "Well, yes. Seventeen. It's just a number. Though I should say, if it is of interest to yourself, I have been forced to don the court dress and the white gloves. I have been pronounced 'available' in that least-available sense."

"A débutante?"

"Quite beastly, isn't it, with the veil and the ostrich feathers? I have done the royal curtsies, two of them actually. It was necessary to satisfy my mother. Part of my penance."

"Ah, a reluctant débutante then?"

"That's the gist of it. Tell me, why do Englishmen need a ceremony? Are they blind? New York boys seemed to know what I was eligible for. I did not have to advertise. Now, the British game is afoot, protecting one's honour while offering it for sale to a man of fortune."

"I am not a man of fortune," he assured her.

"Oh, do not worry, Captain, I would not come parading myself around you. I am quite unsuitable for an up-and-coming gentleman, a banker, so I'm told. You see, I am the blackest sheep of the Buckleys. Expensive but scandalous. I drink with strange men."

"A moment ago, you assured me I was well known."

"Indeed, you are. Yet not all things well known can be allowed to become familiar." She looked him up and down once more, as if reappraising what a captain with medals and a banking job might offer as entertainment. "I shall be the envy and the talk of every lady in Henley – the flibbertigibbet who spoke with the captain, and so brazenly without her chaperone too. I'll soon run out of continents on which to make a bad reputation. Maybe I should find that working class scoundrel John Kelly and sail off into the sunset, fellow rejects heading for Africa, or Asia. Anywhere but here. Here, they only let the great and the good win prizes. Poor Mr Kelly. Let him race, I say, just for the hell of it."

Eustace thought of a bricklayer winning at Henley. He would have liked to see that.

She continued talking, bemoaning the necessity of coming to England until, without warning, her mouth froze in a perfect 'O'. It took him a moment to realise the 'O' spelt alarm.

Looking over his shoulder, he saw a sour-faced middle-aged lady, elegantly dressed but a decade out of fashion, striding towards them.

"Ah, your chaperone?"

"My aunt, the Lady Buck. Stand an arm's length further away if you know what's good for you." Ginny stubbed out her cigarette in the ashtray at her elbow. "Quickly, listen, the Fairchilds have a tennis party tomorrow. Theirs is the big place up by Marlow. You must know it."

He didn't.

"We're all staying there. Come and save me. They want to shove me with some geriatric Earl to even up the teams. It's awful. Do you play?"

"Not really."

"Good, well, that should do. As long as you can hit the ball. Hello, Aunt!" she called as Lady Montague Buckley drew within earshot.

"Virginia?"

The disdainful voice sent a shiver through Eustace. Ginny stood her ground.

"Virginia, who's this you're talking to? You told me you were going out with Caroline."

"I'm recruiting a doubles partner, Aunt. This is Captain Havershall. He's a famous tank driver. That is what you did, isn't it, Captain?"

"Um, yes, I suppose."

"He says he can't come and play, but I've persuaded him. Quite the *coup d'état*, don't you think? That Bessie Cranmer was here a moment ago, inviting him to their place with the Prince of Wales, but he has promised he'll come to our party now, haven't you, Captain? You can't back out, that would be ungentlemanly."

She looked at him, her eyes urging, "Save me."

"I did indeed give my word," he said. "Duty calls the gentleman."

"Really... Virginia," her aunt scolded, but raised no further objection.

Of Eustace's surviving crew, Jones and Blenkinsop died before the end of the conflict in other tanks. Mulgrove lost an arm. Priestley got a medical discharge with Shell Shock. McAllister slunk home after the Armistice and Eustace never heard from him again. Woody headed back to his Northern roots.

It felt odd that those names were once so close, sharing the bound certainty that they would never see England again. Yet now, here he was, Eustace Havershall, invited to visit the Fairchilds of Marlow. He astonished even himself.

The Fairchild Estate seemed to own half the leafy trees in the land. It had deer herds and lakes and monuments without purpose in the middle of nowhere. A drive from gatehouse to main buildings took almost three minutes. The house, which he was assured had rooms for fifty guests, was fronted by a semi-circular forecourt of stone chip, accessible to cars or horse-drawn carriages.

He parked his car, on loan from Archie Hoare, next to other grander vehicles and presented himself at the front door. As per his invitation, he was togged up in flannel trousers which he'd borrowed from Sir John Bowles's son and a tennis racket with a frayed string he'd found in Bowles's billiard room.

The butler greeted him, a severe man who muttered sniffily, "Oh, yes, Sir," when Eustace mentioned Virginia Buckley's invitation. The man showed him around the back of the property to a pair of tennis courts where twenty guests had gathered, picking food and champagne flutes from a buffet table. Half were dressed for tennis, the others — mainly of an older generation — for afternoon tea. Many parasols were in evidence. The place smelt of cut grass and summer.

Other people's tennis whites were radiant, brand new no doubt. No one made an effort to introduce themselves. After several awkward minutes, Ginny bounded towards him in a knee-length tennis dress and blush pink head scarf, her hair pushed back up her pale forehead.

"I had begun to doubt you, Captain," she said.

"I thought I was summoned."

"'Summoned' makes me sound terribly bossy. But, well, you should not mind it," she informed him. "A word of warning before we start. I like to win."

He looked down at his racquet. She touched his arm and said, "I'm sure it will be fine. These people expect me to be genteel. Three New York schools and a Boston finishing academy couldn't teach me the art of losing gracefully, I'm afraid." She giggled conspiratorially. "'Why so many schools,' you ask?"

"I didn't ask."

She seemed to regard this lack of curiosity as good manners, if a little disappointing. They began to discuss the weather forecast for the afternoon's play.

The players were divided into six pairs, but since there were eight gentlemen and four ladies, the teams were uneven. Two had to be assigned as men's doubles. It made no difference once Ginny got on the court. She was the youngest there, but by far the most determined and talented.

The matches played out in a round robin, each over a best of five games. All but three finished 3-0 to one side or the other. Eustace and Ginny won four matches without losing a game.

She insisted they drank water not champagne in the breaks, but accepted his cigarettes. Ginny delighted in spilling salacious details about the party-goers. Some, he was sure, were made up — a distant cousin who lost his leg to a crocodile; another she claimed as the co-inventor of moustache curling tongs.

A couple he recognised from the newspapers arrived midway through the tournament — Winston Churchill and his wife Clementine. They stood talking with Lord Buckley, Viscount Fairchild and a neat moustachioed young man in a suit.

"There, you see," said Ginny. "Bessie Cranmer doesn't always get her own way with the *crème de la crème*. Just because she knows princes. We have the Churchills."

Out of the blue, Eustace said, "I'd like to go over and punch him."

"Oh, you mean, Winston?"

He wanted to explain the urge, but he knew his simple 'I fought in tanks' would make no sense.

"Dear Eustace," she said, making an effort to read his expression. "That's all over... In France, it's all over. *This* is the reward. Can't you let it be over?"

She tapped the side of her head. She suddenly didn't seem so young.

He forced a smile, deciding he should change the subject. "I say, don't I know the man with the silly moustache?"

"That's Mosley, MP for Harrow. One never knows which party he's supporting, that's what my uncle says. Churchill's trying to recruit him for the Liberals, though no one's too sure where Winston stands either. Edward hates him."

"Edward?"

"The Viscount Fairchild, Caroline's chap," she reminded him. "Rather too stiff for my liking. And rather too old for Caroline. Filthy rich, of course. Look at this place of his. Thinks socialists should be shot and we should all be watching Mussolini."

"Who's Mussolini?"

"You are out of touch, aren't you? They were talking about him at Henley, some Italian who worked for MI5 during the war. Edward thinks he'll be Prime Minister and lead the Wops into some great Imperialist age. I can't see that, can you? Italians triumphant?"

"The Italians reneged on their treaties and fought on our side."

"Exactly. Nothing good ever comes of that. But what do I know of politics? I'm a deb. I must look pretty. Say nothing. Stay chaste. I'm a deb. I am a deb."

Her voice descended the scale as she spoke, becoming deep and masculine by the last incantation. She giggled and he laughed. Someone far away shouted their names and told them they were playing next.

The decisive match featured Ginny and Eustace against the unbeaten Ainsley twins, who were twenty-five and looked like Greek gods. Eustace served. Ginny crouched at the net. When Fred Ainsley, the first to receive, cracked a forehand down the line, Ginny sprang forward, skirt billowing behind her, and backhanded a volley between the twins for a winner. Jack Ainsley hit the return from the next serve straight at her. She ducked to the side and blocked the shot with her racquet, the ball falling dead and lifeless over the net for another winning point. The crowd applauded politely.

Despite the evidence, the twins assumed Ginny's success a fluke. They continued to hit the ball in her direction for three games, all three of which they lost. Ginny and Eustace came closest to conceding on a deuce point. A sliced return that Ginny chased to the baseline caught the chalk and skidded, resisting her efforts to dig it up on the half volley.

Eustace, six feet away, distinctly heard the word, "Fuck."

He smiled at her. "That's their Advantage, I'm afraid."

"Fiddlesticks," she said, louder so everyone who hadn't heard her first word would definitely hear the second.

They won the remaining points and the match without Eustace hitting another ball.

"Hurrah for us, Captain!" she cried.

She raised the small winners' trophy and hugged him with childish joy, the tremble of her body like the neurotic beat of hummingbird wings. As Beerbohm's young men, he was fatally smitten.

Only afterwards did he realise he'd not given a thought to his young lady of the yellow bonnet, even though she'd been right there, no more than a stone's throw away all afternoon. How fickle is the human heart?

The tank crew needed a story to explain the bullet hole in Masterson's ruined face. It wasn't hard. With a hundred thousand and more casualties to explain, life was cheap and the expense of mercy easily hidden, so Eustace and his men made Masterson heroic.

In the letter, Eustace had typed one painful keystroke at a time: "… protecting the mechanic working under the tank…caught the side splatter of a grenade…fought on with a German who'd sprung out of nowhere with a revolver…died for his country and his comrades."

In Eustace's own hand, it might have seemed a greater lie. But he typed and typed. He found a rhythm. A release. His grief flowed out with the words and the fantasy.

No mention of how the boy had moaned continually. That wouldn't find a place on the paper.

"Please, please."

He wouldn't stop moaning. Eustace wouldn't stop typing the boy's praises.

"Please, please…"

"Please, please…"

And the bullet made him silent.

After one more war, the son of the once-banned John B. Kelly would win the Diamond Sculls at Henley. His daughter, Grace, would marry the Prince of Monaco and become the most glamorous of all the toffs and aristocrats in Europe.

But not in 1920.

Chapter Three

Arriving from America, Virginia Buckley had a taste for all things modern and London's one advantage over New York was the continued availability of liquor for which she had plenty of appetite. Her educational record which Eustace had refused to probe read something like this: kicked out of one school at twelve, out of a second for insubordination over the length of school skirts, one more expulsion followed before she was finally ejected from a ladies' finishing academy after inviting unauthorised boys for the homecoming dance.

Young Ginny was, by all accounts, a little too 'spirited'.

At her distant mother's insistence, she took up residence in her aunt's house in a private mews off Brook Street, close to Grosvenor Square and a short walk from Hyde Park — six bedrooms, four floors, a basement and more servants than Ginny cared to count.

To a New York girl with memories of jazz and the fashions of early flappers, London seemed mostly tired and grey, full of smoke and fogs and the odour of horse manure. Motorised transport was arriving too slowly for anyone with modern sensibilities, especially for those with a sense of smell.

When Eustace Havershall began calling — a chancer from a family in one of *those industrial towns* — he was immediately branded 'ineligible' by the Buckleys. Nothing could have elevated him in Ginny's mind so effectively. She adopted him as her *cause célèbre*. She thought his silences profound. Gentlemen never listened to women, but Eustace listened to everybody.

He told her he liked the 'new' music. He followed the arrival in England of the Southern Syncopated Orchestra and the Original Dixieland Jazz Band who brought the 'Tiger Rag' as their signature tune. He knew where to find live jazz in London and he carried imported cigarettes, the strong continental brands she preferred. They were impossible to find if you didn't know the city's tobacco shops, and such tobacco shops were impossible if you weren't a man.

He amazed her by guessing her taste in almost everything. One afternoon, he took her to a private art gallery tucked into an unassuming building off Oxford Street. The collection featured, among others, two Picassos, a rare early work by Georges Braques and several canvases by Matisse.

"Don't you love Matisse?" she said, her eye sweeping across the nearest. "The image is so vivid, even if it's not wholly… there, I suppose."

"My impression of modern art is rather like my impression of banking," he told her.

"That sounds like you're trying to be clever."

"No, it's just that both are a wonderful illusion. Imagination is doing the creation. A fellow throws down a few painted strokes and we see a table, a bowl of fruit, a man."

"Yes, but how is that like banking? Now, Eustace, you are being obtuse."

"Banking is an art. The essence is to create 'credit' — the illusion of money, like the illusion of art. A man with nothing can spend wealth he hasn't got, make his tuppence and still have a profit after he's paid his creditor, the venerable banker."

"So, let me understand, you are claiming you are not so much a hero as a conjurer?"

"It is all the more a conjuring trick, because a bank is giving out money it doesn't possess. Not only allowing penniless men to spend money they don't have, but doing it with money that doesn't exist."

"Don't play me for a dumb kluck. That can't be possible. I understand a loan. I have money. I give it to you. After a while you give it back. It's simple and real."

"Not at all. People who borrow the non-existent money pay it to other people who deposit what they apparently receive. Where? In banks. There's the sleight of hand, you see, money has been paid, but money has not moved and no one has had to show that the money exists."

"What if all the people want to withdraw their funds at the same time?"

"They don't."

"What if they did?"

"Then, dear Gin, the whole of civilisation comes to an end. You must never think that way, because even thinking it can trigger the Fall of Man, and of bankers. Credit is a *'dance with the Devil'*."

"And yet you are a banker?"

"I am," he said. "That illusion allows our country to recover… For now, at least."

"You are a funny old stick," she said, shaking her head. "Must we go outside to smoke, do you think?"

"I can't imagine the fog would hurt the focus of this sad work."

They were currently next to the Braques' painting. Nobody else was paying it any attention.

"I think you are a cynic, Mr Havershall. About far too many things. You're not a communist by any chance?" She glanced to either side as if uncomfortable saying the word. "I knew one once. He stole my silver cigarette lighter."

"I do not approve of political ideals," he said.

"It seems you refuse to approve of anything."

"Not true, I think you are marvellous. Of this, I approve. I am yet to be convinced I am mistaken."

She laughed. He laughed with her. They went outside to share a cigarette on the steps of the gallery.

"Do I look awfully like my cousin?" she asked, once the cigarette was lit.

"No. Why? Of course not," he stumbled.

"She was the one you hankered after when we first met."

"Yes," he admitted. "But a man only sets proper standards when he has found the best."

"Nicely said." She pulled a disbelieving face. "So, romantic that you are, you'd go running down pontoons for me?"

"I told you, I am not a fan of Beerbohm. But anyway, you are by far the prettiest Buckley, and have wit and vim with it. That is the truth. There, are you satisfied?"

She squeezed his arm. "I am never satisfied. My beastly uncle says I am decorous, but lack decorum. I am consequently hopeless."

"My father thinks I'm becoming a worthless toff," he said heavily.

"Then we're made for each other," she said as she handed him the cigarette. "My aunt would think a lacemaker's son too ambitious in all the wrong kind of ways."

"A lacemaker's *second* son," he reminded her.

"Doesn't a *spare* have more room for lust and avarice? I'm sure it makes them much more fun to watch," she said.

That was perhaps his favourite day.

The following week, when the knighted industrialist, Joshua Harvey came seeking loans for his new factories, three banks offered him a half million pounds at three percent above the base rate. Refusing to accept defeat, Eustace, on behalf of Weatherstone & Hoare's, took Harvey's shares in Jamaican sugar plantations as collateral and provided the money at two and three-quarters with an extra preferred dividend from profits. Sealing the deal with his signature, Sir Alfred Hoare, the bank's managing partner, called it 'inspired'.

Eustace tried to imagine how Ginny would see it. Surely, the ambition required of a 'suitable' gentleman must be more than one quarter of a percent in a loan. The success left him uneasy, and hungry for more, since this didn't seem enough.

Ginny's cousin Caroline had many opinions now she was engaged. For example, she said that a young woman's intentions with a gentleman can be judged by how long she spends preparing for an evening in his company. Ginny began spending more evenings with Eustace Havershall and more time arranging and rearranging her appearance before each one.

Coming from New York, she had brought several innovations for the control of body hair — a *Milady Decolletée*, Gillette's first razor for women, and two different brands of depilatory cream. Sleeveless dresses and shorter hemlines demanded smooth legs for the summer and the removal of underarm hair. She became fastidious in both, preparing herself to be looked at. She powdered her face lightly and perfumed her skin with hints of the exotic.

She told her aunt she was going with a special gentleman high in a Mayfair bank, the kind who makes money appear from thin air. Eustace's name was hidden behind the illusion.

They went to racy shows like 'The Naughty Princess' at the Adelphi Theatre which featured royals living outrageously among Parisian street artists, and on to late night dancing clubs where a gentleman would seldom venture with a young lady whose reputation was in his hands.

Virginia Buckley surprised him every time. She loved to shock and argue. He hung on her voice in its high dudgeon, the way her cheeks clenched and the agitated way she smoked, cigarette held boldly, eschewing the fashion for holders with long stems. She spoke wonderfully without borrowing the words of others, or slavishly agreeing their opinions. For someone whose background gave her not a care in the world, she cared for everything with unwavering passion.

She possessed a pure and natural vitality. She did not depend on the paraphernalia of her class or her gender. Her beauty needed no advantages from a charcoaled eye-line to enhance the sparkle in the eyes or the deep powder that filled the imperfections in skin or the skill of a couturier to reshape a body line. In her company, he laughed with childish abandon as if he hadn't been doing it properly for a while and had just rediscovered the knack.

The pair became regulars at Ciro's nightclub in Orange Street, with its imposing pillars and a Louis XVI décor in delicious lettuce green and burnt gold. It was licensed until 2 a.m. Often, she danced on when all he could do was sit watching breathlessly. 'Tiger Rag' became their song.

"We must do something wild, preferably illegal," she told him as one such evening finally faded. "That way a lifetime's friendship will be formed, don't you think?"

At that moment, they were trundling around Leicester Square in a horse-drawn Hansom. She shouted for Fredrick, their driver, to halt. After a few short months in London, she seemed to know every Hansom cab driver by name.

She and Eustace leapt down, her leading, him following.

"Bicycles," she announced, pointing at two she had spotted in an alley.

"Oh, no," he replied.

"Come on now. No slacking. Are you sure you're quite ruthless enough to be a banker? Disappointing really. Handsome, I suppose, but not ruthless."

"You think I should be?"

"My cousin Caroline says, all self-made men must be ruthless. They are of an upstart kind — ambitious, desperate, scared."

"If that's me, what about you?"

"I'm not scared, Eustace. Not of anything."

"I am not ruthless."

She looked at him doubtfully.

"No? Maybe you just haven't realised it yet," she concluded.

She ran towards the bicycles, took one and left him with the smaller, rustier of the pair. They rode them back to Brook Street with only a half-moon to lead the way. She pedalled with the same ecstatic frenzy with which she danced, ignoring the possibility of traffic.

The next day, Eustace came to Brook Street while her aunt was out, pleading that they should return the bikes to where they'd found them.

"I steal bicycles and you would give them back?"

"I would," he said.

"So typical!"

She faked a disappointed look, which left him unprepared for the moment she kissed him, sudden and impulsive like everything about her.

"I didn't know the moustache would tickle," she said.

"I could shave it off."

"No, no, it's the height of fashion, I'm sure."

Before she would agree to the return of stolen goods, she kissed him again, her weight submitting itself to his embrace as she hung in his arms, perched on her toes to reach his lips. As much as he wanted all of her, he had never before dared to think of himself as anything but the man who took her dancing.

"Very well. We shall do as you ask and give back the bicycles," she said. "I know when a man must be obeyed."

"Obeyed or indulged?" he asked.

She laughed. "You see, I knew it. Once you have me, you press the advantage and tease me unmercifully. Quite ruthless. I should have listened to my cousin."

They walked the bicycles back to the alley, because being together lasted longer at that speed. He left two sixpences tied to the handlebars in one of her monogrammed handkerchiefs.

Joseph Woodmansey limped into the offices of Weatherstone & Hoare's on November 11th, 1920, anniversary of Armistice. He struggled with a heavy square box tied up with thick string to make a handle. He took off his flat cap and asked for Captain Havershall. He did not have an appointment.

"Tell him, it's his old Sergeant," he urged.

Mabel Perec, the senior secretary, assured him it was 'impossible'. She did not like the look of his cheap suit and the faint odour of pickled onions.

Unbidden, he started to unpack his box.

Mabel Perec was twenty-seven and unmarried, the daughter of a Swiss diamond merchant of Jewish descent who had migrated in a series of unlikely moves to Bristol with his French wife, establishing a chain of jewellery shops across the south-west of England. They were important supporters of the local synagogue.

Mabel graduated from the first ever cohort of the Secretarial Course at St James College, founded by a former private secretary to the Churchills. In 1917, she had been the first woman hired for a clerical position in Weatherstone & Hoare's. War had forced the partners to seek able employees irrespective of gender. Her language skills — she was fluent in three languages — were a positive boon to her employer.

Accustomed to the clacking Remington typewriters that all the secretaries used, Mabel had never seen a 'noiseless' model. All 'those machines' were useless, she told him as the contents of his box became apparent. Typewriters were unreliable American contraptions, spewing out illegible documents, spreading ink, jamming at the worst moments, and even mangling the sheets they were supposed to produce. Unwieldy and loud. How could you put a dozen typists in an office and not deafen everyone?

"I can fix all that," the young man assured her.

Returning from a meeting at the Bank of England, Eustace found Mabel sitting in the centre of the ledger office, three other woman looking on, tapping away at a new typewriter.

"You see," said the salesman, his back to Eustace, his attention on Mabel's elegant fingers as he leaned over, "this mechanism decelerates the typebar before pressing it against the ribbon and paper."

"It's not silent though," Mabel complained.

"Nothing is ever silent, Miss, but the clack-clack-clack that has ruined offices for years can now be banished."

"It is more of a *thunk*," she agreed.

She typed the word, 'Balderdash'.

"Quite satisfying," she declared. Eustace noticed her smile — unusual, because Mabel rarely smiled during office hours. She thought it unprofessional.

The salesman began explaining how his 'Shift Lock' key tipped the paper-holding roller so that a different part of the typebar struck the page. "The key locks in place. You don't have to hold it down while typing in capitals."

Eustace finally recognised the voice. "Woody?"

Joseph Woodmansey turned around. He had grown a beard, lost his acne, wore round-framed spectacles for working this close to his machines. He seemed to have grown an inch or two. There was dirt under his fingernails though, Eustace noticed. That hadn't changed.

"Captain!" he said. "They told me you were quite unavailable, Sir."

"Woody, what on earth are you doing here?"

Woody made a pantomime of checking his surroundings. "Searching for money, Captain. I heard this was a bank."

* * *

Joseph Woodmansey had grown up with farm machinery, apprenticed to Stuart Hobson, a blacksmith in Salford, at age fourteen. Hobson fixed machines at the Endsley Screw Factory and doubled as a motorbike mechanic. He owned an early Rudge Multi, the road version of the bike that won the 1914 Senior TT.

Woody learned as Hobson's shadow. He taught himself to read. He was conscripted at eighteen when the Military Service Act passed in January 1916. By then, he was a skilled engineer.

After the war, Woody made £15 selling the design for a powered laundry mangle. He gave five pounds to his mother and enrolled himself in a night school to improve his reading and writing. His elocution improved; he even lost part of his accent. With the remainder of his money, he bought tooling from the defunct Wainwright Typewriter Company which had never sold more than one hundred machines in its entire existence.

"I thought about it, Captain," he told Eustace. "We all needed something real... after a war. Real and a bit more peaceful. People are going to need to write things down. But see, I'm an engineer, not an artist. I cannot write the fancy words. I can shape them though."

He designed the 'noiseless' prototype from scratch and that was all the hope standing between him and re-enlisting in the army. He needed money to put it into production.

Sir Alfred George Hoare played gatekeeper for all commercial loans to new customers in excess of one thousand and ninety-two pounds and eight shillings. This arbitrary threshold had grown since Sir Alfred inherited his position from his father. The words 'emptying a dam through a pee-hole' had been used at the partners' monthly sherry parties. Sir Alfred had appeased complainants by raising the threshold two percent at a time. He liked to pretend this represented a delegation of authority. Actually, it served to reinforce the unflinching rigidity of his control.

Sir Alfred, now sixty-one years old, was married to the Duke of Devon's daughter, and sufficiently related to the King to have inherited the royal family's hemophilia. His uncle, so company history recorded, had bled to death after an accident with a crystal brandy decanter dropped on the bank's boardroom floor in 1884.

Eustace sat now in that same voluminous room with the white-whiskered Sir Alfred eyeing him over half-moon spectacles. The scent of the room was not blood, but chair leather, polish from the table and spice from Sir Alfred's English cologne.

"You recommend this loan? Almost two thousand for a *new* customer?" Sir Alfred said with the papers Eustace had prepared in his hand. "For this man of your acquaintance."

"Yes, Sir. My acquaintance is noted in my memorandum. I served with the man, Sir."

"A mechanic from a tank?"

"His financial projections are sound. He has firm contracts with profit enough to cover the interest."

"To make mechanical writing machines?"

"Yes, Sir. We have loans at much greater risk, I believe."

"Perhaps," Sir Alfred agreed, "but you must understand the difference between risk and confidence."

Eustace was unsure what the great man was getting at. Sir Joshua Harvey's half million, which had gone through on an approving nod, seemed much the riskier deal.

"These are exciting times, Mr Havershall. The world is expanding, remaking itself anew. But it all relies on confidence. A run on this or any bank in London upon these circumstances could not be defended once triggered. Catastrophe might ensue."

Eustace nodded. This was the point he had made himself when explaining his job to Ginny.

"Excuse me, Sir. The difference between risk and confidence? Surely, in the case of a commercial loan, the lack of one creates the other?"

Sir Alfred shook his head. "Oh dear, no. Perhaps if we were considering a game of cards, Mr Havershall, you would be correct. The noble game of poker, for example. Holding four of a kind reduces the risk of the bet, but cards are not people, young man. We have confidence in our friends."

"*Our* friends…?"

"Sir Joshua, for example. Confidence, to an English banker, Mr Havershall, means backing the clients you know or who are vouchsafed by those same known clients. The breeding of a gentleman is everything. One backs one's friends, those chums you have done business with before. The quality of a business idea matters only so much."

Sir Alfred's smirk made clear that 'so much' meant 'little or nothing'.

One obvious question struck Eustace. "Then how will a man rise in business?"

"How indeed? I am explaining how this bank places its confidences."

"But, Sir…?"

"Ah yes," said Sir Alfred, as if he understood the question of a foolish child. "If I were a cynic, I might say that this Capitalism in whose largesse we bathe is sustained by rich people. They have everything, yet labour on, proving how much they deserve their success by earning more. And believe me, Mr Havershall, we do bathe, and comfortably too. The poor make nothing from nothing and thereby prove that they deserve nothing better. I'm afraid prosperity sticks to old money like a toffee paper to the fingers."

Sir Alfred made the point by rubbing his thumb and forefinger together. "And who's to say we're not the better for it? Consider the case of Rolls-Royce, for example? It has seen something of a rise, I'm sure you'd agree."

Eustace had often heard his father express a dreamy desire to own a Rolls-Royce. No greater testimony to status existed than to be desired by an industrious Nottinghamshire lacemaker who spent most of his dreams craving a knighthood.

"Plenty of working men given employment by Rolls-Royce," Sir Alfred continued. "Formed on the brilliance of Henry Royce's engineering. Henry — I have met him several times — had but one year of formal schooling. Worked on the street corners selling newspapers before his employment with Great Western Rail. He ascended, of course, but to no avail when seeking investment. No, it was Charles Rolls who secured the funding on which Rolls-Royce grew, the third son of the 1st Baron Llangattock. Confidence, you see, my boy. Confidence."

"What if I took the loan? Invested in Woody's… in Mr Woodmansey's company?" Eustace suggested.

"You? You would become one of these manufacturing fellows — another 'typewriterist' no less?" Sir Alfred seemed to invent the word as a rebuke.

"I believe I have something of a reputation to call on, Sir."

"Ha!" said Sir Alfred.

Eustace felt confused. Hadn't Weatherstone & Hoare's told him his wartime reputation was an asset?

Shaking his head, Sir Alfred continued, "Consider the case of Billy Wells."

"The boxing bombardier? That Billy Wells?"

"The same, the boxer and Empire Champion. A soldier who has done service to the King, as you did. I attended his fight only the other evening. For a boxer, he is of the right colour, the right race, which as you know is becoming something of a growing rarity in the noble art. I would parade Mr Wells at a business dinner or make him the hero who represents the bank. Would I loan him money?"

The question was framed such that its answer was obvious.

"You are making yourself into a fine banker, my boy, an administrator of loans, but a suitable loanee? That is different."

Here, their interview ended. The walk from boardroom table to boardroom door seemed long. Eustace thought of the enthusiasm with which he had lauded banking to Ginny. That seemed foolish now.

In his shared office two floors below, Eustace stared out onto Threadneedle Street. The Old Lady — the Bank of England — loomed large in the distance.

"Archie," he said to his office colleague, "do you think your father would loan you, say, a few thousands, if you had a suitable business proposition?"

"Of course, Old Boy. The sum would not be an issue."

"I thought as much."

"What's the problem? If you need cash, I could loan you a fiver or two?"

Eustace picked several pages of the Bank's headed notepaper from his desk drawer and wandered down into the main office to find Mabel Perec. Against the clack-clack-clack of other machines, he attempted his letter of resignation one-fingered on her Remington. He wasted several sheets of paper with his failures.

"I could type it, Mr Havershall, if you'd care to dictate?" Mabel suggested.

"No," he said, more sharply than he intended. He thought of the last letter he'd typed and wondered why this one deserved the same personal touch. "I'm sorry. I have to do it."

That evening, Eustace and Ginny dined at Rules restaurant, Maiden Lane, an extravagance he could hardly afford without a job. The early evening diners were leaving for the theatre as she arrived, gliding in behind the maitre d', late by half an hour, dressed in a coutured green dress, hair perfectly marcelled. The flapper pearls hung so straight she must have strapped down her chest. She let him kiss the back of her hand, where she had carefully dabbed perfume, her smell a summer meadow.

"The staff told my aunt and now you are marked as a bicycle thief. I had the most fearful row getting out of the house," she complained.

"But the bicycles were your idea."

"That doesn't make it better. A gentleman led astray by a lady is more despised than a man who tempts a woman into sin. At least the latter has the gift of the gab. I had to tell my aunt I had a new beau."

"You invented a lover?"

"Not exactly invented, but yes, I went to great lengths. Your name is now Lord Michael. Went to school with Caroline's Viscount, I believe. I met him shopping in Oxford Street. Oh, don't look at me like that, Eustace. I do know a Lord Michael. He's queer as a Cornish banknote."

He laughed and, in this vein, they soon drank several glasses of champagne and a half-bottle of burgundy. The dinner plates were cleared and they sat sharing a warming decanter of port. He had begun to think of the bill, while she continued telling stories.

"This is the oldest restaurant in London, did you know? Founded by a Mr Tomas Rule, who murdered his wife and daughter and was later committed to a psychiatric hospital. There's a fact for you."

He chose not to tell her of his resignation. Not yet. He wanted the good moments to last. He felt he might never deserve them again.

Continuing, she told him how Rules Restaurant had once been swapped with the Alhambra in Paris. The whole Rule family had moved to France.

"I should like to go to Paris and become a dancer myself, or maybe an artist's model," she said. "Ah, to see the Folies Bergère and Zelli's. To stroll along the Champs-Élysées and eat at Fouquet's Brasserie. And maybe to practice my French. That's one thing a finishing school taught me. It seems such a waste not to use it. They dance naked, don't you know, in Paris? And the jazz is not the same. You never hear a half-competent saxophonist in London. I do love the saxophone. I should like to play. Perhaps I could learn."

"You? Play the saxophone? It doesn't seem like an instrument for a lady. Too mechanical," he said.

"Ah yes, that's because the one mechanical thing that suits a lady in the eyes of you men is a parasol. A lady may struggle with it in the slightest breeze until a gentleman comes to explain its mechanism and strong-arms the poor thing into obedience."

"Is this 'thing' the parasol or the lady?"

"Ha!" she said. "You're so… English. I am not one of your toffs, dear Eustace."

They sat there, staring at each other, until finally they burst into laughter.

"Why are we laughing?" she said, trying to control her mirth.

…which only made it funnier, since only the two of them understood the joke, and neither could explain it.

From her privileged position in her aunt and uncle's house, Ginny had seen how her cousin was fastened onto Viscount Edward Fairchild. The Buckley family planned the affair from the outset. Once Lady Buckley decided upon the couple's suitability, Caroline's fate was sealed. He was fifteen years her senior.

Her campaign — masterminded by her mother — had consisted of securing invitations to weekend parties which the Viscount was known to be attending, refusing dances with men of lesser wealth in order to keep slots on her dance card at balls and parties, dropping her work with the suffragettes, joining the ladies' section of his golf club, sending greetings cards and thank you notes to his mother to mark every possible occasion. Properly enticed, the Viscount could not but propose to such a desirable young lady.

His desirability, by contrast, was determined by the effortlessness of his money. When you owned money, you owned land, when you owned land, you received rent. Rent meant income. Steady income without visible exertion was the mark of an aristocratic gentleman.

Ginny decided that she hated aristocratic gentlemen.

A woman well married became a trophy for a man who did nothing, experienced nothing and consequently had nothing to say. Privilege, used badly, was a kind of naivety. It stifled the experience of life. How could such a man understand art or triumph?

As a wife, you wallowed in rich silks and jewels, hopefully producing the required offspring before you became fat and he didn't want you, which would be the luckiest outcome because childbirth became more dangerous as maturity set in. Once married, he was stuck with you and you with him, because no one could afford the disgrace of divorce. With good fortune, he'd die young and you'd be left, the gay rich widow, for a few years before you staggered into old age.

That might be well and good for Caroline, but it was not for her, Virginia Buckley. She wasn't sure what was.

* * *

"Shall I top up your glass, Gin? You seem a little indisposed."

Trying to extend their evening as far as it would stretch, Eustace reached for the port decanter.

Still on the subject of travel, she said, "You know it is not just Paris, I would love to take you to New York. But I suppose we can't go travelling. You would have to marry me."

She clasped her hand across her mouth and giggled at her own indiscretion.

"I thought we were never to talk of that. You were determined not to say yes to any man," he reminded her.

"What I want is scarcely the point. In England, there is never a doubt a woman's knees are sown together like the pockets of a new suit, at least until there's a diamond ring on offer. It seems that's sharp enough to unpick the stitching."

He looked at her, trying to decode the meaning.

"You are outrageous," he said.

"Think, dear Eustace, who but you could handle me? And you're not rich."

She took the decanter, filled her own schooner to the brim. "Cheerio!" she said by way of a toast.

He did not offer to clink his glass.

"What is it?" she demanded.

"I am not rich. I may never be rich. And I have not asked."

"Asked what?"

"For your hand. Must I explain why not?"

"Oh, that! Surely, it's because you are still a penniless potato who drives the girls goofy, but can't spring for the handcuffs."

"*Handcuffs*?"

"The diamond ring, silly," she said. "I suppose, if you can't produce a fortune, well, my family will never say yes and you will have to abduct me."

"Don't be frivolous with me, Ginny, please," he said, his voice heavier. "Not when there is a serious point."

"Fiddlesticks! You usually like me frivolous. Don't you like me frivolous anymore? I wasted my schooling especially. I thought a proper education might ruin me. Yes, I have done the season, failed to attract anyone… well, anyone but you."

"I…" he began and found himself unable to finish.

"Anyway, you do realise you would be mad to think me suitable? You need a wife to do all those wifely things the up-and-coming banker around town requires a wife to do. Networking with ladies. I'd be hopeless." She hesitated. "Good God, what is it?"

"That's just it, Gin, I am mad…"

Now was as good a time as any, he decided. He must tell her.

"I am no longer a banker."

"What?"

"Here's the thing, I am leaving London."

"Leaving London?"

"For Birmingham."

"Birmingham? Why Birmingham? That's north."

"North of London, yes," he agreed. "It's where my business is going to be."

They looked at each other. A second. Two seconds.

"This can't work… you and me. Not as things are," he added.

"You're serious? I can't believe it. You don't have a business. You *are* a banker. How can you say you're not? You make money from money. You told me so. You're not required to make anything useful."

"I resigned this afternoon."

"What?" she said again.

He repeated the phrase. She put her hand to her mouth, but not before her 'f' word escaped.

"You see, that's it," he said. "Yes, I need to make money, but not as someone's lap dog. I want to do things that are useful… so I've agreed on an investment… a personal investment… to make typewriters… assuming I can raise my share of the money."

Ginny repeated the word 'Birmingham' many times, then switched to 'typewriters', repeating that four or five times, then stared in silence at the wall paintings.

Eustace waited. He thought she might cry. He never thought he'd see her cry.

"Birmingham?" she repeated one more time. "To invest in a business?"

"Yes, as I say, I'm hoping to raise the money. Goodness knows how."

"So it's an act of blind faith?"

"Something like that," he agreed.

Her hand was shaking, struggling with the cigarette she had so elegantly lit a minute earlier.

"You don't love me?" she asked.

"I can't love you."

"Well, it seems I was wrong. I thought those things just happened and that was that."

"I'm sorry. It has only recently become clear to me. All that stuff I told you about banking and bankers, it's nonsense. I will not do it for another minute. I will not work for *them*."

"My aunt and uncle will say you've ruined yourself."

"No doubt, but they didn't think there was much to ruin."

She laughed painfully. "Yes, they thought you hopeless."

"I'm rather afraid they are correct."

Suddenly, she gripped his hand across the table. "I'll not have you abandon me in this city. Get on your knee. You should do it now."

They held each other eye to eye for a moment — hers a determined blue; his longing and brown and seeing every hopeless possibility.

"I… can't ask," he said. "Under the circumstances."

"Don't you understand me, Eustace? Don't you understand anything?".

"I thought I did."

"Then let me say it. Whatever anyone else says, whatever I am supposed to be, that matters not a jot. I would fall for you even if you weren't a gentleman and I will wait for you because you are. I do not feel the dust of the shelf upon me quite yet, Eustace. I'm not eighteen for another few days."

"I'm not a gentleman. I haven't the breeding for it and you—"

"Oh, no! You are too noble for your own good. More so because you haven't the arrogance to believe it. If I must agree an engagement unbidden, so be it."

She waited. He considered his options, but it seemed she had left him with none.

"You're sure?" he said.

"I am determined."

"I will get on my knee then, shall I?"

"Yes, I think it best."

He proposed while other diners stared and politely applauded. Virginia Buckley, niece to Lord Buckley, nodded her assent.

The next day, he bought a modest ring without a proper diamond which she never wore around her family, since she had no permission to marry. The marriage itself seemed impossible, yet it fired the hope in her heart and the ambition in his.

Years later, when Eustace asked himself why he'd given up his position in a merchant bank and moved to a city he had never visited, or why he would leave the bustling city where the woman he loved had taken up residence, or why he had decided to become the 'typewriterist' that Sir Alfred mocked, he would not be able to explain it.

Maybe he hoped for that same reckless moment of ecstasy plucked from disaster that he had shared before with Woody and his crew — a mad sense, madder than the mad godless war that surrounded it and the mad generals who sent weltered boys charging towards massive guns with hand weaponry.

Maybe what mattered was a chance to prove himself in something that seemed material. In doing so, might he not prove himself to his father, his family and to everyone else? Might he someday be worthy of Ginny Buckley's love?

Most respectable girls like Mabel Perec, going through St James College, hoped for marriage to their boss or someone of their boss's acquaintance. By becoming 'professional', they believed they might earn it. They too often found bosses married and settled for affairs, too often became pregnant and fell from there downwards.

Mabel hated the flapper pearls that were supposed to hang straight. The new styles were moving her out of fashion and her shelf-life for adventures, of which she had enjoyed a few, was waning fast. "Thirty comes so quickly," her mother warned. She had once been a peroxide blonde, but had never mastered the roots, and now her hair grew out in its natural rich chestnut red, which she preferred whether gentlemen did or not.

Three times a month, she wrote home to Bristol about London's golden streets, but saw them with less and less lustre. Her French mother scolded her on holidays for never bringing a young man home. A nice Jewish boy would be best, but if she couldn't manage that, a nice boy of no particular denomination would now be enough.

She had no one to bring. Few of those St James' girls imagined a Northern boy with a bad foot and a flair for the mechanical. While in London on his search for money, Woody invited her to a Charlie Chaplin movie, claiming, "They never reach the halls up north."

He loved the cinema, he said. She loved it too.

He said he liked it when she spoke to him in French. He did not talk of the woman the language brought to mind — a copper-headed girl near Cambrai, her hair a shade redder than Mabel's chestnut.

Chapter Four

In the week before Christmas 1920, another pompous middle-aged banker elevated from a desk job in the war — this one named Childerson — informed Eustace that he wasn't interested in loaning money to make typewriters. The bank had backed one such company the previous month, Childerson said.

"A British manufacturer, by any chance?" Eustace asked.

"An importer with ambitions to manufacture himself, I believe, but with the best possible recommendation."

"What would that be?"

"His father is a baronet."

"Of course," Eustace whispered, mainly to himself.

"If I may, some advice, young man, there are a dozen ne'er-do-wells opening up factories to make these contraptions."

"Typewriters?"

"Yes, and none as yet holds a candle to the American machines. You would do well to look elsewhere."

"And yet you would back this—?"

"Barrington-Brown. Charlie. His father is a baronet," Childerson repeated.

"I'll remember the name," Eustace promised. He tried to picture the man, hating him already. He had now exhausted the banks of London, asking the Devil to dance, but the Devil was already dancing with this Charlie Barrington-Brown.

He told no one but Ginny of his failures. She said, "Maybe it would help if… I mean, maybe we should announce our engagement?"

"What difference would that make?" he snapped in anger.

They sat in the longest silence of their affair to date and, at the end, she said, "I'm sorry."

He knew what she meant. He could hate Barrington Brown for his privilege. Ginny, at least, aspired to escape it.

He assured Woody he would raise the money for production by the end of January. Woody did not ask how, which was just as well. Eustace had one idea left. It brought him no pleasure.

On Christmas Eve, his father stood before the fire in the library, the room of unread books that spoke everything about his family's social aspiration. The Havershall family had bought this old vicarage at Beeston Fields in Nottingham from the church in 1889. It had been transformed in the better years of lace profits into a minor country house — seven grand bedrooms, two receptions, a dining hall and spartan downstairs quarters for three servants, a cook and a gardener. Its grounds, at two acres, were considered 'adequate'.

"You have a profession, Eustace, a position," John Havershall Senior said. His voice slurred as he smoked a post-dinner cigar.

"I *had* a profession, Father," Eustace corrected. "I was a banker, but a mere unhappy beginner. Other people's money passed through my hands, none of my own. You disapproved, remember?"

"You earned a salary. That at least I could abide."

"Granted, I have given that up by resigning. How else would I pursue my ambition?"

His father thought for a moment, puffed on the cigar. "I wouldn't lend money to family. I would not lend to your brother. I would not lend to you. Never be a debtor, Son. Bad form, you know."

Eustace fought off a sour urge to laugh. His brother, the junior John, was born to a different kind of privilege, had worked in the family firm since the outbreak of the war he'd avoided. Six years in which, as far as Eustace could tell, John had produced nothing of value. He had been put on the payroll the day King George V and Queen Mary visited the warehouses of 'John Havershall Petty Products Ltd' so he might shake the monarch's hand. Grand plans were reserved for his future.

"John doesn't need your money. You've already granted him everything."

"Everything? Is that what you choose to believe?"

"I believe I got kinder shrift from London bankers. What if it had been William asking? What then? Mother's favourite?"

"William? How dare you? Your brother is dead, Boy!" his father shouted. He said other, horrible things about Eustace's choices, but Eustace had stopped listening. It had been a humiliation to ask. It felt like humiliation to be refused.

When Eustace was young — he couldn't remember how young — he and William toiled one morning building the highest tower of wooden blocks the playroom had ever seen. Their brother, John, came in from a cricket match and demolished the tower with his bat.

Eustace could see, even now, the cascade of destruction, the blocks clattering across the floor, the work and the effort destroyed.

Father witnessed the destruction. And laughed.

"Everything is imperfect. Everything fails," he said. "Might as well learn that, boys."

William had cried.

Eustace refused to cry. He sprang across the room and threw himself at his elder brother. Three years was too much of a gap at that age. John punched him and knocked him to the ground. When he tried to pin him down, Eustace bit him on the arm hard enough to break the skin. His father yelled and swore and locked him in a cupboard for the afternoon.

More of Eustace's family arrived after church on Boxing Day — John Junior, wife and baby son; his mother's widowed sister; the paternal grandparents returned from their retirement on the east coast. His grandfather, father and brother now talked of lace, the cloth trade and the family firm of 'John Havershall Petty Products Ltd' that would one day pass down to the baby now in the farthest corner of the room with the ladies. The child also bore the name 'John'. The ladies talked of fashion and the charities of Nottinghamshire.

His grandmother, from time to time, kept returning to the subject of medals and the service Eustace had rendered for his country. She liked to smile at him, because she never smiled at anyone else and it annoyed the surviving generations of 'John'. She was a small hard-faced septuagenarian with a cantankerous wit, a soft heart and grey hair pinned high on her head. The sea air around Skegness preserved her health, she said. She was never to be trifled with.

For the dinner after Boxing Day, Ginny came to join her secret fiancé, bringing presents and her married friend, Matilda. Ginny had spent Christmas at her uncle's estate in Derbyshire and Matilda was her excuse to sneak away. She was supposedly on her way to visit Matilda's people in Lincoln.

No Havershall except Eustace had yet met the 'American'. She was introduced by Eustace as 'Ginny', but reverently addressed by all his relatives as 'Virginia'. Eustace and Ginny laughed about it when they had a moment alone.

Both drank more wine than was seemly in the eyes of Eustace's family. They conspired to take over the gramophone and demonstrate the latest dances to applause from Matilda, indulgent bemusement evident from the Havershalls.

The following morning, Eustace borrowed his grandfather's car to drive Ginny and her chaperone to Lincoln. After the brief high point of the previous evening, he felt depressed and sullen, facing a miserable New Year.

His mother stopped him in the hallway.

"Father says to tell you, you shall have your money," she announced without preamble. "Two thousand pounds, I believe."

Eustace was stunned. His mother played no part in the family business or his father's financial decisions.

"But he refused me?"

"It seems your young lady had a word with your grandmama. And well, matriarch she is, the old lady will not allow it. And so..."

His mother kissed his cheek and turned away. He heard her mumble, "A toff that comes with her threats. The sooner she's gone the better."

As an explanation, it made no sense.

He chauffeured Ginny and Matilda to the village of Cherry Willingham on the outskirts of Lincoln. As Matilda slipped up the driveway of a country house, following a footman with her suitcases, Eustace and Ginny were alone for a moment.

"I'm sorry, you cannot come in," she told him. "Someone might tell my aunt."

"I know, but, I mean, what on Earth...?" he began. "The money? My mother said he changed his mind, but my father was adamant. She said you spoke with my grandmother?"

"Ah, yes, that. She seemed the most amenable," Ginny explained. "Your people are so provincial. In the sweetest possible way, I'm sure. They talk of the Royal visit to their factory like it was a grand event only yesterday. Now, they believe you have become a chancer in London. Penniless, jobless and shamelessly pursuing a Lord's niece. It confuses them. What a gigolo you seem! And as for me? Your grandmother was most impressed that I had met the King. 'At such a young age', she said. I only curtseyed. I did not mention that part."

"I don't understand."

"I said, it was unfortunate the Havershalls had no money. I told her I would put my own inheritance into your business, despite the scandal it might cause. How would it look? A young woman of my status and family — vaguely in line to the throne if a few hundred die off all at once — seduced into funding an adventurer? Especially one who had no hope of gaining permission to marry a Buckley. I may be the black sheep, dear Eustace, but I can play the weak innocent. You see, it would not be good for the Havershalls' reputation when that's spread through London's salons and gentlemen's clubs."

"But the Havershalls have no reputation."

"What? Of course, they do. Isn't the family's patriarch otherwise in line for a Royal honour? That's what a leading purveyor of lace manufactures like your father might be expecting. Your brother's wife told me so."

"My family is hardly leading anything anymore."

"A reputation lingers," she insisted. "As does the pride, and may I say, the ambition to greater recognition." She dabbed an invisible sword onto an invisible shoulder.

"You… you offered to fit my father for a knighthood?"

"Oh, no, no… Quite beyond my reach. I illustrated how his son being part of my scandalous fall might queer the pitch, so to speak. With such gossip, all possibility of consideration would be lost. Your grandmother and I were clear on the *collateral* damage."

"I would never take your money," he assured her.

"A moot point. I do not have any," she said, shrugging her shoulders.

"But, you said to my grandmother—"

"She did not ask me to show her the actual money. You may close your jaw, Eustace," she said, placing her hand under his chin. "It's exactly as you described banking, is it not? The power of money that doesn't exist. But, I suppose, now you know the truth. I have no fortune, merely a pitiful allowance from my great-grandfather's trust fund and my father's indulgence until I am twenty-one. Is the two thousand enough, do you suppose? I see no way of providing more."

"You do realise, Gin, that I am risking everything. If these typewriters don't—"

"Complete tosh! Do not talk of failure."

"You said, we'd never get permission to marry."

"No, Eustace, I said you would not get it. But do I look like I need permission?" she scolded. "I need you to be happy, and successful. You are an ambitious man, Eustace, I always knew it."

"We will have to wait… until the business is stable, at least."

"Yes, I am aware. And I say, 'Very well, if we must.'" She put her finger to his lips. "Hush now. If typing machines and Birmingham do not make us rich, we shall run off and live in a garret and make our fortune as street artists, like they do in the theatre."

* * *

As part of the initial investment agreement of January 1921, 'Woodmansey & Sons Engineering Ltd' changed its name to 'Havershall & Woodmansey Typewriting Ltd'. With no experience of management, Eustace installed himself as Managing Director. Woody became Head of Operations and Engineering. Shares were split 55:45 in Eustace's favour.

Woody had chosen Birmingham, having already moved to the city, declaring that, since the titans of the automotive industry were blossoming in the Midlands — among them Austin, Aston Martin, Hillman, Morris and Rover — this was the place an engineering business must make its home.

Half the city's male population had fought in the war and only two-thirds of them returned unscathed, a disaster followed by waves of Spanish Flu that ripped through the back-to-back slums in 1918 and 1919. The re-emerging Birmingham was, by common consent, the 'city of a thousand trades', its hopes for prosperity lay in metalworking industries. As well as automobiles, there were guns, tools, nails and screws, toys, door locks, buttons, cutlery, and even jewellery.

Havershall & Woodmansey Typewriting — shortened to Havershall's by everyone who couldn't be bothered with the whole mouthful — rented premises at 30 Marmaduke Lane, Bordesley Green. The landlord was a Russian who had fled with his fortune from the Bolsheviks. The street was black with soot underfoot and coated daily with the droppings of passing horses. The same soot blackened the face of every building. The location was not so far from the factories of both the Calthorpe and Wolseley automobile companies, backing onto a branch of an old canal that was part of the clogged veins and arteries of the city. The unmoving waters now crusted over with a multi-coloured scum, reeking of dead fish on hot days, and mildly of decay and dirty washing in cooler weather. That did not matter. In Woody's mind, narrow boats were no longer the transport of the future. What mattered was the 'new' engineering.

The site included a once-white-washed office block that had been part of a workhouse, largely demolished, and an enormous shed-like structure at the back which previous owners had built with walls of tin sheet and from which they had run a metal coating business. Chemical waste had fouled up its drains and its workers had become sick with unknown ailments.

The skyline created by the buildings was dominated by two large chimneys serving the industrial boilers. An abundance of available steam allowed Woody to move in a pre-war press for stamping the blanks of typebars and shaping steel sheet for the typewriter bodies.

In those early months of 1921, the factory produced five typewriters a day. The design in production was not the 'Noiseless', but the old one from the defunct 'Wainwright Typewriter Company'. Woody prepared production drawings and tooling for his noiseless design, while the older model kept revenue trickling in. It sold for twelve-pounds and nineteen shillings, an expensive luxury for most offices.

Upon Eustace's arrival, he secured a modest market among the clerks and secretaries in London offices where old soldiers had taken up residence as managers. They were happy to buy what Eustace termed 'British Twentieth Century Machines', having been accustomed to American imports whose supply was still sporadic and unable to cope with new demand. A war hero was the reliable supplier they were looking for, even if the machine's design seemed ancient.

Unbeknown to these customers, this war hero slept in a storage room at the back of the factory, taking a cheap hotel twice a week when he needed a bath, working shifts in the assembly bays when the firm couldn't afford labour. He drilled metal. He fitted typekeys and spray painted the cases of typewriters. He did not call himself an engineer, but he did what was necessary to become one.

He visited his new fiancée in London by train every weekend. They spent time but not money together. Every pound was his father's until the loan was repaid. He must be free. He had to be rich in his own right and able to marry. And more than that, he had to be fit to marry a Buckley.

A long year followed. Woody made detours to visit Mabel Perec whenever he could. Several suppliers of components and printing inks lay out towards Ilford and Dagenham. Often he'd travel back and forth to the capital by hitch-hiking. Lorry drivers seemed to have a special affinity for spotting a mechanic in need.

He took Mabel to see Buster Keaton's first starring feature, 'The Saphead', on its opening week in London. Harold Lloyd and Mary Pickford also featured in courtship outings. Somehow Woody and Mabel kept up an intermittent connection. She had a weakness for fish and chips, which she pretended were an alien delicacy to someone with her Swiss roots. As a Northern lad, he had a nose for finding the best, though in other ways he tried to play down his roots. He started to copy her accent and even asked her to help him with his elocution.

In the autumn of 1921, he scraped together enough to buy a third-hand Austin 7, drove to London and asked her to marry him. Saying yes to a promise of marriage, she allowed herself to be carried away, all the way, in the back of his new car.

The dice tumbled. Mabel discovered she was pregnant in November, and whether Woody intended his promise or not, he was married by February 1922.

Chapter Five

Ginny's wait for Eustace's success lasted eighteen months before patience wore thin. An invitation to the forthcoming nuptials of Caroline and Viscount Fairchild arrived. Ginny, still living with her aunt, protested that Eustace's lack of money was becoming 'bothersome'.

"Do you wear my ring at home?" Eustace asked.

"Not around my aunt and uncle. It would provoke them."

"Because I am not suitable?"

"I do not care for their judgement. We shall have to work harder to make you rich, that's all. I am determined you will escort me to my cousin's wedding whatever they say."

They were taking tea in a modest establishment on The Strand — stewed Darjeeling, hard scones and waitresses dressed in black-and-white uniforms with darned stockings. Complimentary magazines and newspapers were arrayed for the use of patrons. Brasses and copper kitchen pans decorated the walls. Most of the clientèle were chattering lady shoppers. Not that these got much attention from Eustace when he was with Ginny.

She pushed a page from an American magazine across the table. "Look at how this works," she said.

The magazine was showing an advertisement for the Hayberry-Peats A11 typewriter featuring an evidently-modern flapper in profile, a new-age secretary sitting at her machine. The viewing angle and ruffling of her skirt allowed the camera to capture a glimpse of her stocking tops. She was smiling and smouldering in equal measure.

"'Miss Maybelline Stokes, state champion, types one hundred and thirty-nine words per minute,'" Ginny read.

"Impossible! Those are the machines imported by that company, run by Barrington-Brown. BBTL, he calls it. I saw them at an exhibition in Leeds only last week."

"I don't care much for the machines, but look, look at her. Do you think she is chosen for her typing speed?"

"I find it hard to accept that anyone types at that speed."

"But that's not the point at all. Are you pretending not to see out of delicacy? You need not be delicate with me, Eustace. This is what a young professional woman might aspire to be. Not exactly ostrich feathers, but sending the same message. You can admit it."

"Admit what?"

"That you'd buy your secretary the Hayberry-Peats if you thought she'd raise her skirt and look like this. And more than that, your secretary would beg for the machine if she thought you'd view her this way."

"You are being crude," he said. "Besides we can afford only one secretary and she is forty years-old and almost as wide as she is tall. We wouldn't photograph Glenys for an advertisement."

"What your typewriters need is better promotion. Create an expert to show what the machines can do. And one who looks the part, obviously. Glamour is important. That wife of Woody's…"

"Mabel? Now you want to photograph Mabel?"

"Rather too pregnant in case you hadn't noticed. No, I was thinking that Mabel used to be a clerk or a secretary or something. We should ask her how to set up a competition for speed typing. I could find us the ballroom of a nice hotel, somewhere in London would suit, don't you think? Invite the newspapers and the magazines. They'd love a photograph of girls in, let me think… I know, evening gowns. Yes, we'll make them all wear evening gowns and line them up in rows with typewriters. Everyone would publish."

"May I say, you're being a little fanciful? My company has no money."

"Nonsense. Caroline's Viscount could be head judge and present the prizes. Shall we say one hundred guineas?"

"We shall say no such thing! We couldn't afford—"

"And the contract to be our promotional champion," she added.

"*Our* champion?"

"*Your* champion, if you wish. The Havershall & Woodmansey champion. But let me help, Eustace. I need something to do, something important."

He made the mistake of catching her eye as she pleaded, after which he was always defeated.

By the Autumn of 1922, Woody and Mabel were the parents of a bonny baby girl, 'Celia Jane'. They rented the basement flat of an old Victorian house in Aston. They were happy.

Havershall's were making fifty typewriters a week and Woody's new design, the 'H5 Noiseless', was ready to launch.

The 'H5' raised the number of components in a typewriter from three thousand to nearly three thousand five hundred. It weighed twenty-nine pounds. The added complexity of the key and typebar mechanism was obvious, but Woody's design also added extra gears, pinions, springs, pawls, and fasteners in the 'escapement', the part of the typewriter that controls the precise step-wise movement of the platen.

Woody laid out the production area between component manufacture — mainly on big presses clipping machines, milling and drilling stations, a paint spray booth and a curing oven, all populated by male staff — and various cells that did the assembly, filled with women recruited from the nearby back-to-back houses. This assembly area included stations for the gluing of typefaces to typebars using special jigs built to Woody's specification. Typebars were the bent levers that pressed the letters and numbers onto paper when a key was pressed. Forty-three of them, each a unique variant, were required for each typewriter.

The type-basket containing the typebars and keys was then assembled in a dozen further workstations, multiple pivots and springs were required for each key. Once complete, the type-basket was screwed down into the main steel chassis of the machine, then the carriage subassembly (the platen and its control mechanism) was added before the machine was adjusted and tested. Only when it passed testing were the covers put on.

As a result of the extra manufacturing processes, the factory, now nicknamed 'Duke Works', took on a warmer fuggier smell and a noisy throb that reminded Eustace — standing high on the steps to the production office — of his Mark IV when it was running triumphantly over enemy ground. Ha22ershall's set the initial price of the 'H5' boldly, thirty percent higher than previous models. Eustace trusted Woody's engineering and Woody put his faith in Eustace's selling. Without admitting it, Eustace also put his faith in Ginny's idea. A typing contest was arranged.

The gamble was absolute. Two hundred pounds were left in the company's reserve account. The prize money and the expense of running the event were all the company had. It seemed they were closer to her garret in Paris than any breakthrough in the fortunes of the typewriter business. He did not tell Woody how close they were to failing.

* * *

Caroline became Viscountess Fairchild and the Viscount was recruited as a judge for 'The Grand H5 Challenge'. Ginny's rules were simple:

— *Contestants must be unmarried. (Married women couldn't be expected to travel on the promotional tour required of the champion.)*

— *Contestants must type a memorised script for five minutes. (The script was a promotion for Havershall's typewriters in case any newspapers or magazines were minded to print extracts or take pictures of the finished pages.)*

— *A ten-word penalty was imposed on the score for any mistakes or spelling errors.*

— *Each contestant must use a factory-supplied H5 typewriter.*

— *The finals for the best contestants would be held in the Ballroom of the Rubens Hotel on Buckingham Palace Road. Appropriate dress was required.*

There were five 'regional' heats. Three in London, one in Birmingham, one all the way up in Manchester to give the impression of having conducted a national search. Ginny travelled to supervise each event, dragging Eustace along for company and Mabel as her chaperone and 'typing expert'. She persuaded Woody to attend the Birmingham round, the second on the schedule, suggesting he might find new ideas for making the H5 easier to type on. He was so impressed by the speed of the contestants, he promised special 'racing versions' for the final. He prepared a dozen models with all manufacturing burrs removed and extra grease and polish in the moving parts.

On the big day, the fastest eight young typists arrived at Rubens Hotel. In the afternoon rounds, these contestants fought head to head through quarter and semi finals. An invited audience, provided with free cocktails and canapés, were on hand to witness the contests.

The grand finale, a five-minute type-off, lay between Jean-Alexandra Collins, a rather plain girl from Blackburn in her mother's evening gown, and Margaret Elizabeth Cadogan, a product of the same St James College from which Mabel had graduated ten years previously.

"Fit for a Viscount, if this Viscount weren't already married to my cousin," Ginny declared. She loved Margaret's dress, the perfect manicure of her nails. Margaret was right for the part. Ginny said as much to Eustace.

Two fresh typewriters were produced for the showdown and laid on separate white-clothed tables set on the ballroom's stage. Photographers were allowed close enough to the contestants to take their picture before battle commenced. Viscount Fairchild stood in the background.

In the first row of the audience, Eustace wriggled nervously. Leaning close to Ginny, he said, "I think this may go terribly awry."

"How so?"

"The Collins girl typed almost eight hundred words in the last round."

"You think she will win?"

"I'm sure she will. Miss Cadogan would make the better..." He hesitated.

"Shall we say she looks more like the advert we'd like to print?" Ginny said tartly.

"Yes, I suppose that's it. As you said from the start."

"Do not worry, dear Eustace. The Collins girl, as you put it, is not here to win. She's here for the prize money which I promised to match regardless. Miss Cadogan is here to win."

"You fixed it—?" he began, then realising he might be overheard, lowered his voice. "You meddled with the final... of *our* contest."

"Not the way I would describe it, Eustace. I scripted a good many of the rounds. This must be entertainment, after all. Gritty aspiration versus class, the press love to write that material. Aspiration must rise, but must continue to aspire."

"I don't understand," he confessed.

"I'm sure you do. Miss Cadogan will sell more typewriters."

"Where did you get the money?"

"I didn't. There's a spiv at the back taking bets. I have two-to-one against Miss Cadogan. I smiled at him. My credit is good, apparently. Don't worry, he's already made a fortune on the other rounds. The *hoi polloi* must have their favourites, of course, but the champion must maintain the image... the image suited to Havershall's brand. That is our Miss Cadogan."

"But the girls up there have been typing away for their lives. You can't have paid all of them off with your gambling profits." He nodded towards the stage.

"True, I have other strings to my bow. Equality, dear Eustace, is an illusion. As, may I say, is the idea all typewriters that look the same are the same. Shall we say, Woody's 'special' typewriters gave me an idea. They look the same as a standard one to anyone who hasn't tried typing on one. I tried, you know. Mabel had to teach me. I can't understand why you manufacturers don't put the letters in alphabetic order. It's illogical. It makes it so much harder to get the hang of it."

"You—?"

"Oh, yes, we tested them all. We chose the right ones for the *right* people," she said. "Of course, this being the final, I went for belt and braces, you understand. A few pounds here and there for a much bigger prize."

For reasons unexplained, Miss Collins typed only seven-hundred and forty words with three spelling mistakes in the final round. "Nerves," she explained to a journalist, smiling as the loser.

Miss Margaret Cadogan typed seven-hundred and forty-seven with one error. Three national newspapers, four weekly magazines and a trade paper on the office industry carried her photographs. Orders from retailers and distributers poured into the company offices.

There was no doubt now the world was turning towards 'mechanical' writing. No company, firm, institution, partnership, public body, university, military department or serious charity still thought hand-writing of documents acceptable. Their letters, invoices, orders, statements, accounts documents had to be typed. The once reviled typewriter, with its clanky mechanisms and reputation for ink blots, was coming of age.

There were at least half a dozen American companies with British sales operations, several from Europe and now five manufacturers in England competing with Havershall's for every sale.

The use of 'modern' girls, who were supposedly chosen for their typing and demonstration skills but were always suspiciously attractive and stylish, became a common feature of office exhibitions. BBTL, Charlie Barrington-Brown's company, were the first to employ them in large numbers.

Having bought a metal pressings and castings factory in Doncaster, BBTL had begun making its own machines to the Hayberry-Peats' design and needed to sell in volume to make the investment pay off. Their small army of 'promotional' girls fraternised with the male buyers from large companies, institutions and government bodies which had started to employ pools of women typists. As a result, their female employees were saddled with inferior machines peddled by the most appealing female demonstrators.

"Where does he keep getting his money?" Eustace asked, referring to Barrington-Brown. "He has built up from nowhere and now look at this. He has the banks in his pocket."

Eustace was pointing at a picture in the London Illustrated News. A twenty-foot wide working typewriter had been constructed as a marketing stunt. Models jumped on the keys. BBTL were towing the monster around and displaying it in city centres. The published picture showed the company's owner surrounded by three female models sitting on the 'QWERTY' keys along the top row.

"Oh, that's Charlie," said Ginny, looking over Eustace's shoulder.

"You know him?"

"Yes, I think so. Never knew his second name. Met him at a weekend house party Caroline took me to. Up north, I think. He's quite the socialite. As I recall, she was there with Edward. I think Edward might have gone to school with the man."

"A toff," Eustace concluded. Hadn't that banker, Childerson, told him as much? Barrington-Brown was the enemy, an enemy with the unearned privilege of easy loans.

"Darling, don't be so beastly and sour. We may have spat out the silver plated spoon, so to speak, but we are all in pursuit of money nonetheless."

"Not that kind."

"You do sound preposterous. There are no types of money," she said.

The QWERTY arrangement of typewriter keys was indeed illogical, as Ginny claimed. Woody and Eustace debated changing several times, but concluded it was unavoidable.

Christopher Sholes, a newspaper editor and printer from Kenosha, Wisconsin, applied for a patent on the keyboard arrangement in 1867, claiming his layout was designed to keep letters commonly typed together separate in the type-basket and thereby reduce key jams. He was, however, spectacularly inaccurate about which letters were commonly typed in sequence.

Nevertheless, Remington bought the patent and marketed typing courses based on machines with QWERTY keyboards. The courses were so popular that everyone who learned how to type learned the QWERTY format and machines with the layout were the only ones that sold. For the duration of the patent, Remington were able to extract licensing fees from rival manufacturers.

By the 1920s, the patent had long expired and Remington typing courses were no longer the only way of learning to type, but the format remained ubiquitous. If you wanted to make a typewriter that typists knew how to type on, you had to use a QWERTY layout. Everyone did. So Havershall's did too.

* * *

1923 proved a pivotal year for Havershall's. With the new H5 design and new promotions, typewriter orders soared as office work expanded in the post-war economy. The company appointed Francis Morland Office Fitments Ltd as its northern distributor and the trading house of Corrigan and Corrigan offered to establish an arrangement for India.

Success brought problems. As typewriters flowed out of the factory in Marmaduke Lane, the parasites that prey on others reared their heads. It was petty at first. A few windows windows broken around the back of the property, a small fire in a shed that Jim McCann, the production manager, had built to keep printer ribbons.

A man in a flat cap and donkey jacket visited Eustace in the office the following morning, suggesting that Havershall's might need to buy 'insurance'. Eustace asked who the underwriters might be. The man laughed, shaking his head as he left. The next week, a row of twelve windows in the offices were smashed with bricks. Eustace employed a night watchman.

At the same time, the workforce increased to seventy, half of them women, making 150 machines a week. But problems with quality started rising as sales climbed. Typebars on the H5 started snapping. It was always the ones at the edges of the keyboard. Each typebar on a machine has a unique bend, determined by the need to bring the 'typeface' — the pad holding a particular letter — to the centre of the machine to press the ink ribbon onto the platen.

"You see," said Woody, standing with the two pieces of a broken typebar in his hand. "They're the ones with the sharpest bends. I've had two 'P's and a 'Z' in the last week."

"What do we do now?" asked Eustace. "The returns from Morland's alone are wiping out our profits."

"I'll fix it."

Eustace looked doubtful.

"I'll fix it," Woody repeated. "Haven't I always fixed it? All design is failure. The only question is how and when, and what we do next? Now, go back to selling and leave me to the engineering."

Woody was right about one thing, Eustace realised, they had to keep on selling. If they stopped production because of the problem, the company would collapse.

"Alright, Woody," Eustace said at last.

"I won't let you down, Captain."

Woody lived in the factory for a week. He switched the grade of steel. The snapping stopped and the threat receded. Unsatisfied, he continued his metallurgy studies, convinced an understanding of metal would help future designs. He wrote to well-known professors at universities. At first, his questions were simple, answered in a paragraph. Soon, he was writing four and five pages and receiving the same in return.

Meanwhile, Eustace continued securing sales. He kept a cash box in his office and every week he put a little cash aside for the two thousand pounds he owed his father. Once the debt was paid, he would be a free man, a true businessman. He would be a man who might marry a Buckley.

He drove frantically around the country in an old Rover the company had bought for him. He was exhausted every weekend. He and Woody had never seemed more of a team, but by the time he reached London, he had less and less energy for dancing on a Saturday evening.

There was more to that childhood day he had bitten his brother, deeper scars than Eustace might admit. They were still there, still alive in his head — hellfire and brimstone, just as the church preached from the pulpit. The two thousand pounds was a straitjacket he could not escape.

He remembered the fight with John, his father grasping his arm, a hand like a vice pulling him aside. He was in the air, his legs cycling, a hanged man gaining no purchase. His father was shouting, about biters and devils and the fate God had for sinners.

Eustace was bundled and pushed, left to his fate, which was not hellfire but the confines of the family's cleaning cupboard — the dark, dark place by which all future dark places would be judged and feared. It smelt of candles and dust and old cleaning cloths and metal polish.

He screamed, "Let me out. I didn't do anything."

Nothing except defend himself the only way he could.

He cried long after his father had gone and only his brothers were left outside the door. He pleaded, "John, help me."

John said he couldn't help. He didn't have a key. "You're there forever."

Eustace could see the chink of light around the key hole, in which the blunt end of the key was centred like an eclipse.

He heard William calling his name, getting more distant as John shepherded his younger brother away. That was the first time Eustace felt it — a tightening confinement. The core of his body shrank away as if some inner gravity was consuming him, leaving his skin loose and crawling across the ridges of bone that were his skeleton. He hated the Johns, father and brother both.

Suddenly, he rose into a frenzy. He battered the door with his fists. Took the surface from his knuckles. He kicked it. His foot hurt. His chest was heaving so fast, he couldn't get good air into his lungs. He lay on the floor of the cupboard panting, the salt of his tears dripping into his mouth.

"Never again," he swore. "Never again."

He had already survived two years of fighting when the army asked for volunteers for the new tanks. And that was his moment of madness. Trusting to luck, or in those days still trusting to God, he volunteered for the Tank Corps. His triumph would somehow be revenge.

"To hell with it all." His father couldn't be right.

The same words drove him on now, every time it seemed like he might stop. Havershall's and Ginny stood at the end of his road.

BBTL had been gradually becoming a high point in Eustace's despair. Barrington-Brown's company were securing a monopoly on typewriter sales in important places, particularly anywhere around London that had to do with government or the military. Havershall's bid for these contracts at prices lower than they offered in the Private Sector of banks, financial offices and other commercial enterprises, but never won any of them.

Another picture in the latest 'Illustrated London News' showed the King's Private Secretary receiving his 'BBTL'. Eustace stared at it for several minutes, then vowed to never buy the magazine again.

Havershall's sold a less privileged, yet more elegant, modern image — machines for an office you'd like to work in, not one the King might walk through. Miss Margaret Cadogan was more photogenic than the King's Private Secretary. She appeared in Havershall's advertisements and toured giving demonstrations for years until she married a City stockbroker and was replaced by a younger model, the winner of another 'Grand Challenge'.

Ginny witnessed Eustace's creeping success in Havershall's with a mixture of devotion and frustration. He admitted the growth in sales, but no level of success seemed to generate significant profit or cash in hand. He still pleaded poverty. The debt to his father remained unpaid. Each small setback in the fledgling company fed her anxieties. When would Eustace finally set a date for their marriage?

Every weekend he came to London. Every weekend, with the devotion of a puppy dog, he took her to the theatre or the music hall, to the ballet, to dinner, to outrageous dancing clubs where they played the 'Tiger Rag', to anywhere she cared to go. But their dates now felt tired and therein lay the problem. He showed no sign of ever being anything other than the ideal fiancé that irked her family.

She calculated how much more time Eustace spent on the company than he did with her. She persuaded Eustace that Havershall's should open a London showroom and attach it to one of the typing schools springing up all over the capital. She thought it might bring him more often to the city. It did, but only for a week and the success of London sales only made it 'more urgent' that he be present elsewhere.

When banishing her from New York, her parents had intended her to spend no more than a year in London. By 1923, she had now reached a third anniversary without the husband they had sent her for and the pressure to return across the Atlantic had been growing stronger in each of her mother Elizabeth's fortnightly letters. Her aunt assured her that her mother was in dire need of her return.

Cousin Caroline, recently the mother of twins, counselled her to go. "Ginny, you always lived and died for things that you want. I envy you that. But you should channel a little more practical thinking into what you need."

"I know what I need," Ginny replied.

"No, you know what you want. *Need* is a different kettle of fish. What has he had, three years almost?"

"His name is Eustace."

"Eustace, yes," Caroline said tartly. "He's had the best years of you while other suitors are batted away at the door by your ferocious backhand. It won't always be so."

Behind the words, Caroline dangled the babies, the husband, the title of Viscountess. She was the successful Buckley woman.

Ginny protested, "He wants to make his fortune. I love him for that."

"You can only love a man for so long when your reason for loving him is that he makes you wait."

"It's not like that," she snapped.

"No, your other reason is that we all know he will make you unhappy, and you refuse to admit that we are right."

The slow drip of poison from the Buckleys continued. Another letter came from her mother. It was to be her parents' twenty-fifth anniversary that summer. It seemed it would be the perfect time to visit America. A dutiful month or two in New York and her previous youthful misdemeanours would be forgiven.

"While you are there, you can decide if there is any reason to come back," Caroline said.

Ginny went to especial efforts to make herself attractive that following Saturday — new dress, new hairdresser, getting the eyes charcoaled just so — intending to ask Eustace straight out if he minded her 'holiday'. She'd settled on a blue silk and cotton gown, the first, fifth and last she'd tried that afternoon. She was sure Eustace would now take the bait.

They were sitting in the American Bar at the Criterion, her favourite, waiting for the show in the adjacent theatre. The bar served the finest cocktails in London. They had already consumed three between them.

"Well?" she said, once the proposed trip was explained.

He thought for a while. She felt her heart sink. Silence was the worst possible result.

He said, "The business is at its most critical point."

"Isn't it always?"

"I know. I haven't the money to—" he began.

"But the holiday? I asked you about *my* holiday, not about your money."

He shook his head, failing to see that the question wasn't about a holiday at all.

"Eustace, will you not tell me what to do? My family is all for it, don't you know?"

"I cannot claim the right to say no," he declared.

"Would you say no?"

"You should do your duty by your family."

"Fiddlesticks!" she said.

He had worked seventy hours that week. He was too exhausted to think straight.

Ginny had more than one string to her bow. The show she'd picked that night, 'The Beauty Prize', was part of her message:

An ambitious young man meets a young woman named Carol Stuart, the daughter of a wealthy American. She pretends to be poor. They fall in love and get engaged. When her deception is uncovered, he threatens to marry another. She retaliates by threatening to marry for money. But they are meant to be together, so of course he doesn't. She doesn't either and the real lovers marry, despite the complications of money, presumably to live happily ever after. The story was written by P.G Wodehouse and played for comedy.

"Well?" she said again afterwards as they were taking a Hansom back to Brook Street.

"Well, what?"

"Don't be beastly. Say something," she urged. "Dear Eustace, you and I are meant to be. You are quite removed from the station you were born to and I bear no relation to the well-mannered lady I was designed to be. The over-achiever and the sinner. Don't you see?"

The Hansom turned off Brook Street into the mews.

"Come inside with me. My aunt is out of town."

"That would be quite improper, if you are alone."

"Don't you mean 'inappropriate'? Don't worry, I have servants. They will defend me unless I send them away."

"This, as you know, is not the point."

"Come inside," she repeated. "There is nothing left for it. I wish to seduce you. Half of my family already think I've fallen. So, Eustace, let me fall."

"No," he said firmly. "I do not believe I will. I cannot."

"'Cannot' or 'will not'? Which lie do you wish me to believe?" She shook her head at him. "It worked for Woody and Mabel. Married with a child and blissfully happy. Can't it work for us?"

She stared at him. "You will not rise for a little entrapment? Am I so undesirable? Maybe you'd prefer I play the saleable woman like that Carol and throw myself upon the highest bidder."

"You are being crude. And it does not become you."

"Then set a date. I am decided. Do you not want children? Let's have children. Let us do it tonight. What more have I to offer you?"

The Hansom had now come to a halt, ready for them to alight. "We're here, Sir," the driver shouted from his seat above.

"Wait, will you, Leonard," Ginny cried back. "I'm awaiting an answer. Well, Eustace, say the word."

"I cannot," he said.

The words were tinged with regret. They only made her angry.

"I'd whore myself and you still play the gentleman? Good God! Are you such a pompous ass, Eustace!"

"Not so much the gentleman," he assured her. "I would kill any man who made Ginny Buckley a whore."

She jumped down and slammed the carriage door behind her, shouting, "Don't follow me, then. Don't follow me, damn you."

She did not look back and he thought it wisest not to get out.

She hated his answers. Considerate and cruel. The answer of the impecunious gentleman when what she required at that moment was the swashbuckling chancer. Love must be everything, or nothing at all.

She stayed up all night, packing and unpacking her suitcase in confusion, then left England without even writing him a note. In three years, she thought she had said everything that could be said.

She cried aboard ship for most of the first two days. Not for pain, or loss, but because she could not work out why she was ever so wilful, yet so weak that she would do something she so clearly had no wish to.

How strange it is that sometimes we can't accept the one thing that everything else would be traded for in an instant. Eustace decided that he would explain the following weekend when she was calmer. She would see that he was right. She would see that he was still true. He said as much in a note he sent by messenger before leaving London the next morning.

It was the middle of the week before he realised he had received no reply. She had not written back the very same day as she usually did and they had made no arrangement for the coming weekend. Perhaps he had misjudged her mood.

He tried to telephone the house, something he'd never done before, since his calls would only enflame her aunt and uncle. Sure enough, a stiff housekeeper's voice told him, "Miss Buckley is not home to calls on the telephone."

Birmingham and business were for once pushed aside, sales appointments cancelled. He took the next train to London.

When he arrived at the door of the mews house off Brook Street, the servant who answered looked astonished by his appearance. After she pulled herself together, she asked him to wait. Five minutes he waited. He took deep breaths. He held his hat tight in his hand and turned it so many times he thought it might rip in two.

The same servant came back to inform him, "Miss Buckley is away already, and the Lady Buckley is indisposed, but the Viscountess says you're to come up as she has a message."

"Away? Already?" he repeated, struck by the words.

It was unfair to press staff for answers they weren't permitted to give, so he followed the servant up the stairs into a drawing room. Considering how many times he'd called for or delivered Ginny to the door, it seemed remarkable how little of the house he had seen. It struck him how unfamiliar he was with this life she had outside their meetings. Of her pressures. Of her true reasoning.

The drawing room was themed in brown and lilac. A pianoforte and a floor standing globe were at one end. There were oil painted portraits charting the Buckley lineage on all the walls, everyone captured young, except for the present Lord and Lady who were rendered life-sized above the fire place at approximately their current ages. The fire was not lit. Eustace helped himself to one of two armchairs set far apart, not wishing to occupy the sofa between them. He waited. He took more deep breaths. He found his heart was beating very fast and would not slow.

The Viscountess Caroline Fairchild came in, apologising for the delay. She offered him tea which he refused.

"I'm sorry to say my cousin has departed for America," she said as she took to the sofa. She did not sound sorry at all. "She asked me to tell you of her decision. It was not an easy one. She wanted you to know."

"Oh," he said.

"You seem surprised. Had she not told you she was minded to answer the parental call? To go *home*," she said with emphasis.

"Ginny had led me to believe she was undecided on her trip and that, should she go, it was to be something of a holiday. She seemed somewhat distressed by the pressure on either side."

"I see. Surely, you understand that a lady has a duty. She had promised her parents."

"Yes, of course," he said sharply.

"There is no call to be abrupt."

"My apologies," he said. "Of course, I advised her the same way. These are family duties after all, but…"

He could not go further without revealing their engagement. He bit his lip.

"You must hate me," she said, surveying him carefully.

"Not at all. Your message is delivered. It's simply that… Well, we parted on unfortunate terms. I must consider whether to pursue her."

"To America? Oh, no. Maybe you should consider why she left this message too late for you to stop her reaching the boat. She intended to go, Mr Havershall. To leave you." She shook her head as if weighing up his confusion. "Yes, you must hate all the family. You must think we conspire against you to persuade her."

"Do you claim that you have not?"

"Oh, we guessed you had an unsuitable arrangement. She hides the ring from my mother, don't you know? Rather cheap, I thought."

Eustace clenched his fist. *So the Viscountess did know the situation! Was she being wantonly cruel?*

"I don't have the money. Not yet, I—"

"Precisely," she said.

He did not answer. He began to loosen his tie. "Is that the whole message? That she has gone to America? That's all. No word that suggests she will return, or when that might be?"

"She is going *home*, as I said. I do not know more. She promises to write and explain, once she arrives. I assume she thinks there is something to be explained." Caroline folded her hands, one over the other to place them in her lap. She forced straightness into her posture, as if the discipline of achieving it had been drummed into her from childhood. He was aware of his own tendency to slump.

"I confess," she said at length, "that I have lobbied against you."

"For a time, I was strangely grateful. It seemed to suit my cause. I thought you had only cemented her resolve in my favour."

"For a time, I thought it too. I assure you, in this choice of America, she has decided for herself. In all this time, she always has. I'm sure you can believe that much of Virginia."

In return, he said, "And let me assure you, in all this time, I only ever thought of working for her."

"I believe that might be so. Not that it makes a difference. Tell me, were you *seriously* engaged? I must say I wondered. When I saw the ring, I entertained the thought it might be another ruse to vex the family."

The mention of the ring sparked a thought. Here was his fiancée running off without a word and he supposed that must mean the engagement was over. And yet, she had not given back the ring. That didn't seem like an omission Ginny would allow. Steal bicycles, yes, but not an engagement ring, however poor its value.

He looked down at his hands, comparing them to his hostess's perfect manicure. He'd cut his finger on a box in the factory the week before, not badly, but by the time he got to washing up at the end of the day, the dirty oil from the cutting machines had worked its way into the wound and turned it black. No matter how hard or painfully he scrubbed now, he couldn't remove the tell-tale line across his fingertip. It reminded him of tanks and Cambrai, the scars that took so long to fade and maybe hadn't faded yet.

"She is quite magnificently contrary," he said, uncertain why he felt the need to say it.

Caroline smiled. "I was contrary once. I suppose we all are when young. You don't believe it, but it's true."

She sounded proud of the claim. Some glint of Buckley mischief peeped through. She reined back the accompanying smile before it settled.

"I thought I saw you at a suffragette rally once, handing out leaflets," he told her.

"I am sure you did not."

"It was a long time ago, before the war. You were wearing a yellow bonnet."

"Even if that were true, Mr Havershall — and do not press me to admit it — the Viscount will have no truck with such politics."

"But you were a suffragette?"

"Did she tell you that?" She gazed at him sternly, then softened and said, "Yes, a long time ago, perhaps, before all this manoeuvring."

She offered no more and did not explain what 'all this' might consist of. He wondered whether it mattered. Only Ginny mattered now. Everything else was long ago and childish.

"Whatever you think, it's not your lobbying that's made the difference," he said. "Not having a business that makes money, that's why I delayed. I delayed too long."

Caroline gave a little repressed laugh, that became a snort. "You think a maker of typewriters can rise up and seize the hand of a Buckley? Even if you were successful, do you suppose it would make a difference?"

"She... she led me to believe..."

"I am sure, if she led you to believe anything, it was that the impossible was possible and that nothing mattered a damn once she'd made up her mind. That's her way."

"I think I should go now," he said.

"I thought we were only just getting started. You can tell me how much better I was in the cause for women's votes. Securing a position... a title... is a practical proposition for a woman, even a Buckley woman, Mr Havershall, since the Lord's title must pass down the man's line and I have been sold for money, since I could not have money of my own. That is the truth."

This came without prompting and he did not understand why she was suddenly angry with him.

"Madam, I assure you, I would never say such things, nor think them either. I suppose it is Ginny who says this to you? It is her who accuses you?"

"Yes, I suppose that is also her way. Honest to a fault. I suppose I must credit you this much, Mr Havershall. You have perfected the surface layers. You have the moustache. You play the gentleman well. You would always say the right things."

The compliment was delivered so archly he missed its backhandedness at first.

"Virginia would say that a woman's sacrifice to her husband's character is a condition of entry, Mr Havershall. It is a game with rules, you see. And even she would admit no one controls the rules. Rule One: no one can become socially acceptable by raising their income, any more than that character in the Wilde play can become worthy by changing his name from Jack to Earnest. It's nonsense written by a queer, of course, but it has a point. A child romantically saved from a handbag is belatedly changed into aristocracy, but if you cannot pull off that theatrical rebirth, I am afraid you have no hope."

He stood up because leaving was the safest thing to do. Both fists had now balled so tightly his wounded finger hurt him as it pressed into his palm. He wanted to shout.

It's not you I hate, it's the life you represent. I hate that I want it. I hate it and want it equally. I love Ginny and hate what she comes from. I love that she's trying to escape it. All I wanted was to make a little money, and make her flight easier.

A gentleman could not do that, of course. He was at the door and thought the Viscountess would let him leave unchallenged.

"I do believe you love her, Mr Havershall," she said. "Truly, I do. Because if you are a chancer, you're playing a longer game than any chancer this family's ever dealt with. One piece of advice: don't chase her."

"Why not? What else have I got?"

"I know you want to. You will probably tell me you want to give up your business, buy a ticket, go after her. But don't. You have to be what you are and she has to be what she is. She is braver than me and that's all the chance she has ever wanted, to decide for herself. If she comes back…? Alright, then I will stand at your wedding and applaud. In the meantime, I suggest you make some money."

"I thought the whole point was that money didn't make for class."

"Indeed, it does not. But I suppose, if my cousin is resolved, it can disguise it."

The New York branch of the Buckleys was not as Ginny expected. In the years away, the family had migrated east out of Manhattan and into the Hamptons, a finger of land that looked like it was making a token effort to follow Ginny's journey across the Atlantic. The weight of money trailed a hundred miles back to the melting pot of a sleepless city. Wealth and privilege on Long Island looked not so far different from the wealth and privilege of English society.

The house and the grounds were grand, the upstairs windows looking out over the water from the sheltered side of a bay in East Hampton. There was a swimming pool and lawns large enough for cricket or multiple games of croquet. It had its own tennis court, boathouse and dock.

She was invited to parties, of course. *That pretty girl returned from England.* The New York set had a penchant for driving out to the houses along that strip of land. Here the gay young things danced and consumed booze made in backwoods' stills as if tomorrow wouldn't happen. The air was full of jazz and there was a whole new language to learn, full of *big-timers, sharpshooters, cake-eaters, jazzbos and lalapazazers.*

A seventeen-year-old Virginia — the type who had left for England — would have loved it. The returning Ginny felt only the emptiness at its heart. The first dance partner who slipped his hand a little too low on her hip triggered an electric horror. Every organ of her body seemed to twist around her back bone, trying to squirm free. At the last moment, she struck him open handed in the chest with as much force as she could muster and ran to the bathroom. Locked herself inside for thirty minutes. Stared at the walls as if she could not remember where she was or how she got there.

The moment she most valued on Long Island was when the first envelope from England slipped into the mailbox and she saw Eustace's careful handwriting alongside the stamps and postmarks. He said he had received her letters — she had sent him three — and he was writing rather than typing because he was pouring out his heart. He said he had always loved her, but understood why she needed to be in America and knew he could never hope to marry her without money that might 'disguise his failings'. He concluded by saying that he still hoped for the company's success. She must have read those words a hundred times.

"Oh, God," she told herself, "now I know I am hopelessly gone."

At first, her father's evident increase in wealth seemed to have no explanation. Its source was revealed one evening in Ginny's third week when the house was visited by Mr Luciano Saccacci.

'Sax', as he preferred to be called, drove a Duesenberg Model J, a 6.9 litre with a bonnet so long it seemed preposterous to have only two passengers seats under the folding roof in the middle. He wore a black shirt with a white tie, pink braces and gold sleeve-garters. Success had allowed him to grow out into comfortable obesity. Sax was Sir Stanley Buckley's business partner, dressed to the nines in the vulgar clothes of success, the reality of American money.

The chain of events, as Ginny understood it, was this: Stanley Buckley had arrived in New York on the last dregs of a second son's inheritance, attached to the British Consulate General on Third Avenue in 1911. At one time or another, he had worked in embassies and consulates in a dozen countries, picked up an unmerited knighthood for his services, courtesy of his older brother's connections. In New York, he was employed to liaise between British industrialists and American importing companies wanting to buy in luxury goods. His particular success was promoting the wares of Scottish whisky producers by implying their association with English aristocrats. Stanley himself was a born-again teetotaller.

After the First World War when Ginny had been busy decamping to London, the trade of the whisky producers and their American importers came under threat. The prospect of Prohibition swept through American politics. Sax, a noted Brooklyn 'entrepreneur', had spotted the value of an Old World figurehead with the right accent.

"You see what it is, Stan, I need a name, maybe an English name? Let's say, a Chairman for the Board? No one wants to buy their Snake Oil from a Wop like me. You need a little blue blood, know what I mean?"

Sax invested in a small chain of pharmacies. He and Stanley came to an understanding. Stanley joined the board of what became 'BuckChem Pharmaceutical Supplies Inc.' He was to be its 'front', a five percent shareholder.

When prohibition hit America in 1920, medicinal alcohol was the one legal exception. In six months, some 15,000 doctors and almost 60,000 pharmacists received licenses to prescribe or sell it. Over eleven million people per year apparently had diseases that could be relieved with alcohol.

Scams involving Bootleggers and prescription forms abounded. Pharmacies were the market to be in. BuckChem expanded, buying store after store. Sax provided the alcohol, Stanley the class. The goods never crossed his lips, but Buckley fingers were steeped in the dirty money.

The story tweaked the darkest part of Ginny's humour — she was no longer the blackest sheep of the family. It amused her all the more when Sax Saccacci left a bottle of his best moonshine at the house and she drank most of it in one evening. She wondered if she should tell Eustace. She wondered if he would think more or less of her.

"You see," she would tell him, "with class, it's the thinnest veil. Behind it, just about anything goes."

Chapter Six

Here in the middle of 1923, the barometer of his wealth was still the two thousand pounds owed to his father. Despite the recent successes, the cash box Eustace kept in his office was several hundreds short of repaying the loan.

Every so often, he counted the money, all in used notes of descending denominations down to the odd ten-shillings'. In the weeks after Ginny had left, 'every so often' became every second day. If there were a way to keep score of his success, this was the measure of his failure — even debt-wise, he was not a free man. Not a worthy man. Not a man with his own value.

This, and this alone, obsessed him.

He felt any chance he had with Ginny fading away on his inability to act. His debt and his lack of fortune were the root of every problem. He needed money fast, and fast money always relied on luck.

Clarke Smith, the Managing Partner of the new Manchester office of Solomon-McKensie-Smith Solicitors and Commissioners of Oaths had been a captain in the Royal Flying Corps, a branch of the service as new and vital to winning the war as the tank regiments, so naturally he granted Eustace Havershall an audience for lunch at the Midland Hotel on St Peter's Square.

Eustace presented the advantages of the H5 Noiseless, but Smith wasn't minded to buy. His firm had always preferred American machines, the Hayberry-Peats, and the thirty staff in the new typing pool were going to receive standard No.10s, the same machine BBTL had been selling to the government.

"Much as I'd like to help you out, Old Man, they are three guineas less than your machines," Smith pointed out. He was a thick set man in pinstripes. Despite their noon appointment, they were now swilling brandy and smoking cigars.

"They're not British," Eustace ventured.

"They're made over in Doncaster now, so their chappie told me. And three guineas is three guineas, Old Man. I can't go back to our management board and say I spent ninety guineas more than I needed and removed a supplier we've bought from in every one of our other offices, now can I?"

Eustace knew price was not the issue. If he came down, BBTL would lower their price too. He thought of Ginny's speed contest. He thought of her far away from him and desperation made him bold.

"Suppose I said, I could save you three of your typists."

"What?"

"Yes, three typists," said Eustace, the idea becoming firmer as he worked through it. "You would save on wages and that would be more than three guineas a machine."

"How would you save me three typists?"

"The H5 is not only quiet, it's smoother. The H5 would make them all type ten percent faster."

Smith looked sceptical. Eustace pounced.

"Did you not see our Grand Challenge in the papers? Record speeds, Old Man," Eustace said, aping Smith's manner of speech. "Say, how about a friendly wager, gentleman to gentleman? Your three best girls on these *Hayberry* copies, against girls I bring in from the Bingley and Bolton Bank. Their ladies are using our noiseless H5s all across their Lancashire branches. I'll wager girls from Bingley and Bolton's can produce one hundred and twenty words to every hundred of yours on the Hayberry. That's twenty percent more, not just ten. What do you say?"

Smith started to look interested. "What sort of sum were you thinking?"

This was tricky. Eustace thought of the cash box. The cash box was all he had.

"Five hundred guineas against your commitment to a thousand's worth of Havershall machines."

Smith thought for a moment. Eustace could see the calculations going on behind the man's eyes.

"You have yourself a bet," said Smith offering his hand.

"Word of a gentleman," Eustace replied, taking the deal. "One more thing, the payment terms, if you lose, must be cash up front for the first half."

As it so happened, Jean-Alexandra Collins worked for Bingley and Bolton's, as did two other finalists from the Manchester heat of 'The Grand H5 Challenge'. Eustace paid them at overtime rates for a day. He won the bet. Smith, of course, lost like a gentleman, and handed over his order. Half the money — five hundred guineas — arrived the following day.

Congratulating himself on his cleverness, Eustace wondered why he had started to face every problem with the question, "What would Ginny do?"

He took the company Rover for the drive to Nottingham. He waited for his father in that same family library where the loan had first been asked for and refused. He wore his best suit, his best tie.

His father was slow to appear, unwilling to come until his dinner was finished. He arrived without a jacket, the top button of his trousers hanging undone.

"What is it you want at this hour, Eustace?" he demanded.

Eustace had been to the bank to ensure that the two thousand pounds could be delivered in two piles of crisp ten-pound notes, each eight inches by five, sepia-coloured paper promising to 'pay the bearer'. He had placed the piles on a silver tray.

"I came to pay my debt and be done with it. I never wish to be in debt again," Eustace told him.

His father looked at the money. "Suppose I tell you I don't want it?"

"Why would you not want it?"

"A man need not take from his son's success."

"My success? You sought to strangle it at birth."

"No, I sought to pull you back from foolishness. Like any father should do. You with your fancy ideas. That Lord's daughter has turned your head." His father waved an admonishing finger.

"Niece," said Eustace.

"What?"

"Ginny is Lord Buckley's niece, not his daughter."

"Niece or daughter, your head is turned, Boy."

"And yet my foolishness is here… on the table... paid for in full."

Eustace stood staring, fixed on his father's left cheek, grey and puckering, the return gaze uneven. He had not noticed it before.

"Take your money or not. I want no part of it," Eustace said. "I have never been any kind of favoured son, not like John. William and I volunteered and you bought John his freedom."

"I did not—"

"No, don't lie to me, Father, not now," Eustace raised his voice. "Who got him free? And made a coward of him? A medical discharge? Pah! Who paid the doctor?"

His father shook his head. "You were always a wild and godless child," he said.

"I was the one who did his King's duty, Father. I have the medals. You may burn the money if you do not want it. My business here is done."

He started towards the door. His father called after him.

"The money was not mine. It was your grandmother's. Do you think I had two thousand pounds to give like that? I did not. It was a humiliation. That damned fiancée of yours put it in her head."

Eustace did not turn back.

"It'll never work out, you know, Son… for you and her. Money or not. Never."

His mother hurried down the drive as he was leaving. She caught up as he was getting into the Rover.

"You're not staying the night, then?" she said. "I wanted to talk with you. To hear your news."

"My business here is done," he repeated.

"Oh, Eustace, do not be like this. Be a good Christian son and forgive." She reached out towards him, touched him on the shoulder.

"I said, my business is done." He reached in his pocket for the ignition key.

She blurted out, "I have never seen his grave… William's grave."

The awkward change of subject caught him by surprise.

"I don't want to go there alone, Eustace."

"You mean to go with me? Why would I wish to do that?"

"You are the only one who will. That grey cheek — your father is no longer young. He had a small apoplexy this year, a seizure of the brain. John is now running the lace factory."

"Have him take you then. Perhaps he should see France at last."

She offered such a pitiful look, he felt a wave of guilt at his anger.

"I'm sorry," he said.

"Eustace, you know full well he will not go and he will use the excuse of work and business to refuse."

"I have a business. It may not be lace, or to the family's taste, but it is mine."

"You told me once you wrote letters to the dead boys' parents every time. I never got a letter," she said. "No explanation. You were the one who always understood duty. You will not refuse me."

He knew the moment she spoke it was true. One may as well ask an apple to stop falling half-way down from the tree as to expect a man to reform the shape he was hammered into as a child.

* * *

If it must be done, best it be done quickly, or so Eustace told his mother. He was secretly hoping for a letter that might tell him of Ginny's return. None seemed forthcoming, but it seemed prudent to make the trip immediately and hope for better news on his return.

In two weeks, mother and son were off, taking boats and trains and taxis. The new France they came upon was not the mud-splattered country, pock-marked with shell holes as he remembered. Its rolling hillsides were a carpet of grass and, here and there, a field of poppies, splendidly red, a living carpet, everything so open and endless. In the cemeteries, wooden crosses marked neat lines of graves as if someone were trying to tidy up the chaos that created them. From death comes a new life. The country felt reborn, its colours fresh and vital.

True, the closure of the old world was not complete. The promised headstones had not been placed and the shaky records sent Eustace and his mother wandering the rows, searching for William's remains. His mother dressed in black to mourn her loss, but seemed uncertain what she'd come to find. He worried there would be nothing 'real' to see.

They walked for miles — everything silent, the air shockingly sweet. Twice she broke into tears and threatened to turn back, but with him standing beside her, she found strength to walk on.

Eustace had been granted the rank of captain two weeks before the Armistice in 1918 and, once the fighting stopped, his new status bought him unexpected latitude. The letter from his mother had named the canal; it was all she knew of William's death at the time.

Eustace borrowed a staff car from the camp commander. He needed to know what had happened to William. The war was full of invented stories — the best of them for convenience, but stories nonetheless, like the one concocted to cover Masterson's death. Eustace needed something true in order to believe that William had gone.

All these years later, he supposed his mother needed the same.

And so they searched, mother and middle son, over grass and hillside between endless wooden crosses. The records they'd been shown were patchy. Uncertain.

He wanted to find it. He didn't want to find it. He wanted her to find peace. This, at least, he thought of as another kind of debt.

An hour. Two hours. Small hopes as they approached each possible resting place for William. Bigger disappointments, every time they found a grave that was not the grave.

But then, at last, there it was. A total surprise. Another insignificant cross which was this time not so insignificant.

He tried to clutch her hand. He wanted her to be sure of his presence.

"I remembering him being born," she said, her voice half muted. "William was the easiest, slipped into this life and slipped out. Always so easy with it." She shook her head. "No, I don't think that can be right. You saw men die of gas? Was it easy? You can lie if you must. I don't suppose God would call it a sin."

How easy is it to die? There's a question!

When he had reached the canal at *Sambre–Oise*, Eustace found William's Commanding Officer in a makeshift tent in a makeshift camp. The canvas of the tent had a large brown stain. Its edges were turning green with mould. The inside smelt of stale garlic.

"You know how it is," the officer said. "A stray grenade rolls into a ditch. Accidents happen in war. Gas is unpredictable."

"One of *our* grenades?"

"It was a French grenade. We borrowed a few dozen of the blasted things. No training on how to use them, you see. Rotten luck."

He expected some bigger shock — a turning of his stomach, a gagging in his throat. It did not come. Not then. He stared at the brown stain and the green mould.

"Did he… Did my brother make it to the hospital?"

"Survived three days. Rotten luck," the Commanding Officer repeated. "I wanted to write a letter. I usually do…"

Phosgene was responsible for most of the gas fatalities in the Great War. Unlike other poison gases, it did not kill instantly. It caused creeping failures in the lungs. Fluid built up. A slow death followed.

The Germans introduced it, but the British and Americans used it too, thirty-six thousand tons in total, mainly from stocks supplied by the French. It was often mixed with Chlorine, so that it was lighter and drifted on the wind. Military strategists claimed that poison gas saved lives because it 'reduced the enemy's ability to respond'. Its main advantage was in consuming the enemy's medical resources tending to the doomed.

Eustace had seen a few 'lucky' survivors in hospital tents and holding camps, coughing wrecks of men. If asked, they said the gas reeked like dead horses or mouldy hay. He'd only ever smelt it for himself from far away. On the wind. From the turret of a tank with his head up, escaping another crawling confinement.

He thought about the lie he had written in the Masterson's letter. And about his own luck in surviving.

"Yes, very easy," he whispered in answer to his mother's question.

A gust of wind stirred the French grass.

"Those times we took you boys to church, did you ever believe in God, Eustace?"

"Once. Now I think it's all fate and fortune."

"Yes, I suppose that's how it is. You are off now with your craziness and your crazy American, and you will be rich or poor, I don't know which."

"She is not mine, not any more. Ginny has gone off back to New York, and I am still here. I have…" His hand circled in the air, trying to grasp something. "… no rhyme or reason, I suppose. The money I gave back, he could have burnt it. I told him so. It made no difference."

"You are the one that survived, aren't you? God has given you a gift," she said.

"God? Oh, no, Mother, I told you, not Him."

They took the boat from Calais and trains up through England as far as Coventry where his brother John met them to whisk their mother home to Nottingham. Eustace stayed on the train for Birmingham.

When they parted at the steps of the carriage, she looked through Eustace as if he were not there. Two sons were lost now — William to the war; Eustace by his return from it. He watched the dark line of her mourning jacket, her back to him as she departed with the son who remained.

He saw at last that, of all the childhood things, only the thin Havershall name lingered within him, faint like a watermark in paper. In some way, not of his own making, he had become free. He was alone and alone in all the worst kind of ways.

That evening, he wrote his fiancée another letter. He had got used to writing every week; by now, she had been gone for several months. As a typewriter man — a *'typewriterist'* as the mocking Sir Alfred had put it — he had always ended up hand writing each one, because it seemed so much more of himself would be tucked into the envelope when he posted it.

This time, a whole page described the look on Smith's face when Jean Collins turned in her typescript with one and a half times the word count of the typists from Solomon-McKensie. He told her about the company's profits. He told her he had finally repaid his father. He told her he had made peace at his brother's graveside, though he was far from sure that was true. He got as far as the word 'Masterson...' then stopped. He tore the pages into shreds and threw them on the fire. He drove to Woody's house, needing to see him right away. Some things won't wait.

He parked outside the Woodmanseys' in Aston and knocked at the door of their basement flat. Mabel answered with little Celia in her arms. When he asked for Woody, she directed him around to a garage behind the house.

"His workshop," she explained.

Eustace found his partner working among makeshift benches and piles of old machinery that seemed to have been acquired from junk yards. Oil lamps hung along the walls as in that French pigsty. The guts of several typewriters lay on one of the benches, but Woody was seated on a high stool working at another, drinking his customary whisky from an enamel cup. Before him was the copper-coloured casing of a mechanical woman's head and torso. Her metal legs lay on the floor nearby.

"Captain?" he said in surprise. He reached for a dirty rag to wipe his hands, but offered no handshake. Handshakes were always superfluous between them.

"I didn't know you had this," Eustace said, idly casting his eyes around the cave of treasures.

"I ran out of space at the factory."

"I'm sure we could have found you more, maybe in the new annex."

"This is for my projects."

Eustace raised his eyebrows.

"I paid a shilling for her at an auction," Woody explained, referring to the metal woman. "It's a replica of an ancient Greek invention. A particularly poor replica, I'd say. No one is quite sure how it worked. There's only a few texts that describe it."

"I'm sure you will reinvent it."

"It works on the levels of water and a little bit of air pressure. Principles that Archimedes worked out. You know, the Greeks used it to open their temple doors. *Open Sesame!* An imitation of the power of their gods. Amphictyonis here is a copy made by the Victorians. She pours wine."

Eustace repeated the name. "You called her that?"

"The Greeks had gods for everything... including wine, though some of them had to double up. Interesting, don't you think? Progress gets ever faster. The Greeks had water and air power. Now we're even outgrowing steam and taking to petroleum. Electricity is the next God. You know I—"

"Woody," said Eustace, interrupting. "I'm sorry, I have to tell you something. I need to go to America."

Woody's surprise was evident, but it turned quickly to a nod. "For Ginny, I assume?"

"I know the business needs me... needs both of us... but I can't... I have to fetch her back."

"You mean to go there right now?"

"I decided today. I don't care what her cousin says. I don't care what anyone advises. As fast as I can get a ship."

"I've heard the passage is not cheap. Do you even have the fare?"

"Not really. Not since I paid back my father."

"I see. The company just paid out for new stock. I suppose the second payment from that Smith fellow is due by the month's end. Then we might afford to pay out a director's loan," Woody suggested.

"I cannot wait another day," Eustace replied.

Woody sipped at his enamel cup, gazing at his desperate friend. "I do not see your fiancée as a woman who will be 'fetched' so easily, Captain."

"Then I will beg," said Eustace.

The next morning, Woody did not arrive at the factory until 11 a.m. and when he did arrive, he was riding a bicycle. He laid twenty pound notes on Eustace's desk.

"Will that be sufficient?"

"Sufficient for what?"

"Steerage class passage, I imagine. It won't buy better, not at Cunard's prices."

Eustace looked at the money. "Where did you get it?"

"Suppose I said, I stole it?"

"You didn't...?"

"I didn't. I sold the Austin."

"You sold your car?"

"Needs must. Besides you won't be needing the company Rover for a couple of weeks. There'll be cash in the bank by then."

The money looked very different from the pile he'd given his father. This he would never burn.

"When we are rich, I think I'll buy a sports car. Maybe a Bugatti," Woody said.

"But I—"

"Sometimes you don't understand how it works, Captain. But I understand how you work. Take the train for Liverpool now. You'll make the next boat."

It took almost six days to cross the Atlantic. Time to think and be absolutely clear what he wanted. In New York, Eustace bought dollars with his remaining English money and used nearly all of it to take a taxi along the stringy finger of land to the Hamptons. He arrived unkempt and unwashed, so eager was he to reach her.

He had to give his name three times to the servant who answered the door before he was ushered out onto the patio at the back of the house. Presumably, they wished to keep him downwind from other house guests. He watched the sea glistening off the water far away down the lawns.

She appeared at last, tanned from her Long Island summer. Neat cotton dress. Little make-up. A cloche hat in the same style she'd worn when first they met. She sat on the other side of a patio table, not offering a handshake or a kiss. He looked for the ring, was amazed to see it.

"You look overwrought," she remarked, allowing the faintest smile.

"And you… magnificent," he assured her.

He felt little disgrace at his own appearance. He had come this far and there was nothing more left to care for.

She had been playing tennis every day, she told him. "I am quite the athlete now. Much in demand at the tennis club."

"I imagine," he said and cursed himself for not finding something better.

"I did not expect you, Eustace. You did not write that you were coming."

"I made my decision to travel only latterly."

"You? A decision?" she said, her tone mocking.

"I made no promises before," he reminded her.

"I'm sure you did. I wanted marriage. I wanted to be made love to. You have not yet delivered. When asked, you declined."

"The question was unfair. I was but a poor would-be businessman."

"'Was' or 'are'?" she asked. "It's all stuff and nonsense while this ring sits stone cold upon my finger."

She held out her hand, wiggling her finger to encourage light into the false diamond.

"See, I showed my mother," she declared.

"You did? What did she say?"

"She called it 'underwhelming'. She was beastly about it."

"And your father?"

"He may disown me for all I care. I am twenty-one in December and in my majority. I'm not so much 'on his hands'. Nor on the hands of my aunt and uncle. It does not matter whether I am inappropriately married or scandalously running around London with a man who makes typewriters."

"You think me inappropriate?"

She offered him a pitying look.

"I am inappropriate," he admitted.

"It is your best feature. We are inappropriate together."

"The business…" he began without a plan that would finish the sentence. "I mean, this year is a good year, finally a good year. At the end of the year, we will have made a tidy profit."

"Enough to marry upon?"

"Woody had to sell his car to get me here. Gin, I am a terrible risk." he said.

"Fiddlestick! Everything is a risk," she said. Her face cracked into a smile. "But do not think I will succumb quite so easily. If you will have me, here are my terms. I have not forgotten your promises and I wish to see the Games next year."

The Games of the VIII Olympiad were to be held the following summer in Paris.

"I'm sure you said our honeymoon could be in Montmartre, and this next year will be perfect. Cousin Caroline went last time with our aunt to the Belgian Games. Paris will be so much better than Antwerp. Please, please say you'll take me. I would like to see the Americans run. And that Englishman, what's his name?"

"You have clearly thought about this? Athletics and marriage?"

Ginny rolled her eyes. "I have had a summer to think of nothing else, Eustace. And Paris, the Olympics, this is as long as I will wait. After that, it's a mansion or a garret. I do not much care where it takes us once we have plunged from the diving board, so to speak. I will not flinch at the fall, if fall we must."

For a while, he could conjure no answer, his mouth dry as a desert.

"One moment," he said, licking his lips. He produced an envelope from his jacket pocket. The journey had creased it more than he would have liked.

"What's this?" she said.

"Open it."

"Did you not send letters across the Atlantic, all saying nothing?"

He smiled. "Open it," he urged.

She opened it. Inside was a gold embossed card.

It named the church. And a date, July 4th.

"I thought Independence Day appropriate. Given that America's loss will become my gain. In time for the Olympics, I believe."

She looked at him in astonishment. "How did you know I'd…? I mean, how did you have this ready?"

When he smiled, she slipped her hand across the table to reach for him. He felt the tremble of delight in her hand, the hummingbird heartbeat that was her magic and her radiance, that now was finally to be his.

Woody ran the Duke Works while Eustace was away. They were not the smoothest weeks.

On the first Monday, the receptionist from the office came to tell him that a one-armed man was in reception.

"He says he knows you, Mr Woody, Sir. You and Mr Havershall both."

It took a moment for Woody to register the connection.

"Mulgrove…"

"Yes, Sir, that was his name. Arnold Mulgrove."

"Did he say what he wanted?"

"A job, Sir, that's what he said."

"A one-armed man in a factory full of presses and machinery," Woody mused. He thought about the dangers.

Mulgrove was thirty-years-old now, straggles of dark hair peeping from beneath his cap, a touch of grey in the short sideburns. The six years since the war had created a slight lean in his stance. He wore a khaki raincoat, one sleeve knotted and hanging as if he wished to advertise the lost arm, or maybe to receive due credit for it.

Woody embraced him as a former brother-in-arms and felt a thinness in Mulgrove's muscles that did not seem to have been corrected by peacetime.

"I was training as a setter... once... before I was called up," Mulgrove told him.

Woody could not refuse the man a job. Mulgrove became the only one-armed press setter in Birmingham.

It was not the only employment dilemma facing Havershall's. The rapid expansion of the workforce had brought a diminishing in the care with which workers were vetted. Increasingly, there was interest from those communist infiltrators who had sympathies with the Bolsheviks. The union movement was on the rise, sending organisers steeped in Marxist-Leninist ideals into every factory and trade in Britain. Strikes were common.

The shift supervisors were told to keep an eye open. Every so often, Jim McCann would come to the office with a verdict on new recruit:

"That one, he's from the Worker's Union."

"Let's watch him close then. Let me know when he steps out of line," Woody would say. When the right time came, the man would be removed.

But neither McCann nor his supervisors would dare say a word about Mulgrove. A one-armed press setter had to have a junior to do the real work — the tightening and untightening of bolts, the manoeuvring of heavy press tools. They knew Mulgrove was a pity case.

They also saw that the new employee was talking too much, was too friendly with the other workers, spent too much time chatting with the middle-aged women on the assembly benches. It could not be mentioned to 'management', since Mulgrove was management's man.

Chapter Seven

That fateful year ended with the first substantial profit for Havershall's and, as 1924 began, the sales and administration staff could no longer cope with orders. The company secured a lease on the property adjoining 30 Marmaduke Lane. They built a corridor bridge between the two first-floors with height enough for a delivery van to pass underneath. The offices were now popularly known as 'Duke House' to match the factory area's nickname of 'Duke Works'. A space on the second floor for a boardroom was set aside and Eustace had it decorated in the manner of Weatherstone & Hoare's — leather chairs, panelled walls, the big oak table, a drinks cabinet.

In April, the company paid a dividend to the two shareholders. Along with a small inheritance that Ginny received from an old family trust on her twenty-first birthday, Eustace's payment allowed him and Ginny to put down the deposit on a house — a home in Edgbaston with three bedrooms upstairs, a downstairs suitable for the staff below, should they ever be able to afford any. It was below her class, but above his expectation. A thin back garden looked out towards the cricket ground. It required a mortgage, of course, but he contented himself that his creditor was a Building Society, not a bank.

That same apportioning of dividends bought Woody an updated cabriolet version of the Austin 7 in which he'd once romanced — not to say, 'indelicately impregnated' — Mabel, and which he'd sold to bring the Havershalls together.

Always obsessed with mechanics, he had the car modified for racing and took to competing in local hillclimbs on the weekends. Mabel — at home with Celia Jane — disapproved, especially when he insisted on racing on her Sabbath, and then on the Christian Sunday too.

Eustace and Ginny married, as promised, on 4th July, 1924. There were 300 guests. Eustace's choice was the same church in which Viscount and Viscountess Fairchild had married, though no government ministers or visiting dukes were in evidence. The Buckley family home in Derbyshire was borrowed for the reception.

Ginny's father and mother sailed over for the ceremony. Sir Stanley Buckley, having interrogated Eustace's business and heroic status, gave his tentative blessing to the match and paid for the festivities. Eustace expressed resistance to the cost. Ginny assured him it was all on the lower side of the family's wedding budgets. She had not admitted to him the source of her father's generosity, though buying alcohol with the Buckley fortune rather amused her.

Woody and Mabel were guests, along with fifteen of the senior company staff, and Eustace's mother and reluctant father, who declared the proceedings 'too grand' and 'a waste'. His mother carried an apology from John Junior whose wife was reportedly too pregnant to travel. The rest of the staff at Havershall's were granted a day's holiday.

The wedding presents included two tickets to the opening of the Paris Games and several athletic events, among them the 100 Metres Final.

At 7 p.m. on the 7th July, that sprint final in the *Stade de Colombes* was won by Harold Abrahams in front of 45,000 people. Eustace considered the man a model Englishman. One month before, Abrahams had set a record in the long jump that stood for the next 32 years, but he did not want that medal and didn't compete in the event at the Olympics.

For Abrahams, the youngest of three supremely successful brothers and an outsider by way of his Jewish religion, only becoming the fastest man on Earth mattered. Ginny's American runners were beaten, a world record secured.

However, the new Mr and Mrs Havershall did not actually see the race. They were still in bed, enjoying their honeymoon.

It took the virginal Mrs Havershall one night, one morning and half an afternoon to explore the intimacies of marriage and decide that its physical exertions agreed with her. A handwritten Do-Not-Disturb sign hung on the hotel door.

The bridal bedroom featured a large ensuite and an enamel bath big enough to be shared, so on the second evening, they shared it. Eustace found it quite different from the corroded bath in his Birmingham apartment. Agreeably so.

She lay with her back against the enamel as he reclined into her, head and hair spread against her shoulder, her legs wrapped around his waist as she lathered his chest with a large soap bar.

"I am in love with your feet," he observed presently, grasping one foot and wiggling its polished toe.

"Just my feet?" she said with disappointment.

"I was working on an inventory, feeling my way up to more important areas." He ran his fingertips over the pale instep. "I shall give a more practical demonstration of the ascent as soon as we get out of this bath."

"You only want me clean, so you can make me feel dirty again."

He put his hand over hers, clasping the finger that wore the wedding ring. She dropped the soap. It landed on her calf and continued its slide until it plopped into the water between his legs.

"Hey, be careful," he exclaimed. "A man has delicate goods."

"Delicate?" She laughed, nibbled at his ear and whispered, "It did not seem so delicate earlier. Oh, no, you seemed quite unconcerned by its delicacy then."

At that, he rose from the bath, standing dripping wet and naked. Then he leaned in and plucked her up into his arms. She was surprised by his strength and comforted by it too. All the time, she giggled and protested as she twisted in his grip. Water sloshed about the bathroom floor. He carried her into the bedroom, dropped her onto the bed still soapy and wet and pinned her down with his weight.

"What now, good Sir?" she asked. "You seem to have me at a disadvantage. Must I open my legs and let you in?"

"Yes, I think you must."

"Ah, the ruthless ambition of the man. He commands. I obey."

Five minutes passed until, the pair of them breathless and satisfied, he rolled off her and she found a place to lay her head between his arm and his torso, wet hair against his shoulder in a reversal of their earlier position.

"Tell me something true," she urged, gazing at the ceiling.

"What kind of thing?"

"Something you wouldn't discuss with anyone who wasn't your wife. Something I'm now entitled to. For instance, did I ever tell you how I was thrown out of the first of my schools? I released three piglets in the dining room. I'd painted on their backs, numbers one, two and four. The staff had a frightful time searching for Number Three. I was twelve. They caned me. Can you believe that?"

She stopped to allow him a chance to reply and when he didn't, she said, "Did you really kill people in the war?"

The question took him by surprise.

"You never talk about it and I don't know. You once said you'd kill for me… to defend my virtue," she added.

"There are targets on a battlefield, Gin. And tanks have guns."

"No. I meant, have you killed somebody who wasn't a distant 'anybody'?"

"Yes," he said heavily.

"For your country?"

"I used to believe that. For 'God and King and country'."

"And now?"

"There is always duty," he said. "Even if there is no longer God."

By the time Eustace and Ginny returned from their honeymoon, the company that had become Havershall's was almost four years old. In that time, no one had died in the 'Duke Works', a stark contrast to factories in surrounding streets. The hot dip galvanising plant around the corner burst a barrel of molten zinc and sent its contents across the factory floor, killing three workers and injuring two others. One victim fell into the spreading wave, ending up embedded, a half-coated statue as the metal went solid on the cold stone floor.

Many fingers and hands were lost in cutting machines, lathes and presses. High racks of goods collapsed onto working areas. People were crushed under crates being loaded or unloaded. Those were the quick deaths, but the chemicals in use prescribed a shortened future for all employees of the heavier industries.

Tragedy finally came to Havershall's from the unlikeliest source: their most recent investment, the power press that worked by electricity rather than steam. The mechanism acted using pipes filled with hot oil pumped at high pressure. It delivered several hundred tons of force for forming the metal components.

Press manufacturers were quick to point out the advantages of their 'modern' technology, but not so keen to admit its dangers. Rupture the seal of an oil pipe and the jet of oil is a long thin bolt flying across the shop floor. At 4.21 p.m. on the 13th of August — a day on which Woody had gone out to visit a supplier — the main oil line running to the press cylinder was struck by the corner of a wooden box of finished typebars carried by an apprentice. He had decided to carry two stacked boxes instead of making a repeat journey to the assembly bays. The load was heavy, the stack above his eye-level. The oil line tore from its junction at the top of the press.

Briefly caught in the jet's path, Miss Gladys Jefferies in the assembly area had a chunk gouged from her arm. It struck young Lionel Swithin full in the chest, slashing a deep rut across his body as he fell out of its way. When oil finally hit the far wall of the factory thirty yards away, the jet burst open, taking a mighty divot from the wall plaster. Eustace heard the scream from the office block. There were screams from many people, but none like Lionel's.

The ambulance took a while to arrive. Eustace watched him dying, as he had watched Masterson dying. There was no holster on his belt he could reach for, or help he could offer.

Lionel was twenty-three. He lived with his mother. She had already lost a husband in a car factory at Longbridge. Eustace had interviewed the young man when he joined.

After the body was removed and Eustace had shut the factory for the day, he found Megan Rillett, the office supervisor. She said she knew where the Swithins lived. Eustace needed a guide through the 'backs' of Digbeth, the streets and courtyards of terraced houses clustered around communal privies and wash houses.

The Swithins' home stood last in a blind-ended street capped off by a blank wall. A dozen linked dwellings sat each side of a road of broken pavings, sloping into its centre where the old drains had once run with sewage. An attempt to improve sanitation with underground pipes had removed the open runs, but their smells remained ingrained in the grimy cracks. Working class Birmingham was still canals and sewers and soot and the over-scent of horse-drawn transport. Slack washing lines of grey indistinguishable garments hung between houses, dipping in the middle. A man of Eustace's height had to duck under them. He was wearing his every day suit, the one with the waistcoat. He knew he didn't belong here. It was late afternoon on the warmest day of the year.

He recalled the words he'd written for Masterson's family seven years before, how he was able to say that the boy died bravely for his country, even though the details were a fabrication. He had no doubt the lie brought them comfort. What could he say now to Lionel Swithin's mother?

Perhaps sensing his tension, Megan took two steps back to stand in the road as he knocked on the door and stood waiting. When the mother, her hair tied in a scarf and a pinafore over her house dress, caught sight of Eustace in his management clothing, she burst into tears.

The company had recently purchased a Morris Oxford Bullnose to replace the clapped out Rover Eustace used to make sales trips. He drove it out to Woody's that evening. Woody was in his garage, working on his mechanical woman, a project that never seemed to end. Seeing his partner's state of mind, and hearing his story of the death, Woody shepherded him to the nearest public house, the Barton Arms.

The pub was the flagship of Mitchell and Butler's Breweries, designed by the same architect as the nearby Aston Hippodrome with which it shared a style. It had its own clock tower, all in brick and stone neo-Jacobean trimmings. The interior dripped Victorian splendour — stained glass windows and engraved mirrors, mahogany panels, snob-screens between the public and lounge bars, a sweeping wrought-iron staircase, the whole place tiled and painted with murals. A walking stick displayed on the wall had supposedly belonged to Charlie Chaplin.

"It wasn't your fault. It wasn't our fault, Captain," Woody said for the fourth or fifth time as they sipped their drinks in the public bar.

Eustace had drifted into a fugue. "Do you mean Lionel... or Masterson?"

"Which question would you prefer me to answer?"

"Both... Neither..." Eustace hesitated. "I had to do it. Do you not think I had to shoot him?"

"And you shot him, Captain, you did."

"Death still seems..." Eustace hesitated again. He had hesitated on that battlefield in France. "...Unreal."

Woody lowered his gaze. They had never before talked of those moments inside the tank. Something about this new death stirred it up.

"He'd have thanked you for it, I'll say that. I wouldn't have the courage to do it, Captain, that's the truth."

"Yet you were the one who went under... who fixed the tank? We all waited, me, Mulgrove, all the others... with Masterson." Eustace tried a smile. "I expected it to be peaceful, you know, as I was there, finger on the trigger. You know who put his hand on my shoulder while I squeezed?"

"Mulgrove?"

"Arnold Mulgrove."

"Would that be the same arm he left in France?" Woody said.

They laughed with the black battlefield humour that had once protected them, but the battlefield was far, far behind them. Eustace squeezed his lip between thumb and forefinger, considering his deceptions. "I have never told Ginny, do you know that? She asked me. I would not tell her."

"Aye, well, if that's the only one, I reckon you can call yourself an honest man. There's plenty of things I'll never tell Mabel," Woody assured him. "Most of them I did drunk. That's no excuse. Some I'm ashamed of, but mostly it's worse when I did nothing. It's inactions I feel most guilty about."

"I don't keep secrets from my wife," Eustace said.

Woody went quiet for several seconds, as if his mind had slipped onto a different track, then he said, "I should tell you, Captain, I think Mulgrove's from the Union."

Unlike his commander, Woody remembered little of the tank — he'd blanked it out — but that drunken night in the *maison tolérée*, back when his captain was still a lieutenant, haunted him still. He remembered two of the other men, Blenkinsop and Mulgrove, taking up with the delicate redhead Eustace had refused. After Eustace left, a blonde girl who'd been plying Woody with booze led all of them upstairs.

For reasons unknown, the redhead became a focus for Mulgrove's anger. She had been the lieutenant's choice and now she was the lieutenant's rejected woman. Mulgrove fed on that.

When Blenkinsop was spent, Mulgrove took over. She complained at his brutality and he struck her across the face, yelling, "This is all you are, you whore!"

Blenkinsop had to pull him away.

Woody stared blurry-eyed, occupied by another girl nuzzling his chest. Blood seeped from a cut above the redhead's eye. Her tears diluted the blood. He did nothing.

Woody was the youngest in the party — sometimes he told himself that was his excuse. He had wondered about Mulgrove's violence, of course, but at the time, he had not understood why being an officer's reject had made the girl into Mulgrove's prey.

Afterwards he felt ashamed that he never knew her name, knew neither of the girls' names. That hadn't seemed necessary. He wasn't gathering memories. He expected no time to remember them.

Soon enough, on another French field, Blenkinsop was hit by a grenade.

Following Lionel Swithin's death, Eustace attempted to open a local branch of the National Safety First Association. The attempt alarmed fellow business owners, especially those in the insurance market.

One insurance company said it would not support any campaign for safety, because 'as the number of accidents is reduced... premiums charged to the public have to be reduced.'

Being safer was bad for business. If people didn't keep dying, insurers would see their revenues shrink. Insurance companies hated safety the way other business owners hated communists and unions.

Havershall's was the first company in Marmaduke Lane to put guard shields around its machines. One Saturday, the nightwatchman was assaulted and knocked unconscious. Someone smashed all the windows around the back of the Duke Works. It happened again two weeks later after new windows had been installed. The nightwatchman had his skull fractured.

"It's kids," said Jim McCann, standing in Eustace's office with his cap in hand.

"Kids?"

"Older kids. Local louts, Mr Havershall. Hooligans who never made it to the real fight. Now they're out there and they'll do a little mischief for the highest bidder."

"We have 'bidders' buying trouble for Havershall's?"

"Yes, Sir, I'm afraid we do. I can probably make it go away, if you'd like."

"'If I'd like'?" Eustace repeated

"Plenty of us 'round here think guards on machines is a good thing. And them kids have mothers. They live 'round her too. I have family, a brother, he'd help."

"I see. Would this cost me money, Jim?" Eustace asked suspiciously, thinking of the 'insurance man' he'd turned away previously.

"No, Sir. Maybe a few drinks, that's all. A pound or two behind the bar in the right pub. We'll deal with our own problems ourselves."

Eustace nodded. Havershall's Saturday night problems stopped abruptly and were never spoken of again.

Nevertheless, the businesses in the surrounding streets whose owners had favoured the Safety First campaign began withdrawing their support. The drive for safety survived in Havershall's, but died elsewhere alongside the daily trickle of accidents in the workplace and night-time incidents that weren't so accidental.

Chapter Eight

Entering 1925, marriage to Lord Buckley's niece, albeit his least favourite and most headstrong relation, had elevated Eustace to a new social status, not just the notable war hero, but the leading half of an 'acceptable couple'. The doors of England's finest manor houses were nudged open.

Have you met Mr. Havershall.

Quite the young industrialist, don't you know?

A 'coming' man.

The elegant invitation cards littered the morning mail, arriving in time to be discussed over breakfast in Edgbaston. Three weekend invitations for three consecutive weekends fell through the letterbox as the shooting season approached. He and Ginny were a hit, accepted in a new circle of the comfortably-married, almost-fully-accredited, almost-aristocracy. Privately — in moments not even shared with Ginny — the thought of it made his skin crawl, exactly like the claustrophobia of tanks and childhood cupboards. The walls seemed to come too close.

Elsewhere, the domestic economy was not as a booming stockmarket portrayed it. The unexorcised ghosts of the war hung over Britain still. Stalin had taken power in Russia and communism was on the march.

The government, now led by Stanley Baldwin and riddled with pre-war politicians who had prolonged the fighting, exercised its wounded pride to restore the Gold Standard. The Standard implied that a country's treasury must hold enough gold to redeem all paper notes their current owners wished to exchange. In times of economic slowdown when buying more gold was not an option for the British government, this meant restrictions on the number of notes they could issue.

Effectively, the Gold Standard reversed the banker's magic trick. While bankers created credit by loaning money that didn't exist, Baldwin's government insisted that every pound note was backed by a visible amount of gold. As a result, the money supply stalled and credit was squeezed. The pound, now a rare commodity, showed an artificial increase in value against other currencies.

Politicians bred on the glory of Empire liked the idea of a strong pound, but the country choked. A strong pound made imports cheaper, made exporting impossible, made workers' wages unaffordable. Thus the elevated pound had catastrophic effects on the industrial landscape. Britain could no longer compete.

Pay had already begun to fall for the worst-paid workers. In the mining industry, where depleted coal reserves were making operations uneconomic, wages dropped by a third. The unions, with growing communist infiltration, stoked unrest across industry in general. Activists looked to the Russian revolution for inspiration. Sabotage of machines became a recurring theme.

The inflated value of the pound proved a particular challenge for Havershall's, since the competition, other than BBTL, came mostly from American rivals who enjoyed selling their machines for pounds and converting their revenues into excessive amounts of dollars. On the up over the previous three years, 1925 threatened to reverse Havershall's fortunes just as the company was starting to really grow.

In April, Arnold Mulgrove came to Eustace's office demanding, in the name of the union, a pay rise for all workers in Duke Works. Two other men from the shop floor sat on either side, but Mulgrove was clearly the leader. Eustace had only found out that morning that Mulgrove had been elected as the workers' representative. Woody, it seemed, had been correct.

Eustace was unprepared and too influenced by the growing poverty of Birmingham to give an emphatic 'no', which was what the most recent balance sheets of the company dictated. Yes, he pointed out the malaise sweeping the country, the general downturn in wage levels elsewhere, but Mulgrove told him Havershall's had a duty to do right by its staff.

"I know you know what duty is, Mr Havershall," he said.

"Thank you, Arnold."

"Social duty, I mean. You ain't a toff," Mulgrove added.

Eustace began to ask himself if the old duties had transformed into something else, perhaps while he wasn't paying attention. Now there was this *social* duty.

Mulgrove asked, did he want to be like the company masters who forced shoeless unfed children into the streets? Look at what was happening elsewhere in Europe.

Mulgrove didn't seem to be the same young man with whom Eustace had shared a tank. Or perhaps he was. Hadn't Mulgrove been the one saying, "We're not fighting for ourselves. We're fighting for *them*." An unspoken threat to order was now apparent in Mulgrove's précis of the world order. Democracy was clearly failing, rich bosses tried to hold too tight to their former privilege and the world lurched violently towards totalitarianism one way or another. Maybe you had no stomach for fascism, but do nothing and the communists will rise.

Eustace made the mistake of listening.

Since Lionel Swithin's death, Eustace had often found himself walking around in Bordesley instead of taking lunch. He had seen poverty creeping in, little by little. The metal plating works up the road had burned to the ground one Wednesday night. No one knew if the match that lit the fire came from the owner's side (seeking the insurance money) or from the workers' anger about a disputed overtime rate, or — just possibly — from an act of God.

At dinner in Edgbaston, Mabel and Ginny conversed while Woody and Eustace fretted. They discussed the workers' plight over dinner, quietly guilty at their own profits, even if their profits were now thinning.

Sales were growing, but at lower prices. Consequently, the working capital in the business — the cash that kept the wheels turning — was running low once more. Fairness and prudence could not be reconciled, whatever duty said.

"Still I feel we should do something for them, don't you?" Eustace asked, pleading for support.

"I have started reading Marx," Woody declared.

"Ah, the Russian view."

"Not so much the Russia of today, Captain. Stalin's communism creeps closer to Mussolini's fascism. Idealisms, I reckon, are worthless and everywhere corrupted."

"I have one question," Ginny interjected, breaking from Mabel's domestic chatter. "Will your competitors raise their wages when everyone else lowers theirs?"

"No, but… But the world doesn't seem to be right," Eustace complained.

Woody said, "We've seen enough, Captain, to know the natural state of the world is not order. It is confusion, chaos and yes, poverty. Workers need the company like we need them… to defeat all that."

"Exactly," said Ginny, "but you cannot pay for their bad times. Nothing says the value of labour must always be greater than the price of bread."

"*Let them eat cake,*" Eustace retorted.

Woody and Mabel laughed nervously at the joke. Ginny might have been expected to fly into a rage, but she shook her head and smiled as if some flaw in her husband had been revealed.

"Not so ruthless then. He also wants to be a knight in shining armour," she said with gentle sarcasm. "There are many roads to acclaim and no man — even you, Eustace — can take them all."

At the next union meeting, Eustace granted a three pennies in the pound rise to all staff. Mulgrove withdrew in triumph. Union membership on the factory floor at Duke Works skyrocketed.

Two factories along the road were attacked in a week. Another was set ablaze, but the fire failed to take hold. A handful of working men who had opposed a union convenor were badly beaten in an alley. Woody advised Eustace to dig out his service revolver.

"You need your old Webley to protect you," Woody told him.

"I will not fire that weapon again," Eustace said.

"You do not need to fire it. They only need to see it and they will assume your intention. You get invited to shooting weekends, don't you? You and Ginny?"

Eustace nodded.

"Then they will assume you can shoot."

"Are *you* carrying a weapon, Woody?"

"Captain, I come and go from this factory and sometimes it is past midnight. I'm a jumped-up working man and that's what they hate most. Never ask when you don't wish to know the answer," Woody advised.

Eustace did not ask again.

The last house party of September was at Lord Hailsgam's Yorkshire estate.

Lady Hailsgam was Lady Buckby's sister. The interrelationships were complex. The two Lords had matriculated at Oxford together in 1883, both joined the Guards via Sandringham, married sisters and worked in the War Office in the most recent conflict. Their sixtieth birthdays fell upon the same weekend. A grand party with the friends and family of both men seemed in order. Eustace and Ginny were invited. Even by the standards of other invitations, this was elevation indeed.

Hailsgam House was a wild and beautiful stone building, cut off from civilisation, deep in the dales of Yorkshire's West Riding. It had three wings and nineteen large bedrooms plus servants' quarters and a series of outhouses.

The grouse season was still in full flow and shooting was the centre piece of the weekend. The idea caused Eustace significant trepidation. Gentleman would be required to handle a shotgun, many bruising their shoulders on its recoil as hapless birds, flushed from cover by beaters and dogs, exploded in mid-air above them. Well-dressed women and hangers-on would shout, "Good shot," whenever a bird was hit, though a twelve-bore hunting gun throws a pattern of shot the size of a dinner tray by the time it nears the target. Anyone who can wave the barrel in the air and pull a trigger without falling over would eventually hit something. Dogs and beaters were occasionally reported as casualties.

"Oh, come, Eustace, point the damn thing in the air like you've been doing all along. No one will notice you're not trying to hit anything. You'll still outdo my uncle," Ginny assured him. She had thrown herself onto the four-poster bed they had been allocated — the third best bedroom of the least glamorous wing in Hailsgam House. "I'm sure I could hit one myself, if they'd let me try."

Eustace hovered next to Ginny's weekend luggage, two sizeable suitcases and a hat box, each larger than his own single suitcase.

"I have successfully not hit anything for the whole of the season. I'm getting good at it."

"Do you despise it all so?"

"I don't like to kill anything, Gin."

"Ah, the war hero!"

"Not anymore," he said heavily.

She softened and whispered, "I'm sorry. My uncle is happy we've taken the time. He thinks we are *the* young couple and should otherwise be off enjoying marital bliss. My aunt told me so."

"Happy for you to come, I'm sure. I might as well be a driver to transport the bags."

"Alright then. Lift the cases on the bed, would you, Havershall?" She waved her hand over the area required for their landing. "It's beautiful here. And their chef's the dog's pyjamas. What's not to adore?"

"Thirty guests and I'm the only non-Lord, non-Duke or non-Sir."

"What rot!" She laughed. "Edward's here with Caroline. So there's at least one Viscount. You pretend to hate them, but Eustace, we know it's tosh."

"Do we?"

She crawled across the bed on her knees, cupped her hands behind his head.

"Think of the thruppence in the pound you gave away and consider yourself a good man," she suggested. "Now, show me *marital bliss* before the cocktails are served."

When the hour arrived, the dinner-dressed guests assembled in the drawing room to be introduced. Most knew each other from weekends past. Waiters with silver trays hovered, offering champagne flutes to some, taking orders for Martinis and Manhattans from others.

Edward and Caroline were, of course, experienced hands, as were most of the Lords and Ladies. Eustace and Ginny were the youngest couple on display. Lady Hailsgam — in appearance much like her sister, Lady Buckley — insisted on parading them around. They had been introduced to three-quarters of the room before Eustace came face to face with a couple who seemed vaguely of their own generation.

"… And this is Charlie Barrington-Brown and his wife, Margaret. Charlie, Margaret, these are the Havershalls."

Everything after the words 'Barrington-Brown' passed Eustace by in a daze. He shook the man's hand. He looked at the man's wife and back to the man. He was staring straight at his competition.

"The great Mr Havershall. Hello, Old Bean," Charlie said amiably.

He was not as monstrous as Eustace had imagined. Shorter by a few inches too. He wore his hair slicked back in Rudolph Valentino style, but did not disguise its brownish tinges. His dinner suit was immaculate, a black bow tie smartly executed. He had smooth hands and bright button eyes. Maybe a tad too close together to be trusted, Eustace told himself. And anyway, a man with smooth hands should never be an engineer or a manufacturer.

Margaret was as blonde as ripened wheat with a green gem-stone stare, handsome more than pretty. Too tall for Charlie, she wore flat shoes. When introduced, she explained that she'd grown up not far from the nearest town. Her family owned farmland, lots of it. Lord and Lady Hailsgam were her godparents, she explained.

"How do *you* know the Hailsgams?"

"Lord Buck is my uncle. That's my cousin Caroline over there," said Ginny, pointing.

"Oh, Viscount Fairchild's wife?"

"The same."

"She and I were debs together. What a coincidence!"

Charlie and Eustace stood four feet from one another, stoically unwilling to discuss typewriters. A few agonising minutes later, Lady Hailsgam returned and moved them around to the next couple. Strict rotation was encouraged.

Meeting her cousin again gave Ginny someone to confide in, someone to ask the questions that she could not decently ask anyone else. When the women withdrew after dinner, she pulled Caroline aside. She'd been saving this up for weeks.

The problem, she explained once she was sure they could not be overheard, was that becoming pregnant was taking longer than she had anticipated. She was sure she and Eustace were doing it right but nothing had come of their couplings in over twelve months. Caroline, seven years older, already the mother of twins and pregnant with another child, must surely know the answers.

"Is it our technique, do you suppose?" Ginny enquired.

"I'm sure I don't know what you mean," said her cousin.

For all Ginny's instinct in being forthright, the subject was delicate and ten gossiping women were barely out of earshot. She resolved to whisper.

"Dear Carrie, I'm worried that, when one puts one's mouth to the 'project', so to speak, it might — well — stunt the virility of the eventual outcome. I've tried to look it up, but there was nothing in the library in Birmingham and the librarian was no help at all. I was thinking, the saliva, you know?"

"You… do… that…?" Caroline managed only three faltering words.

Several women turned around.

Caroline took Ginny by the arm and shepherded her further from the main group. "You can't… We can't talk about such things. It's simply not done."

"You don't? I do take it inside before Eustace — shall we say? — *performs*. It's our sort of *hors d'oeuvre*."

Ginny received a look of pale-faced horror.

"Being with a Viscount and so on, I thought he must expect that sort of encouragement rather more," she added.

"Certainly not. We are suitably efficient as it is."

"Oh," said Ginny, surprised. "I want children, Caroline. A daughter. I really do. And I thought, you'd know how to help with such things, being a mother already. One did rather lack instruction, beforehand, what with my mother being overseas, and Auntie... Well, with Auntie being Auntie, I suppose. Daisy Henderson — she was in my finishing school — used to say you couldn't get pregnant if you used rubbing alcohol on it beforehand. She was three months gone when we went to her wedding. I suppose Eustace and I could try without the pre-amble, what do you think? It might be somewhat dry."

"Ginny, keep your voice down, for goodness sake."

Belatedly, Caroline checked the group behind them. One of the louder women could be heard complaining that Mussolini was operating a police state.

Caroline leaned in close, mouth close to Ginny's ear. "I think a young wife should do her duty. Should know what her duty is. And not go beyond it."

"Even if it hurts?"

"Especially if it hurts."

"Fiddlesticks! I like it. I wish it worked for us, that's all. Beyond the pleasure, of course. Did Auntie ever—? I mean, did anyone give you instruction?"

"My husband..." Caroline began. "He was a man of experience. That was all I needed."

"Ah, so, do you...?" Ginny circled her hand in the air, hoping it might convey the question.

"Do I what?"

"Do you have *la petite mort* at all? Ever?"

"Duty," said Caroline, sharply.

...From which Ginny concluded that her cousin did not.

"I had to pretend, once," Ginny said, "but I think he guessed. He paid me particular attention the next time, which was a few minutes after the last time, and then everything was fine."

"No, I do not wish to hear it. You listen to me. It behoves a woman to know what the act is for." Caroline lifted a forefinger in admonishment. "Men want a million little versions of themselves ruling the world. What the women want doesn't matter. A horse breeder pays for the stallion not the mare, Virginia, think on that. He keeps you in clothes, doesn't he? A house? He takes you to dinner, to the theatre... even a little dancing?"

"A little dancing," Ginny agreed. She pulled a face and moved forward to whisper, "If that's our fate, the mare should be well serviced for her trouble, don't you think?"

"Ginny, you're too much. Sometimes, you are the little harlot."

"Oh, *sometimes* I hope I am. Look at us in this room, ladies all." Ginny swept her arm towards the distant group. "The oddest thing is I wanted to throw myself at Eustace from the beginning and only held back because he wanted me as a lady."

She saw — she thought she saw — the vaguest expression of envy spread across Caroline's face. She felt considerably pleased with herself. It seemed she had mastered everything about being Mrs Eustace Havershall except, perhaps, how to have his children.

Typewriters were not discussed until the following afternoon. The dozen shooters and their followers were walking from one beat to another, skirting the edge of a muddy field. As the party formed into a column no more than two or three walkers wide, Eustace found himself next to Margaret Barrington-Brown.

Half the women had elected to stay at the house, but Margaret, like Ginny, had dressed in the English countrywoman's wax jacket and green Wellington boots to join the men. She didn't shoot a gun, but she had every intention of following the action. Eustace wished he could think of something to say to her, but he had exhausted his limited capacity for small talk.

Grasping the mettle, Margaret said, "They told me you were a quiet man. My Charlie is rarely impressed. I'm not so close to my godparents these days, so I had to scheme for an invitation. Charlie insisted."

He turned to look at her, uncertain if he had caught her meaning.

"Oh, yes, I see, still quiet," she said. "And yet…. He hasn't forgotten the Solomon-McKensie business, you know? Or your latest shenanigans over that Newcastle contract."

"I'm afraid I don't do shenanigans, only business."

"So speaks the single-minded man," she said. "Charlie is watching you."

She smiled as if she knew some sort of message had been conveyed. Her mission — whatever it was — had been completed. He nodded to her, noting that the messenger was now watching for his response.

"I don't see why I would worry him. Surely Charlie has all the money and investment he needs. And the Hayberry-Peats is a decent design, even if not a British one," he said. He managed to frame the design issue as if it somehow hinted at a lack of patriotism.

When they reached the next field of heather, the shooters lined up, walking forward with the wind while the dogs were running loose ahead. At one point, they disturbed a covey of a dozen birds who erupted into the air in a flapping, feathery panic.

Shotguns discharged willy-nilly. For once, Eustace stood deaf to the world, waiting for the birds to reach the closest point overhead.

For a moment, he had Mulgrove on his shoulder, he had every Lord and Lady on his shoulder too, but they were brushed aside. Everything was brushed aside. He squeezed.

He let off one… two… barrels a second apart.

Sharp impacts like battlefield explosions. Both shots were kills, the birds plummeting into the heather far away.

The master of the hunt dispatched the gun dogs to fetch them. Everyone was looking at Eustace. It was always slightly frightening to be looked at. He glanced to his right and caught Charlie's eye from twenty yards distant. The message and the response — both were now complete.

Eustace fell from the back of the group as it went off to hunt other things. Returning to the house alone, he slipped below stairs, discarding his boots. His shooting jacket hung open. Mud was splattered above the knees of his trousers. A sixth sense took him to the Servants Hall. A young footman sat drinking his tea at the farmhouse table before the huge fireplace that gave the room its warm, inviting fug.

A teapot and a tray of cups and saucers had been left over from the servants' afternoon break. Eustace nodded to the footman and helped himself to a cup. The footman said nothing except a polite mumble ending with a 'Sir', then finished his drink and hurried from the room.

Alone, Eustace felt better. The space suited him.

After a few minutes, Lord Hailsgam's butler came in. He was a man of fifty with a face like steel, a black suit and white shirt that seemed immune from creases or dirt. A faint scent of lavender trailed him in.

"Sir," said the butler, though no question was asked.

"I came to find tea."

"The Lord would normally ring from upstairs. This is the Servants Hall."

"Yes," said Eustace.

The butler seemed to be hoping that Eustace would understand his intrusion without the matter being explained.

"This is the Servants Hall," the butler said again.

Eustace Havershall was not a toff, except — it seemed — he was to the servants.

"Why?" Ginny asked that evening when she found him loitering in their allocated bedroom. "You pretend to be the most useless shot. You have everyone convinced and then you shoot two birds without even aiming. You made yourself look like a phoney. Everyone could see it wasn't luck. Then you have the effrontery to disappear."

Eustace had seated himself on the edge of the bed. His gaze was inexplicably glassy.

"I want to never come here again," he said slowly. "I want us to never, ever accept an invitation to any of these places. I want to go back to Birmingham and live the life we've chosen."

"'Chosen'?" she repeated, finding the idea didn't fit the facts. She thought better of the question and asked instead, "Why can't we have both?"

"Ginny, I hate the wood panels here, the furniture, the oil-paintings on the wall. I hate that there are so many bedrooms they have to invent reasons for people to come to visit. I hate the fancy dinners and the men they employ to put out knives and forks which are perfectly polished and perfectly placed on the table, fourteen and three-quarter inches from the next knife or fork or whatever, and there is another man who measures the fact that the first man has placed the knives and forks just so and you ask why this ridiculous waste of time because clearly all I need is for my knife and fork to be within my grasp when I want to eat and the polish they use to shine the metal is more likely to kill me than the tiny patches of tarnish that the knife blade might display. And they say, it is the duty of the rich to employ the poor. *Oh, we have so much! Oh, let us be magnanimous by handing a little of it out!* What does it matter if a man is moving a hole from one end of my flower garden to another as long as I'm paying him, today I want my hole a few yards to the right of where it was yesterday, I am doing my duty. I am rich and I am being who I am expected to be. Isn't that right? It's what my father and brother have always wanted to be, and I want none of it. None of it, do you hear?"

He stopped. Breathless. His anger had drained the blood from her face. She felt cold, dizzy as he finished his speech. His hands were shaking. He clenched them together and pulled them into his lap. Still they shook. He hardly seemed to be 'him'.

"I'm sorry," he added. "You were right before. I'm just here to move the luggage. I feel I'm watching the world unfold like the chauffeur's son, nose against a window, staring in at the grand ball."

She sat herself beside him, touched his cheek with the knuckles of one hand. "Eustace, you're so much more than the one looking in. You and Woody, you're shaping the world, don't you see that? Everyone is jealous. I am jealous... jealous and proud."

A steel veil had fallen across his face. She struggled to find the best way to love him through the defence.

"Alright, as you wish," she concluded. "No more of these weekends."

Before dinner, Eustace shaved off the moustache he had sported since his days as a banker and met the Lords and Ladies with his top lip bare.

Driving north and south to prop up the faltering sales growth, the Morris Oxford soon became tired and unreliable, stranding Eustace south of Crewe in a snowstorm. He resolved to join the Royal Automobile Club, which offered roadside assistance to members, and to buy a new car that wouldn't need rescuing.

At a trade association dinner, he forged a friendship with George Hands, who ran Calthorpe cars, a few streets away in Bordesley Green. Calthorpe specialised in high quality lightweight models, long after the market had swung towards heavier alternatives. Hands offered him a discount to £390 and Eustace took delivery of a Calthorpe 12/20, among the last produced before the company went bankrupt.

Calthorpe's failure was another bellwether of an economy that continued to look bleaker, or so Woody declared. The lazy or inactive would perish in the industrial maelstrom. He was now a keen follower of the economic outlook, solemnly predicting that competitors' innovations and inventions would reverse Havershall's successes if they did not invest actively. All modern business must constantly embrace the 'new'. You didn't have to like progress, but success would pass you by if you stood still.

"It has passed Calthorpe's by," Woody concluded. "Your machine's a white elephant. Lovely as it looks."

He walled off an area in the new annex at the back of the factory, which became known as the 'Lab', where he disassembled typewriters from Underwood, Royal, Remington and Smith-Corona — most of the American output. He also collected cash registers, unit recording and tabulating machines. He explained that the technologies were all connected.

At almost ten o'clock one Friday, Eustace was about to lock up for the night. He noticed the dim glow leaking from under the Lab's door. Woody was half unconscious at the bench, perched on a tall stool, a typewriter before him, his glasses half way down his nose. As was his habit, Woody had mechanic's overalls over his suit while working. The top cover had been taken from the machine and his hands were black with ink stains.

"What's that?" Eustace asked.

"The future," Woody said. "A little early, but it's arrived."

The badge said Remington in the usual large font of the brand, but it looked unlike any conventional typewriter. There was a bulge the size of a melon to the right-hand side of the keyboard and a cable leading out.

"It's not a real Remington," Woody said. "Some fellow in Kansas City sold the design to an electric motor company and they made it under the Remington name. Look at this."

He pressed a key with his grubby finger. A motor whirled. The machine struck a letter onto the test paper Woody had rolled into it.

"The future," he said again. "We make good products, I won't deny that, Captain. But a mechanical typewriter is bad for the fingers if you type at any speed. Mabel told me that. Some office girls type eight hours straight. They have to soak their hands at night to get out the cramps. Here an electrical motor does the hard work. You just touch it. Produces always the same identical impression and nobody wrecks their joints."

Eustace understood the advantages well enough. On occasion, he had typed through enough demonstrations in a day to have felt the strain.

"We have to make one," Woody told him. "Think what will happen when typewriters become electric and mechanical like cash registers and tabulating machines. This is a market we have to be in. It's going to change everything. Offices will become electric. Haven't I always said?"

"Woody, we're committed to the H5. We have new presses coming, new tools. All our cash — our future — is tied up in the design. And our margins? Well, we have to make what we make, but cheaper."

"To repeat the past is not enough." Woody shook his head. "I have been watching, Eustace. Electric is taking gas out of street lights. Electric is taking steam out of our presses. Everywhere you look — electric, electric, electric. It makes it easy to mechanise things, creates a process — the sorting of punch cards, the printing of prices on a till roll. Electricity could power a brain. One day, you'll type something and the machine might understand it as an instruction, not the trigger to throw a key at a piece of paper."

"I think that's your imagination."

"Is it? The communists say workers are about to rise and take their rightful places. Others say, one day there'll be mechanical men standing where our workers stand, machines making machines. No need for workers at all." He patted the bulge at the side of the typewriter. "I think this is the future."

Eustace leaned over the bench, tried the 'H' and 'Y' keys. They were always the letters he tested; they had stuck on that first machine in the pigsty at Cambrai. The motor whirred and two soft mechanical 'tinks' produced perfect characters on the paper.

Out of the blue, Woody blurted, "Mabel's pregnant again. So there… another mouth to feed."

The newly formed Soviet Union declared a class war between the proletariat and their enemies. Workers versus toffs, as Eustace would frame it. From Moscow, Stalin steered his fellow Russians towards 'people power' and away from the 'wastefulness' and 'irrationalities' he saw in market economies. Couldn't the West see its own coming collapse? The workers would seize power… everywhere.

Europe watched as Stalin's mother country adopted his planned rebirth, supposedly organised along a long-term, precise, and scientific framework with labour at its centre. But in truth, there was nothing scientific about it. Its methods were blunt; its thinking short term. When applied to Soviet agriculture, productivity collapsed. Famine would soon sweep the country. The middle-class 'industrial specialists', the class of would-be business owners, were convicted of sabotage. Labour camps were filled with Stalin's opponents, the non-labouring management of the old regime.

"That's you and me, Captain," Woody told Eustace. "We're the non-labourers. Do we feel like that to you?"

"Sometimes, Woody. But only sometimes," he replied.

* * *

A handful of screws were dropped into the well of one of the press tools in Duke Works. When the new electric press came down, the screws jammed between the two halves of the tool. By some miracle, a fuse tripped. Another Lionel Swithin incident was averted, but the factory stopped production for an hour while an electrician restored the power and the press was idle for a week until Woody's engineers fixed the tooling and the mechanism that drove it.

Eustace hauled the works representatives in for a meeting. Arnold Mulgrove denied that it could possibly be anyone from the union, got quite agitated when the possibility was mentioned.

"You tell me I should care for your men?" Eustace raged. "They have no care for each other."

"There are them that are with us, and them that are not," said the man seated to Mulgrove's left.

Mulgrove shushed him with a look, but not before the man added. "When it comes to it, they all have to work out whose side they're on."

"Whose side should they be on?" Eustace asked.

"I think you know it's not yours, not anymore," Mulgrove said.

By now, Eustace had established a relentless working pattern. If he was travelling, he would often be up and gone before dawn. Office days began before eight in the morning. He would rise at six-forty, leaving his wife to sleep, wash and dress, be downstairs eating a hearty breakfast by seven-fifteen, out of the door and into the Calthorpe by seven-thirty.

One day in early December 1925, he was surprised by Ginny hurrying into the dining room as he tucked into sardines and poached eggs. She was barefoot, wearing her silk dressing-gown, dabbing a handkerchief to her mouth. Her hair was uncombed.

"Oh, Eustace, Eustace," she cried.

"Goodness, Gin, what is the matter?" He started to rise from his place.

"It's happened. I am sick."

When she caught the smell of his sardines, she convulsed so hard she was forced to grab the edge of the table and vomited over his plate.

"It's the happiest I've ever been," she told him.

"Yes, me too," he said, with the broadest of smiles.

He only called his mother on a Sunday. Without fail, he would telephone at noon after she'd come back from church with his father, though his father never came to the phone. Contact in the middle of a week threw her into a panic.

"Ginny's pregnant."

"Oh," his mother replied.

"It's going to be a boy," he assured her.

There was silence for a while.

"Please," she pleaded, "I know how you think about these things. Don't call him William."

"Tell father if you must," he said, before hanging up.

When Ginny telephoned her cousin, she told Caroline it would be a girl.

Industrial strife in Britain was becoming an epidemic. Jobs trickled away, wages were squeezed, strikes abounded.

Arnold Mulgrove came again to Eustace's office in early 1926, the same two shopfloor representatives flanked him. This time, with three-quarters of the Havershall's staff signed up to the union, Mulgrove demanded paid breaks, extra holidays and another 6d in the pound. Eustace invited Woody to sit by his side to hear the demands. They pointed out the previous rise of thruppence.

"I'm sorry," Mulgrove said with no obvious regret. "It's time for the workers to get what they deserve. We're stronger now. Together with the party movement. Not so easily bought and sold."

"We'd have to increase the price of typewriters, Arnold, accept lower sales and cut the staff to pay for it," Eustace said.

Mulgrove threatened a strike, and many other things without naming them. The only 'reasonable' future was for workers to own the means of production, he said.

They sat in stalemate, none of the five men speaking. Eustace remembered how three of them once sheltered inside a tank, how Woody saved them. He remembered Mulgrove's hand on his shoulder.

"We've taken very different roads, don't you think, Arnold? Different loyalties. Different ideas of duty."

"I've done you the courtesy of calling you 'Mr Havershall', Mr Havershall. I'd trouble you to pay me the same due. Employer and employee... we don't mix." Mulgrove glanced across at Woody, then back at Eustace. "You're the enemy trying to steal our labour on the cheap, like your kind have always done."

"I wasn't aware I was a 'kind'," Eustace said. "Didn't you tell me I wasn't a toff?"

"Maybe I was being flattering. Having possessions, that's being a 'kind'. It's going to be a real war now… like Russia."

Mulgrove departed, promising he would take the strike to a vote. Havershall's could expect the union to be calling everyone out.

"You think I'm a toff, Woody?" Eustace asked when the union men had left the office.

"Certainly not," Woody replied.

"I notice he didn't insult you, though. Apparently you're not the enemy."

"Mulgrove is a rat and a snake. It was my mistake to employ him. I thought I owed him something."

Arnold Mulgrove came all the way to Aston, found Woody in the Barton Arms. They sat across a dark corner table away from the crowd of drinkers at the bar who could be heard discussing Charlie Chaplin's walking stick.

"I have a sort of proposition. I realise you're in trouble, Havershall's and all, if there's a strike," Mulgrove said. "But I'm only doing what I must, Woody, that's all. In the office today, like… I have to play the part. I want you to know I'm sorry… for the trouble."

"There's always trouble," Woody replied.

"Maybe it could go away. You could avoid a strike, if someone knew the right people. There's people in Birmingham, higher up in the union than me."

"Oh, yes?"

"Yeah. It don't take much to stop a strike, if the union says so, you know what I mean?"

"I thought you were all for the workers. Don't you take their subs to look after their best interests?"

"Yes, that's it, the union looks after them. What if we decided it was best not to push for a rise at the moment? Your Mr Havershall, maybe he was right. Jobs lost if the wages go up. The shop floor haven't voted for a strike yet."

Woody took a deep breath and let it out in exasperation. "Arnold, you're just a one-armed man I gave a job to. That's more than everything I should have given you. Are you asking for a bribe now, a bung? Or should we call it blackmail? Did someone send you? You think I'd pay money to someone I can't see… on your say so?"

"I could help you, that's all I'm saying. You think I'm worth nothing? You're going to need help and I know the people in the union who could give it the nod. Folk on the shopfloor are simple. Them who can be persuaded to vote one way can be persuaded to vote another. It wouldn't cost much."

Woody did not reply. He put down his pint glass, intending to leave. But he thought about that red-headed girl in France whose name he did not know, and Blenkinsop and Mulgrove, all those years before. Mulgrove was the worst, and he'd let it go by.

Woody reached into his pocket and pulled out the hand gun he'd been carrying for the previous six months. He placed it on the table.

Mulgrove stared in horror. "Jesus, this is a public bar. For God's sake, Woody!"

"Recognise it? It's a brand new Webley, an officer's gun. Bought with my own money. I'm an employer now. Don't forget. One of them."

"One of them? You think you'll ever be like Eustace Bloody Havershall? Your precious Captain. You think you can get away with what his kind get away with? We knew him when he was a milk-sop lieutenant, you and I. I almost had to hold his ruddy hand when he pulled that trigger. And we kept it quiet, what he done... what never come out... about that kid, Masterson. We never blabbed, did we? He owes me. You both do."

Woody snatched up the gun, pressed its barrel to Mulgrove's forehead and cocked the trigger. Mulgrove flinched and threw up his hand in lopsided surrender.

"Fuckin' hell!"

"Remember who went under the tank and who pulled the trigger. I did and he did. And I'll pull the trigger for him now if I have to. We don't need your help, Arnie. Havershall's will look after its own."

He held the position for several seconds, apparently thinking through options, before he uncocked the gun and pulled it back from Mulgrove's forehead.

"This conversation never happened, alright?" Mulgrove said in a fluster. "I think that's best, don't you? I mean, for you, and for me. It never happened. The strike will just go on."

"As you wish, Arnie. As you wish."

No one in the pub seemed to have noticed. If they had, they didn't care.

In May, a national strike in Britain was declared by the Trade Union Congress' General Council. Though union members within Havershall's were not called out by the national strike, Duke Works held a vote and picket lines appeared at the gates. Some non-union members refused to cross. The few who tried were intimidated and many scurried away. Reports of beatings filtered back to Woody and Eustace. One day, there were only ten workers on the shop floor.

In the middle of the crisis, Mulgrove and the union representatives at Havershall's returned to re-table their demands. A stalemate meeting wasted two hours of a morning.

"What do we do now?" asked Woody, in the recess after Mulgrove had taken his two companions off for a hasty lunch.

Eustace turned to gaze from his office window, out into Marmaduke Lane. Idle workers milled about where cars and lorries usually ran, banners were raised on pavements. Another group of workers on the day shift of the factory next door had turned for home.

"We have lost three orders on price to foreign competition in the last month. What does it matter if they don't come in?" He pointed to the gathering below. "We may as well shut our gates anyway. *Innovate or die*? Woody, we don't even have that option at the moment."

"Then what do you propose? You and I have mouths to feed, Captain."

"They have mouths to feed as well. The pie shrinks and everyone must have a bigger portion so they don't go hungry. Hence, we fight. The new presses, the developments we planned, I'm afraid they must be shelved—"

"No," Woody snapped, his dismay obvious.

Eustace shrugged. "I wasn't asking for a volunteer. There's nothing really voluntary when needs must, is there?"

Woody moved closer to the window, tapped his finger against the pane. "Do you think it's true? All they're waiting for is Bolsheviks and Stalinists to land and put us against the wall. Electric men, that's what we need," he mused. "Machines making machines and all that flesh and blood has to do is watch. That's my future. Our future."

"We can't invest in anything new," said Eustace, emphatically. "Forget the dream, Woody, for now at least, please. We must survive."

"Give me a plan I can believe in, Captain, I'll do it."

"We can't go out with clubs and beat them into surrender. But we can shut the gates," Eustace suggested.

"What? I thought you said we should try to survive."

"I did, Woody, but I also said, '*What does it matter if they don't come in?*' Until they will work on terms that will make us money, why would we let them work? If we let them in, we have to pay them."

"We can't have a lockout."

"Why not?"

"You said they needed the money. It's not their fault. They're led by the union, by the likes of Mulgrove and the commies who sit behind him."

"Whose fault is it in war?" Eustace asked. "I don't want to fight, but I will. You were right before, we have wives and family now. This is our company."

The fear of a general strike turning into a workers' uprising in Britain was real, and shared widely, not just among the upper class patriarchs and factory owners. An editorial in the Daily Mail declared the strike to be 'a revolutionary move which can only succeed by destroying the government and subverting the rights and liberties of the people'. The printers' union refused to print it.

Meanwhile, the courts ruled that any action aimed at the Government did not enjoy the protection of the Trades Disputes Act because it wasn't a dispute with an employer. This was a decisive blow. The individual unions who had called their members out became liable for employers' losses and faced sequestration of their assets to pay the damages.

Nine days into its national action, the Trades Union Congress lost its nerve. It withdrew support for the strike action it had called, spooked both by the court ruling and the revolutionary intent appearing in the communist elements in its own ranks.

The climbdown carried a heavy price. Now, the poor in all industries were doomed to get poorer. Bitter workers turned against their fearful unions.

Eustace and Woody kept Havershall's gates shut for another ten days.

When the two workers' representatives returned to Eustace's office, Mulgrove was not with them. Woody sat at Eustace's elbow. Once he had laid out the new terms of employment — lower wages; longer hours — Eustace said nothing for twenty-seven minutes while the room wallowed in stony silence.

Every now and again, he looked at Woody for support and Woody gazed back with the blank stare they'd agreed before the meeting, comrades in arms once again.

One of the representatives said, "Our people have to live."

"I know they do," said Eustace. "Profit has to feed them. And my typewriters have to sell against everybody else's."

"There'll be hell. I can promise you violence," the other representative said. "You have to give us something to take back to the members."

"There is nothing to give," said Eustace.

"Nothing except their jobs," Woody added.

The next day, the gates opened and the wage rates in Havershall's reverted to the levels of 1921.

"Let's both go home now," Eustace suggested.

"We should leave on time for a while, Captain. No late nights, or working on our own. We both have pregnant wives… mouths to feed."

"I hate what we did," Eustace said. "Ginny thinks I'm a ruthless man."

The police arrived at the house to see Eustace on the following Saturday morning. A plain-clothed Detective Inspector called Idris Davies was waiting at the door when Ginny — now more than six month's pregnant — answered it. He spoke with a Welsh accent.

"We found a body, see, in the canal behind your factory," Davies began, once Eustace was summoned. "One of yours. Beaten up before he was drowned. Man only had one arm too."

"Mulgrove," Eustace said instinctively. "Not many one-armed press setters in Birmingham."

"Quite so. Nasty business. I'm going to have to interview your—"

"Stop! One moment," said Eustace, holding up his hand, palm forward in defence. Shakes he hadn't suffered in daylight since Cambrai had suddenly rippled through his core. He took the moment to let them pass. "I served with Arnold Mulgrove. He was under my command."

"Ah, I see. Management man, was he?" said Davies, as if this might be a clue to the attack.

"Not really, no."

"Lots of displeasure around at the moment. After the strike, see. We had it with the miners back in '21. Same thing. The people on your shop floor, Mr Havershall, at your factory. I was hoping we could go now and do the necessary. Do you have a shift running?"

"Saturday morning? Yes, of course," said Eustace, pulling his thoughts together. "We'll make them available. Jim McCann will release them… whatever you need. I'll get my coat."

"Anything *you* might be able to tell me?"

"No. No, nothing," he said. He took his coat from the rack in the hall and smiled painfully at Ginny. She smiled back.

"I'll go with you," she said.

"No need… what with your condition."

"I want to," she said.

He looked at her inquiringly, but she did not reply. She could not say why she wanted to go. There was something about Mulgrove's connection to Eustace past — to that part of him he never showed — that seemed to make the death important, as if by understanding it, she might find the secret.

Once they reached Duke House, Eustace introduced the inspector to Jim McCann and set off to find Woody, leaving Ginny in his office. Woody was spending the morning in the Lab.

"Mulgrove's dead," Eustace announced, as if still searching for belief in the idea.

Woody responded with a soft, "Oh."

They exchange glances for a moment, and then for a moment longer.

"The police want to know if there's anything we can tell them about him. All I know is he was—" Eustace hesitated, not wishing to say communist. "He was a man of principle."

"If that's what you call him. Do you want to add 'War Hero'?" Woody asked.

"He didn't have trouble that we knew of, did he, Woody?"

"Only the strike."

"Yes, only the strike. The police say it's common…. Afterwards, with the failure."

"There's been a lot of trouble… in the 'backs' all around here. You don't see it, Captain. They hate men like Mulgrove now they've lost."

"No… No, I don't suppose I see it," he agreed. Latterly, the looming threats had stopped Eustace taking lunch and walking around in the streets of Bordesley. He used to have to find a shoeshine boy after every trip, but he was now as alien to the violence of 'need' as he was to the shooting-weekends of privilege. His shoes stayed shined all day. He shook his head, trying to remove the memory of Arnold Mulgrove. The man could not be shifted.

When Eustace returned to his office, Ginny was waiting, cigarette in hand as she slouched in his visitor's chair. Sometimes her pregnancy brought on tiredness unexpectedly. It was early afternoon now and they had missed the lunch he had promised her.

"I'm sorry, Gin. Strikes cause a lot of trouble."

"I thought this man was your friend? A comrade at least?"

"Yes, I suppose he was that."

"You talk like you don't care."

"I care. I just can't let myself... too much," he said.

"I hope they catch them, whoever did this."

"I hope they don't."

"You cannot mean that, surely."

"It's a fair bet he was killed by someone in this factory. Why do you think that inspector came to the house?"

She stared at him in surprise.

"As I say, strikes cause a lot of trouble," he said again.

"You... I mean, you don't know—?"

"You want to ask if I had anything to do with it?

She waited for his answer.

"I didn't have to," he said.

Early the following month — June 1926 — Mabel Woodmansey gave birth to a son. She died nine days later of Peritonitis.

Chapter Nine

The news had not been hopeful for several days, but when the phone call confirming Mabel's death reached the dinner table at the Havershall house, Ginny, seven months pregnant, collapsed in a faint. She was forced to lie down.

Death in childbirth haunted every expectant mother. It struck at around one in two hundred. The rate had not changed much in the previous fifty years. Ginny knew of two distant cousins on her mother's side who had died.

Puerperal Pyrexia is an ascending infection that spreads into the placental bed a few days after birth. In 1926, there were no antibiotics to fight it. Sometimes it led to septicaemia. Bacteria spread into the pelvic veins. Sometimes it became peritonitis, the disease that killed Mabel as bacteria slowly migrated along the fallopian tubes. The death that befell her was both painful and inevitable from its first diagnosis.

Steeling herself, Ginny waddled down from the bedroom an hour after the news arrived, still in the clothes she'd been wearing at dinner. She stopped in the hallway to select a coat from the rack.

"Where are you going?" Eustace asked, watching from the doorway of their main lounge.

"To the hospital."

"Gin, you can't. Not in your state. Not this time of night."

"The decision, Eustace, is do I walk or will you drive me? I don't suppose there's a bus at this hour."

They found Woody on an iron-framed bench in a hospital corridor, a week-old baby boy sleeping in his arms, staring at the opposite wall. The wall had a giant patch of damp spreading from the skirting board. Bare light bulbs hung from the ceiling.

Ginny released her husband's arm, nodding Eustace in the direction of the grieving father.

"Me?" he said.

"Yes, you, dear husband."

"I wouldn't know what to say."

"If you can't talk, sit. You know how to be quiet and listen, Eustace."

He took the seat next to Woody, his outstretched hand reaching for Woody's sleeve. They sat there a while, two men with a baby and no words. Ginny waited across the corridor, found herself a visitors' chair for support.

"Remember our tank, our good fortune," Woody said out of the blue.

Eustace acknowledged with a grunt.

"Die slow or die fast. What's the diff? We could do something. Not Mabel, she died slow." Woody bit his lip hard, held his teeth against the flesh long enough to turn the red to white. "It smells of antiseptic here. Bleach or something. Maybe lime. I don't know what to do anymore. What can I do? It's all blind luck."

The child in his arms started to cry. He gulped for breath. "I couldn't do anything for her, Captain, not at the end. I prayed for God to sweep her up and take her. She was in so much pain. Jew or Christian, that's what He did to me."

Across the corridor, Ginny's head was tipped forward, her face pale, eyes closed. Behind her, the damp patch on the wall hung like a spectre. Soon she would have to go through childbirth, like Mabel. Eustace knew what he had to do. A Havershall child would not be born here.

Around this time, Alexander Fleming began experiments with the common staphylococcal bacteria in St Mary's Hospital, London. Fleming, according to his contemporaries, was an 'untidy scientist'. The uncovered Petri dish of agar culture he left near an open window became contaminated with mould spores.

Another broken experiment. But chance stepped in.

Bacteria around the mould colonies started dying. Fleming discovered it was not the mould itself, but some strange 'juice' it had produced that destroyed the bacteria. He called this 'mould juice' Penicillin.

"One sometimes finds what one is not looking for," he said.

His good fortune came too late for Mabel.

Eustace's mind was made up. Take Ginny to London, consult the finest private obstetricians. No expense would be spared.

Less than two months later, the Havershall baby showed its head to the world in the finest room that same St Mary's Hospital had to offer, white-tiled hygienic walls and a pristine bed of new sheets.

Sixty feet away, on the other side of the brickwork, Eustace sat in a silent waiting room, his hands balled into painful fists. Ginny squeezed too, cool rag on her forehead, biting down on the stick of cork the midwife had provided. Mr Rees, an expensive consultant, looked on. By chance, he was not needed. Her moans echoed from the hard walls, but the delivery passed without complication, or infection.

"Mr Havershall, it's a boy," the midwife told him, emerging from the delivery room.

"My wife?"

He did not breathe again until the midwife smiled and asked if the parents had decided on a name. Only then did he realise the midwife had said, 'boy'.

Boy, for him; not girl, for Ginny.

He found it did not matter so much now the mother was safe. He almost said, "William," but he and Ginny had agreed a boy child would be called Richard. If they'd had a daughter, her name would have been Mabel.

A few corridors further away, Alexander Fleming continued his experiments.

The *'Treatise on Probability'* by John Maynard Keynes now sat alongside *Das Kapital* on Woody's bedside table. Keynes seemed important to Woody, now his family had suffered a senseless death against the odds.

The *Treatise on Probability* said that 'probabilities' are not truth. They did not relate to the simple facts of experience. For example, a half of one percent of women died in childbirth, yet Mabel was wholly dead. The chances that a stricken tank behind enemy lines could be fixed by a soldier crawling beneath and not getting shot were fractional too, yet it had happened. The outcomes could — so clearly, should — have been the other way around.

After his wife's funeral, Woody moved his children to Bristol. Only for a while, he promised, to be with their grandparents, the Perecs. But weeks soon became months and, in mourning, he seemed to develop three personalities instead of one, the divide between them widening by the day. At times, he acted like the northern lad who smelt of pickles and called everyone remotely better than working class by their rank or addressed them as 'Sir'. At others, he was a grouchy limping widower aggrieved at life, who carried a walking stick and viewed everyone with various degrees of contempt. His third personality was the bespectacled genius, who never understood why people couldn't grasp his ideas until he produced examples of the finished product like a magician pulling miracles from his hat.

All three personalities drank heavily. On whisky, the trio would drink themselves almost unconscious. Woody suffered the hangovers. On one bad day, he swore at the office manager and fired McCann and all his shift supervisors. Eustace spent a great deal of time undoing the things Woody had done and the unrest he had caused.

In the night-time backstreets of Aston, Woody eventually found the house of Mrs Bembole, a bordello of local repute. A cut above the *maisons tolérée* maybe, but still rekindling memories that plucked temporary comfort from lasting despair.

On his first visit, he stood outside, pacing sporadically up and down the pavement for half an hour. Not nerves. He knew what money could buy, but that anaesthetic now seemed different and the despair was not that he might be killed at any moment, but that he had chanced to live through all that, only to lose when his luck mattered most.

He went in at last, found himself on top of a peroxide blonde with a Wolverhampton accent and lost his erection in shame before the deed could be done.

Richard was a strong healthy baby who slept well and put on weight. Ginny was happy to dedicate herself to his care, seldom troubling the nanny she'd hired, and forgetting for now that she had wanted a girl.

Meanwhile, with strikes behind them, Eustace renewed his efforts in Duke House. The company recovered its growth, launching its portable version of the H5, called the H5P.

Woody had designed it before Mabel's death. The machine, based on an unwieldy aluminium casting for the chassis, weighed in at fourteen pounds. While the H5 remained the big seller in commercial offices and typing pools, the range now included an H7 — a heavier desk bound machine with a redesigned 'tab' function, better control over line spacing and an ability to take wider paper — and the H10 with a revised key lever/typebar mechanism and a platen covered in hard rubber.

The company now employed over three hundred people in the expanded works, running half the length of Marmaduke Lane. Production varied between eight hundred and a thousand machines a week. Annual sales were racing over a million pounds.

Eustace found himself travelling too many miles for his beloved Calthorpe, which was fragile as Woody had always warned. It broke a piston and Eustace was forced into another car, a brand new Rover. This time, the 9/20 model, designed for endurance.

Within the company, sudden growth put a strain on cash flow. Growth requires cash for raw materials, cash for stock and the wages of the people making it, cash to fund debts when the customers take sixty days and more to settle their accounts. Havershall's didn't have any to spare.

"Take a loan. In any company, cash really is king," the company's bank manager advised, citing the old maxim. "I can arrange it."

"Never," said Eustace.

"You are not making sense," Ginny told him when he discussed the problem at home.

He reminded her that no banker would lend him money when had most needed it. The pain of taking his father's loan still cut deep. She did not push the point.

Further increases in production soon demanded new purchases of equipment. The extension of credit to new distributors and wholesalers stretched Havershall's bank account so thin that Eustace had to turn away orders. He hated that too.

"If you will not agree a loan, why not an overdraft?" Woody suggested when they met to discuss the lack of funding.

"An overdraft is a loan," Eustace pointed out.

"Is it not the opportunity to take a loan if you need it, only if you need it and only for as long as you need it? The bank can arrange it and then…"

"Then what? We don't use it? It's the thin end of the wedge."

"Yes, it is," Woody agreed. "But we'll only need it for the fat end of our growth. No electric model. Not yet, I promise. And anyway, we're owed far more by our debtors than we will ever owe the bank."

Though a grieving man, Woody still provided moments of clarity. In business, he, not Ginny, was the one Eustace listened to. He knew how to persuade his partner.

"Did I not come to your bank for money when I needed it? Aye, and I would have taken it too, had they given it to me. I am not a fool when it comes to growing a company, Captain. I know what oils the wheels."

With Ginny lobbying at home and Woody in the works urging Eustace on, the company secured, for the first time, an overdraft facility of several thousand pounds, much against Eustace's better judgement. He was determined not to use it, or to use only the minimum amount of it and for shortest possible time.

On the back of this liquidity, the factory moved to a three-shift continuous night and day working pattern. Between his drinking,

Woody's new approaches to metallurgy created typebar blanks that had less problems with stress cracking and, through a brilliant innovation in design, Woody created the 'dead key'. This development, introduced on the H33 model at the beginning of 1927, allowed keys to produce a character without advancing the main carriage forward, so that an acute or grave accent could be added with the next keystroke. It avoided giving accented letters their own key, which was a problem in many languages, and opened new European markets to Havershall's products. To Eustace's delight, a French, Dutch and Belgian distributor were soon signed up.

There was yet further celebration when, twenty months after Richard's birth, another Havershall child was due. Eustace imagined a second son; Ginny was convinced she would finally get her daughter.

Few noticed the slow up-tick in the company's overdraft as the growth continued through 1927 and into 1928. There were always debtors on the balance sheet that outstripped debts owed to the bank and reported profits on paper which made everyone comfortable.

Ginny argued for having her second child at home, but Eustace was insistent. They argued. He won. She was admitted to St Mary's Hospital three weeks before the baby was due. Eustace stayed in Birmingham, attending to Havershall's business. He planned to be in London for the final week before the confinement began.

Even with servants to help, he quickly became over-anxious, running both a factory and a home with Richard now toddling. His mind was on Ginny, his imagination turning on all the things that might go wrong.

Woody's mildest personality made an attempt to calm his friend. Maybe he saw it as returning the duty both Havershalls had shown to him over Mabel's death. He insisted the 'Captain' took time off to get away from his worries. The house staff could look after Richard for an afternoon.

Bizarrely, Woody chose the Aston Hippodrome for a Wednesday matinee. In this slot, the theatre showed selections of movies from around the world. "Escape for an hour or two," Woody suggested. "It's what I do."

The film that day was the German, 'Metropolis'. Wealthy industrialists reign over a future empire from thousand-storey skyscrapers, while underground workers toil at the mechanical leviathans that power the eponymous city. The hero — an idealist — attempts to close the ever-widening gulf between classes.

Sitting in a two-thousand-seater auditorium watching the most expansive vision he'd ever witnessed, the film seemed incredible to Eustace, drawing on art schools he had once followed with Ginny through private London exhibitions.

The hero of Metropolis has a vision that the machine at the centre of the future city is a temple and that workers are being fed into it. The progress it depicts — whether industrial, medical or social — drains the humanity from life as much as it bestows on it. The film's central image is of a metallised woman, known as the *Maschinenmensch,* 'Machine-Woman', who is burnt at the stake by rioting workers.

"Look," said Woody, nudging Eustace. "There's my robot."

Woody had never finished his wine dispenser, the Greek goddess in his garage, but Eustace had to admit there was a striking similarity.

Woody, mercifully sober, drove them home after the film. The housekeeper was waiting on the front drive of the house in Edgbaston, holding the leather suitcase that Eustace used for his sales trips.

"What is it, Agnes? You're as white as a sheet," Eustace exclaimed.

"It's Mrs Havershall, Sir. There's been a complication. She's in labour a week early."

Woody refuelled his car and rushed Eustace down to London. When they arrived, a matron barred access to his wife's room.

"What's happening?" Eustace demanded. "I must see her."

"She's with Mr Rees now," said the matron. "It's for the best. They are taking her to surgery. It's rather a complicated Caesarean."

"What? I thought she was just early."

"She is. That's what makes a breech birth difficult."

Sir Ferdinand Rees had been Eustace's choice for Ginny both times. He worked for large fees for rich clients. This time he had to earn it. Rees was the first surgeon in England trained by American mentors to use transverse incisions of the lower uterus for Caesarean sections. They reduced the spread of infections…

…Infections such as peritonitis, a major risk with the old procedure.

For Eustace, no waiting room was ever going to be big enough for this wait. The clock on the wall moved too slowly. He and Woody sat within clean white walls, uselessly waiting. Eustace's knuckles turned pale and the joints of his fingers ached as he gripped the armrest of his chair.

"I should never have stayed in Birmingham. Or gone to that bloody film. Should have been here."

"We are here, Captain. Got you here as fast as I could. You know she's in the best of hands. You picked them."

"Yes, yes, but I didn't see her before... Before *this.*"

"Rees is a good man. You told me so yourself."

"The best," he agreed, but that didn't seem to be the point.

After an hour, Ginny was still in the operating theatre. No one emerged. No message came. He'd never recovered the faith he'd lost in France, but now he thought of praying, of asking a non-existent God to exist for a moment to hear his prayer.

His heart raced. His skin had begun to crawl, as if lice thrived there once more. When he closed his eyes, he saw only the light haloed around a key in a door-lock and heard only voices that mocked him.

"I'm going outside," he told Woody

"But, Captain—"

"Captain, what? You told me so yourself, Rees is the best and I can do nothing. I can't sit here."

"You can't fix this by going outside," Woody said.

Eustace walked anyway and Woody let him go.

The London evening was a drizzling mess. Eustace lit a cigarette. He marched down to Lancaster Gate and across into Hyde Park. Twilight was fading. He told himself it was a ten-minute walk to clear his head so he could be strong again for Ginny when she needed him, but once he had started, he didn't know how to stop. It was half an hour before he felt calm enough to start retracing his steps.

Walking back, he met Woody, the lolloping gait approaching in a half-run half-limp as it always was when his friend hurried. Woody halted, straightened his glasses, caught his breath beneath a street lamp.

"It's alright. It's alright," he shouted. "Another son and they're both alright."

"A son?"

"Yes, a son, Captain."

"Not a daughter?"

"Let's go and see your wife. And your baby."

"A son," Eustace repeated. "Another son."

Back at the hospital, in a white bed with white sheets, Ginny's face struck him like a miracle, her skin matching the linen, her dark hair spread against the pillow. She was snoring lightly on the after-effects of ether and nitrous oxide. He had to touch her cheek to believe she was real.

In a cot by her bedside lay the second Havershall son. According to Ginny, this pregnancy was supposed to produce a girl. A girl would balance the Havershall fortunes. That was not as it turned out. The boy had a bullet-shaped head, swirls of fine hair across the skull, eyes tight shut. But ten beautiful fingers and ten perfect toes. The smell of newness.

"William," he mouthed, reaching for the child. "This time... a William."

He lifted the reborn brother from the cot, supported the head as he pulled new William up to eye level. The blue eyes opened. Eustace traced his finger over the unknitted skull, towards the softest part of the fontanelle.

Taking in the room — his wife, his son — he nodded his head. In all his life, he had never felt such a powerful pull.

Ginny was saved but Mr Rees told her she was unable to bear more children. Ginny cried because she had wanted a daughter. At least one daughter. Failure sent her spiralling into depression.

Chapter Ten

Ginny spent a month in a wheelchair and six weeks hobbling around in pain. The doctor told her it was temporary and prescribed laudanum, but the medication made her into someone else, someone incapable. Observing the world through its haze, she wondered why she was even needed when servants so ably looked after her children when she could not. The observation haunted her.

Every night, she watched Eustace take William in his arms as soon as he came home, slipping more comfortably into fatherhood with this second son. Supporting William's head, the skull seemed to fit so snugly in his huge palm. He would wipe dribbles from his son's mouth. When baby William cried in the night, Eustace would often be the first to rise.

She half-remembered that he had never picked up Richard as a baby or walked him around. She was active then, was always the one with Richard. When the toddler had taken his first faltering steps, Eustace was on a three-day sales trip in Scotland. Now, with William, it seemed that the roles of mother and father had been reversed. And worse, Ginny wondered if she had a role at all.

Eustace denied having any favourite, of course. "I want to be the father my father never was," he said, but she could see he felt the duties of a father to a second son more keenly than to the first. In her worst opiate moments, she found herself filled with jealousy. If Eustace gave his love to William, and what was left to Richard, what did she get? She was trapped by a tiredness sleep could not assuage, her body struggling to recover from the operation that had given her son life, a gift she would have failed to give him on her own.

The laudanum played with her moods, made her unpredictable. She looked down the long opiate corridor stretching into the future and saw a middle-aged wife who had produced Eustace Havershall's two boys. The person she saw there seemed lost and dull and abandoned, and too much like the woman she had always sworn she would never become.

Just before William was born, her mother Elizabeth had written to tell Ginny that her father was feeling unwell and had been to the doctor.

Ginny didn't think much of it, but at the end of July, her mother sent a telegram. Sir Stanley Buckley had cancer of the liver.

"Come now," the telegram said. "Bring my grandsons. So he sees them."

Eustace insisted she could not go alone. How could she handle a three-month-old baby and a near-two-year-old running around on a ship's deck when she was still half recovered from the birth and taking potions for her pain? A row boiled over. She suggested that she hired a nanny for the trip. He said take a nanny by all means, but it was a family matter and he knew he must take charge. Woody could look after the company. Hadn't he done it before? She said she wouldn't be treated like an invalid, but she felt too weak to keep up the argument. She felt she'd lost again.

The doctor prescribed an extra bottle of laudanum 'in case of sea sickness'. Richard and William Havershall were bundled up like reluctant presents and they set off, nanny in tow, from Liverpool on the RMS Carinthia, a luxury liner of the Cunard Line.

The Havershalls arrived three days before Stanley faded out peacefully into the night, unable to speak or acknowledge the presence of either a daughter or his grandchildren. After that, there was a funeral to arrange, a will to be read and a distraught mother to be comforted. Ginny saw it as her new mission. She was determined to take her full part.

After two years, Woody had finally accepted that his children, Celia and James, could not return from Bristol. The Perecs were their true guardians. He was incapable of their care, a widower of selfish habits — movies on his own, football at Villa Park, tinkering in his garage or in the 'Lab' of the factory, occasionally racing a second-hand Bugatti he'd lately purchased around the club circuits and hill climbs of Britain. He was a founding member of the Bugatti Owners' Club. His passion remained engineering. He had begun to develop a fixed hunch in his back from the hours spent at work benches and he'd bought a series of walking sticks to help his limp.

Left once more with Havershall's to manage, he was more interested in developing new machines than selling the current ones. He spent money freely on prototypes and competitors' products. He enjoyed himself. For a while, he drank less.

One extravagant purchase was a Remington cash register, imported from America. Ignoring Eustace's nagging obsession with BBTL,

Remington had always been — in Woody's eyes — the real competitor in the typewriter business. During the Twenties, Remington had diversified, now making cutlery, hunting knives, household utensils and, more pertinent to Woody's interest, machines for handling and securing cash. The model on his work bench ran on electricity. He loved that.

It seemed that British cash registers must always be more complex than American models to accommodate the three-layered money — pounds, shillings and pence. Having twelve pennies to the shilling and twenty shillings to the pound was challenging if you hoped to add up and print a total onto a till roll. He put his mind to the problem.

On a trip into Birmingham which he justified as research, he hovered around cash registers in all the big shops. Here, he met Zoe Fitzsimmons, a rakish Irish girl with curly copper hair, who worked in the dressmaking department of Rackhams store in Temple Row. He'd just turned thirty and she was nineteen with a face like Vilma Bánky, at that time Samuel Goldwyn's most reliable box-office star. An inch taller than Woody, Zoe spoke with a Dublin accent whenever she forgot herself.

She asked him what he was doing. He said, "Inventing the future."

A romance blossomed. She proved willing to see any movie he cared to name and, for the next few weeks, she sat obediently disinterested in the Aston Hippodrome or the brand new 'Picture House' opened by Oscar Deutsch in Brierley Hill. Love proved a negotiable transaction. Zoe professed it to a limping widower still haunted by his dead wife and past sins, because he paid for every evening's entertainment, showered her with gifts and bought her an engagement ring.

The funeral was delayed while Viscount and Viscountess Fairchild sailed from England, representing Caroline's father, the patriarch of the Buckleys who declared himself too old for such travel, even though he seemed capable of standing for hours to make his right-wing speeches in the House of Lords.

As her mother sank into grief, Ginny made all the funeral arrangements while working her way down the last bottle of laudanum. She resolved not to see another doctor for more, so her head wouldn't feel so much like cement when the Fairchilds finally arrived.

In withdrawal, she became restless. The nanny took care of her boys and Eustace had started scouting possible agents for Havershall's typewriters in America. She was left waiting for a dead man to be buried. Out shopping, she bought a board game, packaged in a cardboard box with 'The Landlord's Game' written across the lid and the picture of a mature white-haired woman in the bottom corner. The combination of women and money amused her. She became quite obsessed, forcing the nanny to play every afternoon while the boys took their nap.

When the sombre day finally arrived, a hundred mourners came to the house after the family returned from the graveside. Following Ginny's exact instructions, the lawns were set with black tables and chairs under a dozen canvas gazebos erected to ward off the seasonal showers. A catering company was engaged to provide canapés and waiters. Sax Saccacci had procured crates of premium sherry and six barrels of beer. Sir Stanley Buckley — the great teetotaller who made his fortune on illegal liquor — would go to his grave with an alcoholic send off whatever the law prescribed.

By sunset, the lawns were strewn with paper napkins and dropped sandwiches, the abandoned tables with used glasses. The guests and mourners went home. The funeral was declared a success.

That night, Ginny could not sleep. A death so close after an almost fatal birth, a husband who worked so hard he was never with her and a church full of ageing relatives had made her mindful of the shortness of everyone's time. Now wasn't a good moment to review such things, but she reviewed them anyway. She had wanted to be a wife, and had become one. She had wanted to be a mother, and had done that too. She asked herself if she had managed to make herself happy. She felt only a wearying emptiness in her heart. Even Eustace, Richard and William together no longer seemed like enough.

In the middle of the night, she wandered outside, selected a table and a random chair half way down the grass slope where a garden lamppost threw some light, and started to set out the pieces of her game. She poured herself another glass of the funeral sherry. Her head was spinning.

She was frantically counting spare money into piles when Eustace sat down across the table, dressing gown for warmth and slippers on his feet.

"I thought you would have come to bed by now, Gin. Are you alright?"

"I need an opponent, Eustace. Why have you never played this with me? It's made for you. Besides, it's a terrible game on your own." Her voice was jumpy, full of random highs and lows.

"I thought the doctor said you shouldn't have alcohol with your medicine."

"I've run out, didn't you know? I don't take it anymore."

"I see."

"I can't sleep," she added. "Sit. I'll teach you."

She started explaining the rules with extravagant hand gestures and arm waving. The squares around the perimeter were properties and the idea was to own them all, to demand rent off the passers-by until everybody but you went bankrupt.

"See, you should be good at that, Eustace. I'm sure you can beat me."

He allowed himself to be coerced into playing, but his position became dominant very quickly, partially because her buying decisions were rash, and partially because the dice seemed to like him. She conceded, throwing her property cards onto the board.

"Oh, my head! I can't think."

"I'm sorry. I didn't mean to—"

"Do not say you didn't mean to win. You know you did."

"I'm sorry," he said again.

"Oh, fiddlesticks! It's not apologies I need, Eustace. It's all too boring, isn't it? I remember when we'd still be gay until midnight. I would say, 'Let's dance,' and we'd dance."

He opened his mouth, but didn't know what to say. Ginny was in full flow.

"At those country parties, we used to scandalise those toffs you hated. We weren't part of that crowd, were we? I was too wild and you were too handsome and so, so…" She struggled for a word to describe him, as if finding none with sufficient edge. "You *aspired*, Eustace, and hated aspiring. What was it I said? Ambitious, desperate and scared? I loved watching you try so hard to get back the silver spoon I've always tried to spit out. That was our alchemy. But what are we now? Parents? Parents with a family? A nice business?"

"Parents must provide—"

"Ha! Is that all there is?"

"Gin, I think you're really not yourself, what with your father—"

"Oh, yes, don't worry. I've had too much, that's true. And no medication. Nothing to sedate me. It's a frightful, beastly day and I'm a terrible woman and a bad loser. It comes of being a terrible child. Now… well… I don't know."

She picked up the blue wooden token that had marked her passage around the board, examining it as if it might hold some secret.

"I'm sitting here mourning, but I know what my father was, Eustace. Look at all this. He was a crook. I know the right word for Sax and his kind. Bootleggers and gangsters all."

"So I gathered, speaking to some of the guests," Eustace said. "One of them offered me an introduction to a Congressman, if I cared to sell typewriters in New York. For a price, of course."

She smiled painfully and let the token fall, then took a cigarette from her handbag. With no better response, he produced a lighter to play the gentleman.

"You once stole bicycles and fixed a typing contest to ensure the outcome, as I recall," he said.

"You stole those bicycles right along with me. And the contest wasn't fixed. I scripted it. I paid the actors rather well. Merely an advertising stunt. What Sax is like... I'm not like that. You're not like that, however much you'd like to think you could be. You would never pay the bribes to make it in America."

"The way you say it, it sounds like it might be a compliment."

"Yes, it might be," she agreed. She attempted a smoke ring, but it emerged broken. "The point is I no longer like the liquor business, or anyone associated with it. That makes it rather awkward, but it must be done."

"What must be done?"

"Dealing with Daddy's affairs, of course. He is a dead moonshiner with a fortune to distribute. Mother has spoken to the lawyers today. Daddy's lawyers, I mean. Since there is no one else, it seems I am to be both executor and beneficiary of the will."

"You?"

"Yes, amusing, don't you think? Whatever I was busy becoming, I am suddenly a rich woman," she announced without joy. "I am to receive half the estate, my mother the rest, but I am the executor. I have a husband to guide me so that must have made me a better choice."

"Ginny, I'm sure he didn't mean—"

"Oh, he did. He expected me to turn to you and to be quite helpless. He knew my mother would be. But I will prove him wrong, Eustace. I will not become like my mother, or like my cousin, just because life sprang from my body and made me weak. No, I was never like them, was I? That's why you loved me. I have the list of my property memorised already — half his shares in the pharmacies, a portfolio of bonds, two and a quarter racehorses, twelve acres in Vermont and then, it seems, a villa in the South of France. It's the Landlord's Game for real. I shall need a better grip of the rules."

The struggle to get the words said was plain and her voice was becoming terribly slurred.

"Is that what this nonsense is about?" Eustace asked, gesturing to the board. "Really, Gin, I don't think you know what you're saying, at least not at the moment."

In a whisper, she said, "I think we should both have loved our fathers better. What do you say to that?"

Tears had begun to leak from her eyes.

"So," she continued, gathering herself. "I think I will sell Daddy's share of the pharmacies straight away. Sax would be the buyer. Don't you see, I have my mother's interest to attend to as well as my own? Who else is there to give us a price?"

She sucked defiantly on her cigarette. "When I have the money, Eustace, I want to handle it myself. Perhaps I could invest in your typewriters. You're always worrying about your overdraft, and you say you need investment. Well, here is your chance. You don't need to be beholden to banks."

"I would never take your money, Gin. It wouldn't be right. I told you from the beginning, I—"

"Oh, I wasn't offering to let you take it." She dismissed the thought with an extravagant wave of her arm. "I'm not like your father and I'm not offering you a loan. A shareholding in the company, that's what I want. My shares. *Mine.* Don't you think I can make a go of it?"

"That won't be possible. Woody and I won't sell shares."

"Why not? I can work. I have recovered. I will recover more. I've stopped the laudanum, did I say that already?"

"You did."

"Look at how I've rallied around here these past weeks. I may know little about money now, but I am not some delicate flower. I could clear your overdraft like that!" She snapped her fingers.

"Our overdraft is temporary," he insisted. "It's hardly a loan at all. It's a facility. Havershall's is fine without help."

"No doubt. But Woody told me the bank can recall the money?"

"Yes, but banks never recall money from a healthy business."

"Nevertheless, it seems you are at the mercy of the toffs who run banks, the *Sir Alfreds* you hate. Let's hope you can dance with your devils," she concluded.

She had picked up the box and was packing away the pieces from the game — the property cards, the money, the tokens. She held the lid towards him. The regal woman on its surface looked something like a duchess.

"You know who invented this?" she said. "Elizabeth Magie Phillips. That's her. She has a patent and everything. You try to get all the money and *fuck* up everybody else." The force of the curse word stopped her for a moment. She nodded. "Greed, Eustace, invented by a woman. That's ironic, don't you think?"

"I'm sorry, Gin. At the moment, I think you're just a little indisposed. Best to call it a night. I'm happy you have your money, of course."

"Happy? Yes, happy. I suppose I could invest in a rival company, and go and work there, spread the family risk. How about Barrington-Brown? I understand BBTL intend to float on the stockmarket next year."

"Who told you that?"

"Caroline. She told me Barrington-Brown's raising something he called a war chest… for new ventures."

"Caroline? You could have told me earlier, Goddammit!" He bit his lip and glanced away for a moment. "I'm sorry. I shouldn't swear."

"I didn't mean the news to upset you," she assured him. "But I could put my money there when his shares are on public sale, if you don't want it in Havershall's. Spread the risk. Hedging, they call it, don't they?"

"Ginny… No!"

"No? No, because you won't take a woman's help, is that it, Eustace? You don't want me to have a bit of my own success?"

"I won't take family money!" His voice rose as he spoke. "Not again. Not ever. Not from my family. Certainly not from yours. Woman or man, it matters not a jot."

After a moment, he unclenched his fists and put one hand to his mouth as he spoke. His voice fell quiet as a result.

"You don't understand. I… *I* must succeed in this," he said. "And, Gin, it's not just me. Even if I… No, Woody would never agree to your investment. We started together."

She let him brood a while. The night seemed suddenly cooler.

"If Woody ever says yes, will you agree?" she asked.

"He won't."

"Suppose he does?"

* * *

"Is it right that motherhood changes us all?" Ginny suggested to her cousin at breakfast the next morning. Her head felt like the victim of an axe. She was sure she used to handle hangovers much better.

"Not in the way motherhood seems to be changing you," Caroline replied.

"Perhaps it's the money then," said Ginny. "I used to think it didn't matter."

"Maybe you've finally learnt what the rest of us knew the moment we did the curtsey. Money is everything."

"Oh, no, I don't think it's that. It's just that, now with William and the company and all, there's none of Eustace left for the rest of us... for me. I told him last night that I would handle my own money. I want something to even up the game."

"What?" said Caroline, as if suspected a fault in her hearing.

"Yes, that's right. I was a bit squiffy, probably needed to be to have the courage, but I told him I wanted to learn business, now that I have my own fortune. I seem to remember offering to invest in Havershall's. He turned me down."

"Well, thank God for that! Ginny, you can't. You must go to him right now and tell him you have changed your mind. It's out of the question."

"Why is it out of the question? I'm bright. I'm willing to learn."

"You're a wife. You're a woman. You're a mother. Or have you forgotten?"

"Which of those makes it out of the question? My father's money is mine. Mine and my mother's to be precise. As far as I remember, women had to fight quite hard for the Married Women's Property Act. We're not owned anymore."

"Now you are being ridiculous. Hand the money to Eustace and have him look after it. It's what we all do. Then we can get on with things."

"What things?"

"The things we're supposed to do."

Ginny thought about it for a moment or two. "I've never known what those are," she said.

"You are impossible," Caroline concluded. "Please, Gin, don't do this. It's bound to cause so much trouble."

"Yes," said Ginny, "I think that's rather the point."

* * *

135

Still in charge of the business back in England, Woody convinced himself that everything that hadn't worked at Mrs Bembole's would work with Zoe Fitzsimmons. It was, after all, an act of love. Her red hair enflamed him.

He never got to put it to the physical test. He soon discovered that Zoe's disinterest in movies and conversation extended to any participation in more carnal pursuits. Only marriage, not mere engagement, would open her legs and even then the 'open sesame' moment was set to be brief.

Breaking up, she asked if she could keep the jewellery. He made a lewd suggestion of what she might do in return. He was drunk at the time.

He abandoned her in the lounge bar of a pub at the back of Aston Park. There were plenty of redheads in the world, he told himself. He was, after all, the owner of a company. He could expect certain recognition and, with recognition, should come opportunity.

Chapter Eleven

Havershall's growth slipped and flattened off completely during 1929. BBTL won a large government contract Eustace had been assured was his right up to the last minute. He was outraged. Some underhand deal or higher intervention was involved; someone had spoken to someone and snatched triumph away from him.

Exports of the newer H33 blossomed, but proved a difficult design on which to make profits. Woody said it required more automation in the factory to bring costs down, but automation meant cash, and at the partners' monthly board meetings, Eustace admitted that their temporary use of an overdraft now looked permanent.

At home, he told Ginny that 'holidays' were impossible due to the 'economic circumstance'. She stepped forward to insist that a holiday could be taken on *her* money. She had sold the pharmacies to Sax Saccacci and now they would go to *her* property in the South of France. Loaded down by work, Eustace ceded control of the domestic agenda, thinking it an acceptable compromise.

So off they went in the spring, four Havershalls taking their car on the new Townsend cross-channel ferry between Dover and Calais. Fifteen vehicles were winched precariously on and off the ship, before the family motored for two days down through France. On the first day, they passed the old battlefields; Eustace drove stoically, stone faced. Day Two, through the valleys of Burgundy, his holiday face appeared. He relaxed, became more the husband and father than he had been in months. Ginny found herself leaning towards the middle of the car, resting on his shoulder instead of propping her head against the door post. She felt her insistence justified. The two boys rode in the back with their nanny.

Ginny's villa proved to be a large run-down property on the eastern coast of Cap Ferrat, not far from the Grand-Hôtel and a short walk from the Port-de-Saint-Jean. Built as a wedding present for a Russian countess in 1843, it belonged to her descendants before Lenin and Stalin rewrote the laws of ownership. Stanley Buckley had bought it through a sealed bid at a property auction.

Its outer architecture showed Romanov heritage, while inside it provided four good-sized reception rooms, six bedrooms in the main house and three in a small annexe. The walls were peppered with art, mainly paintings by obscure members of the Fauvist movement. A canvas by André Derain hung in the master bedroom; a Matisse painting of a coffee pot and fruit bowl in the entrance hall used his divisionist technique of coloured dots. Both seemed to be originals.

Cap Ferrat was heaven compared to the grimy streets of Birmingham with its smogs and faltering sanitation. The city of Nice lay ten kilometres to the north west and Monte Carlo was almost visible along the Mediterranean coast if one looked around the peninsula. The family loved the place. They loved its lack of hurry, the beaches and the leafy lane sloping up from the sea where the villa lazed behind its own tree-line. In May, it smelt of pollen and sea salt.

William, now one, took his first faltering steps on the patio. Ginny was there to catch him when he fell. Eustace was there to see it and marvel at their son's achievement. Richard stood and watched, bemused by the fuss.

During the week, Ginny's skin turned brown while Eustace sought shadows to avoid burning after the second day. She got to speak French. She started to teach Richard. She and Eustace splashed around with both boys in the shallow end of the swimming pool.

Fifty lengths before dressing for dinner became Ginny's daily regime. Sometimes Eustace swam with her. He drank wine in the afternoons and at night, they made love with a vigour and ease they seemed to have forgotten. The holiday mood had fully infected him.

His worries about typewriters and money and the politics of England drained away, as the effects of the operation and the overuse of laudanum drained from Ginny's body and the swimming started to restore its former shape.

Woody joined them for the second weekend. In truth, he had rather invited himself. The inaugural Monaco Grand Prix was scheduled for the fourteenth of May. He pointed out what a coup it would be to take some of their better customers to the race. Even though Eustace dealt with sales far more than Woody, he had to admit this was a smart idea.

Woody drove down through France in an open-top Invicta 4.5 litre S-type rented from a collector he'd met at the Bugatti owner's club. The elegant convertible seemed appropriate for the image he intended to portray. He had people to impress.

Patricia 'Patty' Burnett, a new 'lady-friend', sat in the passenger seat. She was — in Woody's eyes — a 'gay little thing' fresh from the 'Peggy Higgins Typing School' in Solihull, though clearly destined to be no one's typist. She kicked off her shoes and put her feet on the side windowsill, cooling her toes in the breeze as her skirt slipped down her legs, revealing an encouraging amount of thigh.

The corporate guests, Mr and Mrs Corrigan, sat comfortably in the back with a picnic basket, a bottle of brandy and a magnum of champagne. Simon Corrigan was the heir to Corrigan and Corrigan Trading, Havershall's distributor in India. He was a thirty-something ex-military man with an extravagant moustache, straw boater and a linen suit a dozen years out of fashion. His wife, Helen, was red-faced, a former flapper, retaining the drooping pearls. They both drank copiously, which suited Woody. The journey was long but the weather remained favourable. They travelled with the top down.

"Explain it to me again," Patty said, cigarette in a holder far too long for use in a car. "It seems like they drive in circles."

"Laps," Mr Corrigan corrected. "One hundred laps."

"Going in circles?"

"I asked the same question," Helen Corrigan chipped in.

"Not exactly circles. There are chicanes and hairpins," Woody offered helpfully.

"And people die doing this?"

"All too frequently."

"Something to look forward to, I suppose," Patty said with a giggle.

Woody kept his concentration on the wheel, imagining handing these guests over to Ginny, who would no doubt entertain them more thoroughly than he could manage. He would then be free to think of Patty. She would be impressed by Monte Carlo, as she had been impressed with the Invicta. She'd love the food he would buy, the wine he would order, the earrings he had brought along as a gift. Afterwards she would, he was sure, soften. She seemed so much more obliging than Zoe.

Holding her champagne in an enamel cup, Patty looked back over the seat for support to her arguments about motor racing.

"You do realise," Helen observed, "that we are being led astray by these men of ours?"

"Oh, yes," said Patty. "Beastly, isn't it?"

After a Saturday by the coast, the Havershalls and their guests drove along to Monte Carlo for the evening, staying at the Hermitage Hotel — a booking Ginny had made and paid for. William and Richard were left in Cap Ferrat under the care of their nanny.

Ginny and Eustace danced. Actually danced! Fit from her swimming, she rediscovered her energy for late nights. The couples swapped partners — Ginny cavorting wildly with Simon Corrigan; Eustace waltzing with Helen and then being lent out to Patty on account of Woody's inability to foxtrot without his missing toe.

The party of six emerged for a brunch late the next morning in a roof top café overlooking the climb from *Sainte-Dévote* to the Casino where, according to Woody, the cars would be at their most spectacular. Ginny walked around with a jug of Bucks-Fizz, topping people's glasses whenever they were less than brimming. She found she enjoyed playing hostess. She was good at it.

The pole position had been awarded by ballot to Philippe Étancelin, a privateer Frenchman whose wife Suzanne acted as his crew chief. Bigger teams with better finances took over as soon as the race began. In the blur of action, the contest at the front was between the Romanian, Georges Bouriano in a Bugatti, the heavily-favoured Rudolf Caracciola in his Mercedes and William Grover-Williams, an Englishman based in France, also driving a Bugatti.

The raw thunder of engines echoed around the harbour front, relentless and claustrophobic in the surrounding amphitheatre. Smoke billowed up from the passing cars. Crowds clustered at every vantage point. In a moment when Eustace's attention was not on his guests, he noticed Woody staring over the railing towards the corner below. He put his hand on his partner's arm.

"It's like a battle, isn't it? I hate the noise too," Eustace told him.

"That's just it," Woody said quietly. "I don't hate it. It's more like an addiction."

A few laps later, an Alfa-Romeo came up the start/finish straight and braked at the entrance to *Sainte-Dévote*. The back end twitched and the flimsy front wheel clipped the concrete kerb on the inside. The kerb stood three inches proud of the road and cars passed within a hands-width of it at astonishing speed. It did not forgive mistakes.

The tyre burst, the wheel crumpled. The car pitched sideways, hit a wall and flipped. The driver was tossed across the track like a rag doll.

Woody stiffened. Eustace, still holding Woody's arm, stared as the flailing doll cartwheeled to the other side of the track, barely missed by two other cars following through the corner.

The wreck rolled one more time, shedding bent metal panels and another wheel. Three marshals ran towards the driver.

Eustace and Woody waited, locked together. They expected the whoosh of flame, fearing the explosion every occupant of a tank had seen at least once... on other tanks.

The battered remains of the car ground to a halt below them on its side. For a second or two nothing happened. Then, with a flash and a shuddering boom, the petrol tank went up.

Woody's eyes were closed before the heat wave and the smell of burning gasoline reached them. Eustace watched the spreadeagled figure of the driver rise, apparently untouched. He was shepherded away by two marshals while others attempted to extinguish the flames. He was limping and holding his knee.

"Woody, he's alive! Lucky blighter! Lucky like us, aye?"

Woody fell back against him and Eustace put his arm around Woody's shoulder.

"I could never sit in that cockpit," Eustace whispered.

"No, maybe not. But it's not the same for me, Captain. I'm watching rich men play with their toys and I'm standing here... me, a boy from Salford. Last night, the Hermitage Hotel. I mean, bloody hell, by all rights we should be dead already. Sometimes I wonder if I am dead. Did I ever come back, Captain? From under that tank?"

"Lucky, as I said," Eustace suggested.

"Something like that, Captain. Some form of luck."

After four hours the race was won by Grover-Williams, a minute ahead of Bouriano. The Havershall party were triumphant and stayed for a champagne reception with the drivers before heading, somewhat drunkenly, back to Cap Ferrat.

Back in *her* villa, Ginny slipped between fine cotton sheets in the master bedroom. Eustace was finishing a late night cigar on the balcony, flicking ash over the side as he took in the midnight sea.

"She's a redhead, isn't she," she said. Statement, not question.

"Who?"

"Patty."

"Well, yes, sort of," he agreed.

"That other girl, Zoe, she was that colour. It's his thing. He's looking for another Mabel, only younger so they don't argue, and redder so they don't seem quite real. How old do you suppose this one is? He has no real intention to marry them, does he? He has two children and he's a widower. Do you suppose he tells them that?"

"You disapprove? I was — what? — twenty-four. You were seventeen."

"Fiddlesticks. That was different. We were courting. We waited. They are at it like…" She stuck short on the word. "I can hear them through the walls."

"You *do* disapprove."

"Don't make me out the prude. Seriously, how old do you think she is? You danced with her."

"I was unaware women have an indicator discerned by touch. Maybe it's like trees with rings?" He laughed and stubbed out his cigar on the balcony rail. "Besides, Woody's more infatuated with cars and machines than young women."

"That's why he's going to hurt them. Now, come to bed," she said, seeing the subject was exhausted. "I want you to make love to me."

"Now? After all that champagne?"

"I'm inspired by this place," she said grandly. She giggled, feeling delightfully wicked. "I think I shall spend my fortune here. You must come and play the gigolo. I want to be — how do I put this? — captivated by your efforts."

Woody's mind was, at that moment, in Madame Franny's. The redhead was that redhead. Mabel had not yet come and Mabel had not yet gone. Time was jumbled and reversed by a day full of alcohol and fast cars.

With something like immortality, he swept up Patty as he wished he had swept up that young girl before the likes of Blenkinsop and Mulgrove took her, the way he wished Zoe Fitzsimmons might have let him.

Patty did not say yes and she did not say no, and somehow the sense of ownership gained from wavering consent was everything he needed. It kept him hard. He demanded that she spoke the few phrases in French she had learnt for the trip and obediently she trotted them out while he groaned and came inside her.

Blenkinsop was buried in France with his sins. Mulgrove, the traitor, was dead. For a few wild moments, everything seemed right in the world of Joseph Woodmansey. The guilt and self-loathing would follow.

Maybe it wasn't Paris — Ginny's youthful fantasy — but in many ways the Riviera was better. Warmer certainly. And it was hers.

She had lived alongside wealth all her life, first under the protection of her name, then under her uncle's roof, more recently with her husband's emerging successes. This was different.

Even if money meant nothing, what one did with it was everything, so Ginny made arrangements to invest in her property. Several thousands were spent remodelling the villa over the latter half of 1929, adopting the Art Deco styling she adored. She hired a landscape architect for the overgrown acre and a half of gardens, putting in a private tennis court and a gigantic patio outside the sun lounge which stretched out to the pool and provided an elevated view over the trees to the Mediterranean.

Havershall's, the company, could use Cap Ferrat for its big 'entertaining' events, or so she told Eustace. She imagined a party there every year, and every year a Grand Prix to woo their visitors.

Back in Britain, the economy continued its wobble. In October, Eustace and Ginny were in London for the biggest office exhibition of 1929. On the 24th, 'Black Thursday', the New York stockmarket lost eleven percent of its value at the opening bell.

The huge volume of share sales overwhelmed the ticker tape machines reporting prices to brokerage offices around America. Remote investors, not knowing the trends, panicked, issuing sale instructions for shares that found no buyer even at a fraction of their previous prices.

Several leading bankers met to pool resources and pour money into blue chip stocks to hold the market up, but the tactic failed — a thumb trying to quell the breach in an almighty dam; the dam broke.

The London exhibition hall emptied as the waves of news arrived. Eustace and his sales team were left on an empty stand, looking at the abandoned litter spread across the hall floor, wondering what this all meant for business.

The following day, while the stockmarket tumbled, Ginny met her cousin for afternoon tea at Simpson's-In-The-Strand. Away from Eustace's business worries, she was hoping for a quiet 'sisterly' chat. It had been a year since they had been together at her father's funeral. Caroline was recovering from delivering her fourth child, only six weeks previously.

She arrived in the most elegant sable fur jacket Ginny had ever clapped eyes on, but when discarded for the maitre d' to deposit in a cloakroom, Ginny saw a Caroline somewhat less suited to her slim-line dress.

Caroline opened with, "Lady Furness is still with the Prince."

She clearly thought this more important than any emerging financial crisis.

"We do receive newspapers in Birmingham," Ginny pointed out.

"I thought you'd be interested… being American and all that."

Ginny laughed. "You know I'm not really American. Neither is she. Born in Switzerland, if I remember my scathing Daily Mail editorials correctly."

"American father," Caroline said. "A diplomat of some kind. I suppose your America does have them, though. Diplomacy never seems to be their thing."

"You, my darling cousin, are a snob."

"Better a snob, Ginny, than one of the grovelling poor. Everyone is so depressed about this stockmarket business, but Keynes says, there will be no serious consequences in London. I've met the man, friend of a friend, don't you know? Quite the genius."

"With respect, John Maynard Keynes is an idiot."

"And what would you know of economics? You're like me."

"I know that rich people get rich when factories are turning and the 'grovelling poor' — as you call them — are in jobs. That seems likely to fall apart if credit dries up."

"Oh, Ginny, you do sound like one of them sometimes."

"As opposed to 'one of you'?"

"Don't be so beastly. I can see he has quite turned you against your class."

"You mean Eustace?"

"He holds you back, Gin. When was the last time the two of you accepted a social invitation?"

"On the Riviera, I may play the hostess. Back home, this Mrs Havershall is looking after her children, isn't that what you told me to do? I'm not going out and I can't be involved in the business, so I'm volunteering at soup kitchens."

Caroline took a moment to recover. "You? Volunteer at soup kitchens? You are incorrigible."

"I imagine I am. Eustace, bless him, thinks only volunteer work is suitable. Being a woman, and especially as a mother, this is what I am allowed."

"I see. Well, I suppose he is to be commended, but I fear he will not take kindly to the message I came to deliver... more of a new invitation, actually."

Ginny eyed her cousin warily.

"Alright, it's simply that I met Margaret Barrington-Brown the other day. Oh, Ginny, it's just an invitation for a weekend away. Up north. Mothers or not, we are *allowed* that. Why, my dear, there are plenty of mothers who are still bright young things — running all over London, leaving their children in the professional care of domestic staff. Costume parties, scavenger hunts, that sort of thing."

"Are you saying *we* should be running with them?"

"All I'm suggesting is that it would do you good to get away." Caroline's voice sank in an air of disappointment. "The Barrington-Browns have an estate. Rose of the Shires and all that. If things are about to get as bad as you say, then surely... I mean, if your Eustace is about to get... surely it would be a way forward... to combine forces. I understand that's what Charlie wishes to propose. I'm only the messenger. He has 'floated' his company, isn't that what they call it? Has oodles of money now. He hardly knows what to do with it."

Ginny remembered how Margaret Barrington-Brown had been an emissary sent to Eustace before. She remembered Eustace's response. She cracked a smile at the thought.

"Things are not that bad at Havershall's, actually. And never will be. If this Mr Brown has raised money he cannot spend, then it is to be hoped he chokes on the interest he has committed to. Havershall's will not be one of his toys."

"You'll not take the message to Eustace then?"

"It would be futile."

"Alright then. I shall deliver your reply. Let's talk of other things," Caroline said huffily.

The waiter had arrived to take their order. While he scribbled down the particulars of their afternoon tea, Ginny reappraised the bitten-down nails on Caroline's hand, obvious now she'd removed her gloves. The shadowy bags below her eyes indicated a lack of sleep or maybe something worse. Caroline squinted through the *pince-nez* she used for reading and lit a cigarette.

"You don't smoke. You gave it up," Ginny said, when the waiter had departed.

"It's nothing."

"Nothing?"

"Nerves, that's all. I'm sure you lose all sense of what's happening in the real world, while you're up there with your soup kitchens in that hell hole."

"Birmingham?"

"Yes, Birmingham. Do you not realise what is happening in the country? In the places that matter?"

"I understand the economy is probably going to collapse, the poor are going to get poorer, and — according to you — our Prince is fucking Lady Furness."

"Don't be crude," Caroline said. She inhaled her cigarette with the indelicate lungs of a veteran, too full of nicotine to remember how the habit once worked. "I meant, what's *really* happening at the root of things. I hear it every weekend in the stately homes where things are plotted and turned, places you and Eustace refuse to go. They fix the fate of England over cigars and brandy. Now everyone has the vote and all is chaos and decay, what's left to impose a sense of order? Who do you think they talk about? Stalin or Mussolini or the rise of this Mr Hitler, the communists or the fascists. Look at what happened with that frightful strike. They say the threat has not receded, Ginny. We lack any control. Only those of class and education can restore it, that's what my father says. Edward agrees. This stockmarket disaster may pass, but it's a beginning. Revolution, one way or another, he says. The trouble with the vote is that it goes to everyone."

Ginny was so surprised, she didn't answer.

Caroline continued, her voice quickening, "The vote is as smart as the fiftieth most stupid person in a hundred. We need principles to hold to, don't we?"

"You no longer sound like you," Ginny told her. "It's your father or Edward saying this. What's wrong with you?"

"My point… my point is, I agree with them. Our other burdens seem quite minor if the order of everything is destroyed. You must admit it, soup kitchens are not the fault of the rich. The masses are their own enemy."

Caroline removed the *pince-nez* and dabbed her cheek with the napkin. Ginny noticed a tremor in her cousin's hand.

"I think this is all distraction and poppycock. You don't care a jot for politics. The cigarettes, the nails, all of it… something is not right with you, Caroline. I will not ask the question, if you don't wish to tell me the answer."

"The answer? Ha!" Caroline put her hand to her mouth as if some secret might slip out. "You want to know what it is to be me? Goddammit, my father is lining up with the fascists and I am getting old."

"Old? What are you on about? You're barely more than thirty."

"Thirty-three. I am losing my looks. I mean nothing to Edward. Oh, Ginny, my husband is having an affair."

The waiter arrived with their order — Darjeeling tea in a silver tea pot, delicate bone china cups alongside fresh baked scones and Devonshire clotted cream. Caroline began to cry and Ginny felt a dark confusion descend over their table. Everything about privilege seemed to matter so little. It was something she'd always believed, but now, as the proof unfolded before her eyes, she didn't know what to say.

A mile away, at the London Stock Exchange, prices continued to fall.

Back in her hotel room, waiting for Eustace to return from his office exhibition, Ginny reflected that only a few months earlier she had lounged in the sunshine of the French Riviera. Entertaining Havershall's business clients, she felt herself briefly 'involved'.

Soup kitchens were hardly the same. Home in Birmingham, things had returned to the way they were. Eustace was off 'doing business' all the time. She had followed him to the capital, freed from the duties of motherhood for a while, thinking of evenings in London, but on three consecutive nights, they had dined with company clients — Frank Morland, the northern distributor and his wife; three intolerable Dutch men; Teddy Hankins, a beastly misogynist who'd made his fortune distributing typewriters and office equipment in Wales. Any one of these commanded more of Eustace's attention than Ginny seemed to do. Did he expect her to be happy with shopping her days away? Was her role in life to frivolously spend money so that Eustace's making of it might seem more urgent?

She thought again and again about Caroline's words, about the financial threat of Barrington-Brown. She wondered how it might be put to use. Did the world not act like 'The Landlord's Game'?

After a weekend to think through their options, October 28th — Black Monday — saw more investors abandoning the market. The Dow Jones Index posted another record daily loss of 12.8 percent. Black Tuesday followed. Sixteen million shares were sold, billions of dollars were lost, thousands of investors ruined. The malaise took hold of stockmarkets around the world. All fell. Keynes was wrong.

"Abandon the Gold Standard, surely now," Woody suggested, newspaper in hand, as he and Eustace sat in the Havershall's boardroom considering the front page stories. Woody was half way down a tumbler of whisky. It was not yet 10 a.m. "Investment is already impossible. There will be more blood over this. Job losses. Wage cuts. No one to sell to. The country's ready to rise, especially in the north."

"We've seen a month of orders cancelled by distributors already," Eustace said.

"Do we know how badly we're exposed?"

"I had Megan check the account this morning."

Megan Rillett was the office manager. Eustace summarised her grim appraisal. "We have nearly topped out the overdraft with all the materials we've bought lately."

"And how much do people owe us?"

"Too much to hope they might pay quickly. I never should have taken that *facility*."

Woody shook his head. "Mosley is saying the government must seize control of banking, raise pensions, increase people's spending. He's right. We rode the last storm, but this—"

"We're strong. We'll be alright," Eustace assured him.

"I know you have a stiff upper lip, Captain, but I don't think even you believe it. It is easy to imagine that we don't depend on the stockmarket, but that's not the way it is. If there is no money on the stockmarket, there is no money anywhere." He sipped at his whisky, then said, "There goes all the future."

Eustace stood at the window, remembering once gazing out into Marmaduke Lane during the General Strike — workers and owners at war over who should own what portion of a shrinking pie. Now the pie itself had collapsed and traffic in the lane was thin. He wondered if it would ever recover. In the future, was there going to be a pie?

While still a member of the Labour Government, having flitted neurotically from Conservative to Independent to Labour during the Twenties, Oswald Mosley tried twice to persuade his current party of a new approach to economic problems. He published the 'Mosley Memorandum'. It attacked the failed monetary policies associated with the Gold Standard, advocating tariffs to protect British industries, state nationalisation of key industries and new public works to create employment. Its intention — so said Mosley — was to 'obliterate class conflict and make the British economy healthy again'.

Mosley had a talent for being ignored, even when he was right. For a while, Woody thought him the smartest man in Britain. Eustace remembered him as the young MP in a suit who came to the Fairchild Estate, but who did not play tennis. He thought it wise to keep an eye on him.

A month into the crisis, the telephone call came from the manager of their bank. Megan Rillett put it through to Eustace's office.

The bank was calling in all overdrafts and Havershall's had stretched to the limits of theirs — ten thousand pounds and more. Profits were simply too slow to materialise as cash, the manager said.

"You can't foreclose on a healthy company," Eustace protested.

"An overdraft is repayable on demand. I'm sorry, cash is king, especially in a crisis."

"You told me that when you wanted to loan me money."

"It is no less true now."

"Yes, but we are invested in hard production assets. We have debtors who will pay us… soon, very soon," Eustace shouted.

"One cannot live on what one is owed," the bank manager said.

"Don't you idiots understand, we can't turn debts into cash at the drop of a hat?"

"The bank needs the liquidity."

"We need the liquidity. Dammit, you've seen the numbers. We make a profit."

"In the past, you made a good profit. At the moment, you break even. An overdraft is temporary. It's meant as a facility. If you check the terms…"

Eustace balled his fist and banged it on the desk. "I don't care about the bloody terms. Breaking Havershall's makes no sense for either of us. You know that. You won't get your money back."

"These times don't make sense. I can give you fourteen days."

The line clicked dead.

Eustace wondered if Charlie Barrington-Brown was having the same trouble. He felt sure he was not. A baronet's son always had bankers in his pocket.

Ten thousand pounds! In the long run, not a problem. In a healthy market, a mere trifle. But right now, in fourteen days, impossible!

Chapter Twelve

There were many reasons why the stockmarket crashed, but the reason it crashed so spectacularly was that old banker's word — confidence. It's either sky high or flat on the floor.

Earlier in 1929, Ramsay MacDonald's minority government had come to power at Britain's first election in which women under thirty voted. 'The Equal Franchise Act' of the previous year gave them electoral parity with men. Margaret Bondfield was the first female Cabinet Minister, ironically in the Ministry of Labour where the most intractable problems would soon lie.

Before the crash, economies worldwide had been slowing, but stock prices had continued to climb, seemingly immune. Investors who could command the trust of their bank had continued borrowing money for stockmarket investments throughout the Twenties. Why not, when you could buy a share for a pound and be assured it would soon be worth two?

Now, despite their habit of loaning money they didn't have, the banks baulked at the diminishing 'safety' stock of cash they kept back. The time of plenty ended abruptly. A frog idling in hot water will eventually jump, and jump it did.

In Britain, the sudden money drought was made worse by the fervour for the Gold Standard and the new government's reluctance to change the policy. Desperate to boost reserves, the nervous banks called in loans and overdrafts from companies. These were the same companies whose shares their more privileged customers were buying. Companies like Havershall's could not pay money back on demand, whatever the terms of their overdrafts might state. They ran out of cash, despite their profits. And failed, seemingly overnight. Eustace's bank manager was right about one thing — in business, cash is always king.

Share prices stalled, so confidence evaporated, so share prices fell further — simple cause and effect.

Now, investors owning shares on borrowed money couldn't meet interest payments and could no longer sell their shares at prices greater than their debts.

Defaults rose. Share prices tumbled still further, so defaults grew faster.

The financial machine was eating itself.

Banks had to call in more loans and overdrafts from healthy companies to pay for the bad debts, which turned the crisis into a death spiral. Havershall's had been sucked in.

Two days after the bank demand, twin telegrams arrived in Duke House addressed to the two shareholders of 'Havershall & Woodmansey Typewriting Ltd.' They expressed the desire of BBTL Ltd to make an offer for a sizeable part of the company. They named a price and offered additional loans to replace the current overdraft.

Woody came raging into Eustace's office, waving his copy. He slammed the door behind him.

"The bloody cheek! The bloody cheek!" he shouted.

Eustace had already had several minutes to think about the offer. "BBTL can go hang but, Woody, it does not change our central difficulty. We have an overdraft and the bank wants it back."

"Yes, but how does this bastard know about our bank? How? We haven't even met him! Doesn't it make you mad? This… This…"

"Charlie…. Charles Barrington-Brown." Eustace provided the answer in parts.

"You've not met this man behind my back?"

"No, Woody, certainly not. I met him once four or five years ago. Seen him at an exhibition since… He was a privileged prig then. I assume he is now. Last month, he bought up Argyle's."

"The brothers? Craig and Eddie, in Glasgow? They make that half-decent little portable?"

"Paid a fair price for it, so I understand."

"Why aren't banks calling in *his* money… *his* overdrafts? Is he so rich that he doesn't need them?"

"I'm afraid he has the advantage. He floated his company when the price was right. Now he has cash in his hands when everyone needs to sell."

"Do we *need* to sell, Captain?"

This was the question, of course, but neither had wanted to ask it. Neither wanted to answer it. Bankruptcy so soon after their recent successes seemed impossible. The crash proved that even the most impenetrable walls sit on shifting sands.

"Havershall and Woodmansey's, that's a family, ourselves and our people. We have protected it all before; we'll protect it now," Eustace said.

"But how? I mean, without new money? Barrington-Brown would keep our people in work at least and we owe them that. It's a sound business. He'd be a fool to do anything else."

"Woody, I don't want to sell. I'm clear on that."

"Me neither. Do we have a choice? A least worst option? Any other *volunteers* hanging around who might help us fix it?"

"I have one idea. Like you said, it's a family matter."

"Not your father… not again. You mustn't ask."

Eustace shook his head. "Wrong side of the family to look for money when the chips are down."

"No," said Woody, grasping what the idea might be. "I mean, you can't. You always said you wouldn't."

"I always said you wouldn't let me," Eustace corrected.

"Don't think of Ginny's money, we can't take it, Captain. It wouldn't be right."

"You wanted a least worst option… a volunteer. I have been sitting here thinking about it. She has volunteered more than once."

"Ginny's inheritance is your safety net. If Havershall's ever goes bust."

"I never asked for a safety net, Woody," he said. "Neither did you and neither did she."

The dinner table at the house in Edgbaston was silent. The wait seemed endless. He had laid out the position after the boys had finished eating and the nanny had taken them both off to bed. Ginny had listened.

"I see," she said at last.

And then said nothing.

"I did not want to ask, Gin. I have not asked in the past."

"A garret in Paris… I haven't forgotten my promise, Eustace. Very well, everything I have is here for you, but I know you will not take it as charity."

"No," he said.

"Good, because I will not offer it as such. I want my shares."

Two days later, Ginny came to Duke House to table her proposal. She insisted she must sit in the boardroom and look Woody in the eye.

"I will invest the sum required to clear the overdraft, plus extra working capital for investment, in return for, shall we say, a fifteen percent stake in the shares?"

Woody twitched in his chair. "Eustace said—"

"In this, I handle my own affairs. Understand me, Woody, only in this matter, otherwise I know what's expected of me," she said pointedly. "My accountant tells me the company is almost forty thousand pounds short of acceptable liquidity, even if you could pay back the bank. In the present climate—"

"This business is sound. It always has been."

"Sound in normal circumstances, maybe. But these are not normal circumstances. I cannot imagine your liquidity will improve in the next seven days."

"I'm sorry, Mrs Havershall, I don't mean to be rude, but—"

"So formal? I am still 'Ginny' and you have no need to apologise, Woody. Business is money and money is always vulgar. A little game taught me that."

Woody looked across at Eustace. Eustace said nothing to help. He managed, "The accountant was Ginny's idea."

"Fifteen per cent?" Woody repeated.

"And a seat on the board," she added.

He huffed. "I would never consider a seat on the board."

"Would you consider allowing Mr Barrington-Brown a seat on your board? I think he would ask for rather more. I am a quieter voice, I assure you, but I intend to do my share of the work to justify the shares I own."

Woody's look towards Eustace became a glare.

Ginny continued, "Think of it this way. Do you always agree with your partner here? You do not. Does he outvote you in those cases? He does, his being fifty-five percent of the shareholding. Now the balance of power will lie with my minority. Maybe I will agree with him… but do I always agree so meekly with my husband?"

"You're his wife, you just said it."

"Indeed," she said. "But I also told you this is business. And I wish to be useful in it, so I will require a seat on the board."

She glanced at Eustace, then addressing Woody again, said, "It seems you may choose the *poison* you prefer — the rich bully, a toff no less, or the heiress who happens to be your partner's wife?"

"Eustace, what do you say?" Woody asked.

"I never wanted Ginny's money, but I would not see either of us ruined. I told her the decision is yours."

"Maybe you would like to discuss it while I retire," Ginny offered. "I can respect that. It is not my business, not yet."

"No, not yet," Woody agreed.

She had begun gathering the papers she had brought with her and pushing them back into her handbag.

"Wait, Mrs Havershall… Please, Ginny, wait."

"Yes?"

"Twelve and half percent," Woody offered.

"Fourteen."

"Thirteen."

"And a seat on the board?" she pressed. She stood, resting her hand on her bag as if undecided if she should stay or go.

After several long seconds, Woody nodded.

Fifty years before, in the 1870s, five percent of the ownership of limited companies in Britain was held by women. By 1920, the figure had risen to more than fourteen percent, driven in part by a war that left the country with a million more women than men.

The Roaring Twenties had then seen an explosion in shares held by women. By 1930, women held a third of UK companies.

Ginny's personal investment in Havershall's was a sign of the times, even if most other women chose the easier routes of stock advisors and the London markets. Both of those now seemed somewhat unreliable.

She stacked the grate in the lounge with apple and cherry wood while waiting for Eustace's return. It produced a smell that could not fail to smooth any conflict. At home, Eustace was still the man. She intended to prove it.

She poured them both a brandy and tipped a little extra into his glass while he was changing out of his workday suit. Kicking off her shoes, she sat before the fire, her bare feet peeping out under the hem of a new dress.

"You're still the cat's pyjamas, you know?" she said, injecting a seductive purr into her voice.

"Havershall's is not a game," he said grumpily after several sips of the brandy.

"No, I'm not playing it as a game. It is life and family. You must realise it is every bit that for me as well as you. Artist or not, I never wanted to live in that garret. I wanted to be here with you."

He hesitated. She said, "Well?" as if the invitation were obvious. "What are you going to do with me?"

She laughed as he pushed her down onto the carpet and tried to kiss her. She wrapped her legs around his thighs. They rolled over and over, ending up in front of the fire with Ginny perched on top.

Ginny was not so frivolous as her celebration suggested. Her plan for investment had begun over a month before. Immediately after her meeting with Caroline, she had telephoned Mrs Margaret Barrington-Brown to inform her that she was, "Terribly worried Havershall's might be having a cash problem in the current climate."

She had never understood business, she said, but a lady could not allow herself to be left destitute.

"I'm sure you would feel the same," she added as she pleaded for Margaret's help.

Margaret asked what the best way to proceed might be. Ginny told her, "If your Charlie is serious about combining forces, perhaps he should call in some favours at the bank before he makes an offer."

She suggested offers by telegram. It might be less painful than facing the management one-on-one.

As much as Eustace loved his wife and admired her determination, Ginny's bailout and his failure to avoid the necessity of her money delivered a heavy blow. He had once been the dashing captain, the chancer. Now, at almost thirty-five, their bedroom mirror showed a pudginess in his cheeks. He was jowly, the stress lines around his eyes caught in artificial light like corrugations. He found grey hairs. He was sure his hair had thinned. The expensive cloth of his suits was more impressive than the contents.

As a man — a gentleman of commerce — he was responsible. For his wife. For his sons' future. For everyone at Havershall's. The long hours trying to maintain appearances in a world where failure was the common currency were extracting a toll, little by little, piece by piece. The ease with which Ginny's money arrived only made his desperation worse.

In November of 1930, the four-year-old Richard Havershall went down with Scarlet Fever. His condition weakened. He was rushed into hospital in Birmingham.

Ginny stayed at his bedside. Eustace visited for several hours every evening. They paid for a private room. In those hours, mother and father held hands, watching their son. The attending doctor shook his head. For a while, nothing seemed to change.

Thinking of the miracle that Ferdinand Rees had performed, Eustace asked for an expert to be summoned — *'The best there is.'*

He was told the greatest expert on childhood diseases was Catherine Chisholm of the Manchester Babies Hospital.

"A woman?" said Eustace, as if there might be some doubt.

"Yes," the doctor said. "She was my lecturer at university."

Eustace hesitated at the idea. He'd rarely met a woman doctor, let alone one who was the best in her field. Before he could decide if he believed it possible, the fever broke. Richard appeared to be over the worst. They took him home in the second week of December, feeling relieved. Eustace and Ginny did not discuss Catherine Chisholm. He contented himself that William had not also caught the disease. He told Ginny, the boys were safe.

But that was not yet the worst of it.

Woody took Patty Burnett to Bristol for Christmas to visit the Perecs. He introduced her to Celia and James as his fiancée, their prospective new mother.

He brought presents. Celia's was a doll; James' a new 'Hornby No. 7 Meccano Outfit'. At four, he was too young to do anything with the small engineering pieces.

"Let your boy use his hands and brains to build his own toys," said the advert.

Both grandparents looked at Woody as if he knew nothing about children. That afternoon, the Perec house was full of tiny wheels and pulleys and strange half-built metal constructions in green and red. They meant far more to Woody than James.

Patty looked on, unable to entertain Celia, horrified to find less years between her and the daughter than between Woody and herself.

Woody looked up from the floor where he had finished the construction of a crane. Patty was trying to amuse Celia by showing her the contents of her handbag. He felt an itch in his head that usually only whisky calmed. A spasm seized his arms like the beginning of a heart attack. He had known that Patty could not be the one. Known, but not admitted.

Suddenly, he saw how everyone else must see him with Patty, how the Perecs must see her. She was not Mabel. The red hair and her youth reminded him of a different woman. The similarity appalled him.

* * *

Back in Edgbaston, William, aged two, was caught up in the excitement when gifts appeared. Eustace was happy to join in, speculating with the excited child what gifts might be wrapped in the next package.

Richard remained subdued. When Ginny mentioned it, Eustace said it was probably the after-effect of the fever. He was weak. That was understandable. He continued playing a game with William.

But Richard's temperature rose again. He cried for no reason, complained that his head hurt. He woke up on the day after Boxing Day wailing uncontrollably and complaining that his left leg wouldn't move. He told his mother there were 'pins and needles'. When she tried to touch him, he recoiled in pain.

Eustace, in his suit and about to leave for the factory, expressed disbelief.

Ginny shouted, "This is my son. We're going to the hospital. Now, dammit!"

Weakened by the earlier infection, Richard was showing the first symptoms of polio.

Waves of polio had been spreading across Europe since the late Nineteenth Century. No vaccine existed. In spinal polio, the most common form, the virus reaches the grey matter section in the spinal column, the part responsible for movement. Muscles miss signals from the brain or spinal cord; they become weak and paralysed. Paralysis comes with fever and pain.

In most cases, the child recovers.

But not always.

In some, the growth of an affected limb is slowed after the disease subsides. One leg may become shorter than the other. The child's gait is distorted — a permanent limp and sometimes deformities of the spine.

All this comes after. Assuming the child lives.

Richard Havershall returned to the best private hospital room Birmingham could offer. Ginny hung by his side, his life in the balance throughout the following week as 1931 approached.

Every hour ticked by slowly. And after that another hour. Ginny's vigil went on and on. In that room. Sitting next to Richard. Helpless. Waiting. Confined.

Her son was pale. He was awake. He was asleep. He cried in pain. She tried to comfort him. She could not leave him. She could not do anything.

Money, investment, her own happiness — the importance of all these faded in the lost moments of that room, until her every thought of Richard felt like a finely honed blade.

Eustace came. And went off to work. And came back. Trying to be father and husband and provider.

Meanwhile, lying in that bed, Richard could not twitch or feel pain, sadness, despair or even joy, without Ginny suffering the same acute sensation. He depended on her. She depended on loving him.

Eustace told himself he should have called the woman doctor the first time Richard was ill. *Why hadn't he done so?* He should have made sure.

He found himself staring across his office desk. A single framed photograph in pride of place. It had been taken on the lawn of the Buckley house on Long Island — Ginny seated and smiling; William a babe in her arms; Richard hanging onto his father's knee for balance, a stuffed bear held in his other hand.

He asked Megan Rillett to find the number for Manchester Babies Hospital. When he hid himself in his office to make the call, Catherine Chisholm would not come to the phone as he requested.

"Mrs Rillett," he said, striding out of his office to find her. "I need a number for Viscountess Fairchild instead."

Caroline had once told him his money could not change his class. And yes, he knew that what Caroline might do with a single phone call was forever beyond a Havershall. So it was with the world and parts of it could not be avoided.

To use the power of toffs would be another humiliation.

Ginny was still at the bedside when Catherine Chisholm arrived at the door to Richard's hospital room the following day with Eustace a step behind. Richard's temperature became stable three days after New Year.

Viscountess Fairchild had asked and help had been sent.

The paralysis retreated in a week, but afterwards Richard's right leg grew faster than his left. He would limp through childhood. He needed leg braces and lifts fitted to the left shoe in every pair. His back constantly gave pain.

For years, Ginny shuttled him back and forth devotedly for treatment, often as far as Manchester. She took lessons to learn how to drive, which she did very badly. In her efforts, she developed a deeper feeling for motherhood with Richard that never quite extended so forcefully to William. William was a strong, healthy, independent child who didn't seem to need anyone. Later, she would come to regret allowing the difference to grow.

Chapter Thirteen

Worldwide stockmarket prices kept on declining, the major indices reaching levels lower than they had entered the Twentieth Century. The resulting cycle was clear: low prices created low investment, which created lower demand, which created less jobs.

By 1931, British unemployment had doubled to over two and a half million. Ramsay MacDonald's government struggled with an impossible contradiction: a balanced budget to maintain the hallowed Gold Standard versus money to sustain the hoards of idle workers.

The pressure for sharp cuts in spending increased. The instincts of the Labour Party held MacDonald back. Catastrophe loomed. Politicians dithered.

The Government introduced a 'Means Test' for those seeking dole payments. Officials would visit families to assess whether they were entitled to help. If an older child or a mother had a part-time job, or a grandparent was living with the family, claimants would fail the test. Family heirlooms and other assets had to be sold and savings spent before the dole was received.

The mood of the country continued to darken.

Once Richard's illness settled into its future pattern of out-patient visits and specialists, Ginny's attempts to embed herself in Havershall's began again in earnest. She allowed herself to spend first one, then two, then three days a week in Duke House.

She took over from Megan Rillett as Office Manager. Megan was pregnant now and intended to dedicate herself to the raising of her child. The irony was not lost upon Ginny, as she left the family home every day, often leaving her own sons to nannies and servants. Her reasons for doing so were alien to most women. At various times, her cousin, her aunt and letters from her mother all expressed disapproval.

Dismissing objections, Ginny approached 'business' with a force of will she had never afforded any other challenge in her life. Since Havershall's was partly hers, she would cherish success as her husband did, and become part of its story. She applied an intelligence which had, in the past, as often been used to avoid things as to embrace them.

First, she promoted Diane Hall to be her deputy. Diane was a plain and efficient woman of thirty. She spoke with a Birmingham accent, except on the phone when her voice had the purest blue-blood plum. Together they coached other young office women to do the same.

Ginny watched and observed and formed her own opinions of the company's operations. It was clear the company's problems had been heightened by its lax approach to collecting from its debtors. Distributors and wholesalers were becoming the dominant route to market for typewriter sales, but they were the poorest payers.

No longer beholden to a bank, Havershall's had accidentally become a bank itself, effectively 'loaning' money to its customers by not collecting what was owed. Worse still, it wasn't charging interest. Even with Ginny's investment behind it, the poor debt collection threatened to strangle the company sooner or later. In the troubled economy, some customers may never be able to pay, she realised. The thought filled her with alarm. It would not be long before her fears were justified.

Francis Morland Office Fitments Ltd had been Havershall's northern distributor since the earliest expansion. It sold typewriters, filing cabinets, hole punches, guillotines, desks, desk lamps, chairs, ink, paper, pens, pencils, pencil sharpeners, rubbers, rulers, punch cards, tabulation machines — in short, everything in a modern office. Its sales had expanded to cover an area from Chester across to Sheffield and all the way up the east coast to Scotland. The company grew steadily until 1928, then fell. In 1930, it stopped paying its bills.

Frank Morland telephoned Eustace as Duke House was closing up one evening. "I'll put it plainly. Morland's is going under," he said. "The bank will be in before the week is out."

Eustace's heart sank, reliving the fourteen days when it seemed a bank-enforced failure might engulf Havershall's.

"What can we do to help?" he asked.

"Nothing," said Frank.

Frank and his wife had been to the Edgbaston house for dinner several times. Eustace and Ginny knew their children and grandchildren. Eustace did not want to let the man down.

"It happens, Lad," Frank said. "Slowly at first, then awfully quickly. You've always done right by me, Eustace. You are my first phone call."

Woody, Ginny and Eustace sat around the Havershall's board table, poring over the ledgers that Mrs Rhones, the chief clerk, had brought from the accounts office. Morland's owed Havershall's over twenty-five thousand pounds.

"Can't we help him?" Woody asked.

"I asked that question," said Eustace. "We can't pay his debts to other people, or to his bank. Just the loss on what he owes us is a body blow. And we'll certainly miss the future sales."

"Frank takes a thousand of our machines a month," Ginny confirmed.

"He did," Woody said glumly. "That's the past now, him buying our machines."

"That is not my point, Woody. The ownership of goods doesn't pass until they pay us. That's the way our contracts work. Eustace is right, we can't afford to lose what he owes, but we can't allow his bank to steal machines from us either."

Woody looked puzzled.

"They will try to claim all stock if it's there when they foreclose," she explained.

"Banks!" Eustace said and swore loudly.

After a pause, Woody's confusion produced a question: "The machines in Frank's warehouses are ours?"

"They are if we can get them back. He hasn't paid for them. Possession is always most of the law," Ginny added.

"You sound like you've been studying this," Eustace said.

"I have. I asked my accountant." Ginny's chosen firm of accountants had latterly become the company's auditors.

"Well, you sound to me like you're suggesting we steal them," Woody countered.

"It's not stealing if they're ours."

"If we take his stock, Gin, that finishes him for sure," said Eustace.

Ginny took a moment, considering what she'd learned since taking up her role. "Yes," she said. "I understand. He already knows it's too late."

They sent Jim McCann and three press-setters to Leeds. Woody took two night shift operators and a shift supervisor to his home town of Manchester. Eustace's team for Newcastle included the driver of Havershall's only delivery lorry, as well as Wilfred McCann, Jim's brother, who boxed as an amateur in his youth, and one other who volunteered for cash in hand.

The Newcastle team set off during the night from Bordesley Green and arrived as the Morland's warehouse crew were clocking onto the morning shift.

"Who are you?" the leading warehouse man asked, seeing Eustace in a suit. He was young, maybe middle twenties. Men in suits didn't usually appear from delivery lorries, it confused him.

"Havershall's. Come to pick up a return shipment," Eustace said breezily.

"There's no returns on our sheets for today."

"That's alright. I have the paperwork here."

The young man looked at the carbon copy of a delivery note for a shipment Havershall's had delivered a fortnight before.

"These aren't returns. This stuff, we've got on the racks. What's it all about? You're not trying to thieve our stock? There's four of us here. If Mr Morland knew—"

"It's not about numbers," Eustace said. "It's about commitment. Me and my men, we fought in the war."

Behind him, Wilfred was working his balled-up fist into the palm of his opposing hand as if it might need warming up. The young man looked at the boxer, then back at Eustace.

"You don't talk like a fuckin' suit."

"No. I suppose not," he agreed. Never quite a soldier, never quite a gentleman, never quite a toff either— this was another way in which he'd prove the things he was not.

The Morland's men stood aside.

Stepping from a hired lorry in Manchester, Woody was feeling the stiffness of travel and the after-effects of a bottle of whisky. He leant more heavily on his walking stick than normal. With his size and his bent pose and glasses, he could never seem a threat. He tried to remember how he'd once watched Eustace stiffen when leading men into battle.

He took out his gun and handed it to the shift supervisor at his side, choosing him as safer than the two bruisers from the night shift who were also on the team.

"That's a Webley, that is. Here, keep it safe and hidden," he said.

The shift supervisor stared as if he'd never seen a gun before. Perhaps he hadn't, Woody thought. These days, Havershall's employed bright young men who had never seen war. If the kid were lucky, he might never see one.

"You wave it if there's trouble, but only if you have to. You can take out the bullets if you like," Woody informed him.

Woody was greeted at the door of a transport bay by a woman with black teeth, the third finger missing from the hand she used to hold his despatch note. She wore working overalls, exercising an unspoken control over the two storemen who rallied to her side.

"This 'ent your stuff," she said, reading the paper.

"I assure you, according to the law, it is," said Woody.

She refused to move.

"If this is peaceful, there's a half-crown for each of you. Not as a bribe. As a thank you."

Woody urged his team forward. When he tried to follow them into the warehouse, the woman caught his stick and tried to pull him back.

"You take our stuff. We lose our jobs. I know where this company's heading, don't think I don't. Same way as the country."

She tried to kick his leg. Woody swung and slapped her across the face. She fell in a heap.

One of the Morland's storemen grabbed Woody and punched him twice before the Havershall's men came to his aid. While they held the assailant, Woody rammed his stick into the storeman's stomach and, as he doubled up, swung it in an arc that struck a defensive forearm with a sickening crack of bone. The storeman screamed in pain.

The sharp report of a pistol split the air. A chunk of the concrete floor next to Woody's foot exploded. The ricochetting bullet pinged off the steel sheeting in the far wall. When he turned around, the young shift supervisor was standing ten feet away, the gun shaking in his hand.

"This is your fault!" Woody said, accusing the woman who was now cradling a bleeding nose, blood leaking around the stub of her missing finger.

"Give me the gun," he shouted, turning on the shift supervisor. "Give me the fucking gun now. I'll have no more of this."

Jim McCann and his press-setters arrived back in Birmingham first, carrying their haul of typewriters. Ginny made sure the office girls who had stayed for overtime made them cups of tea and handed around bottles of beer she'd sent Diane Hall out to buy. They were 'heroes' of the company.

The Manchester team arrived back next. Woody had red stains on his shirt.

"Oh, God," Ginny said, putting her hand to her mouth when he first appeared.

He assured her it was nothing, smiled, took a beer and dropped a pile of crumpled papers on the boardroom table.

"There. We got it all."

The papers too were stained.

"When I said we should take back stock, Woody, I didn't mean we should…"

"And yet, you wanted your property, our property. This is what it means sometimes. Eustace understands," he said, making it clear that she did not. He didn't mention the gunshot.

Woody returned to the basement in Aston. The year before, he had expanded the lease to take the first floor as well, but now he rattled more loudly in the empty spaces. He poured two sizeable shots of whisky before he changed his bloodied shirt and soaked his aching hand in hot salt water. He kept thinking about the woman with the black teeth. Violence left him with a surplus of energy and energy turned to desire.

He considered his options. Who could he call? Patty had gone from his life, having failed to be Mabel. He had memorised the telephone number for Mrs Bembole's house, despite past failures in its bedrooms. He understood that 'special tastes' were indulged for gentlemen willing to spend special amounts of money. He dialled.

"Red hair. French. Young," he demanded.

An hour later a man arrived at his door with a girl. The man was tall and broad and wore a bowler hat and a long dark overcoat. The girl's coat was thin and paler in colour. She looked no more than fourteen or fifteen. As she stood in Woody's porch, she opened the coat far enough to push it back from her shoulders, inviting inspection. Her skin was very white, her hair not quite red, more like burnt gold.

Woody nodded and the girl stepped inside while he paid the man, shut the door and locked it. By the time he turned around, her coat was pooled at her feet. At close quarters, her hair tickled his face and she smelt of face powder and a cloying sweet lavender.

"Are you French?" he asked.

"*Pour Vous*," she replied ineptly.

"And how old?"

"As old or as innocent as you wish, *Monsieur.*"

The morning newspapers brought ever grimmer tidings of civil unrest to the Havershalls' breakfast table in Edgbaston — 'violent clashes', 'running battles of police and demonstrators'. Nowhere was immune — Belfast, Bolton, Cardiff, Coventry, Merseyside, Manchester, Nottingham, Oldham, Porthcawl, Preston, Stoke, Wigan; London, of course, and Birmingham too.

Many near riots followed protests organised by the National Unemployed Workers' Movement — the NUWM — a body whose principles were based on communism and whose membership attracted would-be revolutionaries.

Stirring the pot ever more, the government cut dole payments by ten per cent. The civil conflict avoided in 1926 now seemed ready to reignite.

Ginny trained a new accounts clerk to do nothing but chase payments. It made no difference. The breaches of promises to pay became more flagrant.

"They are all stealing from us," she complained. "It's intolerable. They take our machines, they make a commitment to pay on time. I never made a promise I couldn't keep."

"People are short of money," Eustace reminded her.

"Fiddlesticks. You and Woody want to put more money into development, don't you? We still have almost a hundred thousands pounds in unpaid bills."

"Yes, but they'll pay. That's why we give them credit."

"Like Frank Morland? It's them or us. We need to survive."

Eustace offered her no answer. He already knew too much about survival.

With Morland's in mind, Ginny decided Havershall's needed a collector of the last resort. She asked Jim McCann about his brother. She had come to believe the McCanns were reliable and Wilfred's muscle had proved a great help in Newcastle.

"But I don't know much about money, Mrs Havershall," Wilfred protested when she offered him a raise of tuppence ha'penny per hour above the shopfloor rate and use of the company's pool car.

"Debt is not a question of money, so much as honour, Wilfred," she informed him. "You were a boxer?"

"Yes, Ma'am, a light-heavy, but 'twere always a struggle to make the weight. Starving meself and such."

"That's all the knowledge of pounds you'll need, Wilfred," she assured him. "What about it? Will you work for a woman?"

"Some men won't," he said.

"I didn't ask about some men."

"True," he said. "And 'seems you ain't asking about just any woman either. I'll work for you."

Eustace continued to watch the career of Oswald Mosley. By now, Mosley had twisted and turned many times since that day at the Fairchilds' tennis party.

After his ideas for reshaping the British economy were rejected by the Labour Party, he left to form the 'New Party' on fifty thousand pounds donated by William Morris of Morris Cars. When that failed, Mosley lurched to new extremes. He formed the 'British Union of Fascists'.

His tenacity was astonishing, and also frightening.

Chapter Fourteen

Ginny was now an important part of the business, not just as the source of money but as the company's most reliable manager of its uses. Nevertheless, her idea that this would bring her closer to her husband was failing spectacularly.

At the beginning of 1931, the idea of a national safety campaign had been revived. Eustace was voted in as chairman of the new Birmingham Industrial Safety Group. He told her it would be good for the company's reputation and, ultimately, for its sales. He and Woody had been fitting safety devices on the machines in Duke Works ever since Lionel Swithin's death and now Eustace began giving talks at dinners and conferences about their techniques. He was regularly invited to tour factories. Every manufacturer knew Eustace Havershall. He liked the acclaim.

With his increased absence, Ginny started to notice things around the company that Eustace missed, willingly or otherwise. The things Eustace missed always seemed to have something to do with Woody.

One Monday morning, she ventured into the factory and spotted a young girl sacked the week before for stealing loose change from the coats in the entrance hall. Ginny accosted Jim McCann as he came from the works' office and pointed across at the girl, who was now working on the assembly benches.

"Tell me, does Jane have a twin sister?"

McCann was perplexed.

"I dismissed her Tuesday last, Jim."

McCann's face tightened.

"Sorry, Mrs Havershall," he said, "Mr Woodmansey, he reinstated her."

"Reinstated her?"

"Yes, Madam."

Ginny stared. She noted the fine cheekbones of the girl, a pretty turn to the mouth. Her hair was full of coppery red curls, like Zoe Fitzsimmons, and maybe a bit like Patty. She could have been younger sister to either. A cold shiver ran down Ginny's spine.

"I see," she said. "Always a pattern, I suppose."

* * *

Ginny argued for staying most of spring 1931 on the Riviera, despite the continuing harshness of the economic climate. There was still plenty of money in her own bank accounts, after all. Eustace compromised. It was agreed she would take two weeks with the boys and Eustace and Woody would come later for the Grand Prix, bringing important business clients.

Simon and Helen Corrigan were again on the guest list, though Eustace's real targets were Messieurs Frederic and Bertrand Dupont, partners in Dupont Brothers, whom he'd long coveted as a French distributor.

Ginny crossed the channel on Townsend's 'Forde', a huge ship that transported over four thousand cars that could be driven on board, no more painful winching of vehicles on and off the deck. She travelled down to the villa at Cap Ferrat with Richard, William and a new nanny who shared the driving of Eustace's Rover. Ginny had not driven in a while. Her stints at the wheel were precarious. She lacked any inclination to regulate her speed in deference to other road users. The nanny-chauffeur was safer and got them to the bottom of France without incident.

In the first week, Ginny and the boys explored the coast, sauntering along the *Promenade des Anglais* in Nice. Richard — approaching five — was walking with a brace on his leg but with a diminishing limp. Monthly visits to Manchester for treatment had become quarterly, but still he struggled to maintain his position as 'big brother' when racing William. Little William managed a few hundred yards of toddling before reverting to his pushchair. Richard hurried beyond him, panting with the effort. Honour was satisfied. At least, for a while.

Further along the promenade, Ginny spotted Henri Matisse, taking coffee at the street café outside Le Negresco. The palatial hotel was famed for its architecture. Matisse himself was as regal as she had always imagined — a high forehead, dark beard. He and the building seemed made for each other.

"Look," she told the boys with girlish enthusiasm, "that's the man who painted our picture."

She meant the coffee pot and fruit bowl in their reception hall.

Richard said, "The fruit, Mummy? The fruit's my favourite."

"Yes, Richard," she assured him, amazed that a five-year-old should understand her when she hadn't been at all specific.

She rushed up to Matisse's table, dragging Richard and carrying William. She said in French, "Sir, would you mind shaking hands with my boys?"

Matisse shook hands in a way that suggested some form of magic might be passing. He lingered on Richard who was eyeing him with rapt attention. Matisse drew a cartoon of the boy's face on a napkin with only four pencil strokes and handed it to him. "For a fellow artist," he said.

The guests arrived on the Thursday before the race. Eustace brought the Dupont brothers and one of their wives in a hired Rolls-Royce. Woody brought the Corrigans.

Ginny slipped into her favoured role of hostess, attending to the guests Woody abandoned. Helen Corrigan looked a little plumper and more red-cheeked than before. Simon retained his characteristic moustache and the out-of-fashion straw boater. They proved good-hearted company. They mixed well with the Duponts.

Eustace gave in to expense and secured a yacht and a berth in Monte Carlo harbour for the Saturday and Sunday of the race. "Pushing the boat out," he said, enjoying his own pun. Few others had yet realised the potential the race offered for promoting their business. He relished the role of pioneer, even if Havershall's could scarcely afford it without the base that Ginny's villa provided.

On a walk behind the race paddock during the practice day, Eustace ran into Archie Hoare, his stick-frame clad in flannel trousers and summer blazer. Wire-rimmed spectacles perched on his aquiline nose like scaffolding and he was strolling along arm in arm with a striking young woman he introduced as 'Pam'. Archie was now, at thirty-seven, the Managing Partner of Weatherstone & Hoare's. His father had retired the year before.

Eustace invited the couple to the yacht for the party after the race the next day. He pointed it out from a distance across the harbour. Archie took a second to assess its size, then promised to come. He also said the bank was, "In favour of investing behind new clients."

Eustace laughed, amused by the irony. "Your father once told me I had as much chance of a loan as the boxer Billy Wells."

"That was my father. And that was then. Europe is starting to change. Money is moving. Some rich and sometimes anonymous clients are looking for bolt holes, don't you know? They think there's a war brewing."

Eustace raised his eyebrows, but only partly suppressed his surprise.

"Oh, yes. Certain foreign types think that, sooner or later, they might need to flee and would rather not leave their money behind. They like the discretion of stable banks like mine." Archie shrugged. "I have money to lend if you have the right investment to offer."

"As you can see, Havershall's have ridden the storms. Profits are once again… substantial."

"And cash?"

"Cash is fine," Eustace said with a little less certainty.

"That's the perfect time to borrow — when you are turning every pound into two, or better, three. Think about it. We'll talk more."

As Archie walked away with his young lady, Eustace bit his lip and reminded himself how jealous he'd been when only Charlie Barrington-Brown could borrow money at the drop of a hat. It seemed that Eustace Havershall may at last be entering that club. Looking across the harbour, the yacht didn't feel so much of an extravagance.

On Saturday night, the Havershall party dined at the *Hotel de Paris*, circulating amongst the race drivers at a Royal gala hosted by Pierre de Polignac, Duke of Valentinois, and his wife, Princess Charlotte, the principality's nominal heir apparent. Everyone knew the Duke, not his wife, was the real heir, the one turning Monte Carlo into a playground for the rich. Charlotte, an illegitimate daughter, was adopted by the ruling Prince Louis II to prevent power slipping away to a distant German cousin. In return, Pierre, the son-in-law, had adopted the Grimaldi name to become part of the family.

Their ballroom outstripped all opulence Ginny had seen in her headiest days. She danced with William Grover-Williams, whom she had met after his win two years before, and Luigi Fagioli, a dashing young Italian driver. Their corporate guests were enchanted by the Havershalls' familiarity among the celebrities. Ginny was able to pass Grover-Williams on to Helen Corrigan as a dance partner, and Fagioli to a delighted Eugenie Dupont, Bertrand's wife.

On a bet from Ginny, Eustace, considerably drunk, was sent to ask Coco Chanel to dance. She was seated at a table with Samuel Goldwyn. She refused in perfect English.

Ginny, watching, thought it hilarious. She hadn't had so much fun since the previous season in Cap Ferrat. Afterwards, she wondered why not.

* * *

The view from the yacht was exquisite, but no good for watching the race, so Ginny had reserved a table in the rooftop café the Havershalls had previously frequented, overlooking the cars accelerating up towards the Casino.

While the guests gathered, Woody took the boys to the pits to view the cars. William had taken to calling him 'Uncle Wood'. Richard seemed to like Woody because they shared the same limp. They went along with Mrs Corrigan and Mrs Dupont, the ladies being delighted to drive the two pushchairs.

Their absence gave Eustace the chance to talk business with the abandoned men. Before lunch, Frederic Dupont — holding champagne and a *pain au chocolat* — quickly confirmed the brothers' intention to buy Havershall's machines. The 'Dead Keys' on Woody's H33 model made it perfect for their market. With that alone, Eustace felt the whole expense of Monaco justified.

Simon Corrigan's approach to business was more measured, a harder nut to crack. The Corrigans of 'Corrigan and Corrigan Trading Company' had been traders and businessmen for generations. Simon was the custodian of that family wealth. He sat with Eustace on the café balcony, chiselling spent tobacco out of his pipe with an ivory-handled pipetool and filling the bowl with fresh tobacco.

"This is how it is these days, Squire. I don't know how long India will be India, but that doesn't mean we can't make a pretty penny. Ten, fifteen more years — who knows? Do you follow their little man?"

Eustace did not immediately understand the reference.

"Gandhi," Simon explained. "He's back in the fold, as it were. Last year, marching to the coast and making his own salt so we'd have to arrest him. This year he's in England, negotiating. They call it a 'Round Table Conference', but a few special seats hold all the pointedness of power. They wish to decide the Future Constitution of India, but Mr Gandhi has already signed the pact that matters with the Viceroy."

Eustace might not grasp the politics of India, but he knew of Lord Irwin, the Viceroy. He'd been at Viscount Fairchild's wedding.

"Irwin wants to give India 'Dominion Status'," Simon continued. "If we Corrigans are in the right position, that means lots of typewriters. Don't you see, Squire? Dominion Status — in fact, any new constitution — requires a new bureaucracy of government. What does a dizzyingly complex civil service need? Clerks and typists, that's what. Assuming we can put off the bloodbath, they need typewriters."

"You said bloodbath?" Eustace picked at the word.

"Oh, yes, eventually." Simon lit the pipe with the bold flame of his petrol lighter. "The British can't rule forever. That's clear from everything Gandhi says. My dear chap, only the British could have kept the place from exploding for this long. We Brits have social division honed like a surgical instrument. Make sure the local groups have more reason to fear each other than resent their present overlords — that, in a nutshell, is India. Gandhi is dangerous precisely because he's humble and makes them think he isn't seeking power. God help us if that's enough to unite them behind him. In the meantime, we sell typewriters."

"Listen, Simon," Eustace began, thinking of sales. "Until the British economy recovers properly, I have manufacturing capacity to spare. Suppose, instead of buying your next shipment at your usual prices, I offered you a discount. Woody has done marvels with our manufacturing costs. Could you push us harder into India, and even into the markets beyond?"

Simon puffed on his pipe. "The Corrigans own ships, always have. For years, we moved Indian opium to China and Chinese tea back to England. That great triangle was my great-grandfather's fortune. We shipped whatever commodity fetched a higher price where we sold it than where we bought it."

"I could offer you exclusive rights to any of the countries your shipping arm can reach."

"Exclusive rights? I see you do need sales! But that could be interesting." Simon Corrigan sipped at his champagne. "Another thought comes to mind, Squire. The current attempts to be 'nice' to India and talk sweetness and light to Gandhi will, according to my sources, mean that trade tariffs will be dropped. Then, the floodgates open, especially if the Gold Standard is dropped. I'm told that's inevitable. Suppose I pay a percentage in advance to buy materials and so forth? Could you have machines ready to put on my boat the day the tariff falls? I like an adventure."

Louis Chiron in a Bugatti won the race. Eustace thought he had won the day. He left Monte Carlo with a reinvigorated partnership for Havershall's Indian business, the promise of sales in France, and an offer of money from Archie Hoare.

Coco Chanel came away with a million-dollar contract to design costumes for Samuel Goldwyn at MGM.

* * *

When their yacht sailed back to Cap Ferrat after the race, a drunken Woody was laid in his cabin and carried to the villa when they docked. William toddled behind those helping him, asking why his Uncle Wood wasn't walking and wondering if his leg had gone bad like Richard's.

Ginny was exhausted, but happy.

At bedtime that night, Eustace rested his hands on her shoulders as she sat at her dressing table, putting her face to bed.

"I'm tired. Too tired," she said, thinking she knew the ambition in his touch. She reached for his hand and tilted her head sideways against his forearm.

"No, it's not that, Gin. This weekend, I have the most marvellous crazy idea that things are going to be alright. I may yet justify your investment."

"*Justify?*"

"Yes."

"What an odd word to use. Justification is so—" She hesitated, didn't want to continue.

"Lower class?" he suggested.

"I did not say that. Take me down from your marble pedestal, Eustace. I do not need to be won over and again."

"All I want... all I need... is for the company to do well again. We might yet forge an empire from the ruins of this depression."

She looked at his reflection in the mirror and offered it a smile. "The company is doing well enough, isn't it?"

"I spoke with Archie Hoare," he continued. "He is ready to provide loans for further investments. Investments in other businesses, I mean"

"Wait! You mean the man who came on the boat after the race... with Pamela Mitford?"

His face showed her he had no idea.

"Oh, Eustace, really!"

"Was that—? Of the Mitford Sisters?"

"You didn't recognise her? Sometimes, Eustace, you are hopeless. You served the woman champagne."

"I was thinking about the money."

"You are three feet from one of the most celebrated beauties in England and you don't even notice." She laughed. "Perhaps I should feel flattered."

For a moment, he seemed confused, then he said, "Oh, what? You and Pamela Mitford... scarcely a contest."

"Ha! There is no hope for you," she told him. He hadn't noticed Pamela Mitford, but she knew he'd hardly noticed her either — the way she'd floated between the company guests, the dress she'd selected from a salon in Nice, the way she'd been *the* hostess. "What do you propose to do with your new found ability to raise funds?"

"Oh, nothing," he replied. "Almost nothing. It's nice to know it's there."

"Ah, I see." She turned in her seat to look at him. "You used to sleep in the backroom of the factory and we used to steal bicycles. Now you're in a villa on the Riviera, your business is turning against the tide and it feels good. Am I correct? Why else would you be discussing loans of money you no longer need, and which you say you have no intention of taking? It's the power you like."

"That's about the size of it," he admitted with a shrug. "I always imagined what I might do with Barrington-Brown's cash mountain."

He leant forward, kneading his fingers into the muscles below her shoulders, and pressed his nose against her forehead so the scent of her hair filtered into his nostrils. She smiled, no longer feeling quite so tired.

"Money is sexy, though, I must agree," she said.

During their time in Cap Ferrat, Ginny spent extended periods with her sons. She hadn't done so in quite a while. The gaping divide between them had become inescapable — differences that went far beyond the two inches that separated their heights now that Richard had started a growth spurt.

Richard was like his father in miniature and looked to him for everything, yet never got Eustace's attention as he deserved. When alone, he would sit and watch the world, stare at trees, as if studying the pattern of wind moving their branches. At bedtime, he loved Ginny reading him 'Winnie-the-Pooh', though he could already read it to himself if he tried.

William, by contrast, was a ball of uncontrolled energy. His features were finer — the Buckley blue eyes, the long slim fingers — but he charged around the villa, breaking things if breakable things were in his way. He played football on the lawn. He was already better than Richard. Richard, of course, had the disadvantage of a limp.

As a present for the holidays, Eustace had given Richard the same Meccano Outfit that Woody had previously bought for his own son. It was William who ended up playing with it, and roping in Eustace and

'Uncle Wood' to help. William's own present — a picture book — was quickly discarded.

Back In England, Ginny resolved to redouble the company's debt collecting efforts. If Eustace wanted money for investments, there would be no need for an Archie Hoare. Trusting banks was so 'un-Eustace' like.

Wilfred McCann had become Ginny's trusted 'hand' in all credit control matters. He now added two part-time 'associates' to his team — big, strapping ex-soldiers — and Ginny introduced extraordinary ways of evaluating a potential customer's credit worthiness. Instead of checking a new customer company, be it a distributor or wholesaler, she'd check on its owner.

"Does he have a family?" she'd ask.

"A wife, two sons, a daughter," would perhaps be the reply from the clerk charged with obtaining this information.

"And we know his address?"

"Yes, Mrs Havershall."

"Then give him credit. Family men are trustworthy."

Her credit control instructions to Wilfred were detailed. After two polite letters, Wilfred would go to a debtor's home address and ask for the sum owed. He would address the debtor courteously as 'Sir' or, occasionally, 'Madam', if the situation arose. Should he be given promises that were not fulfilled, he would visit again, arriving as a trio with 'his associates' to repeat the same script.

If a third visit proved necessary, Wilfred was instructed to ask for the money, but throw in compliments about the house, and the children, mentioning them by name and asking if they liked their school, perhaps naming several of their teachers.

A fourth visit was rarely required. The consequences of 'fourth visits' became embellished through gossip. Havershall's debt collections were soon the most feared in the industry, though there was never clear evidence that any fourth visit had ever happened.

Two weeks after Monte Carlo, Woody drove to the Perecs' house in Bristol. He thought it noble to give up another weekend of motor racing with the local Bugatti Club to visit his children. Something about his time as 'Uncle Wood' with Richard and William had left him feeling guilty.

James was now five years old. Woody could kneel on the lounge carpet and play 'Blow Football' — blowing a ball towards an opponent's tiny goal using a straw — or endlessly building and dismantling new constructions of Meccano. That made James happy.

At almost ten, Celia had eyes that reminded him of Mabel. She unnerved him. She called him 'Papa', but he did not feel much like her father. According to his mother-in-law, the girl was becoming a 'naughty' child. She had been dismissed from her school for refusing to join in the Christian prayers at morning assembly and for releasing doves into the school hall. Celia claimed that the doves were a symbol of peace. That had not stopped them perching on the beams above the stage and pooping on teachers seated below during the opening bars of the morning hymn.

"Of course, we're not of the gentile faith, but we don't encourage Celia," his mother-in-law assured him.

Woody thanked the ageing couple for their efforts and told them he would consider a girl's boarding school. He did not discuss it with his daughter.

There was no doubt that Havershall's had turned a corner in 1931. Sales growth returned. Profits followed. Cash followed too, first in a trickle, then in a flood thanks to Ginny's efforts. Havershall's was bucking a trend that continued elsewhere.

The failing UK government, beset by civil unrest and hunger marches, at last abandoned the Gold Standard on 21st September. The following month, Britain lurched into another General Election. A 'National Government' came to power, still led by Ramsay MacDonald, but now held up by Conservative MPs. As the promise to buy sterling with gold disappeared, the value of the British pound fell on foreign currency exchanges by twenty-five percent.

Simon Corrigan made good on his promises. Buying cheap pounds with rupees, he financed a huge stock of Havershall typewriters to be held in British warehouses along the mouth of the Thames ready for shipment. Just as Simon and Eustace had hoped, the countries of the British Commonwealth — a grouping of 'autonomous communities within the British Empire' defined five years previously — agreed to counter the lack of international trade by lowering the internal tariff barriers to each other's goods. The cost of selling goods into India was slashed. The floodgates opened and Havershall's machines were soon leaving the warehouses on the Corrigans' ships as fast as Eustace could make stock.

At the same time as this boost in exports, Havershall's foreign competition started to evaporate. The leading manufacturers of typewriters were American and production on the other side of the Atlantic had fallen sixty percent since the Wall Street Crash. Both America and Britain raised tariffs on goods traded between them in a bid to defend their domestic industries and Havershall's reaped the benefit. In home markets where British-based producers had faced the greatest competition from foreign suppliers, producers like Havershall's now had a freer rein. Although the total sales of typewriters shrank somewhat, the company was able to increase its share. It now fought toe to toe with one serious home-grown competitor — BBTL. *Bloody Barrington-Brown*, as Eustace called him.

Critical public sector contracts for equipping clerical staff in the Home Office, the Tax Office and a dozen local councils were still going to BBTL, but in the private and commercial sector, Havershall's held sway. The factory in Birmingham was running out of capacity and space.

The Midlands Manufacturing Association, a talking shop for owners and directors of companies, held its annual dinner in Birmingham's Grand Hotel and voted Eustace Havershall its 'Businessman of the Year'.

In celebration, Eustace bought himself a Bentley Speed Six, the car of the year for the man of the year. It arrived in time to ferry himself and Ginny to the ceremony.

Havershall's had taken a table for twelve and invited its senior managers. Woody and Ginny sat amongst them, watching Eustace praised for *his* creation of a typewriter business. They continued to sit, looking across the table at each other, while Eustace gave his speech.

Woody's anger at the praise heaped solely on Eustace lasted only a few days. He thought he understood a deeper truth. It was the exchange rate of the pound and the change in tariffs that had made the difference, but engineering was still the real driving force in the company, the underlying thing that created all else.

Despite the heavy drinking, Woody felt he was at the height of his creativity. Now he needed to prove he was still the heart of Havershall's.

He had maintained his interest in cash registers since his purchase of Remington's American design. Now he brought several other models into the 'Lab' at Duke Works. They were dismantled and analysed as he searched for direction.

Cash registers were electrical. Electricity was the obvious future. But the problem of British 'pounds, shillings and pence' still dogged him. He wanted to make a machine that added up British money using electricity, something with a power lead that plugged into the wall.

After months of trying, Woody carried his prototype up to the Havershall's boardroom and presented it to Eustace and Ginny. It came in a large steel box with a mechanical display of numbers on pop-up tags behind a glass window at the top, a till roll printer on the left of a sloping front facia and a stainless steel till at the base that opened when transactions were registered. He called it the HCR380. It was larger and heavier than competitor's machines and promised to sell for a much higher price. It had penny keys for 1d, 1d, 3d, and 6d, which were separated from the shilling keys for 1s, 1s, 2s, 5s, and 10s in two clusters in the middle of the facia. The pound keys on the right were marked £1, £1, £2, £5, £10, £20, £30 and £50. The duplication of certain keys was necessary to ensure that all values were possible.

Registering a complex item, the operator would engage a 'Shift-Lock' key, not dissimilar to that on a typewriter, which then allowed as many or as few keys as required to be locked down until the 'Item Sale' key was pressed. Pressing of this key printed the price onto the till roll and added it to the rolling sum that would be printed when the 'Sum Total' key was depressed. The largest total possible for a single item was £99, 19s and 11d. That involved pushing down a total of seventeen keys, plus the 'Shift-Lock' and 'Item Sale' keys.

The workings of the machine were impressive, but both Eustace and Ginny expressed doubts about Havershall's ability to sell it. This was not the response Woody had been looking for.

Ginny put it most clearly. "Havershall's sales staff are all 'typewriter men'."

"And our 'typing pool' sales girls know how to demonstrate their machines. As a company, we know nothing about cash registers," Eustace added.

"Because we've this notion of being 'typewriterists'?" Woody said, face darkening. "Isn't that what old Hoare called us? Back in the day? An insult. He thought you incapable, Captain. Perhaps he was right. Ruddy hell, I never thought it."

He placed his calculations of cost on the table and proposed a massive investment in production tooling. Support was called for.

Ginny shook her head.

"So you will you vote against my machine, Ginny?"

"I'm sorry. I shall abstain," she said. "I told you when I invested, I would not change the fact your vote didn't carry a majority. It did not then. It does not now. You will need my husband's support."

Woody fixed on Eustace expectantly.

"Dammit. Make a trial run," Eustace said. "Use machined parts instead of forgings, then we won't have to invest in the tooling."

"Yes, but we won't make a profit if we machine parts. It's too expensive that way. We need the tooling. Can't you see that?" Woody pointed out.

"I don't need a profit on prototypes. You need to show we can sell them, that's all."

"No, that's not what this is," said Woody. "It's half hearted backing. This isn't the way we used to do it. What happened to faith… and trust?"

"I believe in your engineering, Woody. Really. I always do. It's just that—" He hesitated for a moment.

"You believe in the engineering, but you won't commit to it? Do you still believe in me, Eustace?"

Not 'Captain' anymore. Woody was making a more direct appeal. Eustace understood the switch.

"It's thirty thousand pounds at least if you're wrong," he said. "It's a thousand or so to make a trial that proves you're right."

Woody stared at Ginny and then back at Eustace. Both seemed to have disappointed him.

"You knew I was right," Ginny said, driving home that evening with Eustace at the wheel. "Havershall's can't sell that thing."

"But, Gin, you didn't vote."

"And you didn't say no."

"I couldn't."

"I see," she said heavily. "I suppose that's understandable. You know, of course, that he is an unreliable drunk?"

"I'm sorry," he said unspecifically.

A run of prototypes had been the least he could agree to when Woody was doing the asking.

Chapter Fifteen

Twenty-five HCR380s cash register were made in January of 1932. They cost nearly three thousand pounds, an amount that could never be recouped by their selling price. They were introduced to the sales staff with a marketing fanfare — a machine that added up British money, all powered by electricity.

"The future," Woody told everyone.

Initially, the sales staff were enthusiastic. Distributors rushed to put the limited models available into stock. The size of the trial run was outstripped two-to-one by orders and the factory mobilised to make a second batch, still at the elevated manufacturing cost. Eustace would not yet relent on the cost of tooling for full production.

Woody sensed a coming triumph. At home, Eustace told Ginny, he thought he might be wrong. Given the decision again, should he have gone to Archie Hoare, put money into the project and planned for success from the beginning? Look at the situation now, making a loss on each sale, and all for a lack of bold faith. Woody deserved faith, even when no one and nothing else did.

Ginny kept her counsel.

Four weeks after launch, reality kicked in. Distributors started returning the HCR380s, describing the product as a 'white elephant', twice the price customers wanted to pay for a cash register and having 'luxury features' that involved pressing a bewildering number of keys. To make things worse, machines that did sell developed niggling printer faults that left many till receipts with nothing in the shillings' column.

Woody swore he could fix these 'teething problems' on the second batch, but that new batch reached the shipping department in time to meet the returns of the unsold originals.

Woody was heart-broken. "All my best went into that," he told his fellow directors.

The drinking spree that followed shocked even Eustace.

In spring 1932, the hardest tickets to obtain were to the opening of the Shakespeare Memorial Theatre in Stratford-upon-Avon, an evening attended by the Prince of Wales.

The previous incarnation of the theatre had been gutted by a fire six years before and the design of this replacement had been the subject of heated competition. Seventy-one entries were submitted. The winner, Elisabeth Scott, was the first female architect ever appointed to a major building project in Britain.

Reactions were mixed. Sir Edward Elgar was to be the theatre's new musical director but, after visiting the site, declared that the 'awful female' had produced something 'unspeakably ugly' and refused to have anything to do with it. George Bernard Shaw declared Scott's design the only submission displaying 'theatrical sense'. He'd earlier sent a telegram to the theatre's chairman congratulating him on having the old building burnt down.

When Ginny saw the pictures, she knew she had to be there for the building's opening. It was a beautiful space to contain the performances of her most favourite of the arts, which only added to the compulsion.

She schemed for tickets. Havershall's had supplied typewriters to the finance department behind the theatre's new box office. She negotiated with the manager over the phone. Two stalls seats for William Bridges-Adams' production of 'Henry IV- Part 1' on Press Night cost her three Havershall H33s.

She bought a new outfit costing her as much again — House of Reville couture from the last collection by Victor Stiebel. She and Eustace would make an evening of it, she told him. He had to cancel a business trip to attend. They travelled down in the taxi from Edgbaston.

"'*Once more into the breach,*'" he offered, as if he regarded the best suit she'd forced him to wear as some kind of battle armour. "I thought you always hated these parades of glamour."

"This is special. And anyway, you're quoting the wrong play. I should like to spend one night with my husband without talk of business... the whole evening, you understand?"

"I cannot help myself. Commerce is my vocation," he protested.

"Ha," she retorted.

"'*Tis no sin for a man to labor in his vocation.*' And that is Falstaff in Act Three, I believe," he said. He felt more than fifty percent certain, having read the 'Complete Works' in his father's library years before.

"I shall take your word for it," Ginny said. She knew he was correct, but admitting it would be wrong.

"It will probably be short," he said sarcastically, "since it's more important to be observed in the foyer and the bar than to observe the play, don't you think?"

"Especially to be seen next to the Prince," she added. "Though tonight, we fear they will be disappointed. Mr William Bridges-Adams has the reputation for producing Shakespeare plays without a single cut. They call him 'Mr Unabridges-Adams'."

"I suppose we must make the best of our entrance, then."

"Oh, I intend to," she said as they pulled up outside. "Isn't the theatre magnificent? Edward Elgar can go hang. Hurrah for Miss Scott."

She gathered her shawl around her shoulders and, emerging from their taxi, stepped onto a red carpet. She felt for a moment all the elegance of a court lady arising within her and played the part she had left behind in 1920.

Ascending the steps of the new theatre, her Stiebel evening dress caught in her sway, photographers turned their cameras in her direction. Eustace walked proudly beside her. The future King, arriving ten minutes behind, merited no more flashbulbs than Mrs Eustace Havershall.

Afterwards, as they waited outside for the taxi to take them home, he told her how beautiful the dress looked, though her shoulders now appeared chilly. He was proud to offer her his jacket to keep them warm.

"I should like to come and live in Stratford and go to plays all the time," Ginny declared. "Don't you see, Eustace, it's pretty along the river. And with this at its heart, it feels right. The house in Edgbaston is too small now we have the boys, don't you think? It's no place to raise them."

"It's far too far from the factory," he said. "Besides, it's quite impossible, what with the delicate state of business."

"Oh, fiddlesticks, don't tell me that. I know more of the state of finances than you do! I collect the money!"

She saw his face change immediately. She knew she had said too much — you cannot tell a man you know more about his business than he does — but, too late, she could not take it back.

* * *

Ginny's picture was on Page One of the local newspaper — 'Mrs Havershall, *Wife of Midlands Businessman of the Year, Eustace Havershall, arrives for the opening of Stratford's Shakespeare Memorial Theatre'.*

Eustace loved the image. He went to the newspaper office and bought the negative. He had it printed and mounted in a 12x8-inch silver frame and sat it on his office desk alongside the family photograph from Long Island.

Ginny hated the headline. It belonged to a woman with a borrowed name and borrowed importance. She never wore that Stiebel dress again.

The change in import and export tariffs continued to do wonders for Havershall's sales, but this was not true for most British industries. Those facing competition from within the Empire lost out to imported goods that now paid reduced rates of duty. Throughout 1932, the economy floundered in its trough of unemployment and poverty. Only misery was on the rise.

The National Unemployed Workers' Movement organised the 'Great National Hunger March against the Means Test' which included thousands of people in eighteen contingents. A petition demanding the abolition of the test had a million signatures. It was to be presented to Parliament when the marchers converged on Hyde Park.

The first contingent, which had taken thirty-one days to march from Glasgow, were greeted by a crowd of a hundred thousand upon arrival in London. The newspapers declared the gathering a 'threat to public order' and pointed to the communist sympathies of the organisers.

The government used the police to confiscate the petition. Lord Trenchard, the Metropolitan Police Commissioner, mobilised seventy thousand officers, Britain's most extensive public order action since 1848. Many people were injured in the fruitless scuffles that ensued.

In Nottingham, John Havershall Petty Products Ltd — after several years under management by Eustace's brother — had lurched from regular annual profits in excess of twenty thousand pounds to a punishing loss in every year from 1929 to 1931. It sublet one of the two storage warehouses adjoining its factory. It laid off a quarter of its staff.

The newly reduced border tariffs between countries in the British Commonwealth let in lace and cloth from the Indian subcontinent. By the early summer of 1932, the company was bleeding away as if it had opened a vein, not just a lack of cash, but a lack of any future.

Eustace's mother phoned on a Saturday morning, not waiting for their Sunday call, to beg him, if he could, to do 'something'.

He was silent for a moment, wrestling obligations, past and present.

"Will they meet me?" he asked, referring to his father and brother.

"I shall make them," she said.

"Did you ever have that kind of sway?"

"In this, I do."

Even with his mother's support, the chasm between himself and his family seemed too wide to breach. He ended the call with a heavy heart.

"It may be a disaster, but what can I do?" Eustace asked Ginny over their Saturday lunch.

Beside him, Richard — now nearly six — was showing some resistance to the fried egg and sardines on his plate.

"Eat up. Fish is good for you. Do you want me to cut it up?" Ginny asked, glancing his way.

It seemed Richard could manage when he wanted to show his father that he could. She watched his improved performance for a few seconds, then turned back to Eustace, dabbing her mouth with a napkin.

"This is all about family," she observed. "Your father offered you a loan when you most needed it."

"Only because you threatened to bring the Haversahalls to shame. And anyway, it was my grandmother who arranged it."

"Fiddlesticks. I'm sure your father wanted to give you the money. He needed the smallest threat to have an excuse."

"That is not how I remember it."

"Then perhaps I choose to remember it that way. We can afford the generosity."

"How can *we* afford any *generosity*? And why should we?"

She considered the question for only a moment.

"We must," she concluded. Then more gently, "You must. Be generous."

"I thought you were set on a house in Stratford?" he said. "Havershall's would have to provide a special dividend for that. It needs to maintain its liquidity."

"You bring that up now as mere convenience. Do not confuse what I want with your family's need, Eustace."

"I am not confused," he declared, straightening his back against his chair. "Oh, no, this is *their* tragedy, not mine, and not ours."

"You don't mean that."

"I think I do. Yes, I'm sure I do."

"Eustace, you are 'Businessman of the Year'," she said with a touch of irony.

"Yes, but I am not a 'John'. Johns are supposed to succeed."

"Damn it, Eustace! They need you. I will wait. Have I not waited before? Besides there is your duty. And that is all."

He hesitated. She said, "Alright, I will mortgage the villa in Cap Ferrat and loan them the money myself then. There! I'll put Buckley money into the Havershalls… again."

"You will not! You will not interfere with your money!"

He held himself back from banging the table, took a calming breath and slowly shook his head.

"I hate this duty. What shall I do? Take a loan from a bank only to give it out again. What would Woody say? What would you say as a shareholder of our company, if you were not such a charitable benefactor?"

"You said you have no more manufacturing space in Birmingham. It seems your family's premises has no work. Offer them a loan, and offer them business so they may make a profit." Ginny opened her palms in a gesture that seemed to suggest an obvious conclusion.

"Make typewriter parts instead of lace? No one could make my father or brother agree. I'd like to see it though," said Eustace, cracking into a wicked smile.

Richard piped up, "Daddy, Daddy, can I get down?" His plate was empty.

Eustace gave his son a sharp 'don't-interrupt-me-stare'. Ginny said, "My goodness what's the rush?"

"It's the cricket. Daddy said we could go."

Ginny looked at Eustace.

"The All-India team are touring. It's just across the way," he explained.

"Daddy says the *Mar-Jar of Poor-band-aar* is playing," Richard said.

"That's the Maharaja of Porbandar," Eustace corrected. "He's the captain, a friend of the Corrigans."

"Really?" said Ginny, trying to sound impressed. "There wouldn't be business associates going, now would there? City councillors who might or might not grant you something or other?"

"I'm taking the boys," Eustace pleaded. "They wanted to go."

"They wanted to go?"

"To see the *Mar-Jar*," Richard said helpfully.

"Be careful, Eustace, where your family starts and stops," she said.

Eustace wore his best suit, a bracken patterned Harris Tweed, and best matching hat. He parked his Bentley Speed Six in a side street off the Lace Market, a distance away from the 'John Havershall Petty Products' warehouses. He offered a rag-footed boy sixpence to watch it with a thruppenny bit in advance.

He started walking, back among the flat-faced brick buildings of his childhood. The Lace Market had grown grubbier in his absence, its brickwork chipped, the edge-eaten signs on buildings of businesses that had gone. A shiver rippled down his spine. He couldn't find a comfortable way to hold his hands. Not locked together, or in his pocket, or balled into fists. He wanted to shut his eyes, but he was afraid of what he might see, or what he might imagine.

His mother had brought him to the Havershall factory a few times, never his grandfather or his father. He remembered one visit with his brothers — Christmas time, snow, and horses and carts struggling on the slushy streets. One poor beast had fallen and broken its leg.

He wondered if he had heard the gun shot. He couldn't remember, only that his mother had shepherded them all away very quickly. Why did he recall that now? And why did he think of Masterson?

Nottingham's Lace Market — a quarter-mile square of salesrooms and warehouses — had been the centre of the world's lace industry in Victorian England. Unlike many processes of the Industrial Revolution, lace making was for a time split between knitting carried out in the home to produce the 'brown lace', and the warehouse owners who organised the singeing, gassing, mending, bleaching, dyeing and embroidering that produced the finished cloth. But as the fingers of mechanisation grew longer, the industrious homeworkers were driven out of business and sucked out of the country air, consumed in a heady brew of production. The so-called warehouses became factories.

At the century's turn, the area around the Lace Market contained two hundred lace making companies producing cloth, their working machines a clunky hell of mechanisation, the shop floor a horrible soup of toxic odours. But the industrialisation failed. By 1932, the contrasts between Birmingham's growth and Nottingham's decline were stark. Along the roads he walked now, the number of lace companies had halved as dominance faded. Fierce world competition had arisen after the war, much of it from Asia, and the Depression and the disastrous early years of the Thirties were busy sending the remaining lace companies spinning towards extinction. Reduced import tariffs dealt the final blow.

The firms Eustace saw now on those streets included a printer, a bookseller, an engraver, a cardboard box manufacturer and a manufacturing chemist. A typewriting agency and a secretarial training college were opening up. He smiled when he saw the temporary signs on the college doors. It was almost as if his proud successes in Birmingham had reached here before him.

He walked in through a loading bay door in a tall brick building, came up the cavernous hall between the ear-splitting clatter, through clawing air and smoke, so different to the manufacture of typewriters. He noticed how the machines here produced a discordant cacophony, not the hum or percussive thump of hydraulic presses.

Down the long wall to his left sat nine upright looms, each the size of a car; up the middle of the factory, another dozen machines, these with a circular base with the area of a large garden fishpond and long arms that circulated over the top on a frame. Elsewhere rows of women at benches beavered away, inspecting or mending cloth. Across to his right were the banks of racking, holding stock. An awful lot of stock, he observed. Wasn't there another company warehouse close by? Was there more in that?

In short, the factory felt ancient. Back in Birmingham, Woody would never be content unless Havershall's had a new manufacturing machine, a faster, better technique for one part or another in the typewriter jigsaw. Here Eustace recognised tired looms from his childhood — the same open frames, unguarded. There were too many young faces barely out of school. He stared at open jaws and spindles waiting to suck in fingers and hands like wheat into a threshing machine.

Hadn't he lectured and campaigned against such things? Why had his brother and father never sought something better when they still had the chance? Ginny's entreaties echoed in his head. *"Be generous. They need you."*

He found he did not feel so inclined.

* * *

As he reached the offices, a middle-aged woman in a hairnet and grey office dress greeted him and offered a cup of tea. She seemed to recognise him. He did not recognise her.

She escorted him up two flights of stairs and into the boardroom. It had one thick window looking over the works and an oak table running up its middle that had seen better days. He was holding a china cup and a chipped saucer when the two Johns arrived.

Greetings were polite and perfunctory. Each asked about the others' wife, the children, their general health.

"I'm sure I don't know why you're here," said John Junior.

"I came at Mother's request."

"She had no right," said John Senior. His father had suffered two further strokes in recent years, both mild. The left cheek dripped like candle wax now. His shoulders were hunched, hair almost gone. To Eustace, John Junior looked more and more a younger version of the same, though without the unmatched halves to his face.

"No Havershall should assume the rights to privilege, or success, or to be kept in the manner to which they are accustomed. I learnt that, Father. I had to, didn't I?" Eustace paused to glance at his brother. "Perhaps I should have told Mother the Johns would have no use for me and saved myself a journey."

"Damn you, Boy," his father interrupted. "If you came here with your impertinence to gloat—"

"Shall we be calm then and talk of money?" Eustace said, cutting him short. "I hear you cannot pay the wages and will soon have to call in the bank and an administrator."

Neither answered. Eustace gazed through the window onto the activity below, the consuming clatter muted by the glass.

"I will buy the business from you," he said, out of the blue.

"What? No. I thought you came to offer loans?" Brother John replied.

"And I thought, you didn't know why I was here. You just said so. Well, Brother, I have decided not to throw good money after bad. But I will *save* you."

His father looked at Eustace. Brother John looked at his father.

"I will buy the business at a fair price, assuming you wish to sell," Eustace continued. "We'll modernise the factory, put its space to better use."

"Better use?"

Thinking of the idea Ginny had planted, he said, "Typewriter parts. This will be a subsidiary of the 'Havershall and Woodmansey Typewriting Company.'"

He knew they would hate that, not just being helped, but being owned.

Eustace walked back to the Bentley and paid the boy his other thruppence. A drizzle had overtaken the streets of the Lace Market. The Harris Tweed was feeling soggy.

He took off his damp hat and sat in the driver's seat with his head dipped against the steering wheel. His body was shaking and, after a while, tears rolled down his cheeks. He could not stop them.

"Did I not tell you? Did I not say, 'Be generous'?" Ginny raged when he reported his meeting. She had stayed up, awaiting his return.

"You did."

"And?"

"Some things were unavoidable."

"I said loan them money and you have bought the whole company. Removed it from their hands. How could you?"

Eustace unpacked the plan he had been formulating. "I am not foolish enough to put my money... *our* money... behind a management that failed. John Havershall Petty Products Ltd has accumulated losses, as well as land and buildings. That's handy."

"What does that mean? *'Handy'*?"

"When I looked at their accounts, I remembered a banker's trick. I rang up your friends, the accountants, to check I had it it right. You see, past losses are more valuable than you might imagine. You add them to your future profits so the sum equals zero and that, dear Gin, is the amount that the tax man demands in company taxes. Zero! Don't you see? Future profit with no tax."

"This was supposed to be about duty," she said.

"Quite so. But, Gin, it is good business. We'll sell the company's spare warehouse and add these tax losses. We may need a small loan from Archie but we won't need it for more than six months. I think I can stand for that."

"You would buy your father's company for its land and its tax losses?" she said slowly. "You humiliated them!"

"You wanted me to save it. I saved it."

She looked at him for a long time.

"Businessman of the Year," she hissed. "This is a petty revenge, Eustace. I'll have no part of it."

"It's good business," he repeated. "Woody and I will vote it through, if you will not."

Ginny had never felt such apoplectic anger in her life. This was too much. How could Eustace do this? What had he become? She slept on it, or tried to. She tossed and turned without finding rest.

The next morning, she took the train to Stratford and looked through all the windows in a row of estate agents until she found the one with the nicest leather chairs.

"Can I help you, Madam?" the office manager asked as she entered.

She offered him a gloved handshake.

"Mrs Eustace Havershall," she said. "I'd like to buy a house. A really expensive house."

That same morning, Eustace tried to telephone his mother. She would not come to the phone.

The fourth property Ginny visited was the one. Not so much a house, in fact, but a small mansion off the Tiddington road with a few acres of garden that rolled down to the River Avon at the back.

It was everything she had dreamed of.

The estate agent named a price. Ginny made an offer.

She arranged a mortgage on the villa in Cap Ferrat and paid a large deposit in cash in her own name. She did not tell Eustace for a week.

"I meant to let you know, I bought a house," she said at dinner, when she was content that enough days had passed to make her point.

He was so shocked he did not register what she meant. With his roast beef on his plate, he had been telling her about a contract in Scotland.

"I assumed," she said, "that with your clever purchasing and selling of land and all that tax manoeuvring, I could expect a return from our profits. The interest on the mortgage is not that much, I assure you, but yes, from now on, I shall require regular dividends from our company to cover it."

"You... You do not understand money," he said blindly.

"I have told you before, I understand it perfectly," she replied. "When one is born rich, one knows how to spend money. Born rich *and* smart, one spends it on the things that matter."

He did not reply.

She continued, "Born without money, it seems its very accumulation becomes the value you place upon yourself. Isn't that so? Spending is so much harder when owning it is what makes you feel valuable."

"What is it, Gin? Are you now trying to become a property mogul? Or are you punishing me? Is this revenge?"

"Revenge? No, Eustace, but I am a shareholder. You make a company decision without me. And I make this decision. I assure you, it's a lovely house. I did not realise how much I wanted a 'country retreat', so to speak. No weekend shooting will be required of you, only the theatre."

Once Eustace had calmed himself and agreed that there was nothing to be done but accept his wife's new purchase, he marked off a room as *his* library and set about filling shelves with books. Unlike his father, who kept books with no intention of reading them, Eustace swore he would one day read every one he collected.

Chapter Sixteen

Stalin held absolute power in Russia; Mussolini tightened his grip on Italy — communism and fascism. Woody and Eustace disagreed on which was the worse extreme, though the 'freedoms' of democracy clearly left other countries teetering in uncertainty. Totalitarian regimes promised stability, even if the battles to achieve it were bloody.

Spain was caught in the turmoil. King Alfonso XIII, for years in the grip of his military, had called an election. On sweeping wins for socialists and liberal republicans, he fled the country, but this new democracy did not serve the country well. Regulation of salaries, contracts and working hours in favour of workers caused increasing friction with employers. Decrees limiting the use of machinery and strikes by unions seeking to restrict women's employment stoked a class struggle. Conflicts escalated. Ultimately, the reforms of a Republican-Socialist government alienated the voters who'd elected it. Fascism fed on the poorly used freedoms a right to vote unlocked. Spain was a microcosm of the whole idealistic struggle.

In Germany, an even more dangerous totalitarianism emerged from its youthful rites of passage. A young Adolf Hitler, leader of the Nazi party, had attempted to seize power in a failed coup back in the early Twenties. He was imprisoned. Freed now, and with free flowing oratory and a mastery of propaganda, Hitler championed pan-Germanism, anti-Semitism and anti-communism. He attacked the Treaty of Versailles and denounced international capitalism. What he was against masked what he stood for. People voted for him. An elected monster. By November 1932, the Nazi Party had the most seats in the German Reichstag.

Eustace's offer for John Havershall Petty Products was, in fact, generous, a little more than he could have bought the business for had he waited until it was officially insolvent.

His father retired. His brother was paid compensation for his redundancy. Eustace took new shares in the name of Havershall's, leaving his relatives only a non-voting minority in the Nottingham subsidiary, and installed himself as Chairman and Managing Director. He injected an inter-company loan of thirty-thousand pounds, half of which had to be procured from Archie Hoare's bank. "There, you see," he told Ginny. "I am borrowing to save the family."

He pointed out that, in this arrangement, part of the profits still went to the two Johns, should there ever be any. She was neither impressed nor placated.

Eustace arrived in Nottingham as the new Managing Director, determined to make something of the factory space, with Woody as his wingman. The failure of his cash register had made Woody's voice quieter. His captain was his captain. He followed.

"These machines need more work than I've got time to give them, unless you want me to move here," Woody declared when first examining the place. "Besides half of it's full of old stock. Maybe I don't understand the cloth business."

"Nothing to understand," Eustace replied.

Standing amongst the racks, they were bathed in the mouldering odours of lace, huge reels of it that weren't quite fresh.

"Rotting money," he declared. "They've always made lace and they don't know how to stop, whether they sell it or not."

He opened his arms towards the racks of lace.

"Sleepwalkers have to wake up," he added.

The following day, Eustace set out to sell the surplus for five shillings on the pound. He found a rival keen to buy on the understanding that Havershall's was about to abandon that section of the market. "Who but a fool would buy excess lace?" Eustace thought. He sold it gratefully, shaking on the deal less than a fortnight after he took control. On paper, it was a sale at a big loss. In reality, it brought the company the lifeblood of cash. The factory floor started to clear. It even smelt better. Only a quarter of it now made lace.

The company's adjoining warehouse, currently sublet to a motor repair shop that worked on trams and buses, was offered to its owner. When the repair shop owner declared he could not raise the funding to buy it, Eustace sold the warehouse to a property investment fund, who took on the repair shop as tenant. Thousands more dropped into the coffers.

In three months, he was able to repay the loan to Weatherstone & Hoare's completely. Eustace felt delighted at his accomplishment. He pointed out to Ginny that this was well in advance of his plan.

"I have my house in Stratford and my mortgage, Eustace. Will I have dividend enough to pay the interest?"

"You most certainly will," he promised proudly.

She looked at the company accounts. "I see we have become asset strippers," she said.

On his next visit to Nottingham, Eustace noticed that two large machines he and Woody had condemned on the shop floor were still lying idle in a row of working looms. On a whim, he inspected their inner mechanisms, expecting to see only ancient history, but he found recent welds and fixes holding the most broken components together. The work exuded quality, as surprising as if needlepoint stitching had been used to mend sacks of potatoes. He noticed some of the gears and pulleys were not original. Holes had been re-drilled and fitted with bushes to make space for different gearing.

"Who did this?" he asked a girl operating the adjacent machine. She could be no more than eighteen, he thought.

The girl took a few steps forward, leaning in to examine the repairs. "Ray Cropper," she said with a nod.

"What? With hand tools?" He had seen no proper workshop in the factory. "That's almost impossible."

The girl shrugged.

"This Ray? Where will I find him?"

"No," she said.

"No, what?"

"No, not a him. Ramona Jean, see." She laughed. There was a gap in her teeth. "Needed fixing, so I fixed it. Me dad taught me welding and that before he scarpered. Here, are you the new gaffer?"

Eustace laughed. "If you're the new apprentice engineer."

Ramona Jean Cropper — already 'Ray' to everyone but Eustace — had her first success in her new role by creating a production line for ink ribbons out of old lace making equipment. Havershall's had previously bought ribbons from specialist suppliers, but all it took was expertise in handling reels of cloth, some tape slitters and a lot of rather gungy ink. The savings to a manufacturer of typewriters were significant.

She soon became a regular and strange sight around the Nottingham works. A scrawny youth, delicate facial bones, a thin nose, sharp eyes, she took to wearing overalls that were always too big and open at the front, showing a white shirt stained with black grease. She had a flat cap too large for her head and walked around with tools weighing down her pockets.

She said she wanted to *educate meself.*

In the next four years, she would go through night school and achieve an engineering degree through part-time study. Afterwards, she enrolled in Nottingham University for a PhD. Her subject was 'Novel Design Materials in Contemporary Typewriters'.

Eustace paid for it all. And told no one. Especially not Woody. All Eustace ever said to Woody was, "Now you won't have to move to Nottingham."

She and Eustace agreed that 'Ramona' didn't suit her and 'Ray' seemed too male.

"How about we spell it 'R-A-Y-E' and you pronounce it like everyone else, Gaffer?"

He found that agreeable. Ray, or Ramona, became 'Raye'.

Reshaping the Nottingham business consumed much of Eustace's time in that next year. Ginny had a house to remodel and typewriter sales in Duke House to look after. She broke her own rules and went in more than three days a week to keep up. The journey into the office was long and difficult and she gave up her twice-weekly efforts to play tennis, which had been rekindled at Cap Ferrat. She didn't tell him, because distance had been one of his objections to Stratford.

The sales handled by the Birmingham office continued to grow rapidly under her influence. She called Woody into the sales office when Eustace wasn't around and offered a olive branch.

"See, Woody, the profits and the cash are up. It's time for a new model of typewriter, don't you think?"

He told her of his dream to make an electric machine. He offered to show her the drawings.

"Not that radical. Not yet anyway. I'm thinking of a compromise," she said.

"A compromise?"

"Let's call it a coalition. We could help each other, and help the firm. The salesmen tell me the H5 has outlived itself. It's more than ten years old. We need something ten years better. Not an electric and not another cash machine, but I'll support you for the money… if it's for a new typewriter."

"Even against Eustace?" he asked. "He's decided he wants to buy more companies. Not make new machines."

"I think my husband is — shall we say? — overly ambitious with money. We will see about his new companies."

Woody was not certain what was being offered. Eustace and Ginny's games baffled him. The hidden conflicts seemed to get more involved and layered every day.

Woody's development of the 'ten-year-advancement', soon named the 'H50', used improved techniques in aluminium casting to form the chassis of the machine. He consulted Wallace Devereux of 'High Duty Alloys Ltd' in Slough, one of the world's leading authorities on metal casting. They struck a deal for technical support.

The prototype H50 was a beauty — finger pressures required on the keys were lighter by a third, making the machine easier to type on. The carriage was smoother and quieter, the casing lacquered with a dark resin that reflected the light as if from depths far within. Ginny joked it was fit to be exhibited in a gallery.

But buying the tools for proper production would cost money. It provoked the perpetual debate in a growing company — too many investment opportunities to consider and only so much cash to pursue them. Which of them should be chosen? It came to a head in the board meeting of February 1933.

Against the H50, Eustace argued a financial point. Wasn't it now obvious how much profit there was in buying broken companies, and how many broken companies like John Havershall Petty Products were there in Depression-era Britain? Now was the time to buy. He had heard that BBTL was bidding for Christchurch, Salt and Bingley Ltd, a small rival typewriter manufacturer in Blackburn.

"They own a corner of an industrial estate, but it's already surrounded by new housing. I know a developer willing to take the land. We could arrange a quick in and out, like we did in Nottingham, and take all their current production into Duke Works for a tidy profit. The residents are crying out for room to build a school and more family homes."

"More *family* homes?" Ginny repeated. His use of the word was too transparent. He seemed to think saying 'family' was all that was needed to persuade her, but Ginny had come prepared, positioning herself an extra foot from her husband along one side of the table, a little nearer to Woody.

"We made more money restructuring the Nottingham business than from anything else in these last six months," Eustace argued.

"Selling assets, Eustace. You can only do that once."

Woody agreed with a nod.

"You want to put money into the future? Well, Woody, this is how we get it," Eustace insisted.

He turned on Ginny. "And you wanted your house in Stratford. How are we paying the mortgage for that? By paying out cash for dividends, that's how. We can't do that and go after every investment. Right now, the shortest term gains, that's what we should keep driving for."

"Whatever you do with Christchurch-and-whatever's, we insist upon investment for the H50 first. Future products," she said, as if stating a campaign slogan.

"*We* insist?" he repeated.

"We," she confirmed. "The *typewriterists*. Those who think this company makes writing machines."

She glanced at Woody and the board room fell silent. Eustace shuffled uneasily, his skin starting to itch. He looked over at Woody. Woody's intentions were plain.

"This time, I *will* vote, should we need a majority," Ginny warned.

"No… No, we will not need to vote," Eustace conceded.

They did not need to vote, because he could not stand to be defeated. Money for the H50 was passed unanimously. The smile she gave him seemed designed to push him away, not draw him in.

After the restructure of the Nottingham business, Woody, the night-time scholar of economics and politics, described Eustace as 'the captain who buys your house, sells its furniture, then sets it on fire, claims the insurance and finally sells off the land.'

As Eustace saw it, all he needed was enough liquidity to buy ailing companies and enough guile to close them down, moving anything of value to the other Havershall's factories as quickly as the land and buildings could be sold. He claimed that a job offered in Birmingham or Nottingham, justified a job lost elsewhere. *Havershall's looked after its own.*

Ginny and Woody had, for once, successfully disagreed. He wondered why this loyal friend she had called a drunk was now on her side. When she had bought her shares, he had never imagined they might team up together. It hardened Eustace's determination. He called Archie Hoare and asked about another loan.

"A big one," he added. His hatred and suspicion of banks could be put aside for this.

* * *

In 1933, power struggles were growing everywhere, not just inside Havershall's, and not just in Britain.

Hitler's minority government put forward the *Ermächtigungsgesetz* (Enabling Act). The act allowed the German Cabinet to dictate laws for the following four years without parliamentary consent. Opposing members of the parliament were arrested to prevent them voting.

A supposedly temporary but absolute power proved irreversible. Hitler changed the law to make the Nazis the one legal political party in Germany. Democracy was *democratically* abandoned.

While this Enabling Act was passing, Albert Einstein, the greatest mind of the age, had been travelling back to Germany from America. He went to the consulate in Antwerp in Belgium and renounced his German citizenship. He saw the future holocaust more clearly than the politicians of Europe.

He acted. They dithered.

After the boardroom argument, a successful H50 launch felt all important. Ginny took control. She centred her sales strategy on improving the company's profile in London.

Havershall's still ran a bi-annual typing competition and owned a trio of showrooms in the capital, though these had recently dwindled in importance. Ginny refreshed the showroom staff, judging that the first wave of employees, now approaching their forties, no longer represented the young single women to be found in typing pools. Their product demonstrations no longer had that 'stylish' impact on the buyers who decided what machines went into big offices. She doubled the prize money in the typing contest, persuaded the Sunday Times and Tatler magazine to run articles on the heats and final.

"Typing on these lighter modern machines will produce new records for speed," she promised the eager journalists. Behind the scenes, she made sure the contest produced speed records and photogenic contestants.

The winner was Amelia Stewart, the twenty-three-year-old daughter of a British diplomat, educated in St Hilda's College Oxford. She had learned to type at Skerry's College in Edinburgh while preparing for Civil Service entrance examinations, but had eventually found employment in the Bank of Scotland more to her liking. Now she was in London. Being tall, she carried off the modern midi-length day dresses — floral prints, puff sleeves, big collars — with aplomb. In the backless, sleeveless Hollywood evening gowns, she shone. Her typing peaked at nearly one hundred and fifty words per minute. To Ginny, she was the winner before she laid hands on a H50 keyboard.

Amelia was photographed a few weeks after her victory on the arm of an exiled Russian Count, twenty years her senior, and then — during a brief trip to England — of Charlie Chaplin, who was forty-four at the time and in-between marriages. All good publicity, Ginny declared.

She chose a picture of Amelia for billboards advertising the new machine, posed not unlike Maybelline Stokes's promotion for Hayberry-Peats. Ginny was fully aware of what she was doing — the physical beauty she was using to sell Havershall's wares. It was the way the world worked and the H50 had to succeed — for Havershall's, for Woody, and for Ginny Havershall too.

Eustace's father died in November 1933. Another stroke, this time much larger, swept him away.

When his brother's phone call came, Eustace was in Exeter at a meeting of Havershall's southern distributor with three of the company's regional salesmen and Amelia Stewart, who was there to demonstrate the H50. He met the news stiffly, said he would drive to Nottingham the following day, then went back to his business appointments. He did not cry.

He called the offices in Birmingham and the house in Stratford, only to find that Ginny was en route between the two. He left a message.

That evening, the Havershall's team went drinking in the Zodiac Bar of the Royal Clarence Hotel next to the cathedral. They were drunk, but he stayed sober. At two in the morning, he was in Amelia Stewart's suite, drinking room-service coffee when the last of the salesmen left. Amelia sat and listened to him talk about Ginny and his boys, the twisted history of the business and his relationship with the 'Johns'.

"It seems that your typewriters were almost to spite them," she observed. There was a soothing Scottish lilt to her accent. She smelt vaguely of poppies and summer fields.

"Yes, maybe they were. At first anyway," he mused.

"What are they for now, then?"

He shook his head. "I don't think I really know."

When he looked at his watch, he said, "I think I should go."

She did not say either 'stay' or 'go', but as she saw him to the door, she kissed him chastely on the forehead. He looked at her in surprise.

They had been together for two working days and he knew nothing of her life. He had failed to ask about her romance with Carlton

Hillaire, the American publishing millionaire, which had been all over the papers when it started and headline news again when it ended. She had let Eustace talk and talk. She was a listener and that was a skill he once prided in himself. It seemed to have gone missing. At least, for now.

He staggered back to his own room. In the night, he dreamt of that moment when a tennis ball dropped on a white line and Virginia Buckley said, "Fuck," so beautifully that only he might hear it, and he, like Beerbohm's young men, was smitten. He woke up sweating, clinging to his sheets, wondering why the dream felt so far out of reach.

The old Havershalls of Nottingham were staunch members of the local church and their collective plot was in a shady corner of the churchyard. The unrighteous masses were denied access or ground space, but John Senior had had his grave earmarked since birth. The only missing Havershall was Eustace's lost brother planted in the French countryside.

On the day of John Senior's funeral, the temperature was barely above freezing. Two dozen of the nearest and dearest stood around the grave while words were said and his body was interred. The wind got up as the first dirt was shovelled into the grave by Eustace's mother. She refused to move after the ceremony was done.

"William had a wooden cross. Only that," he said as he and Ginny stood waiting, long after others had left. They shivered at the bared teeth of the weather and stared at the marble memorial propped up ready to take its final position. It showed the dates 1867-1933. Within that time as the lace business had struck its peak and crashed to its decline, John Senior had produced three sons and the world had graduated from small bloody wars through one war-to-end-all-wars and on to the turmoil beyond. One son was dead, one ruined, and Eustace — who felt himself both the middle and the last — spoke of 'Havershall' as if it were a name invented in Birmingham and typed by machine.

"I don't want us to go back to the house," he whispered to Ginny.

"We have to."

"No, we don't."

"You know we do," she said. She squeezed his hand.

When his mother finally declared herself ready, they drove her back sedately in Eustace's Bentley, spoke with the mourners and received the condolences of neighbours. Ginny stayed close and held his hand loyally, and he loyally stayed close to his mother. He got through. With Ginny in support.

His brother, John Junior was now a lecturer in Nottingham's 'Government School of Art and Design', a place failed lace manufacturers went to teach others how to design new products they had failed to design themselves. As the guests drifted away, Eustace saw him at the bottom of the garden, standing on sodden grass smoking a clay pipe.

"Ginny and I will be going now. It's something of a drive back to Stratford."

"I thought you might be staying over, looking at the Empire."

'Empire' struck a sour note, intentionally so.

"I'm selling out the last of the lace business, now I've spent the tax benefit," Eustace told him.

"That factory is the family's. It's—"

"No, not the factory itself. I'm keeping that. But the last of the lacemaking. To Prestons, the firm up the road. Maybe they can make a go of it. We're making more parts for our H50."

"Parts," John mused. "It's just parts. You've ruined this family, and look at you. You don't even care."

"I didn't break the business, John. You did. You and Father." Eustace pointed his finger for emphasis. "I cleaned up the mess."

"Like I said, you don't care for anything except you and your *society* wife. Your little trophy!"

He waited until his brother's insult had done whatever damage it could inflict. Nothing like the demolishing of a tower of bricks or the denial of the key in the cupboard door — John no longer had power.

Back in the house, Eustace and Ginny stopped only long enough to ensure his mother was settled in a group of her oldest friends, those who had once been guests in the Havershall's house to talk of 'votes for women'. They had come to support her now and he was glad of it. No members of the clergy were in evidence.

"Thank you," he told his wife as they departed.

Ginny seemed surprised, but he had remembered something half forgotten and she had been the one to remind him. She was still holding his hand.

Ginny watched him as they drove out through the outskirts of Nottingham. They reached the crossroads where the road home turned south. He waited for a lorry and a bus to pass. She saw his cheek twitch.

He drove three more miles, then without a word, he swung the car around using a lay-by for extra road width and set off back towards Nottingham.

He had still not spoken when they reached the churchyard, but she had guessed where they were heading. He got out of the car and she did not move, at least not until he had gone through the gate and she could run unseen to the church wall and look over.

From a distance, she saw him fall on his father's grave. He lay down thrashing about and weeping, his fists pounding the earth. He came back to the gate with his funeral suit covered in dirt and his eyes red raw.

She reached for him and pressed herself to his chest. He ran his hand tenderly across her hair and she did not protest, though she knew the hand would be covered in soil from the grave.

"Enough now," he said.

Then he led her to the car and they drove home to Stratford. It had never mattered before that home was so far from Nottingham.

Chapter Seventeen

An English language abridgement of Hitler's *Mein Kampf* appeared in London. Publication by the Paternoster Library was organised in collaboration with the Nazi party. It was added to the pile on Woody's bedside table that already contained books on Marx and Mussolini. He did not think much of the clashing politics.

All totalitarian regimes are the same, he had decided. Freedom is never delivered by regimes in total control and there are always people to blame when no one is allowed a defence.

In Germany, the Nazis seized Einstein's property. They sold his boat and converted his country cottage into a Hitler Youth camp.

Woody saw that he would soon be right about the future — this part of the future anyway.

After the family's move, Ginny's intention had been to commute between the new house and Havershall's. The North Warwickshire train line ran from Moor Street Station in Birmingham, through Bordesley and a dozen other local stations out to Stratford. She knew Eustace would prefer to drive and, on days when they both worked in Marmaduke Lane, he could ferry her back and forth.

As the winter closed in, it became clear the travel arrangements she had imagined when buying the house were impractical. Trains became unreliable, the walk to and from stations became icy and unpleasant; the roads through Birmingham were difficult to drive on in the thick fogs that hung on the city's polluted air.

Eustace declared the traffic problems, "Quite intractable."

His first solution was that they should take a suite in the Grand Hotel in Colmore Row on certain weekdays, but Ginny hated leaving the boys with the domestic staff and missing their bedtimes. On her three days a week, she often took the train back to Stratford while Eustace stayed late at Duke Works.

As 1934 progressed, Eustace booked several nights a week in the Grand, but more often than not, Ginny did not stay with him. Colmore Row was the centre for banks and lawyers and the better parts of Birmingham's night life were in easy reach. He joined the Gentleman's Club at 34 St James' Square and conducted many of his business deals from its dining rooms. He rarely discussed the deals with Ginny. She often found out only when orders for typewriters arrived at Duke House several weeks later. They came with special prices or special payment terms.

"Oh, yes," he'd say, when challenged. "I agreed that in the deal."

When Havershall's chose not to bid, BBTL had bought 'Christchurch, Salt and Bingley'. Charlie Barrington-Brown was cemented as the leading name in British typewriters.

By necessity, after the investment in the H50, Eustace bided his time. He used the travelling days spent as a safety ambassador to visit companies and meet company owners. Visits served as scouting missions for finding new component suppliers and — in Eustace's mind — for future acquisition targets. As if in a hunger, he observed their buildings and factories, their locations, the ease with which machinery might be moved. By the end of 1934, profits at Havershall's were such that buying up small engineering companies started to look possible, even as Woody and Ginny insisted on more investment for manufacturing. Archie Hoare promised that 'additional finance would prove no issue,' should Eustace find a use for it.

Liquidators were auctioning the bankrupt Uttoxeter Stenography Company — USC for short. USC owned a sizeable factory in a high street full of shops. There was no reason for a factory in a town centre and every reason for turning it into retail space.

USC was attractive for other reasons too. Stenotype machines were not unlike typewriters, maybe a distant quirky cousin. They consisted of twenty-two keys, used to record transcriptions of court proceedings and other spoken-word events, their output appearing on narrow rolls of paper, rather than sheets. Pressing keys simultaneously on the stenotype — poetically known as 'stroking' — spelt out syllables, words and phrases in a special shorthand vocabulary. The potential speed was astonishing. Whereas typists could sustain word counts a little over one hundred per minute, top stenotype operators were exceeding three hundred. The problem in terms of selling machines was that few people ever mastered the 'stroking' art and there weren't as many law courts as offices with typing pools.

Whether he believed in the product or not, USC's flagship design had an important attraction in Eustace's mind — it was an early attempt to make a machine powered by electricity. The purchase was bound to have Woody's support. One evening, Eustace took a machine into the Lab with a bottle of whisky, which he and Woody shared. That did the trick. He did not tell Woody that USC's failure was largely down to overcommitment to their new electrical design.

Before bidding, Eustace recruited a property developer he had met at a Chamber of Commerce dinner. The developer was ready to buy the land and build shops if the factory and its operation could be moved. Eustace placed a cheeky low-end bid and bought the company for a price below what he'd agreed with the developer as the value of its land. All he required of Archie was a temporary bridging loan.

Within a month, Eustace and Woody had moved all the manufacturing equipment to Nottingham under the charge of Raye Cropper and the developer was flattening the old factory buildings. USC's 'electrical' model was in Woody's Lab for 're-evaluation'. Eustace asked him to propose a more practical design they could 'invest in'. He did not say when investment might happen.

USC did the one thing an asset-stripped business must do — it generated cash quickly. Eustace floated on the adrenaline rush, grabbing the money to fund his next bid, which was for Renton Brothers in Waterlooville. Renton Brothers was a typewriter manufacturer, if a small one. He had known and drunk with David Renton, the younger brother, at industry events for many years. Eustace stole this second deal from under the nose of Charlie Barrington-Brown. Another triumph, though he needed slightly more of Archie's loan capital to secure it. The thrill was addictive. Eustace had felt nothing like it in years. He had bested Barrington-Brown!

On the evening he purchased Renton Brothers', Eustace arrived home with flowers and champagne, flushed with success. He swept into the Stratford house and lifted Ginny off her feet.

She kissed him tentatively. They fell onto the new Persian rug Ginny had bought for their fireplace, as he tried to remove her dress at the same time. She didn't say no and she didn't say yes. They had done it so many times before, even if the frequency had diminished.

Some of the fabric tore. She swore at him and he paused to apologise. She tried to laugh it off. He was dashing. He was ruthless.

"Fiddlesticks! The dress matters not a jot. Besides, you used to like it when I'd get angry with you. You used to provoke me deliberately. It used to provoke you," she said. She drew him into a kiss and felt him hardening against her thigh.

"Go on then," she urged. "Take me if you must."

"You want to do it here?"

"My goodness, where doesn't matter. You used to have me anywhere you damn-well fancied."

"And you'd let me," he reminded her.

"I'm letting you now," she said. "Remember when I got my shares and we fucked on that old carpet in Edgbaston?"

"You're being crude," he said.

"I'm trying to be," she replied.

He unbuttoned his flies and pushed himself inside her. She wanted to cry out, but some calculation in her head told her submission served her better. She tried to conjure the appropriate noises. When at last, Eustace collapsed, panting against her breast, quite spent, she cupped his head in her hand.

"There," she said. "Done?"

"Did you—?"

"Of course. Didn't you hear me? Good as ever."

Afterwards, she wondered why she'd lied. She realised how desperate she had become for his attention. It felt terrible. She swore she'd never slip back into the role of privileged wife; she'd never be so passive again. Passive was the life she'd been bred for and everything she had always tried to escape.

Eustace's fortieth birthday approached. With new resolve, Ginny decided that its celebration would have to be magnificent. Something to light up the house. It must define for the world what the Havershalls had become. She would play the ringmaster.

His birthday fell on a Friday, but they would make a weekend of it, Saturday afternoon at the theatre and an elegant evening soirée with as many guests as they could possibly squeeze into the new house and its gardens. She began a programme of extended and layered preparations. The band she hired was particularly special. She went to great lengths to tempt them from London for a private show.

The quartet in question was led by the jazz trumpeter, Louis Armstrong, who was presently suffering a lull in his career. When Ginny made her enquiries, his British agent confided that Armstrong was in Europe because the Cotton Club was 'on the skids' and, though he'd tried to make it in Chicago, certain 'characters' suggested Armstrong 'got out of town'. Europe was his temporary hiding place.

To Ginny, who had missed the Cotton Club's heyday in New York, the idea of bringing an all-black jazz band to play in her own back garden seemed appropriately wild. She splashed out the ludicrous fee requested and another for a cocktail dress that would allow her the freedom to shimmy gracefully to the music.

As a prelude to the extended weekend proceedings, she bought Eustace the most ironic gift she could think of, an imported copy of 'The Landlord's Game', its latest edition, now called, 'Monopoly'. The properties were still American and the currency still dollars. Sweeping aside all protest, she set it out in the dining room for a game with the boys after birthday cake on the Friday evening. The rules took some explanation to a nine and a seven year-old, but Richard grasped it well enough and had some luck landing on stations. He and Eustace were the last two left in.

Ginny expected Eustace to let his son win, but he didn't. He owned Boardwalk and Park Place, the two most expensive properties, and planted hotels on both. Richard went down by rolling a double-one, visiting both properties in successive moves.

Eustace seemed to think he was teaching his son a life lesson. She did not see the point. It was already clear her elder son would never be a businessman. She fancied that Richard had the heart of a poet. Would one day write great things about love — a user, not the maker, of the machines that made the Havershalls' fortune.

Monopoly, it seemed, was a failure.

Putting aside the disappointment of the board game, she had earmarked the Saturday theatre matinee in Stratford as time for her and Eustace to be alone, to bond again. She had hoped for Romeo and Juliet, but its run had finished the week before. It was now Macbeth.

She and Eustace swapped their favourite quotations as they waited for the performance to start, but in truth, the production lacked spark. So be it. At the very least, it served as the excuse to get Eustace out of the house while the caterers arrived with a marquee. The stage for the dance band was erected and the firework display prepared. This was to be the main event.

One hundred and fifty guests had been invited. One hundred and forty eight accepted. Ginny had insisted on including Eustace's brother and his wife, though she expected the invitation to be declined and it was. Dismissing the two rejections, she considered the turnout a triumph.

The night proved clear and warm for the time of year, which was as well, because the music and dancing required the manicured lawn that stretched down to the river. The first party-goers had taken to the dance floor before her cousin Caroline arrived on the arm of the Viscount, fashionably late. 'Eight o'clock' always meant nine at the earliest to the aristocracy, but having them at the party at all was already Ginny's second triumph of the evening.

Caroline looked like a different woman. In denial of her husband's continuing affairs, she had spent the previous two years travelling with her husband. Her skin was now tanned, polished with the merest hint of wear and tear. She had lost weight and had a gaunt look which the skin on her bare arms had not quite shrunk to accommodate. She wore an evening dress from the latest collection of Jeanne Paquin and insisted on twirling in front of Ginny to show it off.

"You look well," Ginny agreed.

"And you, my dear, look…" Caroline did not finish the sentence.

"That's a nice idle suntan by the way," Ginny replied.

"I have lain on the beach beds of Europe, while my husband lay with God-knows-who." Caroline dismissed the Viscount with an uncaring wave of her hand. Ginny had the impression her cousin was already deeply intoxicated.

"Caroline, you're not tight?"

"No, not at all." Caroline shook her head without much control. "I have simply become more liberated. Dear Ginny, I never knew what I was missing."

She followed it up with another waved hand, this so vigorous that the motion almost overbalanced her. "Missionaries have so much to answer for."

"Caroline…. You've—"

"Changed? Yes, I should jolly well hope so. Have you heard about the Prince of Wales? Poor Lady Furness, she's been abandoned and now they say he is with another American. He has a taste for them. It's not this Wallis Simpson I blame. Royalty are all the same. Mistress after mistress and we all turn a blind eye. Anyway, while Edward paraded through Berlin with his fascist chums, I was having some fun of my own, don't you know? You must come to visit London with me now we're back. We shall go to the wildest parties. Do you know the Bloomsbury Set?"

"Of course not. I live here," Ginny reminded her.

"*We* could make a scandal." Caroline stirred the air between them with her finger. She tottered sideways.

The intoxication seemed greater than alcohol alone might provide. Who was this new woman before her?

Caroline grabbed the nearest man, called him by a name that didn't seem to be his and, after a moment's confusion, they disappeared into the crowd of dancers on the lawn. Viscount Fairchild was nowhere in sight. It seemed they had agreed beforehand to go their separate ways.

The next time Ginny saw the Fairchilds together, they were leaving unstylishly early. Ginny felt the sleight, of course, but she had the impression their limousine was the only thing the Viscount and Viscountess had shared all evening. They had shown their faces at least — the stamp of aristocratic validation on the Havershall success.

If the Fairchilds were a disappointment, Louis Armstrong and his band were not. Armstrong played improvised versions of his own hits, pepped up with effervescent jive — 'Whip That Thing, Miss Lil' and 'Do That Clarinet, Boy!' Between the songs, he relaxed at the microphone telling bemused guests tales of preachers and gangsters in New Orleans. He showed off his scat-singing.

Ginny could see that few in the audience had heard it before. The lack of words and the variations on scale, arpeggio fragments and riffs twisted faces into frowns.

She asked him to play 'Tiger Rag'. He had recorded a cover version of the tune five years before. She owned the recording on a vinyl disc her mother had sent her.

"An *oldie*," he said with a smile.

He gave an extra verse to the live rendition. She and Eustace danced, reviving memories, close enough to be scandalous. They were both drunk, she more than him.

By the end, the great and the good of the English Midlands were delighted, if a little surprised by Armstrong's 'band of negroes', as several guests described them. At last, the exhausted party-goers dispersed and Ginny lapped up the praise. Who else could have pulled this all together? What a marvellous *asset* she was to Eustace!

She thought about Caroline and her early exit. She dismissed it and poured herself another drink.

The dancing left Eustace feeling awkward. It was nice enough to dance with his wife. But in front of everybody? He was out of practice.

Then came the fireworks.

Huge rockets boomed into the night sky. Rainbow coloured sparks burst high above and showered down. The guests sipped champagne and toasted his birthday. Eustace suffered it, flinching at every whiz and bang, but he kept smiling and accepted the congratulations on reaching the ripe age of forty. As soon as the last firework burst in the sky, he excused himself, saying he needed to 'use the facilities'.

No one was inside the house except Woody, sitting on the bottom step of the main stairs, his bow tie askew, a glass in his hand, the whisky bottle at his side. He had arrived in a pure white dinner suit and accompanied by a new girlfriend — Cassandra, another with red chestnut hair, looking something like a youthful Barbara Stanwyck. Somewhere between arriving and planting himself on the stairs, Woody's white jacket had suffered a stain over the breast pocket.

"Not fond of the war memories either, Captain?" Woody said as Eustace approached.

"Not the highlight of my evening."

"Have a drink with me," Woody offered, holding up the bottle.

"I don't have a glass."

"Well, take this one." He poured more whisky into his glass and handed it to Eustace.

They clinked bottle and glass together.

"Happy Birthday, Captain." Woody took an elongated swallow from the bottle. "You know, I remember, in France, that night you took us all out…"

"After you saved us…"

"After Masterson."

"Yes, after that," Eustace said.

"Did you ever think any of this could happen? I mean, back then, when we were dying and finding ourselves and fucking where we could?" Woody's voice had started to slur, some of his old northern accent returned. "I 'ent forgot, Captain, you refused. You refused that French girl."

"Maisie."

"Was that her name? How do you remember?"

"Temptation, I suppose."

"They did for her badly, after you left, Captain. Arnie Mulgrove was the worst. I should have known then."

"What's that mean?"

"I gave him the job. First, he wanted to open up that whole question… about how Masterson met his end. I gave him the job,"

Woody repeated. "Then he screwed us over anyway. He got what he deserved."

Eustace felt the first prickle of suspicion. "Woody, you didn't do anything—?"

"No, Captain. Not I. But I weren't sorry that someone did. I always thought it was you."

"Me?"

Woody shaped his fingers into a gun and pulled the trigger. "The captain of mercy." His face lifted into a faint smile. "'Ent you always the man to do what's necessary? I wanted to leave that whole thing behind, you know, but I never had the luck. Not the right kind of luck."

Eustace nodded.

Woody said, "And now look at you. You got everything. You married the best woman, Eustace, you know that — the true princess."

"You're squiffy again. You've had too much to talk about women. Besides, I always thought you were never too keen on my choice."

"On Ginny? Pure jealousy, Captain. See what happened to my woman. To Mabel. My Mabel. I loved her. She was the one. None of the ones after, not really, and now this…" Woody waved his hand in the air as if twisting it for exercise.

"Cassandra?" Eustace offered.

"Cassandra is what she is. Which isn't a word I'd use, not in your house anyway. But then maybe all love is like that, though not always for cash." Woody looked at the bottle and then pressed it to his forehead. "Oh, God, what a mess *success* becomes. Is it success because we put fortunes in the bank? Are you happy, Eustace? Forty-years-old, are you happy?"

In the next copy of Tatler, Ginny found a picture of Amelia Stewart. She was demonstrating Havershall's H50 at a grand exhibition in Edinburgh. She was the vision Ginny had employed her to be. In the picture, Eustace stood next to her, smiling. He seemed younger. Younger than forty.

Ginny thought about Caroline and her philandering Viscount. The thought overwhelmed her, filled her with suspicion. She wondered if she was sleepwalking into the same nightmare as her cousin.

Woody's own children, James and Celia, had continued to live with Mabel's parents in Bristol, though Celia was now a boarder at Cheltenham Ladies College during term times. That left James with two grandparents entering their seventies and holding fast to their Jewish faith. In a Christian Bristol, both Saturday and Sunday seemed like dead Sabbath days.

When Woody visited at weekends — once a month at most — he would fill the nine-year-old James with sweets and ice cream. They would rush around the streets and parks and walk down to Bristol docks to watch the boats. James was always running ahead and Woody, hobbled by his lost toe, would be left behind, shouting, "Slow down. Slow down." He'd laugh, because his son was growing up so much stronger and more capable than the runty lad from working-class Salford.

The other three weekends in a month, Woody was racing his Bugatti at circuits all around the country. In advance of the new season in 1936, he bought himself an Alfa-Romeo 8C 2600 of the specification that had won the Mille Miglia the year before. He now had bigger, international ambitions to show what he could do. He was an engineer. He was ever more hungry to prove it. The profits of Havershall's were more than enough to pay for the attempt.

As it happened, the car was never used.

The King died in January 1936. The Prince of Wales, complete with mistress, became King Edward VIII.

That wasn't what stopped Woody's racing.

On a Saturday in February, James Woodmansey came out of the 'Betty-Brunt Special Confectionary Emporium' with a bag of assorted boiled sweets, eating an exotic 'Milky Bar' which the emporium had specially imported from America. He ran ahead of his father.

Woody shouted his usual caution, which James duly ignored.

He watched as his son was struck by the Hotwells-to-Brislington tram.

At first Woody stood there, listening to onlookers screaming and wondering why he wasn't screaming or running or moving or doing something.

His boy was sixty pounds at most. The Hotwells-to-Brislington tram, laden with passengers, weighed sixty tonnes at least.

Chapter Eighteen

Neither Woody nor the boy's grandparents were in any state to make the funeral arrangements. Eustace and Ginny, godparents to both Woodmansey children, stepped in. A godparent's duty never seemed to have meant much, especially after Mabel's death had dropped the children into a Jewish household. Now it did. On the way down to Bristol, the Havershalls detoured into Cheltenham to pick up Woody's daughter from her school.

Celia Woodmansey was almost fourteen. She stood no more than five-feet-three and wore flat shoes. She looked like her mother, but with cheekbones borrowed from a young Katharine Hepburn. Her hair had little of her mother's redness; it rather followed Woody's darker side. At first, she sat in the back of Eustace's Bentley, nose buried into Agatha Christie's first Poirot novel in French translation.

Prompted by Ginny as the miles rolled by, it emerged from her clipped replies that Celia loved crime novels, especially Agatha Christie's, but preferred Poirot in the detective's own language. She spoke perfect French, courtesy of her grandparents' early coaching. She also spoke German, though Ginny was in no position to check. French became their language of choice. The replies lengthened as Ginny pressed more questions on the girl. Soon it was a conversation.

"You like your school?" Ginny asked.

"It has no boys."

Ginny could not tell if this were a fact, a regret or the school's best feature. Celia had eyes that smiled, though the smile never escaped the reins with which she held herself. Ginny imagined a girl's English boarding school to be worse than those she had been thrown out of herself and decided Celia's life must be intolerably dull. This should be corrected.

Ginny had always promised herself a daughter. She had been robbed by the complications of William's birth. Now she might inherit one.

The funeral passed. When the Social Season of 1936 began, Ginny headed back to the South West, lied about her blood relationship with Celia to the head of Cheltenham Ladies College and took the young girl to the Cheltenham Gold Cup where the wonder horse, Golden Miller, won for a fifth time.

In the summer, she invited Celia to Wimbledon. Fred Perry's play was an inspiration. Ginny promised to teach her the strokes. She had just begun to play again herself, joining the club in Stratford. She had found, to her surprise, that she still played the game remarkably well.

Woody's drinking now exceeded the extremes that followed either Mabel's death or his cash machine's failure. Six months in, guilt showed no sign of abating.

He always knew he had been supposed to die at Cambrai. He had lost half a toe, and because he couldn't run to keep up, his son was gone. He dreamt in nightmares of his wife — how she suffered birthing the boy, how she had lingered and died in agony. James, at least, had been quick.

Everything lost its sense in the senseless booze. With a bottle of whisky, it did not seem to matter what he thought once his bargain with alcohol had nightly swept away his reason. He became Mrs Bembole's best client, sometimes as a visitor, often as the visited, though either way the pleasures of the flesh made him viciously angry with himself.

In the summer months, he sat in the movie presentations at the Aston Hippodrome for hours on end while he sweated out hangovers that lingered for days. The Pathé News showed crowds by the million lining the streets to the stadium on the opening of the Berlin Olympics — Hitler, like a Roman god, riding the motorcade, hailed by Nazi salutes and swastikas. Here was the amphitheatre designed to show the supremacy of race.

Woody became familiar with Jesse Owens on news reels, taking 10.3 seconds to run one hundred metres, but the run lasted for hours as it accompanied every show. It stuck with him. Loop on loop. Day on day. For weeks.

This gangly black American outran them all. A man with all his toes. A man who would no doubt have rushed to save James. Woody learned to wait for that perfect moment in the reel, just after victory, when the camera cut onto Jesse Owens' face and Jesse Owens smiled.

The Prince of Wales, now King Edward VIII, abdicated his throne in December 1936 and slipped away to marry the American divorcee, Wallis Simpson. Elsewhere change was more violent.

The day after the Abdication, Brian Fordham laid his resignation on Eustace's desk at Duke House — three lines typed on letter-sized paper that reminded Eustace of his resignation from Weatherstone & Hoare's.

"I don't understand, Brian."

Fordham was an outstanding salesman doing great business for the company in the North East. He had even ventured overseas to promote their products in Denmark and Sweden. He was paid good money.

Eustace read the last sentence aloud, then said, "You want to fight a war in Spain? To volunteer?"

"You have to fight for what you believe in, don't you, Sir? I'm not the only one thinking of going. There's other men in the factory. We're not communists, not all of us, not like the papers say. It's principle."

Comparisons between Brian and his brother William surged through Eustace's mind. Employees were like his family, especially the young ones, those of that rash 'signing-up' age.

"The International Brigades are organised by Communist International, Brian. That's the Soviet Union."

"Yes, Sir. But there's the Workers' Party, the POUM. A lot of British — the ones who believe in the cause — we're joining up with them. Don't you see, Stalin is our ally in this?"

The idea of Stalin as an ally didn't seem right.

"Brian, it's a rag-bag militia marching into hell."

"You think no one should stand up to Mussolini and Hitler, Sir? That's who's behind the Nationalists."

"You don't win wars because you're on the right side."

"Our doorstep next, Sir."

Eustace read the three lines again. "I wish I could describe to you what dying is like, so you could be prepared to avoid it. I'm afraid I cannot."

"Yes, Sir."

"Is there nothing I can say to dissuade you?"

"No, Sir, I don't believe there is."

Eustace watched the young man slip out of his office. He did not expect to see him again. What would he have said to his brother, given the chance? To William with his pen over the paper, ready to sign his life away?

He went to find Woody in the Lab and told him the news. Woody was always spouting warnings about Mussolini and Hitler. He seemed strangely thrilled at Fordham's decision. Eustace suspected he wasn't quite sober. It was eleven in the morning.

"Don't you understand the threat those volunteers are fighting, Captain?"

"I understand war," Eustace said.

"Just because they were the ones stoking up the unions, I don't believe the communists are our threat anymore."

"Why? Because the big strike failed and Mulgrove ended up in the canal?"

"Captain, that was ten years ago."

Those ten years had flown by and perhaps Woody was right, Eustace hadn't grasped the changed ideologies at large in the world.

Italy and Germany sent aid and troops to the Spanish Nationalists who were attempting to install a fascist regime. Behind the embattled government, the Republican side was fragmented. Soviet support damaged its cause as much as aided it.

Unwilling to wade in alongside Stalin, Britain's government maintained neutrality. Like Eustace, it couldn't countenance support for either side. It sent warships to blockade supply lines. It seemed to think starvation might stop people fighting. Volunteering for either side in Spain was declared a crime in Britain, but about four thousand men and women went anyway. Woody said their cause was real anti-fascism in practice.

But as Eustace feared, the volunteers found chaos, a smaller scale version of the futilities of World War One. The English newspapers reported organised totalitarianism on one side and unsupported idealism on the other.

Hope has never been a strategy. In war, it is fatal.

1937 began as 1936 had ended, with rapid growth for Havershall's. Eustace should have been happy, but the news of Brian Fordham's death arrived in May. It hit him hard and he retired to his library to write a letter of condolence to Fordham's mother. He was no longer a soldier or a captain and had no right to judge how another family's son might have given his life. He wrote of Fordham's heroism anyway. By hand, not by machine.

Ginny read the letter before he sealed the envelope. She said, "Eustace, I cannot say I understand why this is so important. So many have gone and so many have died."

"No," he said.

That was all.

The following morning, he held the letter at the mouth of a postbox, hesitating to let it fall. Had it ever been right to say such words?

"...*Died for his country and his comrades.*"

The envelope fluttered down into the base of the iron box.

The Monaco Grand Prix of 1937 was moved back into August and Eustace found himself committed to a selling tour in Scandinavia. He was taking a team of four. Amelia Stewart was to join them in Stockholm as their demonstrator at a national office show. They were trying to follow up leads that Brian Fordham had created, Eustace explained.

It was to be the first time he'd missed the race. Ginny didn't protest at the arrangements, but she constructed her own convoluted schemes. She was always the hostess anyway, wasn't she? She and Woody would handle the event and the invited customers.

She decided she would take Celia to Cap Ferrat. With her fluent languages, the girl was an 'obvious choice' to help her with the Havershall's party. Celia looked older than she was, presentable and beautiful. In short, a lady, even if a 'lady in waiting'. Ginny tried the idea on Eustace and Woody. Neither objected.

Her second decision was enacted with the greatest secrecy. She engaged Mr Carling March of the Field Detective Agency to follow the sales trip to northern Europe.

Ginny was still an occasional driver but, for their thirteenth wedding anniversary, Eustace had bought her a white Crossley 3-Litre Sports Saloon, a version with a special lightweight body made by the famous Beauvais company of bodybuilders.

Ginny insisted on taking Celia into the middle of Birmingham to choose a 'suitable wardrobe' for the Riviera. She maintained the habit of driving recklessly fast, outraging fellow road users in the rush of Saturday morning shoppers. After several close calls, for which she blamed everyone else, she parked outside the doors of Rackhams in Temple Row with one wheel propped on the kerb.

Shepherding Celia inside, Ginny was surprised to be met by Zoe Fitzsimmons. Woody's first post-Mabel fiancée was now the head of the women's dress department and had become Mrs Walker by marriage.

"I didn't remember you having a daughter, Mrs Havershall?" said Zoe, a question delivered among the smoothest of sales patter.

Ginny said, "Oh, yes."

Zoe's look lingered, as if she almost remembered Celia as a child, but couldn't quite bring her to mind.

Later, when Zoe went to fetch a dress in a different size, Celia asked, "Why didn't you tell her I'm not your daughter?"

Ginny shrugged, offering only a painful smile. "Come on, we have money to spend."

In half an hour, they tried on five outfits, emerging with two on hangers and one on Celia, a tailored light grey jacket with more than the necessary number of buttons down the front and a flared day-time skirt in matching charcoal.

"Short is all the rage for the best young ladies," Ginny told her.

"I'm fifteen," Celia objected. Her birthday had been two weeks before.

"Yes… yes, I know."

Ginny imagined how it would be for her young charge when she reached Cannes and Nice. How she planned this reshaping of Celia! Fifteen was quite old enough to be dressed with style. Celia's looks were set to out-dazzle them all.

"And now for the *pièce de résistance*… your birthday treat, Celia."

"I have a treat?"

"We're going on a little adventure."

Celia looked alarmed, perhaps remembering the journey to Rackhams.

"Don't worry," said Ginny. "You'll probably survive."

Ginny explained that there was a H50 typewriter in the Crossley's boot space that needed delivering.

"Don't you ever think about how writers need typewriters?" she said, lighting a cigarette on the move and offering one to Celia.

Celia declined. Ginny decided not to push the point. Not yet. A young girl may be introduced to vices one at a time.

"Owning a typewriter company, my husband made a marvellous study of the machines," Ginny claimed. "Mark Twain used a Sholes & Glidden Treadle Model. He was a pioneer. Scott Fitzgerald — you've heard of him; a terrible drunk and wife as mad as a jail full of suffragettes — he carried an Underwood. We're told Hemingway packed a Royal Quiet Deluxe. No doubt, he has it in Spain as we speak."

"What has this to do with my treat?" Celia asked.

"You'll see," Ginny teased.

They turned south, heading towards Oxford. During the journey, she told Celia of her plan for the Grand Prix weekend and listed out the guests. "Be careful of the ones with hands," she warned. "That means the French and the Italians. Though I'm sure some of the boys of your age are nice."

"Mrs Havershall?"

"Aunt Ginny, please," Ginny corrected. She'd been reminding Celia for the whole morning.

"Aunt Ginny, should I start wearing lipstick?"

"Lipstick?"

"So I don't get — you know — pregnant. If someone kisses me... ever."

The Crossley was cruising along a straight which allowed Ginny enough time to turn her head towards her passenger.

"Lipstick doesn't... It doesn't stop you getting pregnant, Celia. Did someone tell you sex was kissing? O, my Lord! Who told you that?"

"Lucy. She's our Lacrosse Captain."

The memory of Daisy Henderson's misinformed sex education flashed into Ginny's mind.

"I think we'd better stop. This may take a while," she said.

She drew the car to a halt next to a wire fence. Three docile horses were grazing on the other side. Seizing on the horses as examples — male and female — Ginny spent several minutes explaining the proper mechanism involved in reproduction.

"It's obviously more difficult using hooves to cling on," Ginny concluded, once the anatomical details had been explained. "Don't worry, I didn't know either at your age. It's quite pleasurable when he gets inside and—"

Celia's face was screwing itself into contortions, her cheeks reddening.

"Never mind," Ginny counselled.

She offered a cigarette. This time Celia took it and coughed for several minutes. Ginny wondered about the difficulties of mothers and daughters, and relived that moment in front of Zoe Fitzsimmons when she had claimed Celia as her own.

Half an hour later, the car turned into a leafy lane in the village of Wallingford. Ginny parked outside an iron gate set in a neat line of privet hedge. Beyond the gate was a path up to a large detached house clad in grey with reddish bricks making a decorative pattern around its windows. The front door and porch looked newly painted and spotlessly white.

Ginny hurried around to the back to remove the H50.

"I don't understand. Where are we, Aunt Ginny? I thought it was to be a treat."

"Yes, that's right." She handed the machine to Celia, whose shoulder slumped as she took its weight. "Special order. This machine is serial number H50/00001, the first off the line, never been out of its case. I thought you'd like to present it to the new owner. Off you go."

Celia looked up at the house. "Who are they? What do I say when they answer the door?"

"You say, 'I am Celia Woodmansey and my father designs typewriters. I have come with this gift from his company, dear *Mrs Christie*.'"

"Mrs Christie?" Celia repeated.

"Or call her 'Agatha', if you feel comfortable doing that. I assure you, she is expecting you. I telephoned, through a friend of a friend. She said you could come for tea."

"How did you—?"

"Ah well, I don't read her books, but one still has one's connections. These days, I don't care to use them except in a good cause. You do still like Agatha Christie, don't you?"

The advanced party set off for Cap Ferrat at the end of July, having borrowed Eustace's much larger car for the trip once again. It only made Ginny's driving more terrifying. Celia took the passenger seat. Richard and William sat in the back with the same nanny-come-governess-come-chauffeur Ginny had hired before.

They spent their first week around the swimming pool and at the beach. Ginny played plenty of tennis and made good on her promise to coach Celia. She marvelled at how her boys now picked up the game too. Richard could move without much of a limp and his extra size made him a match for his brother. Doubles became possible, as long as Ginny and Celia each took one of the boys and didn't play too hard.

On the first Saturday, Ginny was surprised when Celia insisted on finding the Synagogue in Nice.

"There is a famous one on the *Rue Gustave Deloye*. I promised my grandparents. It's the least I can do."

Ginny had not realised that living with her grandparents had left the girl with even a passing degree of faith. She had always looked at Celia as a fresh-faced English girl. A loose Christianity was assumed. Life was simpler like that. Ginny felt a shiver of unease that she could not put a name to. Celia was gone for most of the morning.

Towards the end of the following week, Woody arrived for the Grand Prix, trailed by two cars full of guests. More arrived by train and had to be ferried to the villa. The weekend brought spectacular weather. The party hired their usual yacht. They sailed over from Cap Ferrat and moored in Monte Carlo harbour. Those who couldn't fit into cabins took rooms at The Hermitage. The Havershall party on race day was twenty-five.

Everyone drank too much, except Celia, who was allowed one half glass of wine by 'hypocritical decree' of her father, as Ginny put it. Celia sat watching with the intensity of a child who intends to learn adult habits and sins.

The Monaco Grand Prix proved a showcase for the war machine mustering in Germany. This one highlighted its industrial muscle.

Manfred von Brauchitsch won the race in a Mercedes-Benz W125. German cars took the first five places. No non-German car finished within three laps of the winner. Britain had no representative in the field.

"It's terrible. Does no one realise what's happening?" Woody asked. "Our engineering has to be better than theirs, or we're lost."

Drunk at the time. And unregarded.

After the race, the Havershall's party left Monaco lowered in spirit by the German triumph, but inflated in number. With thirty-four aboard, ten or twenty more revellers followed them round the coast by car. Several racing drivers were now among the guests

That Sunday night, Ginny had organised a band on the patio next to the swimming pool. She revived her Charleston and Jitterbug with a series of partners, including several titled Frenchmen who claimed to be Counts or better. She was pleased — a wild shindig, and in quite the most elegant surroundings, all without her husband in attendance.

She completed the evening on the patio dance floor, slow dancing with a French Count, Guy de Monteparnasse, who claimed a connection to the Grimaldis. He interlocked one hand with hers, placed the other in the small of her back. When their hip bones met, she realised her hips had not been this close to any man but Eustace for eighteen years, more than half her life. She felt the coldness of her hand in the warmth of Guy's fingers. Too easily his strength might pull her in. The alcohol warming her veins might lead her anywhere. The Count's wife, across the dance floor, looked on with heavy disapproval.

As Ginny turned aside, she saw, two dancing couples away, Celia waltzing with an Italian boy, slightly older than her. The party outfit bought in Rackhams looked wonderful.

"Remember what I told you. Beware of the Riviera boys," she whispered to Celia in French between dances.

"Don't you think they should beware of me?" Celia's arms flailed expressively, the 'R's in her speech slurred.

"Does your father know you're tight?" Ginny asked.

She could see Woody buried in conversation with an Austrian engineer he'd befriended the evening before. This neglect, she surmised, had much to do with Celia's condition.

"I don't mind so much what you do, but do it sober," she advised.

Celia mumbled something incomprehensible and, without the Italian boy holding her up, looked fatally unstable.

"Come with me."

Ginny took her protégé by the arm, excused herself from Guy and nodded ungraciously to the Italian boy, before marching Celia to the house.

Celia was fixed in a vacant stare. Once they reached the master bedroom, Ginny held her fully-clothed under the cold water in the shower. Celia screamed and stamped about on the shower tray. Ginny held her until she saw the vitality relighting in the girl's eyes.

"I think you're done," she said.

She helped Celia unpeel the ruined outfit, then fetched a bath towel to wrap her up. Stealing a glance at the girl's naked body — perhaps not yet filling the fine-boned skeleton that fate had provided — Ginny could play the artist easily enough. Sketch in the final curves. A body and a face, both close to perfection. Celia had everything that once looked back from a mirror for the youthful Virginia Buckley. It shouldn't matter, but it did.

"You're going to have a doozie of a life… but not tonight. Not while you're this way," she told her as she tucked Celia into the master bed.

Celia, half conscious, called her, "Aunt Ginny," as she tried to mutter her thanks and apologies.

"Aunt Ginny, that's about it. That's what I am, an Aunt and an Aunt can't be always the libertine."

She wondered about Eustace and Amelia Stewart, somewhere in Scandinavia now, no doubt. She wondered what she might have done tonight in revenge, if Celia had not been drunk and the jealous stare of Madame de Monteparnasse had not been there to spoil the moment. That frightened her. Long after she'd put Celia to bed, she sat in a chair across the room watching the girl sleep, and turning the wedding ring on her finger around and around, as if checking it hadn't become loose.

Woody's drinking spree on the Riviera lasted long into his return to England. Talking to the Austrian and thinking about the Grand Prix, he had asked himself a question: how had Germany, a nation humbled in the carnage of France, rebuilt itself? It carried the burden of war reparations heaped on it by the Treaty of Versailles, didn't it? Its brilliance in engineering was unfathomable. This was the one subject he cared for most.

The Austrian had friends in the country's government. He had pointed out that, prior to the Wall Street Crash, when the world thought the Roaring Twenties would never end, America and its allies had lent Germany more than one and a half billion pounds for rebuilding, compared to a billion's worth of reparations that were supposed to be flowing in the other direction, much of which had never been paid.

"These cars you see on the circuit are nothing. The loans are now transformed into military equipment, aeroplanes," the Austrian claimed. "Bought on money borrowed from the nations it is determined to fight. Ironic, *ja*?

The Scandinavian sales tour changed one thing in Eustace's mind. He saw a genuine need for a truly portable machine.

Fancy features? No.

Electric power? No.

Just a machine that did mechanical writing.

Company acquisitions could be delayed for a while, but only if he could find a designer he trusted. A new model would be done on his terms, not Ginny's, and certainly not Woody's. Despite his loyalties, even Eustace noticed his friend was now intoxicated more often than sober and incapable of leading any project.

In his fuzzy thinking, Woody had recently become possessed by the idea that the electric stenotype machine was important. Hadn't Eustace encouraged him to believe so when he'd wanted to buy the USC company? Woody was certain Havershall's needed an electric typewriter that used the same technology, so that's the direction his engineering work took him. IBM had recently introduced their Electric Typewriter Model 01 in America, so Woody bought a dozen on import and dismantled them to find out how they worked. In the 'Lab' in Birmingham, his pile of bits had grown and grown, but nothing remotely viable had emerged.

Eustace decided what was needed and he acted. Quietly but with purpose. He asked Raye Cropper to design the new typewriter. He told himself Woody was ill, needed time to recover, needed someone to share the engineering load. He took to visiting the Lab late at night, sometimes easing Woody off his stool and sending him home in a taxi, sometimes driving him home himself. He thought it was for the best. A man who loses both his wife and his son needed time to snap out of it.

Eustace never discussed his reasoning, and for a long time, never mentioned Raye's project to either Ginny or Woody. It was safely hidden away in Nottingham.

Chapter Nineteen

Raye Cropper abandoned the complex 'noiseless' arrangement of Woody's designs. Who cared about noise if they weren't sitting in the typing pool? Eustace had asked for a design to suit people who travelled and typed on the move.

She worked on a simple ratchet to produce a short, lightweight lever mechanism. She bought plastic mouldings to form the tops of keys instead of metal buttons. Her platen was hollow with a three-pronged insert spaced from the central axis. Most radically, her design had a simple cast aluminium chassis that replaced the more expensive aircraft grade alloys in Woody's H50 and a hard plastic case. She experimented with new formulations of paint for UV and corrosion protection, choosing bright primary colours that would match the plastic.

"I want you to look at this, Gaffer," she said when the prototype was ready.

She positioned a bright green machine in the middle of his desk during one of Eustace's fortnightly visits to Nottingham. The desk, having belonged to Eustace's great grandfather, grandfather, father and even to his brother, had never seen a typewriter.

She removed its lid. Underneath, the metal of the typebars was a shiny chrome colour, the new plastic keys black with letters embossed in white.

"Do you know how much our current most-portable typewriter weighs?"

Eustace had a rough idea, but shook his head.

"Fourteen pounds, Gaffer. You know how it is. Think of it as a woman's job — we all do; most typists are. How far do you think the average woman wants to lug a fourteen pound box? Think of me as an exception."

Eustace laughed and considered the question. A woman of Raye's demeanour would probably carry it to London and back.

"Corona have their LC Smith model out now," she continued. "Weighs nine and a half pounds. Mr Woodmansey's got one in the 'Lab' in Brum. Mine weighs a quarter-pound less."

"It's green," Eustace said.

"What colour would you like it? I call this the 'HL1'... or the 'HL1g'. You can have it any colour you like, Gaffer, apart from white. All the whites I tried go yellow in sunlight."

He looked at it for a while, rolled a piece of foolscap into the machine. Resting his fingers on the keys, he tried the usual 'H' and 'Y' keys first. Once he got the feel, he typed, 'The quick brown fox jumped over the lazy dog,' three times over with a line space between them. The letters came out in an even row, all equally black.

"Impressive," he admitted.

"In production quantities, less material, fewer components. It'll cost one pound and seven shillings less to produce. You can sell at a premium on account of the weight."

She leaned over the desk and wrote a number on his blotter. She double underlined it.

"Oh, shit," he said. "What do we do now?"

He had begun to wonder, how would he explain a new design appearing out of nowhere? What would he tell Ginny? Or Woody? He had half hoped Raye's design would be a failure. He had told himself he was testing her skills, but in fact he was testing his old partner.

He confessed to Ginny first. To his surprise, she seemed pleased, as if she had been expecting it and waiting for him to catch up. He asked her for her help when he delivered the news at the next board meeting.

He spent most of a day writing out the words he was going to say. Woody was late on his promises, the expense of the 'Lab' had produced nothing new for over a year and he was a drunk. That last part probably wasn't helpful, Eustace decided. He crossed it out.

In the meeting, his words came out like this: "Woody, we need to make a proper portable typewriter. That's all there is to it."

"Why, when IBM are going for office machines?" Woody replied. On the papers before the board was Eustace's proposal for diverting funds into the new HL1. It would starve any development of Woody's electromechanical models. Woody was already twitchy and agitated. Bloodstream filled with booze no doubt, Eustace told himself.

"Think of our exporters," he reasoned.

He explained why exporters needed a lighter machine. Apart from the Scandinavians, Corrigan and Corrigan had long complained that weight made Havershall's machines seem heavy against an influx of cheap and flimsy machines in Asia. Public scribes moved from place to place. Some would set up in the streets to type documents for a fee. Portability was at a premium.

"You are lying to me," Woody concluded.

Ginny, silent in the corner of the room, offered no opinion, exactly as Eustace had asked of her at breakfast that morning.

Woody stood up. He had to steady himself against the table. He began a rambling speech about the values of their company, values that he — Joseph Woodmansey — had installed in it. It had always been about engineering and craft. It had nobility and beauty.

"Didn't I once say, Captain, I'm an engineer not an artist? I see why you didn't tell me about this monstrosity. You want to replace me... with her. With Raye fucking Cropper. You love her or something... I don't know. That must be it. What do you think?" Woody asked, shooting daggers at Ginny. "Is that what it is? Is he sleeping with her?"

When Ginny said nothing, he said, "Well, Captain, are we about engineering or not?" Then he threw the whisky tumbler across the board room. It smashed against the wall.

"Fuck! Fuck! Fuck!" he cried, palms slapping the table. "What more do you want? You've got everything. You've got everything and I've lost everything. The way everyone calls us Havershall's? Everyone! It's supposed to be 'Havershall & Woodmansey' and yes, we agreed that the names should be in alphabetic order, but I know... I bloody know you were always setting out to be the governor. Isn't that why you had us sell shares to your wife?" He pointed at Ginny as if wishing his finger were a gun. "What happened to my wife? What happened to putting a name on this company for my son, huh? What about that?"

Eustace offered no answer.

"I was the bloody engineer, Captain... Me! Me! Me! Why is your name worth more than mine when I am the one who knows how to make the damn things and you know nothing? You with your finger on the trigger, it's the same again, isn't it? You're the one who fires the gun."

Woody stormed out, crunching over the broken glass as he went. He slammed the door.

Ginny came around to Eustace's side of the table, standing as Eustace pressed his face forward against her. She put her hands around his head as if to steady the world.

"I'm sorry," she said.

"I served with this man."

"I know you did."

"He saved my life. He's my friend. He saved my life and I don't know how to save his."

In 1938, Eustace was the Midland Manufacturers' Businessman of the Year again. 'Havershall & Woodmansey Typewriters Ltd' now employed a thousand staff, split between the main factories in Birmingham and Nottingham, a series of small sales offices and a handful of specialist shops in key cities. The majority of its revenues came from typewriters, less than a tenth from its interest in other mechanical devices acquired from various companies bought along the way. Nevertheless, a sizeable chunk of its profits that year came from the sale of assets — land mostly — stripped from companies Eustace had acquired to add to the Havershall's empire. Its most bizarre purchases were of a manufacturer of apple-coring machines used in big kitchens and another which made a card index cabinet that opened to a particular letter of the alphabet when a key was pressed. Export sales consumed a third of the manufacturing output. Corrigan and Corrigan, now active everywhere from India to Hong Kong, was the company's biggest customer.

During the previous eighteen months, Eustace had travelled to Ireland (twice), Belgium, India, Singapore, Hong Kong and Scotland, as well as taking many two and three night tours to visit Havershall's more remote customers and distributors in England and Wales. He'd given lectures on safety in factories and bought three of them. Having always coveted the brand since he had first driven one, he bought himself a brand new Rolls-Royce Phantom III.

Ginny was not mentioned in the congratulatory speeches, though she sat at his side at the dinner, alongside his boys, dragged along to see their father lauded. She could not work out quite what rankled with her most — the praise Eustace got for everyone else's efforts, the ease with which his acceptance speech soaked up the accolade, or the abandonment she had felt during all his nights away on 'sales trips'. She still awaited Mr Carling March's report. Suspicion and jealousy are two heads to a monster.

Woody did not attend the ceremony at all. He was away that weekend, pursuing his renewed interest in racing cars.

Woody would now happily tell anyone who'd listen that a bigger war was coming. It wasn't just Eustace who had let him down. He started a one-man fight against fascists.

In the mid-year, he sold his unused Alfa-Romeo — too Italian! — and bought a second-hand B-Type ERA. This was not a road car. It was British-built, especially for open wheel racing. He intended to enter the Donington Grand Prix, organised by the Derby & District Motor Club. It was to all intents and purposes the country's 'Grand Prix' and attracted the top foreign teams. He had, he said, seen what the Germans had done in Monte Carlo. He wasn't about to let them do the same in England.

Quite why he thought he was the man to stop them never seemed clear. He was a good club racer at best. Even when he was sober.

The Mercedes-Benz and Auto Union teams arrived in Donington early to prepare. The timing was unfortunate. Germany invaded Czechoslovakia. The race was cancelled.

The French and British governments rushed to Munich and agreed Hitler should take control of the Sudeten territory of Czechoslovakia. They were so scared of the Nazi threat and so keen to appease that they did not invite the Czechoslovakians to the meeting. Their land was handed over to Germany like a tribute.

The appeasing document — the Munich Agreement — was waved by Neville Chamberlain, the British Prime Minister, on returning home. "Peace in our time," he said.

With the crisis apparently averted, the race was rescheduled for the 22nd of October. Woody's ERA lasted two laps before a driveshaft failed. The Monaco result was repeated — five German cars ahead of the rest, the might of their machines proven.

President Roosevelt telegraphed Chamberlain with congratulations. "Good man," he said in response to the agreement.

Hitler told his generals, "Our enemies… are little worms."

On the face of it, Woody put up more resistance, at least for a couple of laps.

The Munich Agreement made Eustace happy. He had always been a great supporter of Chamberlain, since Chamberlain had succeeded Stanley Baldwin whom Eustace blamed for the incompetent handling of the Gold Standard and the abdication of Edward VIIIth.

He drove up to watch the Donington race in high spirits, taking Richard and William as a 'treat' and booked them into The Black Boy Hotel in Nottingham where Woody and his two mechanics were staying.

On race day, Eustace whisked the boys off into the grandstand to get a better view of the chaos of racing. Afterwards in the paddock, he was surprised by the appearance of Woody's latest lady friend. She came out of nowhere, another who — if not yet wearing the ring — was hanging close enough to his arm to secure it.

She was dressed in a plain cotton dress in pastel blue and a floppy but fashionable sun hat, not so much worn as perched. Beneath it, her hair was short and curly; errant brown-black strands spilled down her cheek. It was not red. That was a surprise.

Eustace could see why Woody found her attractive despite the darker hair — a different proposition to Zoe or Patty or Cassandra. Slightly older too. Maybe twenty-two or three.

"Sarah Coles," she said, introducing herself while Woody and his mechanics pushed his broken racing car towards the loading ramps of a lorry.

She shook Eustace's hand with a manufactured self-assurance. Nervous, he could tell, though not so much with Richard and William. She leaned towards them and asked, "Who are these fine young men?"

Richard seemed at first taken aback, then looked up enchanted. "Sh..shame about the race. Jolly bad luck," he ventured.

William said nothing. Sarah smiled at them both.

"We'd need more than better luck against the Germans, I'm afraid. They are rather magnificent. At least, when it comes to their engineering. Even the Woodster admires the godless efficiency of it all. It's a war machine, he says."

"Germans don't want a war any more than we do. Didn't you hear Chamberlain?" Eustace said.

"I wouldn't know. It's beyond my understanding. But if it's only Woody's car that breaks, it isn't the driver, so today I'm relieved. Did you see the accident?"

A bad crash had occurred in the opening laps, the rising smoke visible from the grandstand. No word had been released on the driver's condition.

"On the other side of the circuit from us," Eustace assured her.

"It's always bad when they say nothing. I hate it."

She explained that her uncle had once been a racing driver. He had gone over the banking at Brooklands. Eustace asked if it was through racing that she'd met Woody.

"Oh, no," she said, "I'm at the Barton Arms, rehearsing for the winter season in Birmingham. I'm a dancer."

* * *

Eustace woke early the next morning, disoriented and confused until he realised he was in a hotel, not on the battlefields of France. He told himself he was glad to be up, even if not so glad to be covered in sweat. He had intended to read through some new contracts he'd brought with him before going to the Nottingham factory with the boys. Pressure of work meant he'd missed two fortnightly visits there in a row and Raye Cropper had some new equipment to show off, or so she'd told him on the telephone.

Slipping downstairs, Eustace found few guests around at seven o'clock. The waiters were setting up breakfast tables. He was surprised to see Sarah arrive in the dining room. She wore trousers that might have looked at home on a golf course and an extraordinary hat resembling a small saucer piled with flowers.

As Sarah conferred with the maitre d', Eustace rose and beckoned her to his table. She swiftly ordered fruit juice and asked for toast and a kipper. Her head hung forward over her plate. She offered him nothing but a dutiful, "Good morning."

She had not touched the toast before she said, "I'm afraid he wasn't pleased… about the result. Breaking down, you know?"

"Yes, of course," he said. He noticed how delicate she was. A dancer must be hollow-boned, light as a bird, but it seemed the merest breeze might smash Sarah Coles into pieces.

"He was alright for a while and then… well, we called the room service and we drank rather too much."

He did not understand her confession. Delivered in a regretful tone, almost asking for forgiveness. He reached across under her hat and gently lifted the dark curls of hair from her forehead. She had a bruise above her right eye.

"Oh, God," he said.

The bruise filled his thoughts for days.

Once they arrived at the Nottingham factory, Eustace left the boys with the office girls while he walked the factory floor with Raye Cropper. The area was in full swing, manufacturing parts for the HL1. By comparison to Duke Works or any other factory he had ever visited, it was always immaculately clean — walkways marked in crisp yellow paint; parts and components moved from bay to bay in wheeled carts. They all had labels. Raye herself wore a pristine white laboratory coat.

When Havershall's had arrived in Marmaduke Lane, there was a thin black gunge coating everything from the road outside into and onto the factory floor. He remembered Woody and himself trying to clean it. Eustace felt this brave new Nottingham looked like the future had arrived and it was all Raye's doing.

In recent visits, he had noticed that the under-sixteens in the workforce were disappearing and men were rare. Now there were almost none. When Eustace asked, Raye said, "Women are cheaper."

"You mean, you can exploit them?"

"I mean, we pay our women better than any factory in Nottingham. They work better than men… and yes, Gaffer, they are still cheaper." She smiled awkwardly as if uncertain of his approval.

"Well, I'll be damned," he said and smiled in return.

"Let me show you the equipment you've paid for. I call it a machining centre. It's for the HL1 chassis. We do more with less people."

Her 'machining centre' consisted of four stations set back to back and pointing out at right angles to one another. A moving metal floor in the form of an annulus ten feet wide rotated around the outside, delivering four identical metal tables to the stations, one at a time and in sequence.

Each metal table had a jig to hold an aluminium casting. These castings were the main type-basket of a HL1 typewriter, the heart of the machine that housed the keys and typebars and the mechanisms that drove them. The castings were fixed into the jigs by four clamps, tightened and released on a hand-operated mechanism. A new casting would be loaded at the first station by an operator while unloading the finished casting that had already rotated through the other three stations.

Once a casting set off around the circuit, the second station had four spinning cutters which dropped down on hydraulic rams and milled flat surfaces onto it. These 'flats', Raye explained, would seat and align the type-basket to the base of the typewriter.

The third station was like a porcupine with drill heads instead of quills. She had mounted these at different heights and in exactly the right position to drill all the important screw holes in the casting. The station was sprayed with lubrication fluid. The final station looked much like the previous one, except here the drill heads turned and pushed down 'machine taps' to cut screw threads into the holes.

After a 360-degree rotation, the operator on the initial station was delivered a completed type-basket with tapped holes formed and mounting flanges machined in perfect alignment.

"It's like a monster," said Eustace when he first saw it.

"It's a wonderful monster," he said when he saw what it could do.

"Flat out, it produces a type-basket every forty-five seconds," Raye said like a proud mother hen. "Say, seventy-five an hour; twelve hundred a day when we are double shifting."

"From one operator?"

"One operator per shift."

"How many did it used to take?"

"When we had men, maybe a dozen."

"You don't think a lot of men, do you?" Eustace asked.

"Not many of them. We'll be better when they hurry up and go to war. It suits them." She hesitated, then said, "Sorry, I didn't mean nothing by that. Not my place to say, Gaffer, on Hitler and all that."

His thoughts on a war were well known, though now he pondered on the German engineering he'd seen at Donington. What did it mean? Progress happens and an industrialist — let alone a country — can't afford to stop.

"Could we make more of those contraptions?" He gestured towards the new machining centre.

"For the other models, the ones in Birmingham?"

"Yes, could you make it all look like this?"

"We all thought you was for buying companies, not equipment, Gaffer."

"Well, success changes things, Raye. Let's say we might have money for both now."

She nodded and he wondered how he could possibly explain that change to Woody.

1938 saw great innovation — the ballpoint pen, instant coffee, the invention of Teflon and LSD. At the year's end, Enrico Fermi received a Nobel Prize for discovering a process that involved the fission of uranium. Fleeing the anti-Semitism spreading through Italy, he departed for the United States, taking with him his Jewish wife and the central element of an atomic bomb.

By comparison, the HL1 was a minor advance, though — with the addition of Raye's machining centres — it was an extremely profitable one for Havershall's.

* * *

Just before Christmas, Eustace took Ginny and the boys to see Mother Goose starring George Lacy at the Theatre Royal in Birmingham. Woody tagged along, surprisingly sober.

Richard and William focused on Lacy, the pantomime dame dressed up in a costume resembling a billiards table. Eustace found his eye straying to a girl in the chorus… to Sarah.

Afterwards Woody — still 'Uncle Wood' to the boys — shepherded them backstage. Richard got Lacy's autograph on the front of a pale blue programme that cost thruppence. William pretended not to be interested. Eustace was disappointed that Sarah did not appear.

When he went back to work between Christmas and New Year, the weather closed in, roads got icy and he found himself staying in the city centre on a Wednesday night. The Christmas lights were still up along the streets.

He stood outside the Theatre Royal for a while, beneath the large coade stone medallion on the front wall that showed the face of the Bard looking down. He asked himself what on Earth he was doing. He went inside and bought a ticket.

He chose the left-hand side of the auditorium close to the front. That was where Sarah had her big dance number after the interval. He watched her move. Something close to envy replaced the pity he usually felt for Woody.

He didn't venture backstage on his own, not that first time, but he went back the following week. Twice. Watching Sarah dance. And remembering that he and Ginny had once danced all over London, outraging everyone. Oh, how the young Ginny Buckley shimmied back then!

The weather warmed, leaving slush on the streets. Eustace took another room in the city, another business excuse not to go home. That third time, he went to the stage door and asked the doorman to carry his business card inside. An invitation to visit the dressing rooms came back in reply.

He offered to take Sarah home. She told him she was staying at Woody's apartment in Aston. The Barton Arms had been abandoned.

"It's cheaper. They don't pay the chorus much," she explained. She didn't seem worried by the scandal of it.

"To Woody's then," he replied, because what else could he say? It took him several seconds to come up with, "So you're engaged?" He thought the ring must be somewhere by now. That was Woody's pattern.

"Don't be shocked. No, we are not engaged. He's asked. I said I'd think on it."

"You are unusual," he told her.

"To be so loose I don't even demand a ring?" She smiled at him. Free of its grease paint, her face looked terribly innocent.

"Not the word I was going to use," he assured her.

"Let me change and get my coat. I don't like taxis."

He drove slowly out to Aston, partly because the thawing roads were treacherous, mostly because he didn't want to lose her company or the fresh soapy smell she carried.

When he pulled up outside Woody's apartment, he insisted on rushing around to open the passenger door of his grand Rolls-Royce.

She was almost past him, when he said, "Oh, you've left your handbag," and leaned inside to retrieve it. She reached to take the bag's handle from his dangling fingers.

"Do not say yes," he said.

"Yes to what?"

"When he asks you again."

Taking the bag, she stopped after a step or two as if vacillating between options. Her face caught the street light as she turned.

"I saw you in the audience, Eustace. Not just tonight. All the nights."

"Oh, yes," he said, denial seeming pointless.

"You're most kind, but I think, too clever for all that. And as for Woody, I ask myself what better is there for a girl like me?"

"I could—"

"You could, what? What could you do?"

With a shrug, she was gone.

By the Easter of 1939, Mr Carling March of the Field Detective Agency had collected almost a thousand pictures of Eustace Havershall on his various sales trips and business conferences. In Ginny's eyes, her husband was now woefully neglecting his boys, his family, especially her. Worst of all, the guilt of tracking him made her wonder if she deserved the betrayals that no doubt occurred on those nights away.

Mr March had whittled down the photographs to a dozen that showed Eustace with other women, but all were inconclusive. There was no photograph of Eustace with Sarah Coles.

In the collection were snaps that proved Amelia Stewart had been on his business trip to an exhibition in Dublin and more recently down in Devon too. Two young women dressed like geishas were at his side at a gala dinner in Hong Kong, a promotional tour he'd taken with the Corrigans. Marie Thomas, the glamorous blonde who had taken over as manageress of the London showrooms, was pictured having drinks with Eustace in the American Bar of the Criterion, though Ginny could see an overcoat and hat resting on the adjacent chair. It suggested that Mr March had taken the photograph when another guest was away from the table, a charge he admitted when she pressed him on the point.

"Was he *with* the woman or not?" Ginny demanded.

"It is my view," said March, "that although your husband often deals with women who are — shall we say? — from the 'typing pool', he does not indulge as other men might."

She tried to believe the evidence. She wanted to be wrong; she wanted to be right. She didn't want to lose her marriage, her family. But why had she become so little... so ignored? She couldn't understand it.

"Fuck!" she said aloud. "I own part of the business. That was supposed to be enough."

March looked confused. Ginny poked a finger across the pile of photographs. The smile of Amelia Stewart unhinged her head, and that was all there was to it.

Arriving one Monday morning, Eustace noticed the lights in Woody's 'Lab' had been left on. He nudged the door open. Someone groaned.

"Woody?"

His partner was slumped forward on the workbench, while still half perched on the chair.

"You haven't been here all night?"

Strewn across the floor were piles of metal parts. The chassis of the prototype Woody had been trying to build for the last year was upside down in the waste basket. Wires hung everywhere. Two liquor bottles lay in the disordered mess next to Woody's elbow, alongside a handful of tools, the guts of an electric motor and a three-foot steel rod that provided the leverage for tightening one of the mechanical presses. The rod seemed to have done most of the damage. The room smelt of human excrement.

"You've not...?" Eustace began.

It became obvious that he had. Of all the extremes, soiling himself seemed the worst.

"She's run off."

Eustace couldn't think what to say, couldn't say what he really thought, so he said, "You don't mean Celia?"

"No, no, I don't mean her." Woody tried to balance himself on the seat, but his waving arm made him unsteady. "Not her. Sarah. I asked and asked. She threw the ring back at me. Left town. Took a job on some West End show."

"Oh," said Eustace.

He couldn't call for help — he wouldn't let Woody suffer the humiliation — so he manhandled him out through the back of the factory and drove him home, braving the smell. The Rolls could not be driven in comfort again, without new upholstery.

The drinking didn't stop, or rather it started again as soon as unconsciousness abated. Two nights later, Woody arrived at Mrs Bembole's door. He stumbled up the front steps, asked for the French girl.

Mrs Bembole came to the door to say the French girl no longer worked there.

"Another then, with flaming hair, and young," he demanded.

"Alas, Sir, no. No one of that description."

He knew it was a lie. Even if it were true, an obliging madam always found someone to meet your description, however loosely.

Mrs Bembole watched him. Unflinching.

He had frightened the French girl too much. He frightened them all. Even his money was not good enough anymore.

Ginny ran the offices and her home and worried about her boys. She and Eustace fell further into the silent divide. Only the issue of Woody united them.

"I... I must do something... something more," Eustace said.

"Yes," she agreed.

"I do not know what."

"A sanatorium?"

"He is not insane. His ideas are crazy, but I'll not have it said that he's mad."

"He is an alcoholic, Eustace. There are institutions, discreet places, for the treatment of those with temporary mental illness."

"Is it temporary?"

"It is if he can be cured, don't you think? There is a hospital, beautiful grounds, out in Surrey. Several of my uncle's friends in the Lords have been 'cured' there, I believe."

"A place for toffs. You think Woody would agree?"

"He will agree if I ask him," she said.

"You? Why you?"

"Because I can tell him, as a mother, that Mabel would have wished for his daughter to see him recovered. I do not believe that is for you to say. I will ask him if you agree we should pay."

He flinched, surprised at her question. "Yes, of course."

"Very well," she said.

She did not say he was showing more kindness than to his own father and brother. She was not surprised at his generosity when Woody was the one in need.

Chapter Twenty

While Woody languished in an undecorated room, surrounded by twenty-two acres of Surrey's finest countryside, the war he predicted drew closer.

By the beginning of 1939, Germany was already fighting. England and France remained — like Eustace — consciously unaware, despite their sobriety.

After Hitler had annexed Austria and been handed the Sudetenland, concentration camps opened. The smashing of Jewish businesses and homes sent such a tide of Jews flooding towards Palestine that Britain had to block their entry for fear the Arab population would rise in rebellion.

In March, Hitler invaded the remainder of Czechoslovakia and issued an ultimatum to Lithuania which prompted the concession of the Klaipėda Region, a former German territory.

When Britain and France issued guarantees, assuring their backing for Polish, Romanian and Greek independence, Hitler claimed they were encircling Germany. He renounced his Non-Aggression Pact with Poland and the Anglo-German Naval Agreement. Intelligence suggested the Nazis were building a fleet to match British sea power.

In response, Britain issued leaflets on gas masks and how to prevent the leakage of light from windows during air raids. It did little to invest in actual weapons or military equipment.

Havershall's bought more companies, sold more typewriters. Raye's HL1 swept into the overseas market like a tidal wave and that was as much 'foreign policy' as Eustace thought he needed.

Without Woody, who had been there from the beginning, Eustace felt alone. The days Ginny worked in Duke House did not help. The distance between their offices at Duke House only seemed to get bigger, as did the divide in their marriage. He tried to win her over with his successes; she responded with complaints about his working hours.

In the summer of 1939, the factory of Jethro Moldevine, a Cornish blacksmith who had started a typewriter business on the day of Queen Victoria's death thirty-eight years before, came up for sale. He wrote to Eustace, telling him of his intention to retire. He had no family to hand the business onto. Eustace wrote back, suggesting a visit. Moldevine had not offered a company phone number.

It was a visit Woody would have loved, but Eustace drove down without him. Moldevine was the only independent manufacturer of typewriters left in the country, since Havershall's and BBTL had bought up everyone else who hadn't gone bankrupt. Moldevine made one product, the J1 — big and heavy steel components in a case of polished wood, each one handmade and hand-assembled. The keys had buttons made of polished ivory.

The factory lay in disused farm buildings on the outskirts of Falmouth. Moldevine employed a dozen workers, all craftsmen. The biggest production machine in the place was a drill station.

"What d'you think of it?" Moldevine asked.

The tour had taken no more than five minutes, there being hardly anything to see. There were few windows, several suffering from cracked panes, one punctured by a hole the size of a golf ball. The wooden doors were rotting along the uneven bottom edges. To Eustace, it still smelt like a barn. He and Moldevine stood at the entrance, scanning the rough work benches, each holding a half built J1 and each holding the antique echo of that long-ago French machine.

"Safe," Eustace declared.

Safe because there were no industrial-sized machines to swallow anybody up.

"They're beautiful machines," he lied.

"It's solid British engineering we do here," Moldevine assured him.

The man, like his factory, was from a lost century — a Victorian beard, well kept but grey; his hands great meaty claws; yellow teeth from chewing tobacco. His bottom lip had a worrying black spot in the right corner.

"You said Barrington-Brown had been to visit?" Eustace suggested.

"I said nothing of the sort. I heard you had money."

"You wrote to me, yet you didn't write to him? Jethro, he can call on any bank in the country. You know that. And I know you know that. He could match anything I could offer."

"There's people I'd rather sell to."

"So he already turned you down?"

"That bloke don't know nothing. He reckoned my factory weren't modern."

"It isn't."

"We make good product here, but I reckon Cornwall were too far south for him. He just wanted space on account of expecting to make stuff for the war effort. I mean, damn, who isn't expecting that, Mr Havershall?"

Eustace had been arguing the opposite at a Chamber of Commerce dinner two evenings before. No war, he'd insisted to anyone who would listen.

Moldevine cracked a sour smile. "I've know Charlie since he had no more idea of a typewriter than it were a crate that come off a ship in Bristol. I thought he might've learnt something by now. Well, Mr Havershall, let's be having it… your offer?"

Moldevine would have taken the lowest figure he dared suggest, Eustace knew that. But Moldevine had expectations. He wanted someone who would keep selling his old out-of-date typewriters to people who wanted to look at their purchase rather than type on it. Each bench here would struggle to finish a machine in a day. They were selling art not writing instruments.

"I'm sorry, Jethro. I can't."

"Can't or won't?" The question was sharp, but then Moldevine shrugged and his voice softened. "No, no, I guess not. I'll bet your mucker, Mr Woodmansey would say something different. Maybe I should have asked him. A proper engineer."

"Woody would tell you—" Eustace hesitated. He knew Woody would buy Moldevine's factory, simply for its engineering purity, but Eustace compared the factory before him to Raye Cropper's automated machining centres. There was something both magnificent and sad about progress. Eustace was addicted to the future. Not to the technology Woody fed on, but to the new money it would bring.

The following week, Eustace was offered a property in Radford, on the northern outskirts of Coventry. 'Cartwright & Co. Engineering', the company sited there, was struggling on under an administrator after its owner had died suddenly.

Eustace could send the company's lathes and cutting machines to auction for ready cash — they had no use for typewriter manufacture — and he saw great value in the company's property, which was not far from Daimler's enormous car factory and served by their private railway station, Daimler Halt. He snapped it up, agreeing the deal without a word to Woody or Ginny.

It was, he explained to her later over dinner, the sort of thing Woody would have backed him on unreservedly if he hadn't happened to be temporarily in a sanatorium. The land and property would sell at twice its cost.

"You cannot use Woody's indisposition and inability to vote as a reason to make decisions on your own," she scolded.

"You mean without you?" he said. "How else will we make decisions in his absence, since I own nearly eighty percent of the shares that are in a position to vote? Havershall's must go forward. Besides the financing of this loan is small, almost insignificant. Archie agreed it on the spot."

She scowled at him across the dinner table.

"I did not put Moldevine's company to a vote either. Some things are just good business," he said.

The annual Grand Prix in Monaco had already been suspended due to a dispute over prize money, but the Havershalls took a fortnight in Cap Ferrat in late August. Family bonding, Ginny called it. She hoped to close some of the distance that was evident now Richard and William were in boarding school during term time. The compromise with Eustace was that corporate guests would be invited, but only for the second week; for the first, it was to be family. Family, in Ginny's mind, now included Celia Woodmansey.

When Eustace and Ginny drove down with their boys, Celia sat sandwiched between Richard and William in the rear of the Rolls-Royce. She was now seventeen, the age at which débutantes were presented and at which Ginny had been sent to England in search of a willing husband. Ginny noted the 'coming of age' that had occurred.

Two years before, Celia had needed tennis lessons, but when protégé and mentor returned to the tennis court at Cap Ferrat, Ginny had to play flat out to win. On the second afternoon, Celia managed an honourable 8-6 defeat. Her hostess — at thirty-six — wondered if time was beginning to affect her. Celia didn't seem to sweat.

As they came off court, Ginny spotted Richard and William watching from the garden, some thirty yards away where they could pretend to be examining a flower bed in the villa's garden, but kept stealing glances towards the court, and towards Celia in particular.

The following day, she found the three of them playing tennis together in the afternoon. Richard's leg weakness didn't show now, unless he was tired, and his two-year advantage over his brother gave him extra strength. Every point William lost was greeted badly by the younger Havershall. Celia tousled his hair like some child in need of consolation. After a few games in which balls sailed past him, William found new ways to hold his own. Richard seemed to ease back his effort and, in the end, showed no interest in winning or losing. To Ginny, the afternoon captured her two boys perfectly.

Before any non-family guests arrived, Ginny resolved to take Celia shopping in nearby Cannes. New outfits were required to keep up with the times. She helped Celia choose two pairs of linen trousers — tight waist band, wide-legged.

"Your Katharine Hepburn look," Ginny remarked. As a special holiday gift, she bought Celia a new Roussel swim suit with thin crossed straps at the back and fabric cut high on the thigh. Ventures to the beach now saw Celia trailed by growing streams of teenage boys as the sun turned her pale skin to an inviting tan.

Richard stared at her across the dinner table. William's eyes had started to follow.

"Oh, God, it's Beerbohm all over again," Eustace said.

"It's simply a young girl getting fashionable," Ginny replied. "And yes, I helped. Look at who else she's got, two old grandparents and your drunken partner. I simply had to step in."

For Week Two, Frederic Dupont and his wife Hannah brought a group of French clients. Frederic had been a guest before, but this was the first time he'd brought his wife. Hannah proved to be a squat, dark-haired woman of forty-three. She loved the fact that both Ginny and Celia spoke French.

An American businessman and his mistress who'd been staying in Paris had also been invited. Still convinced that war would be avoided, Eustace was hoping to agree a new transatlantic effort to launch Havershall's typewriters further west. Such expansion was well overdue, he said.

At Ginny's invitation, her cousin Caroline and her Viscount were due to attend, arriving on the second Thursday evening. The house would be full. Ginny hired her jazz bands and a brief party season began. Half of her believed Eustace's optimism about averting war, the other half was now desperate to outrun its looming shadow.

* * *

As soon as Viscount and Viscountess Fairchild arrived, the whole house party developed a dutiful awe for English aristocracy. Ginny thought it vulgar. From the Americans it was, she supposed, to be expected, but even the Duponts were taken in.

She noted that Caroline and Edward presented a respectful and practised compromise to the world. They were convenient to each other, together when other people were watching, apart when no one appeared to be. For most purposes, Caroline continued as the austere and rather prudish woman who had once advised on the wife's duty in marriage, but on occasion, she'd sneak away on an excuse to change her outfit or visit the bathroom, returning flushed and gay and quite without inhibitions.

"What is going on?" Ginny asked when alone with her cousin.

"Oh, nothing. Same old, same old, you know."

"He's still having affairs?"

"Ah, bit of a development on that front," Caroline admitted. She had just lit a cigarette and sat admiring its glowing tip. "Truth is Edward only came here for moral support. I suppose that's what you'd call it. I got myself into trouble. Photographs and such like."

"You? With photographs?"

"With young men. Well, with one young man who proved to be—" Caroline hesitated. "I think they call it a honey trap in the trade. Edward had to buy the negatives from the London press."

"You?"

"Me, yes. Don't look so shocked."

"And that's why you're here?" Ginny asked, seeking confirmation.

"That's why he's here, in case there are more of those beastly men with their cameras stalking the Riviera."

Ginny thought of Mr Carling March, whom she had now dismissed. The memory of spying on Eustace brought a guilty taste to her mouth.

"I think we should parade ourselves... for the record," she declared. "You and Edward. Eustace and I. Along the promenade with the families. Take all our guests. If people want photographs, let them have them. We know the game. You and I were trained to be Buckleys."

"That would be delicious," said Caroline.

At Ginny's insistence, all the weekend guests took a day trip to Nice and strolled along the *Promenade des Anglais*. The men conspicuously dressed in flannels in the manner of cricketers. The women carried parasols, sporting fashionable straw hats with low crowns and irregular brims. No photographers appeared.

"I met Matisse here, didn't I, Mummy?" said Richard, becoming animated as they passed Le Negresco.

"Don't be silly, Dicky," Eustace said.

"I did. He was right there, having his coffee. He shook my hand and drew me a picture," Richard insisted. He looked at his younger brother. William offered no support.

"I'm surprised you remember," Ginny stumbled.

"Henri Matisse?" the Viscount said, sounding contemptuous.

"Yes, Edward, one of those men who can't draw," Caroline teased. Looking at Ginny and Richard, she added, "That's the official opinion from on high."

"He can. He can," Richard repeated. "He's better than anyone. Anyone except Picasso. Do you think Picasso is here this year, Mummy?"

"Not in Nice, Richard," Ginny said. "Further along the coast."

William sighed contemptuously.

"If you want to pursue a real artist, there is Joyce," Eustace suggested, pointing at a hotel up ahead where a cliff rose steeply above a line of buildings. "See there. That's the Hôtel Suisse. Joyce began Finnegans Wake in its rooms. It took seventeen years."

Joyce's book had recently been published and Eustace had worked through it a page at a time since buying a first edition.

"How can anyone take seventeen years to write a book?" the Viscount asked. "I imagine one would get bored reading it."

"It's a large book," Eustace admitted, "with rather eccentric spelling."

"Typical of the bloody Irish," the Viscount said. "Always trouble. Should never have given them independence. We have this idea people know what's good for them. Of course, they don't. See how much better Germany and Italy have done with a proper plan. The fascists have brought back national pride. England has done nothing but plunge into decline since we gave the common man and woman the vote."

Celia piped up, "Of course, it's easy to keep control when all your opponents are held in camps."

Eyes turned. What seventeen-year-old questions a peer of the realm?

"I hear the Nazis have a new one... for female *undesirables*," she continued.

The Viscount recovered from his surprise enough to say, "I assure you, young lady, you are mistaken."

"Ravensbrück, that's it's name. Full of *filthy* Jews, of course? *Krystallnacht*? Is that not true either?"

"That's a rumour, my dear, I assure you." The Viscount turned to appeal to the onlookers. "My goodness, what do they teach schoolgirls these days? Where did you hear these things?"

Ginny was about to step in, but Celia needed no help.

"I speak the German language rather well, your Lordship, with a Swiss Jew for a grandfather. It helps to understand the lies and propaganda."

"I have to say, she is completely right," said Hannah Dupont, her first words in English all day.

Hannah's features, now Ginny chose to look, were dark beyond the Mediterranean. And her nose? Well, Ginny had not considered it before.

Woody was not expected in Cap Ferrat. He had been out of the Sanatorium for only three weeks.

He had purchased a new road car, but found it disappointingly underpowered. A Bugatti 57 Surbaissé sounded fast, he'd thought. It wasn't. He had sent the car to the Bugatti factory at Molsheim in North East France to have the optional supercharger fitted. A trip to the Riviera gave him the perfect excuse to visit the factory, pick up his upgraded car and test it on the roads down to Cap Ferrat. He arrived, declaring himself satisfied with its power. He said he had sworn off alcohol forever.

The American within the house party, and Eustace's would-be American distributor, was a Mr Harrison Verlaine, the forty-something son of a Senator on his father's side and heir to his mother's plantation fortune. He wore plus-four trousers and a tie that hung askew on white starched-collar shirts. Being comically overweight, he looked — to Ginny's eye — rather like a blimp on legs.

"My mother's father owned slaves down in Georgia," Verlaine said during pre-dinner drinks on the patio. He didn't seem to mind the rest of the party sharing his family's dirty history.

Eustace, Woody, Mr Dupont and Viscount Fairchild were sitting around one wicker table with Verlaine. Woody was the only one not drinking. Ginny occupied the adjacent table, Celia and Caroline at her elbow, alongside Verlaine's mistress, Claudette, and Hannah Dupont.

"I'll not say it's an elegant way to get rich, but wealth lasts the generations," Verlaine told his audience. "Gave me the trust fund to come running over to Paris in '24. Gee, I even got myself tight in Gertrude Stein's parlour. I'm a bona-fide Bohemian. And all that's on slave money."

He began lighting a cigar. Between attempts to entice the flame onto the tobacco, he said, "But yes, folks, it's time for a Yankee to go home. I figure trading typewriters and office goods is a noble enough profession, compared to the alternatives. So, Gentlemen, if you want to sell in America, you have to get your product off the boat, you know what I mean? You could do a whole lot worse than Harrison Verlaine."

Claudette, his mistress, had nudged up to Ginny's elbow. She was a willowy woman with a leathery tan, drawn-on eyebrows and false lashes. She claimed she had arrived in Paris after living most of her life in Africa. She spoke English with a Belgian accent.

"My family traded rubber and other things... before the Great War. And rubber is far worse than Harry's plantation stories," she whispered. "When I was growing up, the King of Belgium owned the Congo Free State and claimed everything in it. I saw what that means... to have one man look down as if from heaven."

At the men's table, the conversation drifted on, the Viscount once again attempting to explain the treatment of inferior classes in Germany.

Claudette continued her whisper: "These European men, they don't know what they are talking about."

Ginny started to say, "I'm sure they—"

"They don't understand *atrocity*," Claudette declared. "When even a God who ordered genocide by Jewish Kings will be offended. Atrocity is what this Hitler carries."

"I assure you, my husband went to war," said Ginny. "Battle is enough to school any man."

"*Oui, mais non.* You must know, it is one thing to kill a man who opposes you. You still see a man. When you hack off a child's limbs with a machete because a father does not reach his work quota, you have lost this face, *non*? You see only animals. This is atrocity."

Ginny felt the breath seize in her lungs. No doubt, Claudette was talking from experience.

"The victims scream for a long time. It is worse when they become silent. And still you do nothing. We are barbarians at heart. You think Europe does anything now, for the Jews?"

Caroline said, "You know, I heard Lady Astor saying just the same only last week."

Ginny noticed that Celia had edged a few inches closer to Madame Dupont.

On meeting Stalin, Nancy Astor, a Viscountess through her marriage to Waldorf Astor and the first woman to sit in the British Parliament, had asked the great dictator why he had slaughtered so many Russians. Like most British politicians, she hated communists. She had a softer spot for Hitler.

Visiting America, she told her hosts there would be no war. "The Nazis would have to do worse than give a rough time to the killers of Christ for Britain and America to risk Armageddon to save them."

On the same trip, she told African-American church leaders that slavery had brought them Christianity.

Late that night, the party was lounging by the swimming pool listening to jazz from a gramophone. Pre-dinner drinking had become after-dinner indulgence. Celia had gone off swimming with two local girls she had befriended at the beach and not returned.

Woody was asleep in his deck chair on the patio when Ginny found him. She wondered if he'd secretly lapsed into drink. She scooped a handful of pool water and dribbled it onto his face.

"Shit, fuck, damn… What?" he spluttered.

"I thought you might want to get back to your own bed. Everyone else has long since gone."

The light from the patio windows was leaking towards the pool. He focused on Ginny's face, lit only on one side. He caught its vague distress.

"Sorry," he said, in case the cause was his own behaviour. "I don't mean to mess things up by arriving."

"And yet you arrived. Don't worry. From what I heard earlier, you were the most intelligent conversationalist of the entire evening."

"I was? They must have been talking some—"

"Some awful balderdash, actually," she said.

He tried to sit up but the effort made his head spin. He clutched the sides of his skull between his fingertips. "Maybe I'm getting too old for this. Driving down on my own all in one day."

"You didn't drink?" she said, wanting the confirmation.

"One hundred and twenty days sober. The world seems to be doing quite a fine job of falling apart without me joining in."

"I suppose we're all scared now. I'm sacred. Who wouldn't be? Tell me, Woody, what about my husband? He doesn't say. He won't admit there's a war brewing. You know him better… in this."

"I don't think the Captain is ever scared," he said. "Not like normal men. He thinks… maybe we both do… that we're always living on borrowed time. So this is nothing new. It's all luck. He and I, we know this."

"He betrayed you over the HL1. You wanted to build other things?"

"Yes. I tried."

"But you love him anyway?"

"It's a good typewriter," Woody said.

"And that's what matters to you?" She thought for a moment, then said, "Tell me, if you had the choice of Jethro Moldevine's old typewriter factory and a nice plot in Coventry you could do anything you liked with, where would you have spent our money."

"On Jethro's machines, of course."

"Really? But they aren't the future. You're always the one on about the future."

"I didn't say mine would be the right choice," he said, as if revealing a guilty secret.

"Fiddlesticks! I don't understand either of you. He made the decision without you… without me. Doesn't it make you angry when he's so secretive? He never talks to me anymore. About anything." Ginny lowered her voice. "Maybe he never did, not really. Not about — you know — the tank, or what happened, what you saw together. He's never told me anything. You don't speak about it either."

"It's not my place."

"I think now… I think you're right that there's another war coming fast, and he and I aren't past the last one. Isn't that right?" She looked at him as if she expected him to know, but he offered nothing in return.

As she turned to leave, he called after her, "War's not what really scares you though, Ginny, is it?"

"Why would you say that? War should make anyone fearful."

"True enough, but that's not it. Not for you. You're scared he denies the war that's coming because he might end up taking a place in it. He knows what duty is."

He gave her a moment to consider.

"I'm scared he thinks his place is not next to me," she said. "Because I don't think it has been for a while."

"Those things he does, Ginny… At first, they were about his father. John Havershall Senior was a monstrous bastard. Believe me, I've known my share. Eustace was really the eldest, the best, the heir. His father made him prove that, and by God, he did. Then there was you. You had to give him money. He has to prove he deserves that too. He has to prove he is enough for the new Havershall family. You, Ginny, are his Lady Macbeth."

"That's a hateful thing to say."

"It seems we don't get to pick our parts," he said. "Only to play them as best we can."

Leaving Woody to sleep, Ginny wandered into the east wing where Richard and William had rooms. With all that she had heard in the past few days, she worried how talk of war might be affecting them.

For no reason other than curiosity, she nosed her way into their rooms as they slept. Richard had brought many books, all of them seemed beyond his age. The picture Matisse had drawn was pinned up behind his bed. He must have found it somewhere, its importance now redoubled. William's floor was, as always, littered with a combination of clothes, Meccano constructions and model racing cars. Resting against the wall was a rugby ball and a cricket bat. William was not yet twelve, but already had downy stubble growing on his cheeks and a few stray hairs on his chest.

It was odd, she thought, that now she seemed to understand more about Celia than William or Richard. How had that happened? She wasn't sure the last week and a half had made it better.

By coincidence, her protégé was coming up the corridor as Ginny was closing William's door. Celia's room was the last in the row. She was whistling a tune — the *Marseillaise*.

"Shh!" said Ginny.

Celia halted abruptly, rabbit-eyed as if caught in some act of treachery.

"I'm late. I'm sorry. We got carried away at the beach."

"In the dark?"

"We met friends. I mean, friends of the other girls. Lit a fire. There was a boy who could play the guitar. He tried teach me to whistle."

"So I see," said Ginny.

She noticed the Roussel swim suit beneath Celia's overcoat. Her hair was still damp and tangled, consistent with having spent the evening in a bathing cap.

"Please don't tell my father, Aunt Ginny," Celia pleaded. "I haven't been drinking. It isn't like before."

"Tell your father what? That you had a good time?"

Celia thanked her and said good night all in one sentence. Ginny watched her hurry away towards her room, barefoot and gliding on the balls of her feet as if she hadn't quite forgotten whatever dance step she'd been performing in the sand.

Ginny shook her head, trying to clear a sudden wave of sadness. She started to weep, but could not quite decide why.

In the morning, Eustace found his wife asleep beside him. He decided to let her sleep on, but she woke and followed him down to breakfast more promptly than of late. He was tucking into kippers. Since her first pregnancy, she had tried to avoid the smell.

"Are you alright, Gin? I didn't hear you come to bed."

"Years ago, you'd have waited up. Me in my cocktail dress and then… then you'd delight me in our usual way."

"I'm sorry, too much to drink. With all the guests to entertain. And the business."

"About the distributor…"

"Yes?"

"Do not deal with this American man, Eustace," she said, straight out.

"With Verlaine? Why on Earth not? He has big plans for America, and if they stay out of the war—"

"No, we are better than that."

He looked at her perplexed. "I have never known you be snobbish about business."

"This isn't a question of class, or business," she said. "There will be a war, Eustace, and we will have to fight it. Best we fight with our principles intact, don't you think?"

Two mornings later, the last but one day in August dawned bright and sunny. While the remaining party were swimming, Eustace was called to the telephone. The call had chased him across the Channel.

It began with a voice saying, "Captain Havershall, Sir."

He could not place it until the voice said, "This is Horace Priestley. Remember me?"

Eustace had not seen or spoken to Priestley since Cambrai. He'd heard a rumour Priestley had lost his head before the Armistice and been sent to Craiglockhart Hospital with Shell Shock.

"I've been asked to approach you, Sir."

"Approach me?"

"Yes, by the Ministry of Supply--"

"The what?"

"Oh, we don't officially exist... not yet. The bill's only just gone through Parliament."

"I've not heard of any bill."

"It's Mr. Chamberlain's. A little late, it must be said. He's moved the Minister of Transport over to run it. It already has the approval of the King. We have to make sure that Military Orders get priority and the forces get everything they need."

"Military Orders?" Eustace repeated. He wanted to say, "But we are not at war."

Priestley beat him to the punch. "We need the best efforts of the best men and the best factories. Every advantage we can give them, you understand, and as fast as possible. You have a factory."

"Several factories," Eustace said.

"Your reputation... your Military Cross... goes before you. When would you and Mr Woodmansey be able to come to London?"

Eustace explained the phone call to Woody.

"What do we do now?" Eustace asked.

His rejuvenated partner was sitting on a lounger by the pool, head back enjoying the morning sun, dressed only in yellow shorts. He pulled his glasses down from the top of his head and repositioned them on his nose.

"I suppose we pack," he said.

"We can't just leave. I...We... Havershall's have guests."

"The guests are leaving anyway. Ginny can handle the rest. She's done it before."

"Yes," Eustace admitted, "and now she has your Celia. Her French is marvellous."

"I suppose so." Woody seemed vague about his daughter, as if he had failed to notice anything about her.

Eustace said, "We could tell Priestley next week. Put it off."

"Britain's war preparation is already too slow. Not our place to make it slower." Woody searched under the lounger for the bedroom slippers he'd been wearing when he arrived. "I'll drive you. It's a decent run for the Bugatti."

"I haven't said I'll go. Priestley said he wanted to talk about our 'capacity'. I mean, how useful can we be with our equipment? We make typewriters. Truth is, I've been hoping to avoid all this."

"Like we avoided the last war, you and I, Captain? We'll go. You know it."

"I thought we'd had our war, Woody."

"Wars happen. That's it. This is a different kind, though. *Our* war was not so much won as stopped. Exhausted by the to and fro." Woody used a hand to illustrate the wavering fortunes. "But this next one, Eustace, is an industrial war. A war for men who make things. Manufacture and innovation. You asked how useful could we be? I say we are the most important of all. We can help produce anything. I don't like what will happen if we refuse."

Harrison Verlaine and Claudette had left the afternoon before. Viscount Fairchild had taken the train to Paris along with the Duponts before dawn. With Woody and Eustace's departure, Caroline, Celia and Ginny were left with two disgruntled Havershall boys and a handful of staff hired for a larger party. The departures all seemed so sudden. Ginny felt a terrible hole had cracked open in her life. It had been threatening for a while. The bonding she had hoped might result from the fortnight seemed to have passed her by.

"If this is the last of peace, better make the best of it," Caroline said, cheerily.

Caroline said she knew people who knew people — aristocrats and artists living along the coast. Ginny thought it through, minded to say no, but then she said yes. *Why not?* The Havershalls knew people along the coast just as well as the Fairchilds — plenty of people to invite. She threw herself into it. A last chance, as her cousin put it. The party was set for the 31st of August.

She made phone calls, found another trio of jazz players and a dozen willing revellers who knew how to bring many more. By a combination of cascading invitations and a collection of the local youth provided by Celia, the gathering grew to seventy-five, the biggest Ginny had ever hosted in Cap Ferrat.

The more people who came, the more Ginny's hole might be filled, or at least, that's what she concluded. Before the trip, she had purchased the perfect black dress from a French designer much in vogue. The dress, just above the knee and in silk with zigzag patterns of silver-tipped frills across its front, went with the Rochas' house's signature fragrance, 'Femme'. She looked in the mirror and scolded herself for her vanity. She had been saving it to impress Eustace, but tonight felt like the night to launch it. Black was her colour and her mood in so many ways.

By midnight, dancing spread across the patio. The younger men and women with bodies to show off were changing into bathing costumes and splashing about in the pool. She drank alongside her cousin, bottomless glasses of champagne the waiters offered. Gin cocktails followed.

High on the bubbles, low on the gin, she noticed Celia on the dance floor. The girl's partner, she realised in her haze, was Guy de Monteparnasse, here without his wife. The Count span Celia in and out of his clutches, exposing her tanned legs as her dress flared.

"She is rather enjoying herself, don't you think?" Caroline said, familiar gimlet in hand. "She has gumption, that girl. She told my husband a thing or two,"

"Is Edward truly a sympathiser with all that guff?" Ginny asked.

"Oh, dreadfully. He knows the Mitfords. May even have had an affair with the one who's cosying up to Hitler. I've quite lost track. I think I may have slept with their brother. Or was it a cousin."

"Caroline, you didn't?'

"I'm afraid I did," she said. "Revenge! What is it they say, 'A dish best served cold'."

"He wasn't the one in the papers?"Ginny asked.

"Oh, no. Revenge has been repeated several times."

They were standing at a temporary drinks table on the patio. A penguin-suited waiter was hovering, attentive to whatever might be required. Suddenly Ginny and Caroline burst into howls of laughter.

"What a pair we are," Caroline remarked, sank her drink and reached for the waiter's tray to take another. Ginny did the same.

"Don't you think he's too old for her?" she said, referring to Celia and the Count.

"For her? Yes," said Caroline. "Don't worry, it will right itself."

They lit each other's cigarettes and watched while Celia twirled from the Count to a Spanish boy with slicked back hair. Ginny felt relieved.

She didn't know why. The Spanish boy was the more dangerous. He had a predatory look that Ginny had once known very well.

"Well," she said, "I suppose I once had Celia's legs."

"Nonsense, you still have lovely legs."

"I am thirty-six."

"You are the perfect age for French lovers." Caroline blew a smoke ring. "See the Count. He has divorced his wife, I'm told. Moved to Paris. He is engaged to Isabella d'Genoix and connected in Paris society. I ask myself, did such a man come here for Celia? Or is he returning for someone else?"

"Caroline! You make it sound like—"

"Ah, do not say it. Did we not agree, we must take our chances, snatch a little happiness. Hannah Dupont was right. The French know what is coming to them. They've seen it before. We are hanging on to some beautiful age before it dies — the Last Supper, so to speak. My husband has gone to Paris and you and I are free and far from the London press, thank God."

She glanced towards the Count, her lips pressed together to produce a gentle 'hmmm'.

"Do you remember when we were young, Gin? Henley, when no one would leave us alone. We were so foolish, we would not let them touch."

Before Ginny could form a reply, Celia came bounding towards them, cheeks flushed.

"I am going with the others. Some of us want to go to the beach. Is it alright, Aunt Ginny?"

"Swimming at midnight again? My pool is not enough?"

"It's romance," said Caroline. "They can't feel each other up if they are right in front of us."

Celia glared and Caroline laughed.

In the background, the Count was walking towards them, having left his latest dance partner.

Ginny woke the next morning in her usual bedroom. Her head felt heavy. Light was bursting through the curtains, catching the silver frills of the Rochas' dress discarded on a nearby chair. She stared at it in horror.

Someone had slipped out onto the balcony to watch the sun rising over the sea. Eustace always liked to watch the morning, but it was not Eustace standing on her balcony. The lingering heat of the mattress when she flattened her hand against its sheet was not his heat. Only the wedding ring on her finger was Eustace. She was wearing nothing else.

She remembered the ecstatic uncertainty of the night, that moment when a stranger was above her and it was too late to say no.

If she were careful with the lies she told herself, she was not actually herself when it happened. Maybe she had thought she was proving something, but what it was she couldn't tell anymore.

Guy de Monteparnasse now turned from the balcony. He had stolen not only Eustace's bed space, but the morning newspaper that was always pushed under the bedroom door at six-thirty.

"Ah, you're awake. Something terrible is happening."

It took a moment to realise he was talking about something in the paper. "Look!" he said. "Germany is preparing to cross the border."

"Here? In France?"

As he approached, he pointed to the front page headline. "No, my dear, in Poland. This is how it starts."

She did not speak, but turned her face into her pillow, pressed it down hard, pulled up the pillow corners with her hands so its softness wrapped around her ears.

Eustace had been wrong in the worst possible way. A war was upon them. And she had been unfaithful.

In any seduction, the seduced must give little signs of encouragement and reproach as the boundaries are crossed one by one. War is different. War is built on tiny steps and a large stride. It sometimes needs a substantial nudge to bring the parties across the Rubicon.

Caught in a stalemate over its Polish ambitions, the German propaganda machine had needed to justify an invasion. Troops were massed near the border. They could not cross and be labelled as 'aggressors'.

Of course, if your opponent won't provide the nudge, you can always nudge yourself. At the end of August, prisoners of Flossenbürg, Sachsenhausen and other concentration camps were taken to the border, dressed in Polish uniforms and murdered. Several staged 'incidents' followed. In each, the evidence of Polish aggression was provided by dead bodies supplied by the Germans. There were supposed attacks on a strategic railway at Jablunka Pass on the border between Poland and Czechoslovakia, a customs station at Hochlinde a forest service station in Pitschen, and a German radio station in Gliwice, which broadcast a brief anti-German message in Polish before a former inmate of the Dachau concentration camp and a local Polish-Silesian activist were left dead on the scene, attired to make the propaganda work.

In retaliation for the attacks it had perpetrated on itself, German forces entered Poland at 4:45 a.m. on 1st September. That was the giant stride.

By the time hungover guests appeared for breakfast, the villa's radiogram had delivered a special bulletin about the situation in Poland, interrupting its usual broadcast music. All the villa's rooms had been filled overnight, or — more accurately — been claimed by whoever got there first. As they appeared in dribs and drabs, the French-speaking guests translated the report for the English speakers. Details were sketchy and uncertain, but everyone was in shock.

No one noticed an unexpected face or two around the breakfast tables. The Count's presence was un-noteworthy. He sat with other guests, while Ginny took croissants and orange juice with her two sons. Caroline arrived hand in hand with her gentleman of the night before and plonked him brazenly at her side. It seemed she had lost her fear of photographers. They would soon be off seeking images of a war.

Celia, however, was nowhere to be seen.

When the Count moved to leave, saying he needed to get to Paris, Ginny followed him into the house on the pretence of escorting him to the door, an etiquette she adopted for all departures whether she knew the person well or not. She thought this was safe. War was the only conversation around the breakfast tables.

"Will I see you again?" she asked discreetly as he retrieved his coat from the hall closet.

"Do you want to see me again?" He shook his head as if answering his own question. Once he had the coat settled, his arms in the sleeves, he produced a white business card from its pocket and held it towards her. She read the name, the titles, the address of an office in Paris.

"No," she whispered. "I will not take it."

"I understand," he said withdrawing the card. "But if I may be of service…"

"I am not clear, I'm sorry, I don't know how you were ever invited. I mean, with your wife, the first time. I didn't know you."

"I knew Grover-Williams. Bill and I were friends way back. He told me all about the *Havershalls of Cap Ferrat.*"

"I didn't know we enjoyed that notoriety."

"Not notoriety. I'd call it high regard. Mr Grover-Williams and I are engaged on a project. We are recruiting young men and women who speak French and English and maybe German too. I thought here, among English people…"

"You thought you might find recruits," she said, completing his sentence. "So, in fact, you came on business."

"Yes and no." He switched into French to say, "Mrs Havershall, we both know that we are living under a dark threat. Britain is now sure to declare war. It's time for people to — shall I say? — declare themselves."

"You weren't thinking— Me?"

"No. Oh, no." He shook his head. "I came on business, but in the end, I found something else with you. That is the truth. No, I was wondering about your niece."

"My niece? No, you have it wrong. Celia is not my niece. She is the daughter of my husband's partner."

"Ah, I see. I was mistaken. But I was wondering… you are her chaperone, her guardian here?"

"I suppose."

"She speaks all the languages, and so well. That is unusual," the Count said.

"Her mother was half Swiss, half French."

"And Jewish," he said. "She told me so. No one would suspect. Very useful… for the project."

"Her religion is *useful*? What are you talking about?"

"I meant only that, in these times when there is treachery everywhere, there is no doubt which side a Jew will fight for."

"And you think…? Celia? Oh, no! A seventeen-year-old girl?"

He made no comment, buttoning his coat while she opened the front door.

At that moment, the housekeeper came striding along the corridor. "I'm sorry to bother you, *Madame*."

"Yes, what is it?" Ginny delivered a reprimanding glare.

With her usual cold efficiency, the housekeeper said, "It's the police, *Madame*. About Celia. They're at the side door."

A young officer had come to the villa's tradesman's entrance. Bareheaded now, he was nervously cradling his *képi* when Ginny reached him. After four questions and a similar number of shaky answers, she established that Celia was unharmed. She had, however, been arrested. In the course of her supposed crime, several bicycles had sunk into the waters of the *Port du Nice*. The young officer had been dispatched by his superiors to find a parent. A guardian would suffice.

Caroline and Ginny quickly collected hats and handbags to drive to the police station. Many of the male breakfast guests recovered from their hangovers and offered to accompany them. The Count was the last and the firmest in offering his services.

"This is the Riviera," he said. "Believe me, on this coast, a connection to the Grimaldis is all important in these matters."

"Why, your Excellency, how kind," said Caroline, before Ginny could object.

Caroline threw her a glance which seemed to contain a complete knowledge of the night before. Ginny shook her head, denying nothing.

An hour and a half later, Celia — shaking despite the Count's coat around her shoulders — was sitting at an outdoor table drinking hot chocolate in a street café along the *Quai Rauba-Capeu*, not far from the central police station in Nice. The café stood at the highest point along the Quai. The Mediterranean Sea in front of them rippled vast and blue all the way to the horizon. The world smelt of salt and chocolate.

Celia's face was dirty, clothes somewhat worse for wear, but all charges had been miraculously dropped. She was safe; Ginny was relieved. Five minutes of private audience between the Count and the station chief had proved decisive in securing the girl's freedom.

"They attacked a man. I couldn't stop it," Celia mumbled, hot chocolate cup to her mouth.

Ginny looked at Caroline, who looked at the Count.

"Perhaps you could allow us a moment?" Ginny suggested.

"Come, your Excellency, let's play the aristocracy and take a walk in the *Quartier du Port*," said Caroline.

Ginny was left, looking across the table at Celia. She lit a cigarette. Celia would not take one.

"You pushed three bicycles over the side into the water?" Ginny repeated the story a police detective had given her. "Did you wish to see how big a splash they would make?"

She had noticed Celia's Sunday-best dress, a going-to-church dress, only Celia did not worship at churches and today was not Sunday.

"You were here for the synagogue, I take it?"

"I got up early," Celia began. "There was a man and his sister. I followed them afterwards.... along the road... he was wearing the yarmulke. You know, Aunt Ginny, the skull cap? That's how they knew him. In Place Garibaldi, there were these four boys on bicycles..."

"Ah, the bicycles appear at last." Ginny had hoped the abuse of bicycles might be something akin to her own youthful high jinks.

"They were shouting at him and then hitting him and no one did anything. There were plenty of people around." Celia lifted her head and looked across the table. "The boys... they were shouting, 'Jew, Jew, Jew,' as if that explained it. I thought about what Claudette said, Europe would do nothing to save the Jews."

Ginny stretched across the table, rested her palm on Celia's shaking hand.

"So afterwards, I saw them again. They were going into a café in the port. They left their bikes outside." Tears were forming in Celia's eyes. She wiped them away. "No, I am not going to cry. No one can make me. I managed three of the bikes. I tried for a fourth. But there were people shouting for me to stop. No one shouted for them to stop in Place Garibaldi."

Ginny nodded. "No, no one. I see that."

"Is that how the world is going to be, Aunt Ginny? Now there's to be a war? That's what Guy says."

"Guy? You call him Guy?"

"The Count, then. He said a war is something more than bicycles."

"Yes, of course," said Ginny. "I suppose he thinks you are angry because you are Jewish, and that is enough."

"Enough for what?" Celia's lip trembled. Then, after a few seconds, she said, "I am Jewish."

Ginny could not quite be sure when it happened, when her adopted daughter proved that 'adoption' was an illusion. For all the coaching and the clothes and the invitations to the 'right' events, Celia clung to an identity. Ginny rather admired it. Though she wished it wasn't true.

The Count insisted he could walk to the train station in Nice to catch his train for Paris. As the three women were boarding a taxi, he took Celia aside. Ginny spotted him slipping his business card into the girl's hand. She decided, on balance, that rushing over to stop him was not the best strategy.

"Celia, tell me the truth, did he—?" she asked as their taxi moved off.

Celia had wound down the window and was waving to her rescuer. "Did he invite me to Paris? Yes, he did."

"But you said no?"

"I said I must talk to my father. And perhaps to my grandparents."

"What on earth would you do in Paris?" Caroline asked.

"Finishing school," Celia said. "There are people, he says, interested in placing young people like me in French Society."

"Romantic." Caroline nodded approval at the notion.

"And what might that entail?" Ginny demanded.

"He says, we must anticipate what it is to be a city under occupation. The city lives. The city still has society. Secrets circulate. When the Germans come… Well, things are different in a war, aren't they?"

"Oh, my God! He is a pimp recruiting courtesans," Ginny said. She looked to Caroline for support, but her cousin did not respond.

"Spies," said Celia. "He is recruiting spies."

Ginny retired to bed in the late afternoon, trying to sleep off weariness and guilt. She lay awake wondering what story she could possibly tell Woody about his daughter's arrest, and how she would avoid telling Eustace anything at all about the Count.

Things are different in a war, aren't they?

Celia's words echoed in Ginny's head. Different for Celia. Different for Eustace and Woody. Look at the shameful difference it had already made for Ginny Havershall.

Some time before dinner, there was a sharp knock on her bedroom door. Thinking it must be Celia or Caroline, or perhaps one of the boys, she shouted, "Come in," while gathering crumpled bedsheets across her chest.

Their red-faced English cook stumbled into the room. The cook was rarely seen outside the kitchen and never upstairs where contamination might soil her white aprons.

"Come quick, it's the telephone, Mrs Havershall, the telephone."

"Oh, Lord, not Celia again. I thought she was resting. Is it the Police?"

"No, Mrs Havershall, it's Havershall's… in England. The company. They say Mr Eustace was expected for a meeting in London."

"Yes, what of it?"

"He hasn't arrived, Madam. Him nor Mr Woodmansey neither."

Chapter Twenty-One

On the first night of their drive back to England, Woody and Eustace had stopped in a family hotel near Dijon. Eustace drank the local wine and Woody abstained. The following morning, the car burst a tyre as they skirted east of Paris. Much to Woody's frustration, he couldn't unfasten the wheel nuts with the wrench in his tool kit. They had to wait several hours for a mechanic to arrive.

Once on the road again, they were still a long way from the evening ferry. Woody speeded up. They had promised Priestley to be in London by noon the following day.

The road surface became narrow and potholed. A cart pulled by an enormous tractor that looked no more than chassis, wheels and a naked engine sputtered out from a side road to block their way. No chance to overtake.

"Dammit," said Woody, braking hard to fall in behind.

Eustace lit himself a cigarette. He offered the packet to Woody, but Woody shook his head.

"Trying to give up. One vice at a time," he said. "I know. I haven't done so well with booze, Captain, until now at least."

The road crested a hill. The tractor trundled over the top with the Bugatti following. Fields of grassland rolled away before them down the gentle slope on the other side. Rows of grape vines ran to the left.

"Not quite like it used to be, is it, this countryside? But don't go believing it couldn't be again," Woody said, resigned now to following the tractor. "Whatever Priestley wants, whatever we can do, promise me, Eustace, we must do it, whatever it means for Havershall's. You know that, don't you?"

"It's a rather morbid thought. We don't know what will happen."

"Then why are we here, driving like this?" Woody said. "No one ever knows the future. We can guess. I try to guess. When you see those German cars lapping at Donington, you wonder at their engineering." He shook his head solemnly. "Blitzkrieg, Hitler's war tactic, means moving very fast. Getting equipment to the right place to attack."

"I don't think racing cars win a war, Woody."

"No, but better lorries and tanks will help. Aeroplanes will do the rest. All these things need engines."

* * *

It started to rain as they crossed the junction with the Amiens to St Quentin road. The sun had disappeared behind angry purple clouds. The headlights on the Bugatti worked against the gloom like faint glow-worms, almost useless.

On the twisting roads around Arras, Woody could use the Bugatti's new supercharger to its full potential to punch the car around the corners. He slammed his accelerator foot to the floor. With enough pressure, a missing toe made no difference.

Eustace began to feel anxious as tyres squealed. He calmed himself by closing his eyes, absorbing the lurches and leanings of the car as Woody took the bends in rhythm.

His mind wandered, saw behind closed eyelids the verdant greens turning red and bloody, and the red turning brown, and the brown turning back green with mould and the decay of the dead. If tanks and planes were the new monsters twenty years before, fragile and half-effective in their infancy, what would this new conflict produce? Better tanks? More aeroplanes as Woody predicted? Who knew what else? How terrible and terrifying might it be to fight with the new technologies?

Woody loved cars. He loved their throb, the way rubber scrabbled over tarmac, the way it bit in on turns and the speed of cornering created extensions to gravity, pushing him left and right. Since Eustace was dozing, there was no one worrying about how fast Woody drove. He was determined to keep their appointment with Priestley.

He approached a downhill straight lined with trees, that right foot flat to the floor. The left hand curve ahead could be taken with no more than a dip into third gear, but it was easy to misjudge. The headlights failed to provide much assistance against the gloom.

The bend led onto a humpback bridge, hidden until the car was right on top of it. The Bugatti flew off the crest. In mid-air, Woody saw the tight right-hander which followed.

He braked hard. The road was damp and the car hadn't settled back onto its suspension. They skidded. That was it.

Eustace opened his eyes. Bushes and trees were rushing towards him. He heard Woody's shouted curse word, felt a savage jolt. Then nothing.

* * *

Eustace didn't know where he was. Shocked and groggy, eyes unfocused, silence surrounded him. Prickles stung his body. Confusion and a strange numbness bathed his brain.

He seemed to be held up by a thousand pointed spears jabbing into his arms and legs. He put his hand to his head, ripping through a clawing resistance that restrained him. His hand came away wet. Blood, he thought.

And he was cold. How did he get outside?

Was there a moment when he'd been heading for the windscreen? Had he gone through it?

Without warning, a whoosh of red light and heat rushed over him, making his position bright and obvious. He was hanging in the branches of a tree. His head felt blunt as if half of it had been crushed flat.

But also… Look…

The wreck of the Bugatti, some twenty yards beyond him and below. On fire now, its bent metal frame lit within.

And there was Woody.

Eustace had seen those black figures before, caught like Guy Fawkes' dolls on a bonfire. The victims of tanks looked as Woody looked now, caught half way through the driver's side of the windscreen. Arms flailing as if fanning the flames that burned them.

Eustace struggled to move, to help, to fear, to feel. His own numbed mind would not engage.

Below him, flapping. Desperate. Slowing. Twitching. Not moving. Still now. Flames triumphant. All in half a minute. And still Eustace could not move.

He had been lucky. Always lucky. Lucky now. Not free but not trapped, not confined. To hang here and watch. To hang here useless while Woody died. Like so many other men. No God appeared.

The first voices Eustace heard were French. People shouted. He saw figures caught in silhouette around the burning wreckage, the flames dying from their peak, a terrible smell rising.

Someone was yelling for someone else to fetch an ambulance. He could make that much of the excited French being spoken.

Finally, they spotted him in the tree.

"Monsieur?" someone called. They were looking up from the base of the trunk. *"Vous m'entendez?"*

The woman's voice surprised him. It was always men on a battlefield. But of course he wasn't on a battlefield and, in his confusion, that was the surprise.

"I'm here," he shouted back. The effort hurt and his face was running with a slime of blood and tears. Gravity took the drips from the tip of his nose. His head throbbed. "Where is here?" he asked.

"*Ici?* This is the road to Cambrai."

Far away, the German invasion of Poland progressed while the ambulances came and Eustace was rushed to hospital. The attending doctor moved Eustace to a private room, assuming he would not live long. Remarkable. Fighting. Unusually strong, the doctor told his nurses, though the fight was surely hopeless.

In London, the House of Commons passed an emergency military budget and the War Office began mobilisations of the Armed Forces. Like a procession of sullen eunuchs, other governments — notably in Scandinavia and Italy — declared their neutrality.

The ambassadors of France and Britain demanded that Germany withdraw its troops. At 9:00 a.m. on 3rd September, the British ambassador in Berlin delivered an ultimatum which expired unanswered at 11:00 a.m. Fifteen minutes later, Neville Chamberlain announced that Britain was at war. Before the day ended, France, Australia, New Zealand and the Viceroy of India had all declared the same. Within hours, the SS Athenia, a British cruise ship en route to Montreal had been torpedoed and sunk. Over one hundred civilian passengers and crew were dead — the first 'skirmish' of the 'Battle of the Atlantic'. Polish troops shot a thousand ethnic German civilians in the city of Bydgoszcz — the opening atrocity of an atrocious war.

Britain's first aggressive action was to send a squadron of twenty-seven planes to bomb the Kriegsmarine, the German navy, but they turned back unable to find their targets. On the night, Britain's success came from ten Whitley bombers who — lacking bombs — dropped propaganda leaflets on Bremen, Hamburg and in the Ruhr.

Meanwhile, Eustace Havershall lay in a French hospital, in the town of Cambrai, for the moment unable to remember who he was, or whether he was in 1917 or 1939.

Eustace had broken his leg and his wrist. There was internal bleeding in his abdomen, but it was his head injuries that were deemed fatal. His brain swelled and kept on swelling. He fell into a coma. By the time

Ginny arrived in Cambrai late on 2nd September, attended by Caroline and Celia, he was lying motionless, a body in a bed, eyes closed, alive in shallow breaths and faint heartbeats. So many bandages.

The doctor, a brain surgeon, took her aside to tell her they had done all they could. They had operated to try to relieve the pressure inside his skull. *Would she like them to call a priest?*

The question astonished her. The doctor delivered it in English, as if translating the bad news were the last small thing he could offer.

"No," she said. From the moment she had met him, Eustace never seemed to need God. He had, at one time, needed only her.

She stared across the table at the doctor. White coat. Oiled hair receding in a way that gave his opinion a heavier weight. His office was bare. A fan clattered in the background.

"He's not going to die," she said. "Who is the best man in your field?"

She watched the doctor stifle a laugh, a smirk. Who would laugh at a soon-to-be-widow and her hope? She stiffened herself, balled her fists as Eustace would have, forced the shakes to stop.

"It is the question my husband would ask, if he were able. He always asks it."

"Then I shall answer. Antoine Dubarry. He's a professor at the medical school in Paris."

"Alright then."

"But, *Madame*, he's at the Sorbonne, in Paris," the doctor repeated, as if the city were somewhere alien and far away. "It is impossible. There is to be a war now and everyone is running home."

Celia, who was sitting silent in the hospital corridor, who had lost a father, who didn't seem to know what her future might be and who didn't seem able to cry, said, "I'm sorry?" as if the urgency of Ginny's sudden demand had caught her by surprise.

"I said give me his business card. I know he gave it to you," Ginny said.

"The Count?"

"The Count," Ginny confirmed.

"So now you need his help, he doesn't seem so terrible. If I give it to you, will you help persuade my grandparents? I don't want to go back to England. I could be useful here."

"You know I can't allow—"

Celia held out the card. For a second, Ginny's hand hovered short of it, but there was no refusing the terms; her need was absolute. She smiled painfully as she accepted the bargain.

"What are you going to do with it?" Celia asked.

"I'm going to call him and beg," Ginny said.

Professor Antoine Dubarry appeared in Cambrai the following morning and the regime treating the comatose Eustace Havershall changed. He took a week to show signs of proper consciousness, but at least he showed them.

"Full recovery in such cases is rare," Dubarry warned her.

"You do not know my husband," Ginny said.

"There may be changes in personality. This is… *natural.*" He used the last word as if he were uncertain of its meaning. What was natural about the effect of damage?

She shook her head. A more unchangeable personality than Eustace could not be imagined.

"You do not know my husband," she repeated.

The two-minute telephone conversation when she had asked and he agreed was the last time Ginny ever spoke to the Count.

She said, "It seems I must give you Celia. Was my honour not enough?"

He replied, "You wrong me. I did not take anything not willingly given. By you. Or her."

"You are an 'honourable' man, then?"

"I will do you the favour you ask," he promised. He did not press further for any assurance regarding Celia.

"Guy," Ginny said, after a pause. "You and I, it wasn't because I don't love my husband."

"Yes," he said. "I don't suppose he could hurt you so much if you did not."

The body of Joseph Woodmansey was transported to England for burial. Caroline escorted Celia. With no surviving relatives in Manchester, he was buried in Bristol, next to his wife and son.

Eustace was still in hospital at the time, though by then, Dubarry had moved him to Paris where he could keep a personal watch on his recovery. Ginny followed.

Celia remained determined to take the place the Count had offered. True to her word, Ginny tried to persuade the Perecs it was for the best — *Paris was fine; she was there nursing her own husband.* She spent almost two hours on the telephone in the attempt, calling from the matron's station of the hospital.

"Thank you, Aunt Ginny," Celia said when she took back the receiver. "You know I will do it anyway."

"Yes, I do not doubt it. If I had been given permission for all the things I was going to do 'anyway', my childhood would have been easier. It softens my conscience, but only a little. Better on both sides if you go with your guardians' permission."

"You know, sometimes I wish you really had been my guardian."

"None of us get everything we wish for," Ginny said.

Celia must take a new name, her Svengali declared, and she jumped at it. She was to enter French society. She was to tell no one in her old life. She was to tell no one in the new life either her religion or her old name. She packed for Paris, having nothing left that mattered to her in England.

The old Celia, about to be reborn a French woman, met her 'Aunt Ginny' in Fouquet's Brasserie on the Champs-Élysées.

"I debated not coming. Disappearing and telling no one. I decided to come for you," Celia said as she stood in front of Ginny's table. The maitre d' had just escorted her across the restaurant.

Ginny, between visiting hours at the hospital, sat with an orange juice in one hand, a cigarette in the other, examining the outfit Celia had chosen — the trousers they'd bought together, the Hepburn look they had conjured, expecting a different future at the time.

"Guy says, I mustn't write. He does not know how long it will be until it happens… I mean, when this war will arrive in Paris."

Ginny nodded and pulled on her cigarette. "I was sorry about your father's funeral. I wanted to be there, you understand?"

"I understood why you couldn't. I am so sorry about the accident. And about Eustace." Celia slumped against her chair. "For Papa, well, I think it would have happened. It was inevitable."

Ginny started to deny it. Hadn't he come through the rehabilitation? Celia cut her off. "He didn't care about anything. Nothing that mattered. Not after James. Perhaps not even after my mother."

"Oh, no, don't ever think that," Ginny said. "Woody was pulling himself together. He loved you."

"Did he? I never saw it."

"I never saw it in my own father either, not until it was too late," Ginny assured her.

They ate a Parisian lunch together — a bowl of soup and fresh crusty bread washed down with a half bottle of Chablis — a glimpse of a life Ginny had once imagined for herself. Over *Pears Belle Helene* for dessert, she explained the details of Eustace's faltering recovery and Celia spoke about the school the Count and his contacts had arranged — one looking forward, the other back.

Afterwards, they walked along the *Champs-Élysées* to the Métro station at *George V*. Ginny watched the young girl stride up the platform, whistling the *Marseillaise* as she went. She was out of tune, but it didn't seem to matter.

The train approached and Celia mounted a carriage in a confident, gracile step. She leaned through a window and waved 'Aunt Ginny' farewell.

"*Au revoir*," Ginny shouted optimistically.

"Good-bye'" she mouthed under her breath.

Ginny bit her lip. The Riviera and her French fantasy were over. She could not admit it, even to herself, but she did not expect to see Celia again.

Chapter Twenty-Two

Eustace was moved back to Birmingham at the end of September, but his recovery was slow. He stayed in hospital another nine weeks.

Ginny had to abandon working part-time. It required all her efforts to run both the business and the family. She occupied Eustace's office in Duke House, commuting back and forth between the company and her husband, and occasionally — on weekends — saw her boys.

In her first week in charge, the shift engineers cleared out Woody's 'Lab'. The disassembled components of a dozen competitors' products were tossed onto a scrap-metal lorry. Jim McCann summoned her to make a ruling on the remains of the company's first typewriter, the prototype Woody had carried into Weatherstone & Hoare's bank in 1920. It looked like a clunky monstrosity now, but somehow it had escaped Woody's rage when he'd destroyed everything else.

"It seems a shame, Mrs Havershall?" he said, the question evident, as they stood in the Lab's doorway.

"What would you do, Jim?"

McCann looked surprised, as if he'd never expected to need his own opinion. He shifted uneasily from foot to foot.

"Woody and my husband, they've relied on you," she said. "You kept everything running through all this, so tell me, does this typewriter need to stay? For 'old times sake'?"

"You have to keep it, Mrs Havershall. Him and Mr Havershall, that's what they built the company on. It's a beauty."

The strength of his pride surprised her. Absolute and unconditional.

"You've always been loyal, haven't you, Jim? I mean, to the business."

"This place saved me after the war, Mrs Havershall, that's the truth. Four of my family. All of 'em have worked here. You know Wilfred, my brother."

"Wilfred has served me well," she agreed. "Now I have more than debts to think about while Eustace is recovering. I shall need factory managers, not just to run production, but everything; the engineers as well. Raye Cropper for Nottingham, of course; you for here."

"I'm not half the engineer she is," he admitted, blushing bright red.

"Perhaps not," Ginny said, taking a moment to recognise his honesty. "She can have Woody's title of Chief Engineer, but the factory here is yours to run. You've always given your loyalty to my husband. Will you give it to me?"

"Wilfred, me brother, he worked for you. Said you were always decent. He also said you were hard. There ain't no half measures. Havershall's is life and death for some of us."

She nodded thoughtfully. "I'm sure that's what Woody and Eustace always believed."

She put her hand on the wreckage of the prototype. The keys were sticky when she pressed them down. Dust coated her fingers.

"Do you think you could clean the casing, at least?" she asked. "I don't suppose anyone has to type on it. Maybe Eustace would like to display it in the library at home... when he's recovered."

The situation Ginny inherited was impossible. Men were leaving for the war. Supplies of raw material had already become erratic. Havershall's were struggling to keep the factories turning. The shop floor was filled with half-finished machines short of one component or another. Orders for the completed models had fallen sharply.

When one of the women missed her shift, the message came to Duke House that she'd 'received a telegram'. Ginny insisted on going to the house, taking comfort and money. Diane Hall was charged with making sure the grieving widow was looked after until she felt ready to return 'however long it took'. The bereavement was the first of many, even though the war was just getting started. Ginny went to all the houses, as Eustace had once gone to Lionel Swithin's. She tried to act as he would have done.

She found herself following Eustace in other things too. She got used to rising in the dark, going to work in the dark, leaving in the dark, always fighting another crisis. She could never seem to sleep, either because there was no time, or because her body was racked with tension, or both. She did not like to look in mirrors. Everything rested on her shoulders. She did not like 'being Eustace', as she came to think of the duty she'd inherited. Her sons were back at their boarding schools. She was alone.

In office mode, she called the Ministry of Supply trying to rearrange the fateful meeting with Priestley — if the Ministry needed manufacturers, Havershall's would step up. Raye Cropper could relay the factory to produce anything the war called for.

Ginny tried five times. Priestley always seemed to be busy.

On the last call, the receptionist told her, "Mr Priestley hasn't the time to speak to women."

"Fuck him then," Ginny said.

Ashamed of the outburst, she apologised profusely. The receptionist wasn't the problem. Afterwards, she told herself, she needed more rest. She was losing her self-control.

To Ginny, 'rest' meant doing something different, rather than doing nothing. Stress brought a nervous energy she needed to relieve. She started playing tennis at the club in Stratford again, hitting balls with wild abandon. She found a sense of identity on court, a Mrs Havershall who wasn't the acting Managing Director of Havershall's. She would leave her wedding ring in the lockers with her other jewellery while she played; she would never take it off anywhere else.

The assistant coach at the club was Martin Van Devere. Devere became her regular partner. They played every Saturday.

After the third doubles match in which they were partnered, her car wouldn't start. She sat stranded in the car park, racked with frustration as the starter motor refused to offer another effort. Suddenly the idea that tennis was unburdening her troubles or easing her tension seemed absurd, the idea that she could take over from Eustace and Woody seemed equally so. She burst into tears and couldn't stop.

Devere appeared from the club house at the best and worst moment.

"Trouble?" he asked, peeping in through the side window.

She sniffed and wiped her face. He was kind enough not to mention it when she opened the door.

"I'll call a mechanic, Mrs Havershall. I can drive you home. The receptionist will wait for them to come out. I'm sure it will be fine."

It was a long time since she'd felt looked after.

"Ginny," she said as if already giving him far more than access to her name.

At home, she invited him in for a drink. The accident had changed things, and yet it actually changed nothing. She was right where she had been when she'd danced with Guy de Monteparnasse and now she was weaker not stronger in the face of temptation.

Devere presented himself as a blonde Adonis who looked Scandinavian but spoke with a vague Black Country accent. She was twelve years his senior, which seemed to suit him. On the court, his serves and smashes had shown a delicious violence, but off it, he was a boy. She appreciated the gentle obedience. It did not add much to her physical exhaustion to lie back and accept his attentions. It helped her sleep. It seemed she hadn't slept properly since sharing a bed with the Count.

One night spent with Devere quickly became several nights. For practical purposes, she needed to be in charge, saying when and where it was safe to meet, often an hour here, a half hour there. She was the boss of a company and commander of a twisted life when all the other things were unravelling.

That command seemed to suit him also. Devere told her that he was in love.

She said, "That makes it all the worse for you."

After the Count, and with Eustace lying in the hospital week on week, half what he'd been, the infidelity never quite seemed real, more like falling into a comforting safety net.

The death of Ginny's uncle, Lord Montague Buckley, came as another shock, not only because it was unexpected, but because she found she cared. Her contacts with the man had been few and far between, even when she'd spent those years living in his London house. They had hardly spoken in the years since.

"Dead," she found herself repeating into the telephone.

"Dead," Caroline confirmed.

Ginny heard discomfort in the silence on the other end.

"Ginny, it's so awful. He shot himself."

The funeral took place in Chesterfield Parish Church, the largest in all of Derbyshire, famous for its distorted spire. Eustace's doctor advised against the trip. He wasn't strong enough to support himself, let alone a grieving wife. Ginny went alone.

MPs and Lords came to be seen. Winston Churchill was in attendance, recently reappointed First Lord of the Admiralty, a member of Chamberlain's War Cabinet. His wife did not accompany him.

Caroline and her husband, Viscount Fairchild, stood with the bereaved Lady Buckley greeting mourners as they filed out of the twisted building into the churchyard, all paying their muted respects.

Ginny spotted Lord Hailsgam and his wife. And then there was Margaret Barrington-Brown, hiding in funeral black, Charlie nowhere to be seen. Margaret made a point of picking Ginny out, came over with her hand extended. Ginny accepted it as a peace offering, shook it glove-on-glove.

Margaret launched into a speech about how saddened they were, she and Charlie, to hear about Mr Woodmansey's death and Eustace's injuries. Was he recovering? How was the business? Was there anything Charlie could do to 'help'?

Ginny assumed Margaret meant another attempt to buy Havershall's. She glared in return. Margaret spent a minute and a half on the benefits to an engineering company of a lengthy war. Governments were spending so much on manufactures and Charlie was expanding BBTL into 'absolutely everything'.

At the end of her monologue, Margaret added, as an afterthought, "Of course, I was so especially sorry about your uncle."

Ginny was thinking about the business BBTL was doing for the war effort — at a handsome profit, no doubt. She missed Margaret's sudden switch in the subject matter.

"It was so terrible. We shouldn't talk about it. They're keeping it quiet."

"I'm afraid, Margaret, I do not know any details."

"Oh, my, Virginia. I shouldn't say. There would have been the most beastly terrible stink, my dear. They were about to arrest him. Oh, didn't you know? He was a member of the Right Club. You know, the one started by Ramsey, that Nazi MP they've had to lock up."

Ginny felt the horror spreading. Did Caroline already know this? Had she somehow avoided it with the blind-folded discretion of the British aristocracy?

Margaret continued, "Charlie says the Right Club had infiltrated the police, the government ministries, even the War Cabinet. He's heard they were compiling a list of opponents to be removed when the country falls."

"This country won't fall," Ginny snapped.

"Of course," Margaret said, correcting herself. "But what did it for the plotters, you know, was they found Ramsey's collaborators were working on a dossier — stolen telegrams, papers we'd shared with the Americans, that sort of thing. There was a go-between."

Margaret stopped. Ginny was clearly supposed to fill in the blank.

"Not my uncle?"

"He was the one Lord in the House who was openly for Mosley."

"Yes, he was, but—"

"And look where Mosley ended up, marrying that Diana Mitford with Hitler as his witness. When we cover up these things — for the good of morale — we make a job of it. We have to."

Ginny was struck by an unexpected thought. *Who could organise such a 'cover up'?* She looked across at Lord and Lady Hailsgam.

"Oh, no, not him," Margaret said, following Ginny's gaze. "It takes more power than that to keep such things from the press." Her eyes strayed to the left and alighted on Churchill. Ginny suddenly understood.

It took some loyalty, she decided, knowing what was known, for a politician to turn up at a traitor's funeral. Churchill stood there in his dark suit and Homburg hat, covering a betrayal by showing support for the dead man's honour. To Ginny, this *duty* paid to the Buckleys seemed in contrast to the one her uncle had not exercised. She saw now the reason Mrs Clementine Churchill was not in attendance.

Churchill had removed his cigar and bowed with grace when he took Lady Buckley's hand and said whatever words of comfort he could offer. He loitered now by the churchyard wall, no bodyguards surrounding him. The security cordon had set itself up on the other side of the wall. Rather trusting, Ginny thought. If there were that many sympathisers, wouldn't the Nazi's have assassins around every corner, infiltrators even inside a churchyard?

In a moment of madness, she walked towards him. Churchill was relighting his cigar. He lifted his eyes and watched her approach. The gaze exuded a beady, intimidating concentration.

"I am afraid," he said, "I can see the Buckley features but cannot place the lovely face they produce. Have we met?"

"At a distance," she assured him. "Virginia Havershall."

"The niece, if I'm not mistaken," he said. He did not offer a handshake.

"I now run the factories of Havershall & Woodmansey, the typewriter company? During my husband's absence, of course."

"Your husband is a soldier? A volunteer?"

"A car crash. Eve of the war. He is recovering."

"My sympathies, Madam." Churchill raised his eyebrows as if asking a question. *Why was she telling him this?* Ginny was ready.

"I wanted to inquire of you… to ask… to ask if we might not do more for the war effort."

"More?" he repeated.

"Sir, I have several factories. Engineering companies with our expertise might be utilised for a greater benefit than typewriters, of which we currently have a surplus."

"We already have typewriters. I own several myself. We need weapons."

"Which is why I would prefer Havershall's to be making something more useful. Guns and bullets, perhaps."

"You should talk to the relevant authority," Churchill suggested. "I am at a funeral."

"With respect, Sir, where shall I talk with you other than at a funeral? I have spoken to the Ministry of Supply, or I have tried to. It seems it does not want my help."

Churchill chewed on the end of his cigar. "If the proper channels have turned you down, Mrs Havershall, I am sure it must be because your factory was found unsuitable."

"My factory, Sir, was found to have a woman in charge. If the proper channels will not give us satisfaction, then — forgive me — I will try the improper ones."

He nodded faintly as if he had begun to see her point.

"Do I look incompetent to you, Sir? I can show you our current accounts. My greatest rival, Mr Barrington-Brown, is already engaged in making war supplies. My foreign competitors, so I am told, are preparing to make parts for the American effort even though that country has not yet entered the war."

"Nor is there any certainty that it shall," he reminded her.

"There is certainty that it will enter soon enough, or fight the Germans alone when we lose. I'm sure that is what Mr Chamberlain tells Mr Roosevelt."

Churchill smiled. "When he asks him for money… yes."

"Now, I understand, Longbridge has abandoned making cars. It is inundated with orders for ammunition and parts for tanks. It cannot cope. My husband once served this country in command of tanks, tanks you yourself helped put on the battlefield. Now I, as his wife, am denied an opportunity to contribute to any manufacture. Have we women proved unreliable in some way? Am I perhaps a spy? My father was a moonshiner and my uncle a traitor. I have the breeding for it."

"Keep your voice down, woman," he hissed. He turned to look around, but the nearest group, some ten feet distant, were still engaged in their own conversation. "Have you no decorum?" he said, smiling as he said it.

"In winning, I have neither decorum nor shame, Sir. Of the Americans, I understand that Underwoods will make the M1 carbine, Smith Corona will make rifles and Remington is setting up for the manufacture of pistols. So what would you have me do with a hundred-thousand square feet of the country's finest production space?"

"You are well informed about the intentions and manoeuvres of your rivals."

"I am a business woman, Sir," she said. "You are no doubt well informed about your enemies, and of their intentions. It is necessary, in business and in war."

"Ah," he said thoughtfully. He stared at her for several seconds. "Yes, I remember now. You were the tennis player."

Ginny walked away, appalled at herself, yet exhilarated. She had confronted Churchill. She had spoken her mind. She had held her own.

Ten days later, Havershall's received an order for the cylinders of military handguns. She sent Churchill a black HL1 typewriter with a thank-you note that said, "I trust this will prove superior to your other models." He never replied, but an invitation to tender for the supply of typewriters to the Civil Service in Whitehall arrived the following week.

Eustace was discharged from the hospital in time for Christmas. During January and February of 1940, he started to become mobile, but was still housebound when rationing began. He was presented with a ration book and, by the time he could go out to see what was happening, sugar, bacon and butter were becoming difficult to obtain.

In March, he felt stronger. He exaggerated the progress of his recovery, told himself he wasn't struggling with his limp, he didn't get headaches and his heart rate didn't go screaming out of control when he overexerted himself. All three were necessary lies. He bought himself a walking stick, which reminded him of the one Woody once used. He tried visiting Duke House.

The staff cheered him through the door. He took the Managing Director's chair and Ginny moved back up the corridor, but he quickly found that the company's core activity had moved with her. Ginny was by now so thoroughly in charge that Eustace couldn't feel the same about either factory or offices. That morning, he sat alone, feeling his weakness, and did nothing, waiting to become useful again.

He remembered how certain Woody had been about the coming war and the part that machinery and manufacturing would play in it — an industrial war. Making office machines didn't seem enough. Certainly, watching others make office machinery would not suffice, even if a few handgun cylinders were now in the mix.

That evening, Eustace said, "Please, take me to his grave, Gin. I feel ready now. I have to see it."

They picked the following Saturday for a trip to Bristol. They stood in the graveyard, saying no words.

There lay Mabel, died 1926. And there James, from ten years after. Here now was Joseph, nickname 'Woody', a 'loving father and husband', gone in 1939.

"My luck," said Eustace, out of the blue.

"Was it luck?"

"He had none, Gin. Not after Cambrai. It has stuck to me like a smell." He shook his head. "He always smelled of pickles."

"Luck or not, in another few months, we shall sell our two millionth typewriter."

"No, not 'we', not anymore. *You* will sell that machine. I feel useless. More useless than he was as a drunk."

She linked her arm with his. It used to be easy to know what to say, but he was expressing a truth she couldn't admit. There were many secrets she couldn't admit now.

"Maybe we should commission a statue. Something to always look on everything Havershall's does," she suggested.

He smiled vaguely. "He deserves that. I think I let him down. You tried to warn me what was happening. It was you who got him to the sanatorium. Now you're having to run the company."

When he turned from the grave, she felt him sag against her arm and she tightened her grip to hold him up. She remembered how he'd thrashed about over his father's grave, wondered if — given ruder health — he might have done the same for Woody.

Germany invaded Denmark and Norway in April of 1940. They fell too quickly. Britain's failure to support Norway brought down the British Prime Minister. Neville Chamberlain resigned; the King called for Winston Churchill. Many had expected Lord Halifax to be chosen, but Chamberlain convinced the King otherwise. This proved to be his last great act. Chamberlain would be dead before the year's end.

In May, Hitler's Nazis launched an offensive aimed at France. To circumvent the fortifications on the Franco-German border, Germany attacked the neutral nations of Belgium, Netherlands, and

Luxembourg. Out-flanking defenders by rapid manoeuvres through the Ardennes, the Germans — perfecting their Blitzkrieg tactic — reached the coast, cutting off British and Allied forces in Belgium. Most of the 'Allied' troops were evacuated from Dunkirk by the desperate use of small boats, but their equipment was abandoned and lost.

Soldiers, however brave, could not fight an industrial war empty handed. The factories that might supply them were now the only thing that stood between Britain and defeat.

Havershall's next order from the Ministry of Supply was for the rollers of a Comet tank.

Chapter Twenty-Three

Richard watched his father limping around the house, using a stick for support. Although his own leg had strengthened, the thirteen-year-old limped again for a month, in the hope of bonding.

"Dad, do you get pains in your back?" William asked. "Dick always does. He moans about it all the time."

Eustace shook his head. William seemed content with the answer. Richard seemed deeply disappointed.

William turned twelve at the end of the Easter holiday in 1940. He had lost his fascination with Meccano and, while at home, filled the house with 'Skybirds', model aircraft kits that he assembled devotedly.

The kits, made by A. J. Holladay & Co, contained shaped wooden blanks and detailed cast metal parts, ideal for beguiling a would-be aviator. First World War planes, all in 1:72 scale, dominated the range, supplemented now by those being readied for the new battle.

The manufacturer published a quarterly magazine, 'The Skybird League'. William's great ambition was to win their photographic competition for completed models. The winners were displayed within the windows of Hamleys toyshop in London. His limping father seemed less of a hero than a dashing young pilot. In model dogfights, a British plane would always win.

On the few evenings the family ate together, Ginny sat measuring distances in her head. William's chair was a little closer to his father, but not so close as it used to be. Richard's had turned away towards the far wall. Both the boys sat between her and Eustace.

She had to force the family conversations, because Eustace often seemed to drift off, his thoughts somewhere distant. The boys still called her 'Mummy' and told her how their days unfolded. She told them nothing of hers. Increasingly, they called him 'Father', or — worse — nothing at all.

The next time Ginny drove him into Duke House, the previous pattern was repeated. Eustace sat alone. His telephone never rang. The business had forgotten it needed him.

Just before lunch, there was a commotion audible up the corridor. He hobbled out of the Managing Director's office, along to the open area with the sales desks run by Diane Hall. Usually, twelve women in three rows of four sat demurely answering phone calls and typing up orders. On this day, Diana Hall was waving a telegram in the air and jigging around in delight. Two of the younger women were unstacking glasses they'd carried from the canteen. Ginny brandished two bottles of champagne that had appeared out of nowhere.

"What the devil is going on?"

He thought, for one crazy moment, some miracle must have ended the war.

Ginny turned, foam overspilling the uncorked bottle in her hand. "Why, Eustace, the most marvellous news. We won the tender for the Civil Service."

"But that's Barrington-Brown's contract. It always has been."

"Yes, isn't it wonderful?"

"Yes, wonderful," he said.

"Come on, ladies, let's celebrate," she shouted, sloshing the wine into the glasses, careless of how much ended up on the table.

He felt the energy draining out of him.

To Eustace's knowledge, the Civil Service contract had been tendered four times in twenty years. Under his management, Havershall's had got on the shortlist once. He had put immense efforts into the chase. And always failed.

In a few chaotic months, Ginny had taken it from BBTL. The world had changed beyond his comprehension.

Eustace stared at the box of business cards he kept on the front edge of his desk next to his two beloved photographs. Music drifted from down the corridor. Ginny had found a radio and the tipsy office girls were dancing on their lunch break.

His box was stacked with names. Over the years, he had been on committees, attended dinners, given talks on safety, bought components from a hundred different engineering suppliers. He knew everyone. *How come he was now unneeded?*

The first card he picked out of the box belonged to Wallace Devereux of High Duty Alloys. Devereux had been Woody's contact to begin with — a relationship forged when the H50 was designed — but

Eustace had met the man at several trade dinners. They were both keen on better safety standards. They had found they liked each other.

It took three phone calls — receptionists passing him from pillar to post — before he found Devereux at a number in Westminster.

"What are you doing working in London?" Eustace asked after the pleasantries were done.

"I've joined the war," Devereux announced, sounding pleased with himself.

"Ministry of Supply, by any chance?"

"Old hat, my friend. No, I turned that ministry down. I'm Director of Forgings and Castings at the new place."

"What new place? Isn't 'Supply' the new place?"

"It was. Now it's the 'The Ministry of Aircraft Production.'"

Suddenly, all Eustace could picture was his son's Skybirds and Woody's prediction of the coming importance of aeroplanes. "Oh," he said in surprise.

"If you want to do something useful, my friend, come and talk with Beaverbrook. We could use men like you who know where and how to get things done."

After he put down the phone, Eustace gazed at the box of business cards.

…Where and how to get things done…

He had always known how to do that.

Winston Churchill's idea of the value of planes was much like Woody's had been, less romantic than for a boy who loved Skybirds and the glory of the pilots, but reaching the same conclusion — Britain needed planes.

The Ministry of Aircraft Production was created in the first month of his premiership. Chamberlain's pre-war government had ploughed money willy-nilly into aviation projects, paying for new factories to be built. These were so-called 'shadow factories', managed by motor car manufacturers but making aircraft parts. The investment was not fruitful. Aircraft failed to appear.

Lord Beaverbrook was appointed first minister of the new department. He set up headquarters in his own home, 'Stornoway House', a stone's throw across Green Park from Buckingham Palace. He had less than two months to revitalise preparations before the air battle began in earnest.

* * *

Eustace felt compelled to offer whatever remained of himself in the war effort and Devereux was insistent, making sure a meeting was arranged.

"Don't worry, my friend. Beaverbrook's one of us. He makes things happen. He'll like you."

Beaverbrook's name, when unwrapped from its aristocratic title, was William Maxwell Aitken, a Canadian. He had made himself a millionaire before the age of thirty, moved to England, bought the Daily Express newspaper and been an MP before elevation to the peerage at the age of thirty-seven.

He was now sixty-one years old. Eustace assumed he would have slowed somewhat, and that a newspaper mogul would know more about typing and printing than engineering. He had seen the man once before, at Viscount Fairchild's wedding, but never spoken with him. He imagined another stuffy English Lord, a toff, maybe an ageing Barrington-Brown. He did not expect the meeting to go well. He agreed for one reason — Woody.

Ginny was away that week at a two-day exhibition of office equipment in Liverpool. The organisers seemed not to have noticed the outbreak of war and forgotten to cancel it. Havershall's were committed, she said. She needed to grab what typewriter sales were still on offer.

Eustace didn't tell her about meeting Baverbrook. She would have doubted his fitness to drive to London. Perhaps he doubted it himself. He had driven no more than five miles on his own since the accident.

The appointment was scheduled for 9 a.m. on the following Friday. He left home before dawn. Arriving at Stornaway House fifteen minutes early, a man in a butler's uniform greeted him in the vaulted hallway and told him, "Lord Beaverbrook has gone to breakfast with the Prime Minister."

The butler seemed quite pleased at the delay. Eustace sat in an armchair next to a grandfather clock, staring at paintings, high decorated ceilings and a pair of carved wooden lions that guarded the bottom of the main stairs.

Beaverbrook appeared at 11.27, flanked by two security guards whom he dismissed as he walked through the door. He was shorter than Eustace remembered, stooping in gait, not unlike a miniature Churchill, same receding hair on a big head, though decidedly slimmer in the body. His stiff arms hung at his side as he loped across the entrance hall. Under his flapping overcoat, he wore a dark tailored suit in the style of an undertaker. Rolled up beneath his arm was a set of engineering drawings.

He approached Eustace with hand outstretched. "Devereux's man?" he said. "Tanks and typewriters, isn't it?"

"Eustace Havershall," said Eustace, rousing himself from his armchair. He tried not to grimace as he fought the stiffness in his leg.

The two men shook hands. At that moment, the Lord's private secretary appeared unbidden. He stopped at respectful distance, waiting for the Lord to remove his coat. Beaverbrook seemed in no hurry to do so.

"Tell me, Mr Havershall, where would I find the finest castings in '1503'? In your experience, of course?" Beaverbrook asked.

1503 was a grade of steel. A test, but rather a pompous one, Eustace thought. It was easy enough to pass.

"Baggards in Newcastle, or perhaps Markett and Johnson of Sheffield. I could give you addresses," he offered, wanting to make a point.

"I know Baggards. That would be Granby Street. And for aircraft grade aluminium? Who do I go to for that?"

"Ah," said Eustace. "I could not look beyond Wallace Devereux's company as the finest. We've dealt with them for years."

"Let's suppose for a minute, Wallace's people are at capacity. I have a problem with the propellers on the new mark of Hurricane. Can't get any for six weeks. Our battle will be lost by then. Where do I go for help?"

Eustace racked his brains. "Luton," he suggested. "Luton Premier Castings, Bryn Rothgear's company. He opened a new subsidiary there last year."

"You know this Bryn character, do you?"

"I sat with him on a committee when he had his first factory in Birmingham."

"I see," said Beaverbrook. "I can't abide committees myself. They take the punch out of war. I've shut down as many as possible. Still, come on. Needs must."

Beaverbrook made a half turn as if urging Eustace to take the lead. Eustace was confused.

Sensing hesitation, Beaverbrook said, "No time like the present, man."

"But... you mean, go there? I'm not part of the department. You haven't interviewed me yet. And I'm not cleared for this, not for plans to new aircraft." Eustace nodded towards the drawings under Beaverbrook's arm.

"Nonsense. I finished interviewing you two minutes ago. You know everyone who counts. You're a genius. Devereux assures me of the same." Beaverbrook turned to the private secretary. "John, find a number for — what was it? — Luton Castings."

"Luton Premier Castings," Eustace corrected. "Bedford Street, I think."

"Yes, call them, would you, John? Get hold of this Bryn Rothgear and tell him I'm on my way with Havershall here. We'll be there after lunch. Oh, and then call the home securities chappies and get Mr Havershall some clearance so I don't have to shoot him after I've shown him these drawings. There's a good man."

"It takes a week or so to get a clearance, my Lord… normally."

"Then remind them this is abnormal. Use whoever's name you need to get it done."

"Yes, my Lord."

Beaverbrook turned back to Eustace. "Always stir up trouble. In this job, ask for the impossible, plus a little. They told me that if I turned every relevant manufacturing machine in the land onto aircraft parts, I might make two thousand planes a month. I said, 'Well, give me the irrelevant ones as well, because I have a war to win.' Do you have a car handy?"

"Parked down the street."

"Good. What is it?"

"A Rolls Royce."

"Ah, yes, good cars. I used to own them," said Beaverbrook brightly.

"Oh, really, which version?"

"No, not models, the bloody company. Charles Rolls sold me his shares. I had to sell them on, though. Not my thing. Propaganda, that's what I'm good at. I need engineers for this job. Come on. Chivvy up."

Beaverbrook smiled and Eustace led him out of the door. He was about to become chauffeur to a Lord, but he didn't feel the usual distaste for privilege. He didn't feel tired either.

"You have a limp, man," said the Lord, spotting the obvious.

"A car accident. I'm still in recovery."

"No time for recovery. This is a war. Last week, I had them release all the Jewish engineers we had in internment camps. I mean, the German Jews we were holding. You know why?"

"Because there is a war?" Eustace suggested.

"Too bloody right. We need everyone who wants to fight Hitler to be fighting Hitler. Some damn good engineers in those camps. Manufacture is going to win this war."

Eustace thought of Woody. Woody would have been delighted.

"Know any jokes," Beaverbrook asked as they walked down Cleveland Row, Green Park to their left. "Winnie told me a belter about Goebbels this morning."

Ginny's train back from Liverpool was late that night. In her absence, and in the spirit of mad energy inspired by Beaverbrook, Eustace had helped the housekeeper tidy up the boys' toy boxes and get them to bed. They were home from school for a long weekend.

He and Ginny had resisted talk of evacuating them further west, perhaps into Wales. So far, a German bombing campaign that might touch Stratford felt like no more than a distant threat. An afternoon with Beaverbrook brought even the distant threats into sharp focus. Perhaps that's why he kissed them both before he left them to sleep.

Exhausted at last, he was dozing in an armchair, listening to the news on the radiogram when Ginny's taxi arrived. He roused himself and met her at the door. He made her a drink, a gin and tonic, while she went to hang up her coat.

Sensing his change of mood, she kicked her shoes off and sat on the armrest of his chair. The newsreader was describing another setback in the Allies' military campaign.

"It is getting worse and we are still losing," Eustace observed.

Ginny reached out to run her fingers through his hair. He had several scars on his scalp from the accident, around which hair now grew unevenly. He felt her fingers trace the imperfections. She smelt warm and soft and vaguely of sweaty exhibitions.

"You're not going to ask about my day? Hankins showed up. I hate that man. He wouldn't give us the order. Not on acceptable terms."

"Then do not deal with him."

"He is a big customer, Eustace. He has what's left of the market in Wales. We have to deal with him. And anyway I got the order… in the end."

"You sound like me." He put his hand on Ginny's thigh, resting its palm against the fabric of her skirt, and turned towards her. "Gin, I have volunteered myself to the Ministry of Aircraft Production in London," he said, seizing the moment.

"Volunteered? Volunteered! But... You can't fight. Not in your condition."

"It's not fighting. Not active service, Gin. It's a desk job, for manufacturing. Wallace Devereux got me in. I helped get new Hurricanes built... first day."

"First day? What do you mean, first day?"

"I've been to London. For the interview. Ended up in Luton with Bryn Rothgear. Do you remember him?"

"Eustace, you're not ready to go back to work, and if you are, then there's Havershall's. I can't manage forever. Why are you springing this on me now?"

"I thought we agreed, you'd sell the two millionth typewriter. Didn't you just say you dealt with Hankins? You got the Civil Service contract, Gin."

He did not tell her how useless it made him feel to watch her succeed. Especially at things where he had failed.

"I'm ready. I told Beaverbrook I am."

"Lord Beaverbrook? Isn't he newspapers?"

"He's the Minister in charge of making planes, or making people make planes. It's classified. I wish I could tell William, but—"

Ginny looked at him as if he'd gone mad.

"Eustace, there is a factory... three factories with Nottingham and that new one of yours that no one wants to buy now there's a war..."

"You beat Barrington-Brown," he said, as if this were decisive proof of her competence.

"Oh, no... No, I can't run a company, Eustace."

"You already are."

"But that's temporary. I... I can't... I won't be put upon like this."

"I thought you'd be pleased. It's a desk job. No danger. Like those cushy jobs the toffs got in the last one. And look how it helped them after."

Ginny's face darkened. "This is just as Woody told me it would be. Don't lie to me, Eustace, please. This has nothing to do with 'afterwards'. You aren't one of those cushy job men and you know it. Don't tell me this is all to help Havershall's."

"But it is," he insisted.

"You did this without asking me. Again!" she said.

"I'm sorry. Today, I just felt... ready for duty."

"Then come back to Havershall's, for God's sake. Do that first. You are still the Managing Director."

He shook his head and she trailed off into empty silence.

"Gin, say something," he urged. "I didn't want to go to war."

"Pah! You didn't want to go to war!" she shouted, as if the real truth were obvious. "Woody warned me, dammit! You're like a sad man who says he doesn't want to breathe anymore. He breathes anyway, Eustace, that's the way of it."

"A war is happening. I prayed it wouldn't."

"Rather a hollow prayer from a man who has no God."

That stopped him for a moment and he paused to gather himself.

"Afterwards, it'll be better. We'll fix everything when the madness stops," he promised, lowering his voice.

"Which madness would that be, Eustace? Tell me that."

They sat silently as the background voice on the radio moved onto the weather, neither offering a response or a further question passing until a tear leaked down her right cheek and, a moment later, another down his left, neither able to explain the silence or the tears, or how the feelings of one so closely matched the other, or even why they were sad.

She unhitched herself from his armrest.

"So be it," she said as she headed for the door.

On 10th June, Italy, Germany's partner in the 'Axis' alliance, invaded France from the south. German forces came rushing in from the north and took Paris on the fourteenth. France signed an unworthy armistice. It divided France into German and Italian occupation zones, and an unoccupied rump state under the Vichy Regime.

In the House of Commons, Churchill announced, "... The Battle of France is over. I expect that the Battle of Britain is about to begin."

The British stockmarket crashed. Traders saw it as the beginning of the end.

One thing now stood in Hitler's way. A successful invasion of Britain would require the Luftwaffe to cripple the RAF. A German advance required seven hundred thousand tonnes of shipping to cross the Channel. That shipping had to be protected. Until air supremacy was established, Hitler's Blitzkrieg tactics were stalled by twenty-two miles of water.

As the weeks passed, Ginny read the headlines about France and tried frantically to contact the people she knew in the country. The one postcard she'd received from Celia had arrived seven months before.

There was now no trace. The remaining Woodmansey was gone, under whatever name she and the Count had concocted as disguise, or whichever new zone she may have disappeared within.

Working for Beaverbrook, Eustace was busy, trying to make aeroplanes. Ginny did not see him more than two days in the next month — not just a man returning from an accident, but a man so far away it felt like looking through a telescope for land on a sea voyage.

She made Havershall's two millionth typewriter, ten thousand handgun cylinders, the rollers for a hundred tanks and spent five nights with Martin Van Devere in that same time. She wasn't good at loneliness. He was the cure for that disease. But also her revenge, she realised. Exactly as cousin Caroline had played out the tactic against the Viscount. It wasn't so difficult after all.

On 10th July, the Battle of Britain started in earnest — the first major campaign ever fought by air power alone. To begin with the Luftwaffe targeted coastal-shipping convoys, ports and shipping centres, tempting Britain's Royal Air Force into a fight. Twelve days later, it shifted to direct attacks on airfields and infrastructure.

How could a recovered man demonstrate his recovery, his value? Not in Havershall's. The Ministry was Eustace's chance. *Pain and weariness be damned!*

He worked with the vigour Beaverbrook demanded. The organisation was characterised by chaotic management and crisis aversion. Willpower drove output. When you went somewhere, you arrived like a pirate — Beaverbrook's Bully Boys, they were called — using past connections and influence to plunder manufacturing capacity. Eustace quickly gained a reputation as the best of the raiders. He had once commanded tanks, he explained. The principles of attack were similar. The Ministry's name provided the biggest possible weapon.

From invalid, he rose again to become a man of action. The Battle of Britain must be won. As fast as the British built aircraft, the battle swallowed them up.

Eustace charted their brief lives as new planes roared throatily overhead. Occasionally, on his travels, he would get to witness a dogfight — what he came to see as *his* fighters taking on the Luftwaffe's finest. Sometimes he saw and felt the joy of victory, occasionally the heart-wrench of defeat.

He would see a plane go down and focus on the list of parts that had put it together — two wings, one engine, one propeller, landing gear, fuselage, ailerons, rudder. He'd be haunted afterwards, imagining the smoke and falling flames. Another life — two arms, two legs, one head. But that's how war was, wasn't it? What had they always called it, a sausage machine of youth? These air battles were in fact like all other battles, the threat to its participants too great to stop, even for a moment. He did his job.

He liked factory visits best, walking in unannounced. He usually knew the owners, having bought from them, or met them on safety committees and at manufacturing associations for many years. He knew how they thought. Like him, they were men who could not bear defeat, so he implied that the war would be lost without them. They had a *duty* not to fail, same as he did. Call it God or Patriotism, he didn't care. Anything that worked.

"You're giving our boys what they need to win."

Like a magician, he found manufacturing capacity that didn't seem to exist. He conjured up parts that couldn't be made in a year and delivered them in weeks. He got aircraft made with energy he hadn't shown since he was sleeping in store rooms at the back of the Duke Works and visiting his society fiancée in London. He missed those days. He missed Woody and Ginny. He missed the life that had given him his boys. They were the future. He missed them too.

The Castle Bromwich factory on the edge of Birmingham was one of Beaverbrook's biggest headaches. It had been set up before the war using four million pounds of Government money under the Shadow Factory scheme. It was supposed to transfer technology from the motor industry to bolster capacity for the new Spitfire.

But Castle Bromwich under the stewardship of William Morris of Morris Motors was a disaster. Morris had been elevated to the peerage — 'Lord Nuffield' — but he had not delivered one Spitfire by the time Beaverbrook became Minister for Aircraft Production.

On his appointment in May, Beaverbrook had raged at him over the telephone. Sarcastically, the other Lord replied, "Maybe you would like me to give up control…"

Sharp as a snake bite, Beaverbrook said, "Nuffield, that's generous of you. I accept!"

...And promptly handed the factory to Alexander Dunbar, a man he had poached from Supermarine in Southampton, the original manufacturers of the Spitfire.

"Ten in June," became Beaverbrook's motto, a promise that the first ten aircraft would roll out within a month.

The required number of Spitfires were indeed shown to the public in June 1940. It was unclear on where they came from. Castle Bromwich was probably not the source.

"And that's how you do it," Beaverbrook told Eustace.

Propaganda was the thing he understood best, being a press man rather than an engineer.

There were — when Eustace turned to statistics — some hard figures to be proud of through the summer of 1940. Between January and April that year, Britain had produced only two and a half thousand planes of which less than six hundred and fifty were fighters. From May to August, under the new Ministry, over four and a half thousand planes were produced, of which nearly two thousand were fighters.

The turnaround was an unprecedented industrial feat. The rate of new aircraft production in Britain was now two and a half times better than Germany's. At the same time, the Ministry sourced parts to repair and recommission one thousand nine hundred grounded aircraft. Eustace Havershall was an unseen hand, relentlessly pushing them out of workshops and repair hangers.

In the dog fights and onslaughts of anti-aircraft fire, the number of active German fighters in operations over England fell to a third of its former total, while the RAF's complement rose. The sky-fought Battle of Britain was won. The country had out-manufactured its German enemy, not by providing better planes, or suffering lower losses, but by building planes more quickly.

Eustace thought he understood the price of war, but, in detail, it is always too high for memory to retain. War re-proved its horrors to Eustace. He saw more and more of those dogfights, emblazoned in smoke and fire in the skies above his head as he travelled from place to place. Each day, always worse than anyone could remember.

When he had volunteered for the new-fangled tanks of World War One, the average soldier was thirty-years-old. In World War Two, the fighter pilots he provided with aeroplanes were, on average, twenty. More than half were teenagers. By August of 1940, the life expectancy of these boys was four weeks — the price of victory.

Eustace felt guilty, felt safe. Safe, when the tank commander in his head knew he should be long gone. Yet here he was, steward of that sausage machine. He carried that burden alone.

As he turned fourteen, Richard had started writing poetry. When he was home for a weekend, Ginny found it on typed pages next to his bed while the boy was asleep. At first, she assumed it had been written at his school.

The content was in the protesting style of World War One, like Sassoon and Owen, though Richard seemed to be imagining things he'd never seen himself. There was a fear to it, though the rhymes and rhythms were smooth and the words lyrical.

She sat on the floor with her back against his door, holding the pages. By and by, she noticed something odd. The letters didn't all sit quite straight on a line. As a poet, he had typed his name as 'Dick Havers', but the 'i' was always too high, the 'c' and 'v' too low.

Finally she realised. Its source must be the old prototype in the library. Its inspiration came from among his father's books, not from his school. She stared and stared — her son's fears of imagined war set in the mechanical print of those who had fought the old one.

"How did you manage to type on that clunky old machine?" she asked him at breakfast the next morning.

At first, Richard seemed coy, as if he wanted to deny ever being in his father's library.

"It's alright," she said by way of encouragement.

"I… I took it apart and oiled it and everything. I was careful. I wanted to do something nice for when Father is home again."

"You fixed it?" she said. It didn't quite make sense to her.

"The letters are still wobbly," he pointed out.

Ginny shook her head. "This from the boy who never played with his Meccano?"

"I never liked making things," he said. "Making words, that's different."

She realised, right there and then, that the poems were more important than the machine to Richard. She saw also the yawning gap between father and son, and how badly Richard would be disappointed if he presented Eustace with poetry. A serviced typewriter was a better gift.

* * *

Eustace drove up to Sheffield to see the Managing Director of Hillsborough Engineering & Supply Ltd, a company famed for drop-forgings in difficult grades of steel. He was procuring components for a project so secret even he understood only part of its purpose. A thousand pieces were needed in the next twenty-one days.

The Managing Director's name was Eric Andrews, but it was not Andrews who sat waiting for him.

"I'm sorry, Mr Andrews is indisposed, but the Chairman is here to see you," the young woman had told him as she led him up the stairs. The chairman, large as life, was Charlie Barrington-Brown.

The Barrington-Brown facing him had changed since their last meeting. He was distinctly overweight. His hair had turned grey, a thin colourless mass of wiry clumps. The face had reddened. Veins like a local roadmap burst across his cheeks from the sides of his nostrils. The moustache tried to hide the facts, but one small patch right of centre refused to grow with any colour. He wore a suit styled for a country squire and squinted in the manner of one refusing to wear glasses long after corrective lenses were required.

"Well, well, the notoriously ruthless Mr Eustace Havershall. How are you, Old Bean? I assume you are hoping to steal more capacity. From what I hear, you and Beaverbrook must be winning this war on your own." He grimaced as he rose to shake his visitor's hand. "Excuse me, won't you? I have a touch of gout. My doctor says, lay off the sticky puddings, but I always liked puddings."

"You own this place as well?" Eustace asked. On previous projects, the management had been dealt with by someone from the Ministry of Supply. Nevertheless, he was surprised not to have known about BBTL's interest.

"Bought it as the war broke out, Old Bean. One of our biggest investments. I thought — you know? — engineering companies make money when there's planes and tanks and ships and guns to be made. Regretting it now. I'm afraid I had to fire your Mr Andrews."

"But I spoke to him two days ago to make this appointment."

"Yes," said Barrington-Brown, as if the reversal of fortune was much-regretted.

"And?"

"We make the engine mounts for that new bomber, the one that's always in the news. Inherited the project when we bought the company. Inherited the liability too. It's hard to say when so many are being shot down, but it comes out in the end."

"What does?"

Barrington-Brown hesitated. "Drop forgings have the habit of developing cracks… inside… if you don't get them right. And planes fall from the sky if their engines are no longer attached." He mimicked a falling plane with his hand. "We've only just realised. Frightful business."

Eustace watched the hand plummet to the desktop, unsure what he should feel about the tragedy. *Hadn't he always wished disaster on Barrington-Brown?*

"Sorry, but this might be a wasted journey. As soon as it hits the headlines, this particular subsidiary will be toast." Barrington-Brown smiled unconvincingly. "It will cause something of a bird's nest for BBTL too, I suppose. Congratulations, by the way. I hear you won the latest Whitehall contract."

"Havershall's? Yes, I mean, we did." That victory — Ginny's triumph — seemed far away. Out of curiosity, he said, "You held that contract for years."

"I had it with Hayberry's. Waved it at the banks to get my first loans. I'm afraid I lost my *influence,* shall we say? These things happen, during a war, what with all the unpleasantness." Adopting a reflective smile, Barrington-Brown pointed towards the ceiling.

Eustace tried to work out what the cryptic reference meant. He returned a blank.

"Think about my wife's Godfather, Old Bean, don't you remember?"

"Lord Hailsgam? But he never goes to London or dabbles in politics. Almost never takes his seat in the Lords. He's no *influence.*"

"It's all water under the bridge now, I suppose. We're all on the same side, you and I, now we're in a war." Barrington-Brown wiped his mouth with the back of his hand and said, "You are right, of course, Hailsgam's always abstained from high places, hasn't he? But his best friend—"

Eustace felt the penny drop. "Good God, Lord Buckley? You don't mean Lord Buckley?"

"Lord Buckley, the fallen fascist," Barrington-Brown said regretfully. "He was rather useful for me."

"So, all those years, I never stood a chance on those tenders?"

"Not a prayer, Old Bean. Buckley hated you. Why wouldn't he? I mean, you and his niece? Whereas I? Well, time was, I introduced his daughter to her husband. Got me rather a lot of business in the end. I scrubbed his back. He scrubbed mine. Until, well... it's all terribly unfortunate."

Terribly unfortunate? Eustace had believed he had ceased fighting the toffs and their class wars when he stopped attending their weekend parties. It seemed they had never stopped fighting him.

Chapter Twenty-Four

In the shadow of war, the staff at the Havershalls' house in Stratford had been reduced to a housekeeper, a maid, and a part-time cook. The boys were at boarding school most of the time. To Eustace, it made the house feel empty on those dwindling occasions when he made it home.

He drove there for dinner that Friday night after his visit to Hillsborough Engineering. He and Ginny shared a perfunctory kiss in the hall. She seemed surprised by his presence.

He took a bath, put on a lounge suit, even chose a tie. She didn't dress for dinner, he noticed, sat waiting at the table, still in her office clothes. A candle in a silver candlestick and a bottle of Malbec from their dwindling cellar stood watch on the table between them. Glasses were filled and they toasted the memory of Lord Montague Buckley and Woody and lost family. The tradition had become rather stale.

She told him the news, first from the letters of their boys, then of another big order for tank wheels.

"The return rollers on the caterpillar tracks, for the North African campaign," she explained.

He nodded and prepared himself to make an announcement. "I want us to take a shot at buying BBTL."

She looked straight through him for a moment. "Good grief, you're serious!" she said. "What makes you think Barrington-Brown is ready to sell?"

"BBTL has hit trouble. He told me so himself. His shareholders will do the selling for him."

Ginny shot him an incredulous look.

"Bumped into him while trying to buy Ministry components, Gin. He's dropped the most beastly clanger. Planes are falling out of the sky. It's a matter of time before it hits the headlines."

He dashed off the particulars, including which newspapers were planning to run the story. The repercussions on the Stockmarket would be ruinous to BBTL's share price.

"You sound happy that planes are crashing. Listen to yourself, Eustace."

"I.. I didn't mean it like that. But don't you see, it's an opportunity? I told you all this would set us up for afterwards. Owning BBTL would make us the most powerful typewriter manufacturer in Europe, let alone Britain."

"Yes, maybe, if there really is an afterwards."

He shook his head gravely. "Gin, I've seen one war that seemed never ending, but there's always an afterwards with or without you. I telephoned Archie Hoare, asked him if he could find us five million."

"A loan? For five million! You seeking a loan?" She laughed as if he had tipped into the absurd. "Is this why you've come scurrying home on a Friday? To tell me this, not to see your wife?"

"The opportunity…"

"To hell with opportunity! Is this another thing you've decided on your own, Eustace? Wasn't running the company the job you dropped on me?"

"I only knew there was an opportunity because of the work I'm doing. Didn't I tell you—?"

"There is no 'opportunity'. No opportunity because I will not allow it, and you have no Woody to take your side."

"But, Gin.."

"Damn you, Eustace! You are the one who hates loans." She shook her head and repeated the five-million number. "We used to discuss everything, even when I wasn't part of the business. Now, I'm running it with you *in absentia*, and it seems I know nothing of our plans. How is that?"

She dabbed her mouth with her napkin and dropped it on her plate.

"I'm sorry," he said. "I want BBTL. I have to have it."

"Of course, you do," she said. "I know what you are, Eustace. Your next deal is still like the last one, which will be like the next one, win or lose. Just a bit bigger every time. That's you. You cannot let anything alone."

"You knew—"

"If you're about to say, 'I knew when I married you,' then yes, I knew. It was more romantic then. But this pursuit of Charlie Barrington-Brown is preposterous. It always was."

"Gin, I need your support in this," he pleaded.

"You…need…*my* support."

"There's things to be done. The money can't be raised unless I… unless we… put up sureties from the company."

"Ah, I see, I was right. This is why you're here on a Friday night." She paused, making sure she had the picture straight. "You can outvote me, but not act on a financial reconstruction, isn't that right? Something of the five-million scale requires more than half of all the shareholders. Yes, I have read the shareholders' agreement, Eustace. This is about Woody's shares, of course. With those still uncertain, you are scuppered, aren't you?"

They sat, unspeaking, on opposite sides of the great wooden dining table. He put down his wine glass. A nerve in her cheek twitched. The gently-formed crow's feet beside her eye cushioned its tremor. She fumbled with her cigarette case — something he'd given her for a long-ago birthday — and managed to extract a slightly misshapen cigarette.

"These damned things. I can't get my brand now the war is on," she complained.

The neurotic beat of her presence seemed somehow arrhythmic to him now. He offered her a light, but she turned away and used the candle from the table for the purpose.

He was about to take up his wine glass again when she said, "I suppose we must divorce then."

He had never been more shocked.

Eustace took his overnight case, repacked it in the bedroom, then drove himself to a hotel. As his car splashed through the wet Stratford streets, he reflected on all the things he had ever wanted and taken from life. He told himself he'd been fighting for a war that ended well. It seemed he could not have it.

When she had asked for a divorce, he had sat there, staring at her. Eventually he had said, "A divorce is impossible. I do not want a divorce. Ginny, for God's sake! This is about how it can be… afterwards."

"Ha! Appealing to God, Eustace? You, the non-believer? We're broken *now*, Eustace. Not afterwards. Can't you see that?"

"I will not divorce you," he repeated.

"Then I shall prise myself away, one way or another," she promised.

The legal and commercial tangle created by Woody's death was this: he had created a trust in favour of his children after Mabel's death to be released when they reached twenty-one. The documents had not been updated in fifteen years and thus included 'James Joseph Woodmansey, Celia Jane Woodmansey and any further issue.' James was dead. Celia was missing.

Eustace, advised by Archie Hoare, knew this produced an unholy mess. When Ginny had taken her thirteen percent of the company in

1930, it left just under forty-eight percent and just over thirty-nine percent in the hands of Eustace and Woody respectively. No one held a majority.

While this was not an obstacle in the day-to-day running of the company since Eustace's shares outvoted Ginny's, it created a problem now because the shareholders' agreement that ruled the company demanded specifically that 'any restructuring involving greater than twenty percent of the company's net asset value' required a 'majority of the issued shares' to vote in its favour. Eustace held less than fifty percent overall; Ginny's and the 'floating' Woodmansey shares held the rest. He needed one or the other to vote his way, and since those floating Woodmansey shares belonged to an eighteen-year-old spy who had disappeared with the French Resistance, a big loan could not be approved without Ginny's agreement.

On Monday morning, Ginny phoned the most prominent solicitor she could think of.

"Mrs Morrison, I understand you are a woman solicitor," she said on being transferred to the correct extension.

"You are misinformed, Madam, I am a solicitor," came the reply.

"Then you will do nicely for my purpose," Ginny said and engaged Carrie Morrison within a minute and a half.

Carrie Morrison's was one of the first four women ever to qualify as a solicitor in England, though she had not begun her career in the field of law. When the Sex Disqualification (Removal) Act of 1919 allowed women into the profession, it changed everything in her life, except perhaps the attitudes of men around her.

Once asked on an official form if she suffered 'any physical disability,' she replied, "No, except being a woman."

She married and refused to take her husband's name.

In 1931, she had been the first woman invited to speak at a Law Society annual meeting. Having campaigned for reforms to the divorce laws for years, the chosen subject for her talk was the 'Benefit of Dispute Resolution' and the 'Courts of Domestic Relations'.

Unseen and unmet at the time, Ginny took all these background facts as recommendations. Morrison's gender felt the most compelling.

Ginny drove herself to Carrie Morrison's Chambers in Broxbourne, Hertfordshire. Morrison's office was twenty feet by twenty laid with nearly-new Axminster carpet, featuring one desk with neat piles of papers, two bookcases against the back wall, a leather chair for the solicitor and three cloth-upholstered visitors' chairs. It smelt of law books and lavender. Ginny selected the middle chair.

Morrison, in person, was a stern short-haired, fifty-something woman of formidable intellect. She wore a prim dark jacket and skirt, in appearance like the headmistress of a school several degrees stricter than a convent. Her voice chimed with Oxford-perfect clarity. Resting her palms on her desk as if the world needed her steadying guidance, she examined the photographic work of Mr Carling March from the Field Detective Agency. Useful, but only circumstantial evidence at best, she concluded.

"Let me warn you, Mrs Havershall, even in these circumstances, divorce is difficult. I might observe that Henry VIIIth enjoyed the advantage of having the church in his pocket and even so, he was forced to change its Managing Director, so to speak. Twice after that, an axeman was employed. Divorce can be messy. And socially damaging to the woman... if that's what this comes to."

"I fear there is nothing left for it."

"Yes, indeed." Morrison adopted the expression of a caring teacher. "Do you know how many people marry every year?"

Ginny shook her head.

"In this country, half a million couples last year. It was a boom year. It always is when there's a war on the horizon. Do you know how many divorces were granted?"

"No, I—"

"Seven thousand, seven hundred and fifty-five," Morrison said, lingering on each digit. "It makes one think, doesn't it?"

"It makes me think there must be a lot of people living unhappily."

"Quite so," Morrison agreed. "Though we are quite lucky. It is not just adultery now that can bring about the end of a marriage. Since the Act of '37, we have cruelty, desertion or incurable insanity to choose from. This accident of his—?"

"My husband is not insane," Ginny said. "Neither am I, I think."

"Is he cruel or has he deserted you?"

"Only in pursuit of money. And duty to his country."

"Let us hope, then, that he is sleeping with other women, and — more importantly — that we can prove it."

* * *

Eustace adopted a nomadic lifestyle through the late summer of 1940, living in hotels and officially 'designated' accommodation, while doing the Ministry's bidding. He was no longer welcome in Stratford and rarely went there. He would work Saturday mornings in the Ministry's London office, a proper office now, no longer Beaverbrook's house. In the afternoons, he would visit one of the theatres. The matinees were quieter. He didn't feel so trapped.

He had a ticket for the Old Vic on Saturday, 7th September. He bought a programme and a double brandy at the theatre's bar and sat among the throng of ticket holders, leafing through the cast list as he waited for the bell. He spotted a name — Sarah C. Black. In an instant, he guessed that Sarah Coles had taken the name for the West End. He felt certain of it, though his certainty came without evidence. He realised he'd been looking for her in every theatre show he had visited. He simply hadn't admitted it.

When the show started, she appeared in the chorus line, dancing next to five other girls. From the second row of the dress circle, he watched that curl of her hair dripping over her eye.

She had a short solo before the interval, singing not dancing. Her singing voice was unexpected, low and jazzy. He thought of the long-ago bruise and wondered about the name. Was she afraid that Woody would come after her, unaware he had passed on?

After the performance, he found he had been paying so much attention to Sarah, he had missed the commotion brewing outside. It must have been possible to hear the distant thuds during the show, but he had been lost in the music of the accompanying orchestra. Belatedly, an air-raid siren started.

Once in the street, he looked up. Fresh explosions flashed through the towering smoke clouds already blackening the sky a few miles east towards the docks. A few seconds later, their chest-pounding thuds would arrive. Dots of planes were now scudding towards him, orange trails shooting up, reaching for the dots. Even compared to frantic dogfights of recent months, this felt both more and less unreal.

One dot dropped, growing larger and darker. When it was close enough to have shape, it grew wings and engines and the smoke trailing behind it became a tail. It went right over his head.

He watched it, a toy from his son's model Skybirds, until it disappeared behind the line of rooftops and exploded somewhere over in the direction of Chelsea. The sound hit him in the ribs like a medicine ball, took the breath from his lungs. The ground seem to unhinge itself from the Earth's mantle and shake and shake. People were screaming. He could not understand it. He thought he'd seen the pilot's face. It was wrong. All wrong. Wars were muddy fields with young men posing as soldiers. London was everything he still believed was civilisation, and yet war still came here, this close.

Blind to his own reason, he limped around the theatre into a back alley, trying to hurry. He stumbled upon the Stage Door. He banged hard and when the Stage Door Manager answered, he said, "I have to escort her home. The Huns have started bombing."

The stage manager asked him what he was talking about. He said, "Sarah Coles." And then he said, "Miss Black."

Two more distant bombs exploded and sent another hefty shudder through the theatre walls. The tremors convinced the stage manager. He stepped out of the doorway.

Eustace continued lopsidedly down the corridor towards the dressing rooms, calling, "Sarah, Sarah."

Quite by chance, Sarah appeared around the corner ahead, flanked by three other chorus girls, all now in civilian clothes.

"What the hell is this?" said one.

"Eustace?" Sarah said in surprise.

"Come with me. They've started bombing."

She did not move. He told her, "It's alright. Woody is gone. He can't hurt you."

He reached for her hand. "Come with me," he repeated. "Please…"

"But my digs are around the corner. I'll be fine."

"No, you don't understand. We have beaten them in the dog fights — the Spitfires, the Hurricanes, all those fast planes. Now they're trying to flatten London. I have a car."

"Don't talk stupid, Mister. Is he mad? Shall we call Wally?" said another of the chorus girls.

"No, it's alright," Sarah said. "He can take me if he wants… wherever it's safe."

He drove fast but not as desperately as Woody might have. He and Sarah reached a hotel south of Hampton Court. He told her they would be alright.

"Hitler seems to have it in for the East End. The docks, I imagine," he said, referring to the chaos they had left behind.

He took off his wedding ring and offered it to her with a sheepish smile. Far too big, but she squeezed her fingers into a fist to hold the ring in place while they booked in under the names 'Mr and Mrs Smith'. She handed it back to him in the first-floor corridor as he fumbled with the room key. She stood kneading the skin it had touched as if it had already burned the sin in place.

Their room looked over the river, and beyond the river, back towards London. She took to the bathroom. To make herself 'presentable', she said. She surprised him, having no words of regret when he told her about the dead man who had once stood between them.

From the window, Eustace gazed at the boats tethered to their moorings, bobbing on the current. It was evening, the moon a quarter full. Towards the horizon, a darkness that seemed to mark the edge of everything had arisen, soot black on the twilight greys as if the half-world to the north-east was being swallowed.

The bombing entered a second wave. Fire red cracks arose like flares. Licks of flames danced up towards oblivion. How great must the fireballs be to reach so high at such a distance? He swore he could still hear and feel the thuds, the screams of Londoners. Perhaps the war was being lost this night. He had run from it. Escaped again. *How shameful was that?*

He wondered about his factories and Stratford and his boys and Ginny, and all the other things he ought to be defending. He had not seen his boys in almost a month. They didn't know about the threatened divorce, or his chance to break Barrington-Brown, or ten thousand more aircraft parts he had spent the week pursuing from Glasgow to Colchester.

He rested his forehead against his balled fist. He had nothing to hope for, except to prove that *he* could build the planes. When Barrington-Brown fell, Eustace Havershall would still be standing.

Sarah emerged from the bathroom, was tiptoeing naked across to the bed. She slipped between the sheets and called his name.

Grasping consolations had never served his purpose, or sat easily on his conscience. He turned his head away.

"What is it?" she asked.

"I'm sorry. I'm sorry. This cannot be."

"I will give you anything you ask for," she promised.

He shook his head. She did not have what he needed. Perhaps no one did.

The Blitz on London began. Hitler had seen that Britain's fighter aircraft could not be defeated and the country could not therefore be invaded. He turned to his bombers, seeking to pound its capital into submission.

There were twenty-four plays and musicals running in the West End on 7th September. One week later, two remained. The Old Vic was one of the first theatre buildings to be hit.

But the effect of the Blitz on other business was surprising. Theatres closed for war and professional sports stopped playing, but the London Stock Exchange closed for only a week. Money — its circulation — and the healthy continuation of commerce was vital to a war conducted through manufactured goods.

Woody had said, "The next war is an industrial war."

He would have thought the achievement of Eustace and the Ministry impossible.

When Eustace had first made his call, Archie Hoare had agreed there was money to be made in a war and investments to be shuffled. Wealth was flowing through the secret channels of Europe, made fluid by the shifting geography of power. Banks in countries that remained neutral were popular. Switzerland did well. But even Swiss bankers and their clients needed investments in places that hedged their bets.

"A smart investor might put money in both camps," said Archie. "Some on the British side of the fence; some on the German. You can never tell who's going to win. Of course, the smart investor tries to win either way."

With the right banking connections, money could be provided for the enterprising industrialist, he promised, those prepared to dance with the greater devils.

For nations, however, the finances of war provided a different challenge. Money was burned like confetti. Without it, a country could not fight. Fighting this new war, a Britain that so recently measured itself on its possession of gold shipped out its last cargo of the precious metal in return for armaments. The country's treasury went bankrupt. It was borrowing to fight on and needed both a stockmarket and rich allies to borrow from.

Ginny renewed her search for the evidence that might force through a divorce. Amelia Stewart, whom Ginny had once assumed to be her husband's mistress, was now married and unlikely to admit any adultery. She must look further afield.

She settled her suspicion on Raye Cropper. When angered, Woody had once made an accusation. Unlikely as it seemed, who had ever known Eustace better than him? And why not Rate Cropper? She was young and smart, even if not society's idea of beautiful. The bootstrap ambition was probably part of Raye's appeal to a man like Eustace.

Ginny called Raye down from Nottingham on a Friday morning to discuss the future of Cartwright & Co, Eustace's last acquisition before the war. It had stumbled along, mostly unattended and unthought of for a year. The two women drove across to Coventry together in Ginny's Crossley.

"He wanted to sell the property before the war started," Ginny explained, pulling into the company's car park at the front. Norman Street contained a row of factories of similar age and shape, each a low-roofed manufacturing building with a floor space no more than a sixth of Havershall's facility in Duke Works. The Havershall's property was Number Four along the row. Unlike its neighbours, it came with a sizeable empty yard at the back.

"That has to go," said Raye, pointing to a wobbly 'Cartwright & Co Ltd' sign that still hung above an unpromising entrance porch.

The sign's second line added, 'Established 1842'. The last Cartwright owner had been the fourth generation to run it.

"Just short of its centenary," she noted.

They toured the building, witnessed machines that weren't making anything and storemen who seemed to be moving stock from one shelf to another without shipping any product to customers. The accounts showed sales levels a quarter of what the company had managed at its height.

"So? Shut the company? Sell the land?" Ginny asked as they wandered back to the car park. "We could use some of the manufacturing machines and sell off the product line. Maybe the land too. That was the original plan."

"That's what Mr Havershall would do," Raye agreed.

"And Woody would have let him."

"Yes, I suppose he would. But you don't want to do that, Mrs Havershall?"

"I want to know if you think it the right thing to do."

"Alright... Then, no, I don't think it is. With the war work, we're gearing up Nottingham and Birmingham to run three shifts now. We could do more with more space and more labour. Why give up a factory here? Mr Woodmansey — Woody — he always said he had come to Birmingham because that's where all the best engineering was done. Well, Nottingham's not bad and Coventry's better, I reckon, especially if you're going to make parts for tanks. This is a motor city, what with Daimler up the road."

"Could you bring it up to scratch, if I gave you the job, and the money?"

"You want to put investment *here*? With me to run it?"

Ginny nodded.

"Because Mr Havershall would do the opposite?" Raye suggested.

"Well, perhaps. But you told me it was the right thing to do anyway."

"Aye, it is."

Ginny greeted the judgement with a bright smile. "Call me Ginny. We'll get along famously."

She offered to buy lunch, assuming they could find somewhere open. Neither of them knew Coventry well.

"I need to ask one honest question," Ginny said as they drove away. "You see, Woody, bless his soul, always told me one thing I didn't believe. And now I need to know the truth. Get it down in writing, so to speak. So tell me…"

She stopped as if a question had been asked, her eyes on the road so she didn't have to look at her passenger.

"Tell you what, Mrs Havershall?"

"Tell you what, *Ginny*?" Ginny corrected. "I assure you, your secrets are safe. This isn't about the past. It's about the future."

She left a moment's hesitation. Not deliberate. The next question was hard. "My husband has been having affairs. This is certain. Did he ever have an affair? With someone in Nottingham?"

Raye didn't answer. Her mouth opened but nothing emerged.

"I'm sorry," she managed at last. "You didn't think… with *me*?"

The car stopped at the junction of Norman Street. There was no traffic but Ginny made no attempt to proceed. She turned in her seat to face Raye.

"We are divorcing, you see. The future of Havershall's, our factories, lies in the balance."

"In the balance?"

"Who gets what. Does Havershall's continue as it is today, or does it revert? I wouldn't like it to revert."

Raye's eyes ticked left and right as she made her calculation. "Are you threatening me, Mrs Havershall?"

"Ginny," said Ginny.

"Mrs Havershall," Raye insisted.

"I have the bank records, Raye. He paid for your night school classes. He paid for your tuition on your degree and for your PhD. He educated you. You see how it looks?"

"The company paid."

"My husband signed the cheques."

"Yes, he was the managing director so I suppose he did."

"And hence my question. I have no grudge to hold, I assure you. I just need the truth."

"No," Raye said and repeated the word three times. "I don't like the way you people get away with it all the time, that sort of thing, but your husband, he was always the gentleman. Never treated me as anything but an engineer, which is what I am."

"I'm sorry? 'Us' people?" Ginny queried.

"Like your Mr Woodmansey."

"'*My*' Mr Woodmansey? I confess, Raye, the possessions in this conversation have left me at a loss."

"Management, if you like. Classes that reckon themselves better than the rest of us."

"But Woody was—"

Ginny found she could not bring herself to say that Woody was not one of 'us'. Yes, he was an outsider, a 'working class lad', or had been, but he was certainly raised to 'management'. She had never considered what that made him in the eyes of anyone else.

"It don't do to speak ill of the dead," Raye continued. "Forgive me, I shouldn't have. That ain't my way, Mrs Havershall."

Ginny noticed how the elocution slipped out of Raye's voice when she became agitated.

"On the contrary, please, say it all. We both know Woody was… problematic. It's been a year, Raye, enough reverence for the dead."

"He didn't marry 'em, that's all. When he got them up the duff, I mean. Why would he? He had money. He could afford to send them, you know?"

"Send them where? Now, you have really lost me."

"There's women who'll do it for you, make it go away, for a price… when you're in trouble."

"I'm sorry, Woody arranged for these things? For *abortions*?"

"Makes college fees seem irrelevant, doesn't it?" Raye said. "Except for his last one, I'm told."

"How many were there, for God's sake?"

"I dunno. Three or four I know about. But the last one, she was the one who *had* the child. Nancy... Nancy Jarvis. She didn't know, not 'til he was gone, see. And then what's a girl to do?"

A car pulled around them and honked. Through a wound-down window, its passenger called out, "Women drivers. Why don't you get a ruddy move on? There's a war, you know?"

Ginny was busy, replaying memories of things in which she should have seen more than she'd seen at the time — Woody's string of women, always younger; the girl he'd reinstated on the shop floor after she'd been caught stealing. She should have asked more questions.

"I am sorry, Raye. I apologise for the question, for my accusation. It was wrong. And I'm sorry for Mr Woodmansey too."

"I thought you'd know all about it. You only had to look for the red haired ones. He always preyed on them."

"This last one, I'll go and see her. Believe me, Raye, I'll put it right. I've been to see all the war widows, not that this Nancy is a war widow, but Havershall's looks after its own, that's for sure. Eustace taught me that."

"I heard she died. After the baby, see. An infection, that's what I heard."

Ginny put her hand to her mouth. "Oh, no, not like Mabel!"

"Mabel? I wouldn't know about that. But the baby was a boy, I heard. You don't know half of it, do you?"

Ginny shook her head, shouldered the guilt. She took it on behalf of Havershall's. "Did my husband know? Does Eustace know about Nancy? About any of the Nancys?"

Raye did not answer. Ginny repeated the question.

"Why would he, Mrs Havershall? You didn't."

Ginny thought about the sixteen years she had slept next to Eustace Havershall, felt him kicking against history, often heard him murmur, *"You can't go outside, Woody. I wouldn't send anyone–"*

Turning back to Raye, she said, "We will never tell him about Mr Woodmansey, about Woody. Promise me that."

Radford was, on the face of it, a great place for a new manufacturing venture. It claimed to be birthplace of the British motor car industry. The 'Great Horseless Carriage Company' started there in an old cotton mill in 1896. Its growth paralleled the industry it served. The company was quickly renamed Motor Mills, stuck between St. Nicholas Street,

Sandy Lane, and the Coventry Canal. A red-brick office block with stone banding was erected at the turn of the century. The design included an electricity power house, a revolution in its time, replacing steam as the main industrial driver. Soon after, the company had changed name again. It became Daimler. Ironically, given the company's role in both wars, the name was licensed from Herr Gottlieb Daimler, founder of Daimler-Motoren-Gesellschaft of Cannstatt, Germany. The companies were not linked.

When Raye stood in the back yard of the Norman Street works, the Daimler buildings dominated the skyscape. She thought the new Havershall's location perfect. She promised a working factory with modern equipment in less than sixty days, in much the style that Beaverbrook's Bully Boys had adopted when seizing Castle Bromwich and other commandeered facilities. In return, Ginny promised she would signed the cheques for the investment.

The sad failure of Hillsborough Engineering & Supply Ltd in the matter of drop forgings with inner cracks was revealed in the Daily Mail.

Two whole squadrons were grounded for checks. More would follow. Someone high up in the RAF had leaked the story. Apparently an engineer in the aeroplane manufacturer's design department had been bribed to wave through the normal pre-production tests.

That evening, 26th September, the nineteenth in a row, London was bombed, but not before the share price of Hillsborough's owner, BBTL, had fallen by a half on the stockmarket.

Ginny had arranged a *tryst* with Devere for that same evening. He was to meet her discreetly in the car park at Duke House after office hours and drive her into Wales, to a delightful country hotel over the border near Shrewsbury.

"Listen, Martin, I know I said I would, but now I just can't, not tonight," she said as she greeted him next to her car.

"But Ginny, darling, we're booked…"

"I changed my mind. I have a headache. I feel unwell." She reached for a piece of paper in her pocket. "There, see. I have to go there. That's the truth."

Ginny had consulted the files in the wages office, found an address. Devere read it aloud from the paper.

"You shouldn't hang around in Birmingham at night, not on your own. There have been bombings, like in London. It's getting worse."

"Then drive me, Martin, please. Only don't ask me questions. I'll make it up to you."

"You will?"

She smiled at him. "I will. I always have what you want."

She knew she was lying, even though she didn't know what the truth might be. Devere was a convenience. He always had been.

He drove her through Digbeth to the address. They parked at the top of the street, looking down its slope past the terraced housing. The spot was a few hundred yards from where Eustace had stood talking to Lionel Swithin's mother in 1924.

Ginny sat waiting, hoping and yet dreading that someone — maybe Nancy Jarvis's mother — would come out, pushing the grandchild in his pram, so that she would see him and not have to speak.

Nothing moved except the grey washing lines strung across from house to house. It was half-moon dark and the street-lamps hung unlit overhead, predatory statues whose lights were victims of gloomy war. In the distance, the reports of bombs could be heard. A night time raid was beginning.

"We're looking at a bloody street. Are you getting out?" he asked.

"No, Martin," she said. She had thought about it every possible way and found no solution. "What good would it do?"

"Havershall," said the stern voice on the other end of the telephone. It was Beaverbrook. A knock on the door had summoned Eustace to the hotel reception in his pyjamas. It was seven in the morning. He had been visiting Middlesborough the day before.

"Southampton had it bad last night. Sixty Heinkels. Lots of nasty munitions. Seven incendiaries hit the Woolston plant. One blew the buggery out of Itchen. Vickers say they don't know when Supermarine will be back in production. I need you down there," said Beaverbrook.

Supermarine, still the largest manufacturer of Spitfires, was owned by the Vickers company. It sounded to Eustace as if Vickers were in crisis.

"I can't lose the production, Havershall. We can't shoot these new buggers down if we can't get in the air. We have to find a solution."

"Were people killed? In the raid, I mean?" Eustace asked.

"Not as many as if we don't have Spitfires."

Chapter Twenty-Five

Beaverbrook's team descended on Southampton. Eustace got no sleep for seventy-two hours. In five days, the manufacturing equipment salvaged from Vickers' Woolston and Itchen plants was moved into three large garages around the city. Spitfires were back in production. Beaverbrook came down from London to offer his congratulations.

Sipping tea from enamel cups outside the Woolston factory where lady volunteers had set up catering for the rescue workers, Eustace thought of everything Woody had preached about the future — big factories, infinite automation. Suddenly, conjured out of nowhere, his mind reversed all the equations.

"The Germans will always bomb a factory," he said.

"Of course," said Beaverbrook, who was sipping from his cup

"Suppose there wasn't a factory."

"What?"

"Suppose there were hundreds of little workshops. Not one factory. What we've done here, suppose we did it everywhere, like it used to be when my great grandfathers made lace."

"Lace? What has lace to do with it?"

"Small workshops was how they made it. Before they had factories. Hitler can't bomb everywhere."

Beaverbrook thought through the idea for a moment. "Lots of people would have to give up their spaces. They wouldn't like it."

"Yes," said Eustace. "But we're Beaverbrook's Bully Boys."

"Ah, well… always cause trouble. They'll have to lump it," the Lord agreed.

During the following month, the Ministry, led primarily by Eustace with teams of engineers as the worker bees, re-sited entire factories along the south coast using twenty or more different locations instead of one.

Eustace drove from place to place, looking for the Holy Grails of aircraft production — anywhere with a ceiling tall enough for the enormous frames used to lay out an aircraft's wings. The buildings and small factories commandeered included a laundry, a bus station, a lighting factory and a series of outbuildings connected to a cemetery.

Once it was all done, and Beaverbrook declared himself satisfied with the new supply lines, Eustace was sent to Bristol, Oxford and Derby to perform the same trick.

Eustace, the industrialist, reversed the Industrial Revolution. Factories had replaced cottage industries. Now cottage industries made production safe.

At home, Ginny took to sleeping in the newly-installed Anderson Shelter in the garden, though air raids, now reaching Birmingham and nearby Coventry, rarely came close to Stratford. The Anderson Shelter had a floor area of four-and-a-half by six-and-a-half feet, buried in the ground and covered with six corrugated iron sheets bolted together at the top.

On the one occasion Eustace came home for a night, the Anderson Shelter saved all the embarrassing questions of who should sleep where, or how close their bodies should come. The shelter was too much like a stranded tank for Eustace, whether it kept him safe from bombs or not. He tried sleeping in the spare bedrooms that seemed most comfortable. After passing from one to the other, he was found by the housekeeper unconscious in William's room. Both the boys were away at school.

When the bombing of London had begun, the government feared widespread 'shell shock' among its citizens, similar to that seen in previous wars and among soldiers at Dunkirk. An earlier committee of psychiatrists predicted three times as many mental as physical casualties from aerial bombing. In preparation, the government hastily set up a special network of psychiatric clinics.

All predictions proved wrong. The clinics soon closed because of a lack of patients. The number of suicides and drunkenness declined and London recorded a mere two cases of 'bomb neurosis' per week in three months. If anything, the cheerful crowds visiting bomb sites to offer assistance hindered rather than helped the rescue work.

Each new reverse of fortune brought forth more volunteers for Local Defence roles. Workers endured longer shifts and weekend working. The number of days lost to strikes was the lowest in history. London was bombed fifty-six times in fifty-seven days. Quite what the Luftwaffe were doing on the other day was unclear. Newspapers reported that a third of all roads were now impassable due to debris. On every journey, a new route had to be taken.

A Gallup opinion poll showed that only one in thirty Britons expected to lose the war, despite the reported military setbacks everywhere except in Britain itself. Churchill had an approval rating approaching ninety percent. Society did not collapse.

The Germans attacked other cities. The industrial heartlands of the Midlands were becoming a principal target, though any town or city with a manufacturing base was on the Luftwaffe's list.

Eustace became used to those mysterious knocks on his door. A hotel receptionist, a bell boy or a Bed & Breakfast landlady would be calling to tell him that Lord Beaverbrook was holding on the telephone line. He would be instructed to go here or there to view some new disaster affecting production. Horror became his staple. Broken and burnt buildings — those that were not well hidden — and broken and burnt workers.

Each time, he would do what he could to put production back on track, move it to his model of smaller workshops. He could not put the people back together.

A typical day: he was in Huddersfield in the morning, looking at castings. By two o'clock, he had driven to Salford. Henry & Henry Ltd had been hit by a bomb the night before and part of their roof had collapsed. The bomb failed to explode. The smashed rafters were hanging down onto the shop floor where four Norton presses were normally stamping out metal blanks on a twelve-hour shift.

"There's a low loader and a crane on its way," Eustace told Jake Henry as he came off the phone. "The army have commandeered a school gymnasium they're not using at the school on Moss Side. You can have that."

"We haven't moved those presses since the day they were installed. It won't be easy to recommission them in a new place."

"Don't worry. I've two men who know how. Here by tea time."

"We're lucky," Henry told him. "Arkwright and Spears, them on the corner, caught one that went off proper the night before. Two girls on the night shift got it. Black like sticks in a fire when they found them."

These female victims were all too common, since women had become the principal workers in factories.

"I'm sorry. It's terrible," Eustace said. He had a special tone for delivering the words. He spent the next ten minutes talking to Henry about his family, the things worth fighting for. He had become used to dealing with managers shaken by the unspeakable sights of war and finding ways to get their thoughts back on production.

By four in the afternoon on this typical day, he had moved on to Bolton, wielding drawings of a new valve housing for the upgraded Spitfire. "I need the first hundred tomorrow."

"That's a six or seven hour set up, is that," the production manager complained, examining the design. "We can't start 'till the morning now. It's too late. You'll have your parts Tuesday at a pinch."

"Ernie, he's your chief setter, isn't he?"

"Aye," the man agreed. "You remember him then?"

"I do. His leg's too bad for the army, but he knows his duty. Ask if he'll stay tonight, if I stay with him. We'll have the machine ready for you in the morning."

Eustace received the astonished look he received from managers and supervisors all the time. It was inevitably followed by a reverse.

"Oh, no, that won't be necessary. We'll get it done for you, Mr Havershall. I'll stay meself."

Eustace had learnt not to smile.

Meanwhile, he kept his eye on the nightly news — war reports and the stockmarket. Share prices rose and fell on the war news, up on every small victory, down on each German triumph. His main interest, BBTL, limped on at its new low. Archie Hoare called him one evening when he was in Newcastle. The five million he'd asked for the month before had been raised.

"There's a rumour we're interested, Eustace. Hard to keep a lid on raising five mil, don't you know?"

"And so?"

"Better move quick. I'm afraid people will have twigged we work for you. The speculators will buy and the price will shoot up again."

"I..I haven't got agreement to the terms of the loan. Not yet. My wife…"

He did not say he saw no way to procure an agreement. The idea of finally besting Charlie, being the industrialist who somehow emerged triumphant in an industrial war, was something he couldn't let go. It was a dream. Ginny had made her position clear, yet he couldn't un-dream it.

Ginny had worn the same dress three days in a row. That was a first. Her hair was tied up in a scarf. She had been home with her boys on the weekend, but since Monday, she had been travelling back and forth between Nottingham, Birmingham and the factory at Radford that Raye Cropper was refitting, her overnight belongings in a small case.

The varnish on her nails was beginning to chip; two of them had broken.

She had hardly noticed this condition until Caroline came to visit, arriving in the reception at Duke House in her ostentatious furs. The Viscount and Viscountess Fairchild had graciously handed over the use of the old Buckley estate in Derbyshire to the army that week, and Caroline had insisted on a detour en route back to London to help celebrate Ginny's birthday, 'a little in advance'. The actual birth date was the following week.

"My, my, so this is the place he has you slaving?" she said with a dismissive glance around the reception hall — a clutch of visitors chairs and two typists with telephones gathered behind a desk; behind them, a large sign that read, 'Havershall and Woodmansey Typewriters Ltd, established 1921'.

"In Eustace's absence..." Ginny began. "We are both directors. I am in charge now."

"Yes, but look at your hair, your face. It's a mess. I should take you straight to the finest hair dresser in Birmingham, if there is such a thing."

"Here where civilisation dare not say its name? Really, Caroline."

"Birmingham was always such a dirty, grimy little city. This is what I always warned you about, Gin."

"You mean that I might one day do something useful here?"

"Poppycock. You sound exactly like him. Don't you dare say it's a duty. He's led you to this." Caroline took another look around, clearly unable to find anything of merit. "Are you ready to come? I have a birthday lunch arranged for us and my driver is outside."

"I must fetch my coat," Ginny said.

"Very well. And remove the scarf. You look like a land girl."

A few minutes later, Ginny was sitting next to her cousin in the back of a chauffeured Bentley. She had done her best to brush out her hair, but her dress remained creased.

Caroline began reporting the latest gossip, all of it gloomy — whose son had signed up, whose had avoided service, whose had been killed.

"You're not listening, are you?" Caroline complained when she noticed Ginny's vacant gaze. Her eyes were filling up with tears.

"Oh, dear, what is it, Gin? Is it that beastly factory?"

"Nothing. Nothing really." She fixed her gaze on the broken nails. "Someone telephoned me this morning to say Eustace has been voted the Midlands' Businessman of the Year. Third time in ten years."

"But you run his business?" Caroline said.

"Yes. Precisely. It's his war service, of course, that attracts the vote. Our office has seen him less than a dozen days since the accident. I'm more of a 'typewriterist' than him."

Caroline raised her eyebrows into a questioning arch, not understanding the reference.

"Caroline," Ginny said, "I have asked him for a divorce."

"A divorce?"

"Yes. And he has refused."

Caroline looked alarmed. "Of course, he has refused. Divorce is out of the question."

"But I—"

"Oh, no, Gin. This must be the American in you. We do not divorce in England."

"England makes it terribly complicated, it's true. My solicitor explained it. But why not? We are driving each other mad."

"Then live apart. You're practically doing it by the sounds of it. Goodness knows, Edward and I have coped. Buckleys do not divorce. Society would not approve."

"Though it approves of the sordid affairs?"

Caroline allowed herself a thin smile. "I rather think it sees them as colourful, gives gossips something to talk about without giving grounds to remove you from the conversation altogether."

After a moment of reflection, the smile was supplanted by a frown. "But this I do not understand. If you wish to divorce, why run his company for him? Leave it to rot. Why this?" Her gesture turned Ginny's appearance into a question.

"Have you forgotten? I own part of the company."

"And which part of it do you suppose you will get in any settlement?

When Ginny had asked for a divorce, she had not thought about anything but getting away. She had no destination in mind, or ideas on ownership.

"Suppose I do not want any part," she said.

"If that is really true, I'd say indifference was to your advantage, assuming you wish to pursue this mad notion of a legal separation. Maybe I am foolish. By comparison to you, Ginny, I almost certainly am. But you may play on the fact he has always needed his company, needed it more than anything else. A 'Society' wife was never more than part of his scorecard."

"That's not true," Ginny snapped.

"Dear Gin, all men, even Edward, are the same." Caroline shook her head judgementally. "Forgive me, but whether the company rots or not seems the perfect bargaining chip. Threaten the company. He will give you up, I'm sure of it. You'll get anything you ask for, except Havershall's. Wouldn't you like to be rid of that place? You cannot tell me you're happy like this?"

Eustace's discomfort with hotels escalated. Beaverbrook could find him at random hours of the day anytime he stayed in one. He couldn't stand the silence, waiting for a telephone to ring or a door to be knocked. There was the loneliness of it too, of course.

He spent several nights on the platform at the Elephant and Castle Underground Station with hundreds of others who were sheltering there, sleeping head to foot, side to side, humanity packed into a warehouse, waiting for the order to start life again.

Sirens wailed. The ground shook with each nearby bomb. Fear crept in. And went out. Like lungs breathing.

But people were together. They told jokes. He liked their blind confidence in the war effort. He listened to their hopes and dreams for the end of the war, and always said, "Yes, yes," with the greatest conviction.

A girl of eight or nine, who had at some time lost her right arm at the elbow, chalked out the squares for hopscotch on the platform with her left. She hopped and skipped in perfect balance. She gave up the game when three old women arrived, looking for somewhere to lay down.

People sang too:

The Lambeth Walk.

The White Cliffs of Dover.

God Save the King.

A young couple brought a wind up gramophone and danced in a space no more than two yards square.

Sometime after midnight on his third visit, a deafening thunder shook the tunnel. Large chunks of masonry fell from the ceiling. The word came, shouted down from above that a pub and two houses nearby were on fire. The able bodied men, Eustace included, and a few of the women ran up the stairs and out into the street to help.

Eustace spent two hours on a bucket line, throwing water at the flames because the fire-brigade couldn't be spared from whatever larger buildings were ablaze that night. Afterwards, without sleep, he felt strangely refreshed. He slept on the same six feet of platform the following night and all his neighbours knew him by name. The place had an unfathomable spirit that rode through every crisis. He found to his surprise that he was not concerned by confinement anymore, or about dying in these crowds, if that was what luck dictated. His claustrophobia had gone. That Mark IV tank and that locked cupboard in childhood Nottingham no longer echoed.

Chapter Twenty-Six

The next time Eustace and Ginny met was in Carrie Morrison's chambers in Broxbourne on the morning of 14th November 1940, the day before Ginny's birthday. One of three visitors' chairs remained empty since Eustace had come without representation. He and Ginny chose the chairs farthest apart.

She first congratulated him on being 'Midlands' Businessman of the Year'. No one had yet told him the news. He stared at her blankly and then said, "Sorry," as if he understood his victory was stolen.

She saw how wretched he had become. The unceasing effort had creased his suit, frayed his shirt collar and mis-fastened his neck-tie. His hair needed a trim. She remembered Caroline had said much the same about her own appearance.

"Eustace, are you quite alright?"

"Ministry business," he said.

"In London?"

"Everywhere," he replied.

Carrie Morrison coughed to attract attention. "We are here to discuss various impasses that frustrate the matter in hand. You want to make certain business decisions but you cannot agree. You cannot declare Miss Celia Woodmansey dead for seven years, since she is merely missing in an occupied country, though given her disappearance, this seems the probable outcome."

"She is not dead," Ginny insisted. Eustace nodded agreement.

"Quite a hornet's nest," Morrison concluded. "Mr Havershall, I understand you might wish the company to secure funding for the purpose of buying this rival."

"It is secured," he said.

"Yes, but lacking the support of fifty percent of the shareholding, you are frustrated." She stopped to read from the papers in front of her.

"Archie Hoare and I have discussed a personal loan. I will buy BBTL shares myself."

"Understandable," Morrison agreed. "But unwise. I assume you would need your current shareholding in Havershall's as security?"

He nodded.

"Alas, any attempt by you to purchase BBTL shares personally would breach the covenants in your shareholders' agreement."

"What covenants? I don't understand."

"I refer to the 1920 agreement between shareholders," Morrison said, tapping her finger on the relevant papers. "According to its principal restrictions, no shareholder may hold a stake in a competitive business. It also states that 'no shareholder may sell or otherwise put at risk their shareholding without first offering to sell said shares to other shareholders at a fair market price.' That is Section 17, paragraph 'd'. Mr Havershall, you cannot use your shares as security for a personal loan without first offering them for sale to both Mr Woodmansey's heir and Mrs Havershall."

"But Ginny's not a party to the 1920 agreement. That was between myself and Woody."

"Indeed, but the obligation is to offer for sale to 'other shareholders'. Whilst Mrs Havershall was not a party to the original agreement, we believe only the legal heir of Mr Woodmansey could release you from that obligation to 'offer' once his estate is out of probate, assuming an heir can be established."

"'We believe'," Eustace repeated, noticing the collective term. "This is absurd. There is no heir and my wife does not have enough money to buy out my shares."

"A hornet's nest," Morrison repeated. "Of course, things would be a lot easier for you if your wife were to agree to the company taking the loan necessary to purchase BBTL. Your vote and hers would then represent more than fifty percent of the 'issued' shareholding."

On cue, Ginny added, "But I won't, not at present."

"We've been over this many times," Eustace replied. "Why are we sitting here?"

"We are proposing a solution, Mr Havershall. My client wishes to divorce you and in order to do so—"

"No," he interrupted. "If Gin has a proposal, she can speak for herself. She always has."

Morrison looked from Ginny to Eustace and back, seeking instruction.

"Very well," Ginny said at last. "If you wish to hear it from me, you shall. I am willing to vote through your loan and sell my thirteen percent in the settlement. You can have your company. I want my divorce and, of course, there is the question of grounds. 'Wanting to be divorced' are no grounds at all, apparently. One party might be cruel or mad, but whilst we may both be candidates, we are neither of us certifiable. That leaves adultery."

"And?" he prompted, refusing to see the point.

"Oh, come, it's a simple enough process these days, Eustace. You book yourself in a seaside hotel with a mistress of your choice. A detective takes a few seedy photographs. We get an honourable separation. It is what's expected."

"I don't care what's expected. I don't have a mistress. No one, Gin. No one to take to any hotel."

"Pah! Ambition is your mistress. I think it always was." She put her hand over her mouth, because the next thing she might say would be damning. She said it anyway: "Eustace, you must know, *I've* taken lovers. That's the truth."

His face looked as if he were tumbling into a hole. A deep, deep hole.

"Only since you abandoned me," she said.

"I was doing my duty. I didn't abandon you."

"It felt like you did."

He felt his body start to shake. He couldn't stop it. "Shouldn't I be taking the photographs?"

"Maybe, then at least you'd be paying attention. But you do realise, because the world is the way it is, you must be the one to admit the adultery. It's the only thing half acceptable. Look at me, Eustace, I'm broken. You have broken me."

"Mr Havershall," Morrison said, commanding his attention. "We can provide a stand in, if required. I think you'll find the judge is willing to be gullible in such matters. If you give Mrs Havershall a divorce that preserves her — shall we call it? — social standing, she will vote for a loan in Havershall's of any amount you may need to buy back her shareholding and pursue this purchase of your rival. We thought that is what you wanted."

Sitting back in her chair, Ginny thought, *"This is the bargain Caroline expects you to take."* She waited to see if he would.

Eustace sat silent for several seconds, until the silence felt terribly empty.

"I don't have a mistress," he repeated softly. "And I don't wish to fight any more."

"Then, you *will* grant the divorce?" Morrison pressed.

"Gin, I don't..." he said, turning to her. "Is this what you really want? To let go of the company... our company?"

"Our company?" Ginny said sceptically.

"Yes, ours. Our family. That's the way Woody and I always saw it."

"Your family has not seen you for a while. Your factories have not seen you in a while either. Have you ever visited the new one at Radford since you bought it? Come with me this afternoon. I'm going there. The Havershall engineers have been there a month, night and day."

He shook his head — it had become unusually heavy — then muttered, "The war. The war." Repetition gave it some special meaning that remained unspoken.

"Due in Reading. Beaverbrook's orders," he said. "I don't know how else it can be, Gin, at the moment."

"Oh, Eustace," she said. "It's not this moment I worry about."

He had come with the birthday present he intended to deliver. Unable to decide on the gift — something big, something perfect; if the gift could be perfect, could he not still be the perfect husband? — he had settled on something rare, a box of cigarettes of the French brand Ginny had smoked when first he met her.

He found the gift still in his pocket as he drove away from the meeting with Morrison. With his work, his current obsessions, it seemed that the realisation of what matters always came too late.

What had she said? That she was *broken*? That she had taken lovers? Weren't they both broken then? Hadn't he nearly taken Sarah Coles?

And then there was today's evidence to consider: what sane man would buy a thoughtful gift and forget to deliver it?

She wanted to be home, but there were duties of her own to attend to. She drove back through Coventry to visit Radford as promised. Eustace would have done the same in the days he still felt himself to be Managing Director. If he couldn't be there, she would go. She was still his stand in.

The machines were close to beginning manufacture. Raye Cropper and several of the Duke Works' engineers had been staying in a guest house up the road.

"A thousand tank rollers before the end of the month," Raye promised again. It had become her mantra. She had read about Beaverbrook's Spitfires in the newspapers. "Tonight and a few more late nights, we'll get there."

Ginny thanked them for their work. The emotion of the day stayed bottled. She said nothing about Eustace when they asked, nothing other than that an old soldier feels the pull of duty.

Don't worry, he will be back leading you again. I know I'm only the reserve.

That same night — the fourteenth — under a bright full moon, the manufacturing heartland of Coventry, eighteen miles from Stratford and a little over twenty from Birmingham, took the single most concentrated bombing attack of the war. Five hundred Luftwaffe bombers carrying an 'improved' type of incendiary device descended on the city.

Back in Stratford, Ginny woke on her birthday morning to a sinister cloud hanging across the eastern horizon. It interrupted her walk from the Anderson Shelter to the house. She paused at the patio doors, goosebumps growing on her arms. Not so much a cloud as a dark angry mouth. So wide. So high. It seemed like the world might have ended within it. She clutched the dressing gown around her shoulders.

"Coventry, ma'am," the housekeeper informed her as she appeared from the house. "It's on the radio. All of it... gone."

"Oh, God," she said. "My people at Radford."

Two minutes later, she was in her car.

The heat haze cut a shimmering mirage across the cavernous horizon as Ginny's Crossley neared the city. It was a winter morning, but the temperature, stoked by the Coventry fires, was as warm as summer, the air so darkly clogged it seemed night had decided to stay.

Ginny had read reports of other bombings, of course, even seen photographs, but in flat monotone words and black and white images. Here, a three dimensional horror, colours sucked dry but lingering and lifeless; the smell and the taste were not held back by a flimsy canvas roof. Ashes fell in showers of burnt confetti, leaving speckles on the windscreen that her clacking wipers would not remove.

She wondered why the German bombers had kept pounding for so long. Once you've ruined a city, there's no point in ruining it more — piles of brickwork, pools of shattered glass, the water flooding onto the streets from broken mains, collapsed lampposts, upturned cars and lorries, a bus nose down in a bomb crater, whole blocks of the skyscape now mazes of random walls in parks of smouldering dust. A bomb, she remembered Eustace explaining, blows outwards, takes down weaker structures until there's nothing to retain the pressure waves, the last strong surface stands. There was nothing miraculous about it. Just a wall or two that survived.

Here and there lay a charred body yet to be recovered, twisted in the surprise of death, and all the time in the distance, the remains of the great cathedral, its roof gone, a pall of smoke rising in a column from its wreckage.

Skirting the centre, she turned north out towards Radford, but half a mile short, she was stopped by a roadblock. The terraced houses beyond the wooden barrier had been strafed, every third one hit. The contents of rooms had spilled out of wrecked upper storeys into front gardens, garden walls had toppled into the street. And beyond all that, the sky above the vast Daimler plant was licked by tongues of orange flame.

A volunteer policeman had been trying to organise cars into three-point turns. He came to Ginny's side window. When she wound it down, he said, "Better turn around, Missus. You can't get through here. Might get round the east side if you're lucky."

"But my factory is along the road. See!" She pointed into the distance.

"Road's got a hole ten feet deep. You know how it goes, if you want to get there, it's no good starting here. Best keep safe, aye? Besides, it's not good for no one to see, 'specially a woman."

"Our people — my people — are up that way. Norman Street."

He did not seem to believe her. The ownership she claimed surprised Ginny for a different reason.

Stiffening her voice, she declared, "My name is Virginia Havershall. I run Havershall's."

The man balked. "Suit yourself. You're not getting up this road in that, that's all I'm saying."

She swung her car around and deposited it on the pavement. She began her own personal march. Several passers-by were staring. She was not sure why she'd become so abrupt. An armour had descended to keep her safe, an illusion to dull the senses.

On top of the rubble, a few houses beyond the roadblock, Ginny glimpsed something white sticking up like a defiant sapling tree. But it wasn't a tree…

Impossibly, because everything now seemed impossible, it was a child's arm.

For a second, she wondered at the numbness of her own reaction. An arm. An arm. A child's arm, like Richard's or William's. She felt dizzy with uncertainty. What could she do? Screaming would have no point.

The arm moved. Weakly and desperately.

* * *

Two hours before, Eustace had woken in a Bed and Breakfast establishment outside Loughborough. His landlady told him the news.

"We have a factory in Radford. *I* have a factory... or rather Havershall's do." He remembered what Ginny had said the day before, the suggestion they should go there together. "Oh, Gin," he whispered.

"I thought you were a Ministry man," the landlady said.

"Sometimes, yes. But I make typewriters. I need to use your telephone," he told her. When she seemed reluctant, he said, "Military business," because he knew that would work.

He telephoned Diane Hall in Duke House, asking first for Ginny and then for Jim McCann. He was told neither were in. The Coventry factory had been hit. No one had heard from his wife.

He paid for his room without waiting for change and left without eating the landlady's breakfast. As he was starting the car, she came rushing down the drive to catch him.

"Here, my house isn't a telephone exchange, you know. There's some fella on the phone now says he's a bloomin' Lord."

"Tell him I already left," he said.

He was surprised he felt no guilt at the lie.

Coventry came into sight from miles away, a vague roiling darkness above the horizon. It dwarfed even the blackness over London on that first night of the Blitz. He could feel its heat and smell its poisonous gases, even with his windows closed and even at this considerable distance.

He'd known battlefields, driven tanks, always with the same senseless determination to charge towards, not away. Only a coward turns away. He felt that familiar fear crawling across his skin, but this time for his wife, for his company, not for a tank crew under his command. Somewhere outside Bedworth — his car the only traffic the road — he felt the engine begin to struggle, becoming a clanking rattle as his fuel ran dry.

"Fuck," he shouted. How could he have not realised? He had spent his last petrol coupons two days before, and somehow lost track of the miles and the consumption.

He stepped out onto a grassy bank, coughing as he tasted the air. There was an iron gate and a field stretching out behind it. Two late season flies landed on the gate post. They created a familiar tremble — the memory of a tank commander.

The world before him lay perfectly silent, still now but for the veil of slow smoke, its violence spent, burnt out as if the ruined land were waiting for God to reappear from Armageddon. He knew well enough not to wait with it, or expect any mercy he did not provide himself.

A volunteer ambulance came for the girl beneath the rubble. They carted her off. Bloody faced, half conscious, crying for her mother. To live, to die — who knew? The girl's eyes were open as the stretcher disappeared behind the ambulance doors.

Ginny walked on.

She was here to find her people. Havershall's people. It seemed she had never fully felt that responsibility before. It struck her that the same weight had hung on Woody and Eustace since the beginning. She remembered Lionel Swithin, Brian Fordham. There were others since the war began, and she had done her best to do the visits Eustace would have done. But this time, it was her crisis, her tragedy. She had decided on the investment in the Radford plant. She had sent the Havershall's people here. They were her people now.

Ashes still fell. Smells became dry and sulphurous in her mouth. The skeletons of burning Daimler buildings appeared and disappeared, eclipsed by the lines of felled and remaining houses as she passed. A baptist chapel had escaped intact apart from its windows. Beyond it, a village hall had lost the greater part of one corner.

A clutch of ARP wardens hurried past her in the other direction. Reaching the corner, she stared along Norman Street. Transformed from the afternoon before, the first factory had been flattened, its red-brick remains gently smoking. A bent metal sign on its fallen iron gate had been twisted so the only words visible were, "…and Sons Ltd."

Further up the road, the Havershall's factory looked undamaged at first glance, but as she quickened towards it, she saw that its far end, where they had been commissioning the big presses, had collapsed and an ugly crack extended along the brick fascia of the front wall.

A Havershall's lorry was parked outside. Several faces she recognised were grouped in conversation at the front door — Jim McCann and his brother among them. Raye Cropper too.

"Are you alright? Is everyone alright?"

"Mrs Havershall?" McCann exclaimed, turning first.

They all turned after that. They smiled to see her. Raye even hugged her. It seemed right to embrace and be embraced with the relief.

Ginny scanned through the faces she'd talked with the day before. All accounted for, several now blackened with sooty smears.

She marvelled at the Birmingham crew. "Jim, Wilfred… shouldn't you be at Duke Works?"

"Came across on the lorry soon as we heard," McCann said.

"We can start the presses by the next week, Mrs Havershall, if we move them down the other end, assuming someone can get the electric working by then. And of course, as long as it don't rain too much or too sideways," Raye added, gesturing to the roof. "We'll need someone better at heights than me for that."

"People are dead… back behind me," Ginny said, this still a surprise to her. Perhaps saying it would make it more true, or better still, less so. "I…I've seen bodies. A girl survived…"

She looked around the group, unable to finish what she wanted to say.

"Mrs Havershall, we're all OK here," said McCann. "All of Havershall's. We're all OK."

An army truck with a broken silencer roared up the road behind them and pulled to a halt in a screech of brakes. The passenger door opened and Eustace jumped down. Business suit and army boots. A camouflaged backpack over one shoulder. He looked exhausted.

"Gin?" He shouted her name before any of the others.

She replied with his, as if some handshake of words were necessary. How else to check that the two presences were real?

"Can you help us out, Mr Havershall?" McCann asked. "We're going to need one of them small cranes."

"You're making aircraft parts here, right?" said Eustace, knowing the answer was 'no'.

"Tank rollers," Ginny informed him. Beside her, Raye nodded to confirm the claim.

"That's good enough for the Aircraft Ministry. I can pull some strings. We have to get producing… soon as possible. It's an industrial war."

Nazi propagandists invented a word for it: *Coventrieren*, meaning 'to raze a city to the ground'. Half the eighty-thousand houses were damaged or destroyed. The important factories had been consumed in an inferno.

Havershall's would be up and running by Tuesday.

* * *

When they had finished their initial assessment of the clean up and the army truck had carried Eustace off to view a dozen other burnt out factories, Ginny found the cigarettes and a gold-embossed card on the seat of the Crossley. It was his invitation to the 'Midlands Businessman of the Year' ceremony. Handwritten in one corner, it said:

"*Dear Gin,*

The gold is not quite so fancy nor such a surprise as a wedding invitation and I know you have many reasons not to wish to be there. But I tell you now, I deserve nothing of this award. I will tell the Association so. I must refuse it, if you will not accept it with me. E. xx."

She laughed at the cigarettes. She had been trying to give up smoking for a month.

With the boys away, the prospect of a birthday alone seemed too bleak, so she had invited Devere to the house that night. The invitation had been issued the week before when she had been expecting to be celebrating a divorce. It didn't feel right now.

There was Coventry to think about — the people who'd rallied around because they worked for Havershall's. Eustace included. It seemed it might mean something, perhaps everything, but she couldn't work out how.

And now here she was, in the twilight of the birthday evening, dressing for someone else to undress her. That was wrong.

Sex with Devere had become mere habit. Her body did things without her, and maybe that's why she had let it continue until now. He brought her flowers and a card. He told her she was beautiful. She knew it was not true. Caroline had made it plain enough what hard work did to a lady's appearance. Ginny kept thinking of Eustace's cigarettes — the right brand for the wrong time.

The coupling that evening, with all the attentive mechanical proficiency, brought no pleasure. Devere's bony knee caught her thigh. His stubble irritated her shoulder. She felt dry, even after what he called his 'special attention'. In the distance, she heard, or thought she heard, the thudding of bombs, more bombs. Danger had once made it all the more exciting, but now it only made it frightening. She watched the ceiling. It seemed to take an age until he climaxed inside her.

"Martin," she said, "I believe this is over."

He was perched on the bedside. She possessed the bed's space, laid out on the sheets, her hair askew on the pillow. When Devere reached for her forehead, she pushed his hand away.

"You see, I am trying to fight a man who will no longer defend himself."

"Your husband? Surely, darling, he'll see he must free you, if he's a gentleman."

"He was always a gentleman," she said. "Worthy not wealthy. And at the beginning, I thought, if he wanted to measure his worth in pounds, that was alright. I encouraged him. What a mistake that was. Does that make any sense to you?"

"Not a word of it," he said.

"No," she agreed. "Not a word of it."

She turned to the wall and waited. She felt Devere's breath, heavy on her skin.

"You don't want to be free of him, do you?"

"I suppose that's right. I would say, I'm sorry."

"But you're not?"

"No," she said.

She watched him leaving, fumbling beyond the end of the bed as he wriggled back into his clothes and she balled herself up in the farthest corner of the bed. Devere disappeared from her life in the same way as he had entered — with timing of her choosing.

She and Eustace were a madness. Quite incurable. She saw that.

Wandering downstairs, barefoot, dressed only in a slip, freezing cold, all the fires were out. She passed the mirror in the hall, saw herself thirty-eight years old, a wealthy woman on the cusp of divorce. How had that happened when she had loved so completely, and they — those other women of the Buckleys' class — only constructed their marriages for economic advantage? Trades for privilege, one way or the other.

She found the cigarettes, the one beautifully illicit thing left of her birthday. She lit one with matches she used for candles and headed for the Anderson Shelter, staring out into the night as she walked down the garden, thinking of Eustace, of their children, of Woody and Celia and Woody's women, and the boy Woody had sired. The boy suddenly seemed important. And something which, in Eustace's name, she knew she could fix.

Ginny Havershall took the train into Birmingham on Monday of the following week. The winter rain pelted down as she approached the house in Digbeth. With the cowl of her raincoat pulled forward over her head, she felt like a hunched medieval friar, about on God's grey business, or — worse perhaps — the grim reaper. She knocked at the appointed address, a knock she had failed to deliver on her previous visit. A sour-faced middle-aged woman in an apron opened the door.

"Mrs Jarvis?"

The woman nodded.

"Nancy's mother? Grandmother to…" She paused. She had the name written on a card. "…Michael Luther Jarvis? Do I have that right?"

"Yes, what of it? Who are you?"

"In this matter, my name is not important. What matters is a financial settlement for your grandson."

"What? Financial settlements? My husband's not home. I'm not in the business of selling children."

"Not selling, Mrs Jarvis, and not buying either. I don't suppose we live in such Dickensian times. This is quite another century. It's more a question of securing a future… for *afterwards*. My husband always promised there would be such a time."

Chapter Twenty-Seven

Eustace sat with his H30 typewriter on a desk at the Ministry of Aircraft Supply. He had been sitting for half an hour and typed nothing. Six months of seven-day weeks, eighteen-hour days and then some — this for a man who should still be in recovery — he had no more to give. It would be better on the other side, when there was no longer a war every day.

Beaverbrook pushed his head through the crack in the office door. "Might have known it was you still here. Have you any idea of the time?"

"No, Sir, I don't suppose I do."

"Writing a letter?"

"Resigning," Eustace said.

When the word came out, Beaverbrook did not seem surprised. He stepped into the room, close enough to peer over the typewriter's platen.

"Not exactly prolific. I hear the girls can do one hundred and twenty a minute on a decent Havershall machine."

"That and more, some of them. I'm out of practice."

"This bombing of Coventry… This is the last of it… a beaten enemy spitting his last venom," Beaverbrook assured him.

"Yes, Sir,' he replied.

"The Luftwaffe have half the planes they started with, half the air crew. No spare parts for the planes they have left. Whereas we, according to my reports, have out-produced our losses every day since the summer. We have won the Battle of Britain, Eustace. Lasted out the Blitz, more or less. And for you, 'Businessman of the Year', quite an honour?"

"You heard about that?"

"Indeed, they have asked me to go up and present the award."

"That's impossible. I—"

"Nonsense. I told them, yes, of course. I only wish it could be something more substantial, a sword on your shoulder perhaps?"

"I never did it for the honours, Sir. I tried to convince myself once that I did it for the connections… for afterwards." Eustace trailed off with the shake of a head.

"Most men, when they say they did something without want of reward, are liars. Not you. You were compelled from the beginning. Duty, don't you see?"

"My wife kept the company running when I came here. If anyone deserves an award..."

"Quite so. Virginia, isn't it? The old Buckley family?" Beaverbrook smiled rather smugly. "A newspaperman knows about everything. Part of the job, don't you know? If it helps, I know how to type. I could sit and you could stride about and dictate your resignation. That always works for me."

Eustace took several seconds to process the joke. The delay led to a proper laugh.

"That's better," Beaverbrook said. "I think we may leave it to others to win the rest of the war. There is a time when men must decide to stop fighting."

"Is that what you intend to do?"

Beaverbrook lowered his head. "I too shall resign from the Ministry of Aircraft Production. I confess I have had the mistaken notion of tempting you over to the Ministry of Supply. They need good men. I see I was wrong. I release you, Eustace. You need releasing and that's my word, for what it's worth. For myself, I will take a rest and then, who knows? I'm getting old."

The boys' term finished early and Ginny had them home at the beginning of December. She was amazed at William. Not quite a teenager, grown two inches, he looked like a man in waiting, though there was still a boy's collection of Skybirds in his room. If he could have had anything in this world, he would have been a pilot.

Richard remained a more delicate flower, now no taller than his brother. His history with polio was hidden, but denied him William's physical prowess. Poetry and art filled out his life. One day, Ginny snuck into his room to find out what he was working on. He had covered his easel with a sheet. She pulled it off.

Richard's painting borrowed from Munch's 'The Scream'. The sky was a bright blood red, the figures of his men and women shocked pale by the falling world they saw. She found it disturbing, more so than the typed pages of poetry she'd found before.

She was still sitting on his bed, gazing at the painting when he came back into his room. "I thought you loved Shakespeare and his ilk. When did that change?"

"Don't go through my things anymore," he said.

"I beg your pardon. I'm not 'going through' anything. It's a painting."

"Mother, please. I'm trying to express something. You don't question William when he builds planes."

"He is not you," she said, without explaining the double standard. "I was looking at your work. When you start thinking about these things, that's when it becomes real."

"War is real. Your factory makes parts for it, doesn't it? That's real."

"Yes, it is," she agreed. She wanted to tell him about Coventry, but thought it too much. She offered nothing, no rationale for pride or duty, or why one must make things that kill in order to live. Eustace might have understood that better, she thought, maybe spoken to Richard, if he'd been here.

Her son looked at his feet, still half a room away from her.

"How do wars end?" he asked, both younger and wiser in one question.

"I suppose, Richard, the sides pull back. They stop fighting."

"And who decides that?"

She did not answer. Nothing felt certain anymore.

"Will I get to fight?"

"You're fourteen," she said in surprise. "Nearly fourteen and a half," she conceded when she saw his grimace.

"We won't give up, though, will we?" Richard lowered his voice, adopting the Prime Minister's gravelled tone: *"We shall fight on the beaches... we shall fight in the fields and in the streets... we shall never surrender."* Then, in his own voice, added, "Do you think Germans don't believe the same? It goes on and on. Won't we have to kill them all? To win?"

"What do you mean, darling?"

"William is just like Dad. They would have us kill them all. It's just slaughter. We have to stop."

When he had finally found the strength to type, Eustace had given a month's notice. He laid back in his office chair, thinking he would take a nap, but once released, he slept right through the night. It wasn't the first time he had slept there in a sitting position, leaning forward with his cheek on the desk. He told himself it was the last.

He met the new day with a new determination. His first phone call was to BBTL in Doncaster. He asked the receptionist if Mr Barrington-

Brown was yet at his desk. He was surprised and a little impressed to be told that he was. It was one minute past eight.

"Tell him, it's Eustace Havershall."

"Is he expecting you, Sir?"

"I don't know what he's expecting," he said.

After a minute of limbo punctuated by the clicks of a telephone exchange, a familiar voice appeared on the line.

"Well, well," said Barrington-Brown. "Is this the moment when you make the offer, Old Bean? I heard from my bank that you've had Archie Hoare running all over London. I suppose I should be expecting the cold morning call. When the boot was on the other foot, I tried to spare you. Sent my bid in by telegram."

"Woody and I did not take it too kindly at the time."

"Oh, really. I apologise. Your wife's advice, I believe."

"My wife?" Eustace hesitated. The claim seemed bizarre at first. "Ginny asked you to send a telegram?"

"Ah, yes, that's how I remember it. Did she never tell you? I hear she may not be behind you in this, or is that just a rumour too?"

Eustace withdrew his ear from the receiver for a moment and rested his forehead against the hard plastic of its case, as if that might help him grasp the implications. He laughed to himself.

"Listen," he said, "how would it be if the next order for drop-forgings came Hillsborough's way? We could make something of a song and dance about it for the press. 'Ministry asserts faith…' and all that."

The other end of the line hung in silence.

"Would that help you rescue your situation, Charlie?"

"Yes… I suppose… yes, certainly, anything from the Ministry would help with credibility in the City. It's what we need in Hillsborough Engineering. Can you do it?"

"Oh, I think I can misuse my authority one last time," Eustace said. "And, Charlie, I will hold onto my five million. We will make sure the rumours circulate. Your share price will rise. That should give you time and maybe protect you from others who might like to take a cheap bite at your company. That's all I have to offer."

"Thank you." The uncertainty was evident in Charlie's voice. After a moment, he asked, "But, why?"

"Maybe to make you suffer a bit longer. I am notoriously ruthless." Remembering Ginny and remembering Woody, Eustace said, "No, it's not that. We're all on the same side, now we're in a war. Besides, I'd miss your rather ugly typewriters."

Charlie Barrington-Brown allowed himself a knowing chuckle. "Bravo, Eustace," he said. "Bravo."

Curfews turned the annual 'Businessman of the Year' dinner into a luncheon. Beaverbrook had arranged to meet Eustace at the Spitfire factory in Castle Bromwich on the same morning.

"I've a hankering to see the plant. I haven't been in a while. Since I stole it. You do still have the Rolls, don't you? You could pick me up."

"The luncheon is at twelve."

"I'm in Castle Brom for ten. A quick inspection to boost morale and keep them on their toes. Walk around with me. Shouldn't be more than an hour."

The tour ran late, of course. There was always too much to see in a factory. Too much to discuss. Should some of the production be moved out as they'd done with other factories? What would Beaverbrook's Bully Boy advise this one last time?

Eustace ended up speeding through the streets of Birmingham to reach the Grand Hotel Ballroom. Despite the jolting ride, two minutes hunkered in the passenger's seat and Beaverbrook fell asleep — his usual trick.

Eustace's Phantom III had a tiny rear window and wing mirrors mounted far forward which restricted the view behind, but he was certain the same car — a grey Rover — was stuck behind them, keeping a constant distance, despite his speed. He drove on. He took a left hand turn and then half a mile later, a right into a backstreet heading nowhere in particular.

The sharp turns and the rougher surface roused his passenger. Eustace was firing furtive glances at his wing mirrors. The Rover had not gone away.

"What is it?" asked Beaverbrook.

"I believe we're being followed."

Beaverbrook raised himself in the passenger seat, stuck his head through the passenger window to get a better look.

"Ah, yes," he said. "I forgot about those. They are supposed to be discreet."

"You know them?"

"Winston insisted. Something about assassins from over the channel. Two attempts on Churchill and one on the King since Easter. They don't get into the newspapers, not even into my newspapers. Now, I have security everywhere. And I have to carry this thing." He patted a bulge beneath the breast of his jacket. "Most bothersome. It's a Webley. Officer's gun, so I'm told. I wouldn't know how to bloody fire it."

An arm out of the window, he waved cheerily to his security guards.

"Pays to be polite," he said, "if one expects them to jump between you and a bullet. It's Eric and Vincent today, I believe."

As the honoured guest, Lord Beaverbrook rose at the top table to give his speech and present the award, an engraved silver salver. Only a few minutes late. Those who served the lunch to ninety-eight Midlands' industrialists plus guests — a smaller turnout this year for obvious reasons — had done a fine job of catching up the twenty minutes delay the guest of honour had caused.

The lesser numbers and the midday timing gave the event a more personal air, though perhaps a more sombre tone. Chandeliers in the great ballroom had been removed to protect them from any bombing that might swing them off their mountings.

The business-suited diners on their round tables of twelve turned their chairs to hear the great man speak. There was applause and an approving clink of cutlery against glasses. Beaverbrook's speech, as was expected, rallied the war effort, emphasised the role of factories and workers. It praised the women who had stepped up to the work men had been forced to abandon. It acknowledged the sacrifices of Birmingham and the Midlands in particular. He mentioned Coventry.

Then, turning to the award, he began by saying he had come to honour a great industrialist and a great company, one that had served its country well.

"Let me present the man to you..."

Beaverbrook caught Eustace's eye, two seats along the row, and urged him to stand.

"This is the most worthy man in England," he declared. "Each plane we have produced more than the Germans has a piece of Eustace Havershall within it. Few men can say that, Ladies and Gentlemen, few men indeed."

"Go on, say something," he mouthed in Eustace's direction. "They expect it."

Eustace felt under-prepared, having spent the last few hours rushing around a Spitfire factory. He had written some notes the night before, but it struck him now that they would miss the point entirely.

"Thank you," he managed. An opening that played for time, allowed him to think. "I... I suppose I should also say something about the war. That seems to be what everyone's concerned about. I don't know why."

The audience laughed. A few diners clinked cutlery against wine glasses.

"We will win. Because we must. And that is all of it."

He took the easy applause that followed without a smile. He knew, better than anyone, that winning was bitter, not sweet.

"Joseph Woodmansey — Woody, as many of you will know him — and I came here in 1921. We stood in a street no more than five miles from here, looking up at a building with a Russian landlord at our side. It was a mess — a dirty, grubby mess. You all know how Birmingham was back then. We didn't know what we were doing. All the money we had was a loan my father gave me, which was given because he believed I might end up as a family scandal otherwise."

This confession drew a small cheer and a few catcalls from the audience.

"Yes, yes, I was the 'spare' and the rebellious child, so to speak. I wouldn't make Nottinghamshire lace. Woody convinced me that people needed typewriters, because after a war, a great number of things need writing down. At the time, two other great things were said to me, things that should be remembered when all else seems impossibly bleak... and sometimes now, I know, things seem impossibly bleak.

"The first is, '*I can fix it, Sir... if I go outside.*' Woody said this while we were trapped in a tank on the fields of Cambrai. It taught me something about survival. About courage. About resolve. The second, I have thought more upon lately, because it means everything to me. It was something like this, if I may paraphrase: '*When typing machines do not make us rich, we shall run off and live in a garret and make our fortune as street artists.*'"

Half his audience fell into silence. The other half tried to laugh again.

"I cannot draw," he told them. "So I decided that typewriters had to succeed. I am happy to honour the two people who made that possible for me."

He looked for Ginny who was sitting a table and a half away with his sons. Jim McCann, Raye Cropper, Diane Hall and a handful of others — the Great War veterans whom Havershall's had employed from the beginning — were at the same table. Ginny smiled back at him. Her eyes glistened.

* * *

She had been at work at seven-thirty that morning dealing with a new contract for the navy which needed both Jim McCann and Raye Cropper to modify production lines in the factories. She had meant to buy a new dress but hadn't had the time and, anyway, there was rationing to think of.

So Ginny stood next to Eustace, dressed for work, as the newspaper men demanded pictures of the couple responsible for the 'Havershall's dream'. She noticed that, for once, he urged her forward, that his shoulder tucked behind hers when the photographers asked them to step closer together. She didn't know that she'd ever seen a picture of herself with Eustace where all of her was visible. She was visible now, even though she looked more ready for the typing pool than a fancy luncheon. Maybe this was what a business leader looked like. She didn't care. She decided she looked like Virginia Havershall — a *typewriterist*. And so did her husband.

As the ceremony wound down, Beaverbrook circulated the tables until the business men started to disperse. He sat with Eustace and the rest of the Havershall's party regaling them with tales of the newspaper business, describing encounters with Charlie Chaplin, H G Wells and Wallis Simpson. William and Richard paid rapt attention. There was something magical about Beaverbrook as a raconteur and their interest egged him on.

"Baldwin called me a man who wanted power without responsibility. 'The prerogative of the harlot throughout the ages', he described it. I suppose he had a point. I was trying to start a political party at the time. Free trade within the Empire! That was my slogan. The Empire is a great thing, you know. It will help us win this war."

"What's a harlot?" William asked.

Ginny turned to Eustace, who turned and looked at Beaverbrook. The great man smiled mischievously in return.

After a while, as the tales got increasingly bawdy, she invented an excuse to shepherd the boys away, saying she must must introduce them to 'other people'. There were few people left except crusty old business men.

Alone with Beaverbrook, Eustace said, "Gin says I am to invite you back with us for supper in Stratford."

"That is most kind, but I have a train to catch. Besides, you two should be together." Beaverbrook was lighting another cigar. He'd already bitten off the end. He pointed it vaguely in Ginny's direction. The Havershall boys were next to her, talking with the mayoress.

"As it happens, I believe it is the condition on which I get invited myself," Eustace assured him.

"Ah, the threat of divorce. For all the chaps who have worked for me, it's an uneasy time."

"Yes," Eustace agreed. "But with Ginny and I— Well, when you recruited me, Sir, I was already in a long, dark convalescence. My partner in this business had died."

"This Mr Woodmansey?"

"Yes, that's it. He always knew we had a duty. I didn't quite know what it was."

"And do you know it now, do you suppose?" Beaverbrook glanced once again towards Ginny. "On second thoughts, I'll come with you to Stratford."

"You will?"

Beaverbrook nodded thoughtfully. "I lost my wife. She died. Who am I to advise you? But this stuff we do, trying to earn what we've already got, it does pile up if you don't say stop, doesn't it? That is the truth."

Beaverbrook puffed on the cigar and reached out his hand to grip Eustace's arm. "You, Old Boy, are a man who cannot fail. That is your best and worst feature. Your wife is charming. Your children... they would make any man proud. Whatever you've done to her, Eustace, *fix* it. Even if you have to '*go outside*'. That's the phrase you used, I believe."

The Havershall party finally broke up. Raye set off back to Nottingham. McCann drove the others back to Duke House.

Beaverbrook offered to take Richard and William to Stratford in the Rolls-Royce. He 'understood those cars', he told the boys, bragging, "I used to own the place, don't you know?" By now, the boys had quite taken to him. Ginny thought it a matter of time before he had a new nickname — 'Uncle Beaver' or some such. Ginny could drive Eustace in her Crossley, the new uncle suggested. He was persuasive, as always. He winked at Eustace when the arrangement was agreed.

They set off in convoy, Ginny and Eustace in the lead, Beaverbrook behind with William and Richard, the security men at the rear in their Rover. For the first mile or so, Eustace could not think what to say. He thanked Ginny for the day — all the people she'd got to come, the older employees who would have known Woody.

Bomb damage from the previous week blocked part of the Stratford Road near Highgate Park. A man in ARP uniform on traffic duty diverted them onto a back street.

Ginny turned into a road full of local shops closed for the afternoon. A blast crater had undermined and demolished the wall outside a church. There was no activity but for a few pedestrians.

Eustace tilted his head to get an angle to see in the wing mirror, checking the Rolls and the Rover were still in convoy. At that moment, a big delivery van came across from a side street and stopped in the middle of the road behind them. When he looked forward again, a blue low-loading lorry with 'Toohey & Sons Merchants' written on its side had stopped too, blocking the road a hundred yards ahead.

Before Eustace had realised what that meant, a man in a cloth cap ran from behind a postbox. He carried a grenade in one hand, a pistol in the other.

"Put your foot down. Go straight at him!" he shouted.

Ginny hit the brakes.

"No. Don't stop!"

A bullet pierced the windscreen, high and to the right, spidering the glass. Eustace threw himself across the car, his body shielding hers.

At that moment, Beaverbrook's bodyguards came speeding past the door, lurching across the front, scraping the driver's side wing of the Crossley. Their Rover hit the man, tossed him in the air, scattering gun and grenade, caught him again on its bonnet before smashing into the postbox. Blood splattered as far as Ginny's windscreen. She screamed.

The grenade had bounced into the road in front of them. Eustace ducked as it exploded. Glass showered in. He felt the car lifted. He remembered his tank — the same lurching nightmare. It tottered on the two driver's side wheels for a moment, then slapped itself down hard. The suspension broke with a crack and liquid started spreading out from beneath.

He saw that flames were engulfing the Rover, saw the liquid trickling towards it across the uneven tarmac.

"Get out. Get out, it's petrol," he shouted at Ginny. She did not respond, even with his face right up to hers. Her eyes were closed.

He tried the passenger door but the door wouldn't open. He shouldered it. It was caught. He was caught. They were caught. The flames grew. The liquid from the Crossley tricked ever closer to the burning Rover. He thought of the burning tanks at Cambrai, but only for the briefest second. He didn't want to die here. He didn't want anyone to die here. He didn't want to live without Ginny, the thing he had always loved most in this world.

He wriggled in the seat to get more purchase and kicked the passenger door again and again, ignoring the pain in his leg. Frantic and out of control, he kicked. For her.

The bent metal holding the door catch gave way. He scrambled out onto the tarmac in a heap, dragging Ginny behind him. He struggled to manhandle her unconscious body towards the pavement where he thought the fire could not reach. *Just get away from the car!*

He cried out her name.

He thought she might be dead. She might be dead… *Oh God, no!*

A second. Two seconds. No response.

He said her name again.

Then a wave of heat seared against his back. The fire had reached the Crossley. It had gone up with a whoosh!

An eyelash fluttered, a nerve in her neck twitched.

"Eustace…" He heard her murmur. Then she said, "The children…"

He looked sharply to his right. William and Richard? Where were they? Of course, he must save them too.

Some yards off, the Rolls-Royce had turned towards the kerb and escaped the blast, except for a broken side window. A faltering Beaverbrook was helping Richard and William out of the rear seats.

Adrenalin pumping, Eustace spotted two men running from the delivery van behind the Rolls. He saw their rifles. More assassins for sure. He pounced on Beaverbrook, urged his boys into cover on the far side of the car while grabbing for the holster inside Beaverbrook's jacket.

"Give me it!" he demanded. A rifle shot ripped into the car's panels.

Eustace gripped the gun. Beaverbrook's Webley. A handful of memories.

The leading runner slowed, taking a steadier aim. Eustace clicked off the safety catch. The next rifle shot struck his upper arm. The gun spilled across the tarmac. But then, before the pain of the bullet even registered, the assassins fell. Both of them. Crumpling as two sharp reports split the air.

Confused and clutching his bleeding arm, Eustace looked around for an explanation. Beaverbrook's security guard — the Rover's passenger — was poised on one knee, elbow propped on the other, his gun still in hand while the petrol fire raged behind him. This saviour rose, smiled wanly, and began walking towards Eustace.

Eustace glanced at the blood oozing between his fingers. Only for a second. When he looked up again, he saw the lorry driver, ghosting through the thinnest part of the flames.

He shouted a warning. Too late. Someone fired. Someone unexpected.

Ginny was only half conscious. When she had picked it up, the Webley moulded to her grip. She saw her boys and she saw Eustace. She pulled its trigger, as natural and inevitable as flinching. She did not see the target, not properly, only its danger. And that was enough.

That British officer's revolver had a particular sound. He'd heard it night after night for years. In Eustace's mind, the gun was always out of its holster. Masterson had fallen sideways, the death splatter across the bulkhead where his body had been propped up a moment before. Now the boy was quiet. Above his smashed cheekbone, the eyeball was drooping as if trying to examine the damage.

A small piece of white bone dressed with pink fat had landed on Eustace's boot. He did not know what to do. Mulgrove had pried the gun from his hand, the knuckles locked and white.

That was 1917. And that was now.

He walked over to her slowly, not wishing to cause more alarm.

"It's alright," she said. "It's alright now."

Her wobbly legs would hardly hold her up. He reached for the gun, eased her fingers from the handle one at a time.

"I shot him, Eustace."

"Yes."

"I shot him," she said again.

"Sometimes that's all there is."

A doctor came to the Police Station and declared the bullet had passed straight through Eustace's arm. He was lucky. Always lucky. The doctor stitched his wounds and bandaged him up.

Four German assassins — the postbox man, two from the van and the lorry driver — were dead, along with the driver of the Rover who had broken his neck when the car hit the postbox. The survivors lingered at the station making statements. Beaverbrook and the surviving bodyguard swore that Eustace had shot the German lorry driver and the police were willing to swallow the lie.

No woman wanted to be branded a killer, the Detective Inspector said. He had asked Ginny what she remembered. She thought for a moment, then said she remembered nothing. The powder burns on her hand were obvious, but she kept repeating that her husband was a hero.

She refused to go to hospital despite the doctor's recommendations about amnesia. After the first hour, she and the boys took a taxi back to Stratford.

Someone in Whitehall, probably at Churchill's request, sent a car from the nearest army barracks for Beaverbrook. This time, travelling back to London, he would be in the rear seats with two armed soldiers in front.

"You know," said Beaverbrook as he departed with a handshake, "I could arrange security for you, Eustace... in case. Even for you and your family."

"Why would we need security?"

"I think we must consider the possibility that I was not the only target. Perhaps I was not the target at all."

"Why on Earth would you think that?"

"No one knew I would be with you after the ceremony. Yet everyone knew this was the day for Eustace Havershall, Businessman of the Year, quartermaster of Spitfires and Hurricanes. And where would he be going... *afterwards*? Home to Stratford with his family, they might assume."

"That's rather fanciful, don't you think?" Eustace pointed out.

"Perhaps, but the route you'd be taking would be obvious. All they needed was a false ARP man. Tell me, who else could they be expecting in a unique white Crossley and a Rolls Royce Phantom but the Havershall family? Certainly not Lord Beaverbrook." He patted his chest to make the point. "I was supposed to be on a train. But you are well known, my friend."

"No," said Eustace decisively.

Beaverbrook smiled. "I'll admit I'd be rather jealous if they wanted to eliminate you but not me. I thought I was important. Being shot at by Germans, quite a validation. Never mind, the matter is closed. But, Eustace, if you change your mind, about anything..."

Eustace shook his head. "You were right. I am done. I need to be home..."

"Very wise," said Beaverbrook. "To add to everything, today, the Havershalls saved a peer of the realm. Enough for one war, I think. Other things to do now."

"Sir?"

"Yes," said Beaverbrook.

"Thank you."

A policeman in plain clothes drove Eustace back to Stratford that evening when the paperwork was done. At first, he couldn't find anybody but the cook inside the house.

William and Richard were at the bottom of the long garden beyond the Anderson Shelter where the grass started sloping towards the river, trying to dig up worms to attempt fishing in the darkness.

Ginny sat on the patio step, smoking again, watching her boys. She was drinking too, though the glass perched on a stone tile was filled with tonic water. A bruised sky had developed far off in the distance, lit by a sliver of moon.

"Look, it's enough to bring brothers together," she said with a tinge of irony.

"No alcohol?"

"Beastly, bad headache," she explained. She lifted the cigarette that lay smouldering between her fingers. "I've taken these up again though. Someone bought me the right brand and now I can't stop myself."

He sat next to her an arm's length distant, examining her strained face. "Perhaps we should take you to the hospital after all?"

"No. It's not that sort of headache."

"What then?

"I've been trying to think why I didn't keep my foot down, at the beginning when you were shouting, 'Go on.'"

"And yet you fired the gun when I did not. I should have—"

She leant sideways to be closer to him. He rested his hand over hers.

"Perhaps the time for secrets is over, Gin," he said. "I should have told you. Before, in the other war, there was a boy. Herbert Masterson. I think that's where it all started… Woody and I… all that ambition. If we were going to survive, we were really going to prove we deserved to, that we deserved our share of everything."

He told her, for the first time, how he pulled the trigger at Cambrai, helping Masterson on because it seemed a task God had forgotten to perform.

At the end, he said, "You had to. Today. But look what you were saving. All this."

They had a view down the expanse of garden to their sons, two outlines baiting hooks on their fishing rods.

"They would have shot us all, I know. I am no fool, Eustace. I think, when I realised, that's how I managed to do it."

"Gin," he said, interrupting her flow. When she gave him her full attention, he told her, "I do not want to be divorced."

Her face cracked a smile. "Well, at least, we haven't had to live in a garret and paint for a living. For a while, I thought that might be a serious possibility."

"For a while, it was," he agreed.

He remembered how the young Virginia had twitched with the nervous energy of a hummingbird. Now she was composed, focused far down the garden on the two boys. On the future.

"Lately, Eustace, I have tried too hard to be you. Why? Because it seemed the only way you'd see me."

"I see you now, Gin. Life-sized and real."

"I know what I want now, Eustace. I have wanted it always. I wanted a man who knew he was worthy. Worthy not wealthy."

"Is being a bit of both those things alright?"

"Yes," she said. "It's definitely alright."

She took him into the sun lounge where they kept a private bar and a gramophone. After she poured him a brandy and herself a dry Martini, she lit another cigarette. They shared it.

She shuffled through a shelf of vinyl records and found Louis Armstrong's recording of 'Tiger Rag'.

"I thought you had a headache and couldn't drink," he observed.

"It's gone now," she said.

When they danced, he noticed the turntable seemed too slow and Armstrong sang too deeply, but it suited their mood.

"It's been broken for ages," she told him.

"Yes," he said.

"Yes," she agreed in return.

After a moment, they both burst into laughter.

Epilogue - 1941-45

Beaverbrook resigned from the Ministry of Aircraft Supply at the beginning of May 1941. With the Battle of Britain conceded, the Blitz continued to fade away, producing one last spectacular encore over London the 10th of the month. In that raid, the Luftwaffe dropped eight hundred tonnes of bombs, created two thousand fires, killed one thousand four hundred people and injured a similar number. Westminster Abbey and the Law Courts were damaged; the Chamber of the House of Commons was destroyed. But the Nazi strategy was spiralling into incomprehensibility. In June, Hitler turned from Britain and began Operation Barbarossa, the invasion of the Soviet Union — fascist against communist. It was a Hitler's fatal error. Whatever sanity he had was gone.

Beaverbrook came back into office that same month. Unable to stay idle, this time he was heading the Ministry of Supply. His aim now was not to build aircraft for a rearguard action to defend the shores of Britain, but enough military weapons and equipment to win an industrial war overseas.

Eustace played no part in it, other than accepting orders for military parts at Havershall's. He returned to work full time and vowed never again to be Businessman of the Year.

Ginny continued to run the sales and administration staff at Duke House, but cut her working week. She and Eustace agreed there was a duty in wartime. She accepted the presidency of an injured soldiers' charity. It vowed to raise the money for a private rehabilitation hospital by the end of the war. Beaverbrook made the second largest donation; the first was in the name of Joseph Woodmansey.

Richard's 'Red Scream' hung on his bedroom wall throughout the war, next to a sketch by Matisse. He was eighteen in 1944 and called up. He failed the medical examination, was excused combat training, and taught clerical duties and typing in the navy.

His brother William spent the war with a wooden model of a Spitfire hanging from the light shade above his bed. Too young to be a pilot.

Celia Woodmansey was still listed as missing.

Acknowledgments

Firstly, let me acknowledge that all historical fiction is, by definition, made up. All my main characters are therefore fabrications, except the public figures who obviously aren't, like Beaverbrook and Churchill and a few others. The actions of those characters are roughly historically accurate, though not where they interact with the novel's fictional cast list. In giving Eustace, Ginny and Woody a significant role in history, I have occasionally stolen from the real heroes who should be lauded for those feats. For this, I apologise.

Secondly, I'd like to mention the people who have helped and supported me in getting this novel completed. I could never forget the huge impact my mentors, first readers/critics and family have had on my work. A novel requires a formidable support group.

My teachers, through various courses and workshops, have included Graham Joyce, John Harvey, Sara Maitland, Chris d'Lacey, Jacob Ross, Rod Duncan, Helen Cooper, A L Kennedy, Jake Arnott, Carys Davies and Suzannah Dunn. I've learned and adopted ideas and techniques from them all. Those things were also unashamedly stolen.

My work has been extensively workshopped with two distinct groups whose support and expert guidance have been critical. I'm indebted to the Leicester Writers' Club, in my view the best and most helpful writing group in the country; I worked out recently that I had driven over fifty thousand miles to attend the Thursday night sessions since I joined in the 1990s — twice around the world. More recently, the support group formed from a course with Curtis Brown Creative have become a major influence on my writing. Thanks are due to all of them, and also to Jennifer Kerslake at Curtis Brown who organised our course.

Finally, but most importantly, my family makes life and everything else possible. All my thanks and love go to Rebecca, Jonny and Kathy. This book is for you.

David N. Martin — 2024

About the Author

David N. Martin comes from Peterborough and lives in rural Northamptonshire. He has been an entrepreneur and industrialist, as well as an author. He has worked with more than fifty small and medium-sized companies throughout his career and many of the scenes in The Typewriterists borrow from that experience.

His creative influence appears in many places, especially through his input as a first reader and coach to fellow writers, but his own most important literary works have always appeared under pseudonyms, until now that is. The Forged Truth Publishing project has finally persuaded him to allow his latest novel, 'The Typewriterists' to appear under his own name.

Printed in Great Britain
by Amazon

58438513R00199